THE RED DEATH

Kevin plunged into the lake.

I've got to try to save him!

Beyond him he saw the nose of the boat disappear; saw the old man's arm, black except where bloodied flesh showed through, thrashing the water; saw the straw hat float innocently away; saw bubbles dance and whirl. It was like a shark attack.

He pulled up and treaded water, whipping his head from side to side. He swatted at the dark objects—hundreds of spidery creatures, clinging to one another—swarming around him.

I have to try to save him!

The old man's body seemed almost too light as the boy locked his elbow under an armpit and began towing him to shore.

He lifted the body out of the lake and carefully turned it over.

A skeletal face lurched up at him, bearing a rictus smile. All the flesh had dissolved. Or been eaten away . . .

DEMON'S EYE
STEPHEN GRESHAM

ZEBRA BOOKS
KENSINGTON PUBLISHING CORP.

ZEBRA BOOKS

are published by

Kensington Publishing Corp.
475 Park Avenue South
New York, NY 10016

First printing: July 1989

Printed in the United States of America

Prologue

Winter, 1829

Dear God, let it be healthy!

The young woman clawed at her distended stomach, lurching forward as the contraction gripped her entire body, jerking her as if she were a marionette manipulated by some invisible master.

Dear God, please!

And the pressure from the push she could not resist held her; her wrists went limp from exhaustion; from her pelvic area down she felt nothing except the energy-draining thrust of the living thing within her.

At the height of the contraction, she cried out.

Something in the cool shadows of the wine cellar shifted, but of that movement she was unaware, every ounce of her concentration given over to the inexorable drive of Nature.

Then release.

She eased her sweat-soaked back and shoulders onto the horsehair blanket; her tattered and blood-stained dress rode up immodestly from her knees to her waist. But this was no time for ladylike pretensions. She panted, breath coming like stabs in the chest. Sweat trickled into her disease-swollen eyes. She shivered, and her shoulders trembled involuntarily from the dankness of the womblike pocket of the cellar where she had come during the night, knowing that the waiting was over.

Her mouth formed a frozen circle which she fought against. She struggled to bring the lips together and shape a word, to call for help or assurance from the woman who hunkered near her, holding a torch.

"Portisha!"

She twisted her head toward the looming presence, mindful that another soul-wrenching assault would be launched at any moment. But she needed to see her companion. Weakly she lifted a hand and spider-walked her fingers, hoping to touch warmth and the strength of another human being.

"Portisha, will it be healthy?"

She searched the shadows for the old midwife, but saw only an amber smudge within a black matrix. Disease and the violence of giving birth had contorted the young woman's face as if it were made of clay; a few of the brightest flickers of torchlight seeped through the slits of her eyes. Nothing more.

The old woman beside her studied the grotesque face, the bloated skin, the running sores; and, even in the meager light, she could detect the scarlet-colored patches dappling the young woman's cheek and chin and forehead. Those marks announced to the world that a horrible sickness — a red death — had seized another victim.

Pity in her eyes, the old woman rose and crept to a far wall where tiny rivulets of a chalybeate spring needled into the cellar from some underground source. Into the mineral water she dipped a rag torn from the young woman's dress. Then she returned and laid it onto the stricken woman's forehead.

"Portisha?"

"Save your strength for the child," the midwife whispered.

"Will it be healthy? Dear God, I wish it to be."

6

"Sh-h-h. Only a little longer. A little longer."

Again, the young woman surged forward, caught in the thralls of something which completely controlled her. And again she cried out.

The midwife watched. And prayed that the rapidly emerging child would not survive the experience.

The birthing cries filled the cellar.

Near a large wine barrel, an echoing moan was issued; a sleeping form mixed whiskey dreams with the young woman's pain. The drummer, weary from too many miles of travel and oblivious from too many bottles of strong drink, tossed and turned. In a reflexive gesture, he reached to one side, making contact with his livelihood — a bulging sack of pots and pans and assorted wooden toys.

His day had been profitable. The long journey to Alabama had been worth his while, for the wealthy Southerners who had gathered for the opening of the magnificent Blackwinter Inn spent freely. He had celebrated, and the kitchen servants had offered him refuge in the cellar for the night.

"Push," the midwife commanded. "Push, dear girl."

And the young woman could hear her own bones and joints pop. Her loins shuddered. One violent surge and a burning emptiness. Warm, steamy tendrils embraced the insides of her thighs.

The drummer squinted at the scene, dismissed it as an odd dream, and returned to the land of the homewinds.

"Portisha!"

It was a weak and helpless exclamation.

The old midwife lifted free the wet bundle of flesh and placed it upon the young woman's stomach.

"Portisha, tell me this only," she gasped, sucking in gouts of the damp air. "Is it healthy? Dear God, I wish it to be."

And she wished more in her secret heart. She longed for a handsome boy and dreamed of the child stamping his impression upon mankind. Perhaps, she imagined, he would

7

become a politician. Governor of Alabama one day? Or wealthy. As wealthy as Jacob Manley Blackwinter, builder of Blackwinter Inn and progenitor of the lakeside, bustling town also named after him.

She trembled with joy at the warmth squirming upon her.

"It is a boy," said the midwife. "Here. Touch its man parts."

But the young woman could not move her hands. Shadow-strewn light swirled above her. She was bleeding much too heavily from the birth. Consciousness dimmed. And the disease, worsened by her weak condition, redoubled its attack. Blood pulsed from her nostrils, ears, and mouth. She managed to speak, though her words threatened to drown in the blood.

"Call him Joshua. The conqueror."

She swallowed and prepared to speak again.

The midwife leaned close to her hideous face and nodded.

"Portisha, is he healthy? Why doesn't he cry?"

"He is healthy, dearest girl. He is. I will let you hear his heart beat."

The young woman coughed; her chest suddenly heaved; her body stiffened.

"Dearest girl," whispered the midwife. "Rest in peace from the pain you have known."

She cleaned the child's body and wrapped it in a blanket. Then she positioned the torchlight so that she could view its face. She held her breath, anticipating her own revulsion.

But what she momentarily saw brought a sigh of relief. A firm, handsome face, centerpieced by dark, intelligent eyes, greeted her.

"Joshua," she murmured.

In a flickering of torchlight the face changed.

And the child began to cry. It was not, however, the high-pitched wail of a healthy baby, rather something deeper, something raspy like exhalations of fire. Scarlet splotches appeared, pocked here and there with angry sores. The right eye suddenly swelled shut as if an invisible fist had smashed the cheekbone; and the left eye opened wider, dominating the center of the face, a large, liquid eye—like that of a vulture—which stared, never blinking, up at the midwife.

She reeled back and screamed.

Several feet away, the drummer stirred awake and wiped escaping strands of whiskey-flavored saliva from the corners of his mouth.

The midwife clutched at her throat. Summoning courage, she lowered herself near the squirming child as it lay upon the corpse of its mother.

"Dragon's voice and demon's eye," she whispered. "You will carry the red death in your touch. God forgive me. You must not live."

Calming herself, she methodically tore a long strip from the young woman's dress and began to wind it around the child's neck. She kept the blanket between her hands and the infant's skin.

"God forgive me. I *must* do this."

In the torchlight, she hesitated.

The child twisted to one side and cried its hoarse cry.

And the midwife tightened the strip of cloth.

"Stop, woman! Hosts of angels, stop!"

The drummer clasped the woman's wrists; surprised, yet resolute, she struggled free.

"Let me do this!" she hissed.

"Merciful heaven, why?"

"Demon's eye," she pointed. "This child, Joshua, carries the strain of the red death. It must not live."

Surveying the child's face, the drummer dismissed the woman's explanation.

"No. No, you must be wrong. The Almighty wouldn't visit such a thing upon a wee baby. It's more likely it had a hard birth that reddened and bruised the face."

The midwife gritted her teeth.

"The mother died from giving life to this little beast. She carried the scarlet killer, and now this child will if it's let to live. It must not."

The drummer pushed the old woman aside. He stared at the child. Then smiled.

"All my days I've prayed for a son. Back home in New Orleans, I have a wife and four daughters. Pretty daughters. But no son to join me on the road and lug my heavy sacks. I'm growing older. I'll take the child if no one claims him. Joshua. Joshua will comfort and aid me in the years to come."

Winter, 1842

The drummer reined his horse to a halt at the top of a pine-clad rise. Behind him, wheels creaked and another horse snuffled loudly as a boy guided the animal up next to the drummer, then climbed down and unhitched a knife sharpener's cart.

"Joshua. Son, come see it. Our destination. Come here where you can see."

The boy, very tall and slender for his age, clambered to the man's side.

"Weeks ago, Joshua, when we crossed the Mississippi, I promised you we would see it. Your birthplace. Blackwinter Inn. See it? Wouldn't you like to live there?"

Something of surprise and awe registered in the boy's red-splotched, misshapen face. Below him, the dark, coffee-colored water of a lake shimmered, and in the midst of it an island jutted forth as if defying the presence of the lake. And atop the island, surrounded by a high, rock wall and giant pines stood Blackwinter Inn, bathed in stately grandeur, capped with a stunning bell tower. The edifice commanded the scene as if it were a medieval castle.

"Ain't it a grand piece of work?" the drummer prodded.

10

"Oh, my boy, if you could talk I know you would spout praises of it all the way to its very gates. I know you would. What a grand place to live it would be."

The man smiled broadly and arched and then relaxed his shoulders, shaking his head in wonder. In return, the boy fashioned a smile, and when the drummer gestured for him to sit, he obeyed.

"A rich and powerful man operates that grand thing. Jacob Manley Blackwinter. Oh, a man he is who can stand on the very shoulders of the earth. The very shoulders."

He paused a moment, and from one of his trinket sacks he retrieved a small blanket obviously wrapped around some object or objects.

"Mr. Blackwinter will allow us to sleep in his wine cellar. That cellar—there's a story there, but . . . but our journey here has a special design, Joshua. Special design."

Edging closer to the boy, he gathered himself for solemn words.

"When I look upon your face, Joshua, I do not see the ugliness others see. I, Silas Butera the drummer . . . I see a son who has kept me fine company on the road. I see a handsome face shadowed there below your affliction. And, yes, I know . . . in the streets of New Orleans, you are feared and hated. You used to cry when we had to hide you from those who wanted to kill you."

Rubbing his fingers nervously over the blanket, the drummer shook off images from the past and mustered a fatherly determination to speak directly to the boy.

"Joshua, you never need be feared or hated again. Ever. Beneath Blackwinter Inn there flow mineral springs—healing springs, Joshua. People—wealthy people from up north, from everywhere—come here to drink this, this *magic* water, to bathe in it and be cured of whatever ails them."

Then he raised a hand as if to temper the boy's sudden excitement.

"Yes, it may cure you, Joshua. It may even give you a voice. But I can't promise it. Can't promise it."

The wind skipping off the lake soughed in the pinetops, a chill winter wind, and it drew man and boy into a warm knot.

"I have something for you," said the drummer. "A gift. When we present ourselves and display our wares tonight, you will use this gift."

He unfolded the blanket and handed a fine pair of leather gloves to the boy. A merry tinkling filled the scene. The boy appeared pleased.

"Those tiny bells on the knuckles of each glove will help me to know where you are if we should happen to get separated. Wear them, Joshua. Wear the gloves, and no one will fear your touch."

The wind continued to sough softly in the pines.

Drummer Silas and the boy gazed longingly at Blackwinter Inn.

That evening

The festive license of the night held sway.

Costumed phantasms waltzed, flooding the gaily decorated ballroom with color and breathtaking movement. The heart of life beat to the strains of beautiful music. And at intervals an ebony clock chimed and the dancing ceased and the conversation of the masked ladies and gentlemen created a music all its own.

Cloaked by a heavy curtain, Joshua viewed the spectacle. His eyes followed the swirl of gowns, his ears captured every sweet note, and his nose found perfume in every molecule of air.

The hour having grown late and the drummer having confided in wine, the boy had been drawn to the sights and sounds. He would not stay long, he told himself, for the drummer might awaken and become alarmed at not discovering him near.

In the excitement of stealing away from the wine cellar, Joshua had forgotten his fine new gloves. But no matter, he reasoned. The tiny bells could not truly signal his location, could not be heard above the magnificent music, or the conversation and laughter, or the resonant clamor of the clock. And so he watched on, drinking in the gilded bustle of Blackwinter Inn as if it were a life-preserving elixir.

"What are you doing here? You! Your face is the face of an ugly brute! Be gone from here!"

Joshua turned to the sudden challenge of a handsomely bedecked gentleman.

"What are you doing here? Answer me at once," the gentleman persisted.

But the boy could only emit a hoarse cry.

The moment kaleidoscoped when the gentleman clasped Joshua's hand and pulled him from behind the curtain. The scene blurred as almost immediately the man collapsed. A woman looking on screamed. Voices of concerned and curious and startled men chorused. And the boy stood, shocked, in utter disbelief that events had so transpired.

"God in heaven, see to the gentleman!" someone shouted.

There was, however, no agent on earth powerful enough to assist him. Stunned observers could only stare in horrified fascination at the gentleman's transformation: the scarlet splotches leeching across his pale face, the erupting sores, the eager streaming of blood from his ears and nose and mouth.

"Seize the boy! He did this! I saw him!"

Amidst the continued screaming of the women and the haranguing of the men, Joshua was wrestled to the floor, then roughly dragged from the room.

It may have been Jacob Manley Blackwinter himself who directed a half dozen men to remove the boy to the wine cellar where they covered him with a burlap sack and bound it tightly with rope.

A moment of private history repeated itself when the drummer shook free of his stupor to witness Joshua's life threatened. But this time he was knocked unconscious before he could defend the boy.

"Put him on the next rail north," a silk-suited gentleman called out. Others agreed, seconding the suggestion angrily.

Despite his tall and meager frame, Joshua fought them like a wild animal. Blinded by the burlap sack, he stumbled deeper into the cool depths of the cellar.

"Don't let him escape!"

Suddenly the cellar echoed the sharp report of a revolver. A bitter puff of smoke drifted over the small mob. The silk-suited gentleman's aim was deadly.

Struck in the back of the head, Joshua lunged forward, crying out in agony only once.

The cellar gradually lapsed into silence.

The men, after pronouncing the boy justifiably a corpse, returned to the ballroom to recount an episode of a civilized legal code in action.

In the morning, the grief-stricken drummer, aided by a Negro kitchen servant, dug a shallow grave for the boy in the most remote corner of the wine cellar.

Try as he might, Silas Butera could generate no words of parting.

Days later

Trickles of the mineral water have pooled for hours on end at the point of the recently hollowed-out gravesite. Through the moist earth, a hand breaks free. Fingers curl. The hand flexes. Animated, the corpse of Joshua Butera

14

struggles from the darkness of its repose.

The face of the boy is handsome. The eyes are dark and intelligent.

He clears his throat.

And though no one else hears him, he speaks.

"I am here," he exclaims. "I am here."

Chapter I

1

"It sounds so romantic. Like an adventure. The old hotel must be absolutely charming. Think of the stories it could tell—it's nearly a hundred and sixty years old."

Kathy Holmes bubbled on, glancing from her husband, Alan, who was driving, to her stepson, Kevin, who was scrunched against a door in the backseat.

"You'll lose some of your enthusiasm when you see how much work we have ahead of us. We're using this weekend for a down-and-dirty closer look at the property so we can agree on some repair priorities—plus, it's officially the first weekend we've owned the place, so we're going to celebrate our debt."

With that concluding line, Alan smiled at his new wife, but when he caught a glimpse of his son in the rearview mirror, the smile dissolved. Then Kathy reclaimed his attention.

"What are we calling this venture—joint ownership? Us and the Bozics and the Davenports?" she asked.

"Mostly the Goldsmith National Bank owns the property, but they let us put our names on the fancy-worded deed. Sorta like those false diplomas you got in high school

17

before the real ones came in the mail."

Kathy tucked her knees up under her and surrendered her gaze to the deep, woodsy landscape.

"You know what's amazing to me? That three couples have stuck together over the years. Seems unusual that adults could enjoy each other's company so much. That's nice. Terrific, really."

"Hasn't all been peaches and cream. But I've known Larry and Gina Bozic for ten or twelve years, and Mike and Sarah Davenport for about as long. Of course, I met them through Dora, and I think she and Gina cooked up the idea for all of us—three couples—to vacation together every year."

The late afternoon sun, a high, November sun, dappled the road, hitting and tossing off intense glints of light from the station wagon.

Uncomfortable with the sudden lull in the conversation, Alan reached for Kathy's hand, squeezed it, and gained a return smile.

"Sorry, Kath. I said the *D* word, didn't I?"

She shook her head.

"Don't apologize. She's been a part of the group from the beginning. She was your wife. The other couples knew her and obviously liked her. Still do. She'll be like . . . like a ghost this weekend, haunting relationships that you're all familiar with."

"Look, Kath, the others have only known you for six months. Six months. Damn, that's a blink of an eye. Give them time. They'll warm to you. They're good folks. They've been good friends. Great friends. Dora can't be one of us anymore. They realize that."

"But it means I'm the new kid on the block." She sighed. "I'm just no good at making first impressions."

"Made a good one on me."

She leaned across the seat and kissed him on the ear, then turned self-consciously toward Kevin, but he was staring

18

out the window, seemingly oblivious to any conversation or activity in the front seat.

"I want this to work," she exclaimed, raising her voice so that the boy would be sure to hear. "I want your friends to accept me. Maybe I can win them over this weekend . . . win everybody over."

"If you're alluding to my son as well as the others, good luck. Turning thirteen has given him license to be even stranger than usual. Plain and simple bad manners are the heart of it."

"Alan, don't, please."

"Kath, he's gone out of his way to be as cool and indifferent to you as possible. Well, if he knows what's good for him, he'll change his tune this weekend."

Father and son made eye contact in the rearview mirror.

"I believe the headaches and dizziness are still giving him trouble, Alan."

She rested her chin on the seat and let concern seep into her voice.

"Are they, Kevin?"

"Yes, ma'am. Some."

"Oh, for Christ's sake, how much mileage is he going to get out of that accident? It happened early in the summer. The doctor gave him pretty much a clean bill of health."

"A shock like that can have long-term effects. I know, Alan. I've had nurse's training, and I've read case studies about severe electrical shocks."

Kevin dropped his eyes in apparent embarrassment.

Conversation waned for a mile or so. Tension held, then lost strength by degrees.

Through the pines and hardwoods, a lake loomed to the right. The station wagon dipped suddenly downhill, crossing a long bridge near a marina.

"Look at that!" Kathy exclaimed. "It's a Mississippi riverboat, isn't it?"

An expression of delight and surprise on her face, she

19

sought out confirmation.

"Yeah, it's the Catlin County paddle wheeler," Alan responded. "Every Saturday afternoon until around Christmas, it goes from here on Jackson Lake north to Blackwinter Lake and back. It'll circle our island on Sunday morning if the drought hasn't lowered the lake levels too much."

He winked an apology for his harsh tone moments earlier.

"Oh, it's such a gorgeous boat. Have you ever ridden on it, Kevin?"

"No, ma'am."

2

It was happening again.

That indescribable lightness. A floating free. A vantage point on some scene projected from the context of the present. This time the boat, the gleaming white paddle wheeler trimmed in red and gold, triggered the flashforward.

From somewhere high above the boat Kevin watched the carefully restored vessel glide along, its huge wheel churning, generating small, eager waterfalls. And its decks were thronged with people on each of the three levels, smiling people, pulling away from view as if flowing into a previous century.

He focused on one passenger.

A mixture of relief and abject terror coursed through him.

But he could not understand why.

The passenger was a complete stranger to him.

The present reasserted itself. He was once again in the backseat of the family station wagon. He pressed fingertips onto his forehead, fought a wave of dizziness; then, seeing that his stepmother had noticed, quickly lowered his hand.

He hoped she wouldn't say anything.

The woods swallowed the sunlight; an occasional roadside sign would appear and race by, vanishing, only to be replaced by another farther down the road.

Everything about this trip feels wrong.

That morning he had considered going to his dad and pleading with him not to spend the weekend at Blackwinter Inn. But for the inevitable question—Why?—he would have had no convincing answer.

There was no point, he reasoned, in creating more friction between them.

He would keep quiet. Survive the weekend. Be a mouse in the corner.

Yet, confrontation with his dad loomed, a band of threatening storm clouds in the guise of a report card—a very poor report card. He hadn't shown it to him.

It's not my fault. I can't concentrate at school.

Though it promised to be easier than the seventh grade, the eighth grade was proving more demanding academically and socially. Not only was he losing points in the classroom, he was losing friends out of class—his curious lapses into silence, his blank stares, his bouts with disorientation; the accident had wrenched him from the orbit of his peers.

Mom would understand.

But since she and his dad had divorced, she had been living and working in Birmingham, a hundred miles away. Of course, there was now a new member of the household, and he really didn't mean to be so cool to her. Kathy had pluses: She was smart, energetic, pretty; she obviously loved his dad and he loved her—and yet . . .

At school last week a teacher intern from Auburn University had taught his English class; like Kathy, she was blond and attractive. But she was still a college student—not even ten years older than he was. How could such a person possibly fill the role of mother?

21

Bottom line: Kathy hadn't been there. Hadn't been there as he was growing up, hadn't bandaged a skinned elbow, hadn't read Golden Books to him, hadn't taken him to Little League practice, hadn't saved him an extra piece of pie, hadn't baked him his favorite cake on his birthday, hadn't hidden Easter eggs for him, hadn't made Santa Claus come alive on Christmas Eve.

Hadn't loved him for as many years as he could remember.

If I could only stop time . . .

His head buzzed.

He studied the face of his wristwatch.

The second hand swung slowly but inexorably, carrying him from a comfortable and secure past into a future he feared because, while it could be glimpsed, it could not be fathomed.

Stop time.

Lightness.

His stare locked onto the delicate, circling hand.

Pain danced behind his eyes.

The inside of his mouth dried.

He flashed forward. And found himself in a ballroom, floating above music and waltzing and splashings of color. A clock chimed; its deep voice echoed and all movement ceased.

And the second hand on his watch abruptly stopped.

3

"It's stopped!" he exclaimed.

Immediately Kathy glanced at him, her curiosity tapped. She laughed nervously at the intensity of his outburst.

"My goodness. What's going on back there?"

He met her smiling eyes.

"Oh . . . it was . . . my watch . . . it stopped. It . . .

22

hasn't been running right."

Then he caught the full bore of his dad's disgusted look.

"Are we going to have to put up with a whole weekend of that kind of thing?"

"No, sir. Sorry. I . . . I'm sorry."

Kathy gave her husband a bemused grin which seemed to say, Be tolerant. You were thirteen once upon a time.

"Will the others already be there?" she asked, gently guiding his attention away from Kevin.

"I expect so. The Davenports will be out on the lake in their houseboat."

"A houseboat? Sounds like fun."

"Yeah, they love it. Mike believes he was a sailor in a previous life. Well, not really. But he and Sarah spend a lot of time on that boat. It has all the comforts of home."

"Don't they have a cabin on the lake, too?"

Alan nodded.

"A trailer. Larry and Gina are supposed to set up our base camp there, and between the houseboat and Larry's fishing boat we'll transport people and everything else over to the island."

"Larry's certainly a pleasant guy. 'Laid-back,' I guess, is the right word for him."

Alan chuckled.

"Or maybe lazy or shiftless or unambitious. Larry lets life come to him except when food is involved. He'll go to great lengths there. You'll see. He'll fix a gourmet meal for us before we go home. And he and Gina will fight. They always do. At least, Gina fights and Larry sorta makes like a sparring partner who never throws any hard punches. Their marriage seems to work, though . . . so what can you say?"

"Sarah's the one who's kind of a puzzle to me," Kathy responded. "She's nice, but very quiet."

"She and Mike have been going through a tough time."

"They thinking of splitting up?"

Gripping the steering wheel more firmly, Alan said, "I'm not sure. Anyway, I told you about the nightmare they experienced a couple of years ago, didn't I?"

Kathy thought a moment.

"Nothing's coming to mind. No, I don't believe you did."

"Tragic business. You see they had adopted a boy—twelve, thirteen years old. His name was Richard. Very bright. Always seemed comfortable around adults. Always seemed, you know, older, more mature than other kids his age. Well, one evening Mike and Sarah went out—to a party at the Bozics', in fact—and came home and . . . Mike found him. The boy had hanged himself in the shower."

"My God," Kathy exclaimed and then pressed a hand over her mouth.

"Really tore them up. In ways, they haven't recovered. Blackwinter Inn is like a new lease for them. Sarah's a Blackwinter—I may not have told you that either. She remembers visiting the inn years and years ago when her grandparents were living in it. So . . . like I said, maybe it's a starting-over place for them. Maybe that's what they're searching for. Maybe that's what they need."

A quarter of a mile passed in silence as Kathy let shocking images mirror forth, then fade mercifully.

"Alan? What about you? What are you searching for at Blackwinter Inn?"

He glanced at her to see whether her expression matched the apparent seriousness of her question.

"Hey, Kath . . . isn't that a pretty heavy question for the start of a weekend away from our jobs and the depressing nightly TV news—and telephones and taxes and all the other little daily atrocities we'd like to forget?"

"Yes. But will you answer it anyway?"

He shrugged his shoulders.

"OK. It's simple. The place fascinates me. I want to find out why."

Kevin touched the glass on his watch.

No, dad, you won't want to.

Stop time.

He wished the drive was a reel of film he could reverse and the station wagon would race backward to Goldsmith to the Holmes' garage, and they would frantically unpack and find themselves in front of the television watching Peter Jennings and the Friday evening news and all the world's horrors.

Horrors safely removed from them.

Chapter II

1

"They're late!"

Gina Bozic scanned the lake road, one hand on her hip and one saluting to shade her eyes.

"Dora would never have been late," she added. "Dora was on time. In control. On top of things. Miss Rah-Rah Fluff probably had cheerleader practice and made Alan watch her."

In a plastic chaise lounge, Larry Bozic nursed a Stroh's. He followed the nervous route of his thin, dark, waspish wife as she buzzed from the deck of the trailer to the driveway and the stack of groceries and camping gear and tools.

"Come on, babe. Why be so damn hard on her? She's Alan's wife now, like it or not."

She wheeled and pointed a revolver-shaped hand and finger at him.

"Not! I miss Dora already!"

Larry shrugged. He guzzled another inch of the Stroh's, musing at how a cold beer could taste every bit as good on a crisp autumn day as in mid July. The world was replete with such wonders, he decided. He unwrapped the first of two chocolate-covered Zingers, patted his substantial stomach, and bit enough of the end of the snack cake to reach the creme-filled center.

He chewed, swallowed, and belched. Dark crumbs resembling ants clung to his lips.

Beer and Zingers . . . ah, life! Ah, humanity!

"They were supposed to be here at four o'clock. It's nearly four thirty, and the sun's about down and we don't have stuff organized. I bet she's making Alan late on purpose. It's a slap at the closeness we've all had as couples—that's what it is."

Oh, Lord, Larry thought, she has that tone going. And that finger.

Managing to crook his neck a bit, he located the white, ghostly form of a houseboat gliding toward shore.

"Davenports are docking. They can help."

Pocket computer and notepad in hand, Gina fumed into a lawn chair next to him.

"*You* could help! Instead of lazing about, feeding your face. What are you eating? Zingers and—! Larry, dearest, sweetheart, love of my life, you are repulsive. A lout. A perfect lout."

He smiled at her and wagged a finger.

"Thank you, babe, but don't count on being able to butter me up. I'm not one of your clients."

Gina punched at the computer, translating numbers as rapidly as possible onto the notepad.

"If interest rates don't drop before spring, how in the hell will I reach my quota?"

Larry frowned at her.

"Can't you put that away? Lord have mercy, babe, you know you don't have to be realtor of the month every damned month. You're depressing your colleagues. And me. And the kids."

He gestured vaguely at their two daughters, one of whom was walking atop the deck railing as if it were a balance beam.

"Wish I had a cigarette. *That's* what's depressing *me*. I'm not going to be able to quit," she snarled.

"Sure you are," he insisted before taking a lengthy draw on the Stroh's. "Will power. Main thing, you need to get the hooks outta you. Your damn job has hooks, Gina. It's gon' drag you under if you let it. Relax. Follow my example."

"Perish the thought," she muttered.

She bit at her bottom lip as she saw something more in the figures she didn't like. She flailed a hand wildly, the action of a one-armed orchestra conductor. Then she sighed.

She slammed the computer onto the notepad, puffed out her cheeks, and searched the heavens for solace. Apparently she found none. But she did witness the antics of her eldest daughter.

"Look at this!" she exclaimed, pointing again. "She's your daughter, Larry. Explain to her that the Olympics were over in September. It's too late to go to Seoul."

Her husband laughed and the laugh provoked another belch.

"Maria, your mother says she wants to see you do a backflip into a splits."

Gina glared at him.

Maria, going on twelve, deftly balanced herself on the railing.

"Oh, Daddy, you know Mom hates it that I like gymnastics."

She had her father's blond hair, blue eyes, rounded cheeks, and yet, unlike him, a reasonably athletic body.

"It's a waste of time," said her mother. "Young women today shouldn't try to become jocks or beauty queens. They should mold themselves into competitive businesswomen. It's certainly not too early for you to start considering a career orientation, Miss Somersault."

"Lord uh mercy," said Larry. "First we have 'Miss Rah-Rah Fluff,' and now we have 'Miss Somersault.' Be careful,

28

Sophie, you're next."

Their youngest daughter, nine, sauntered up to her mother and climbed onto her lap.

"You got a funny name for me, too?"

Gina smiled expansively at her. Sophie's dark eyes, black hair, firm and very attractive features were small replicas of Gina's.

"Yes, I have."

She squeezed her daughter's waist.

"I will call you 'Sophia Bozic, chief executive officer,' or 'Sophia Bozic, chairwoman of the board,' or 'Sophia Bozic, congresswoman.' How are those?"

"They'll do just fine. Lot better'n 'Miss Somersault.' "

"Jesus," Larry muttered, "when does she get to be a little girl?"

"She's beyond that. Aren't you, Sophie sweet? No, this one—*this one*—is not going to fiddle away her time foolishly jumping and tumbling around. She's going to make something of herself. You'll see."

2

"Why does she hate me, Daddy?"

"Hey, no . . . listen to me, kiddo. Your mother doesn't hate you. Donchoo be thinking like that. Why, that woman would fight all the demons and devils in hell for you. I'd bet my next beer on it."

Maria tried to force herself not to smile, but when her dad touched the icy can to her nose, she couldn't help it. Giggled, too.

"You drink too much beer, Daddy. You'll be out of shape to play church-league basketball."

"Nay, child. Oh, say not so. This somewhat rounded exterior but hides a lean, mean, slam-dunking interior. Why, even now I could trip lightfootedly upon yon deck railing."

She giggled again.

"Not without breaking your neck or the railing."

"Very perceptive, kiddo," he responded, smiling, hugging her to his side. "So you ought to be able to see through your mother if you can see through me. She just wants you to be your best."

"But what if I don't want to be a person who sells houses or is always interested in making money? I'd rather be a gymnast, and I could be 'cept I have a hard time staying thin."

"You inherited your father's metabolism for sure. Ever think about going out for the track team and throwing the shot put?"

"Daddy! Quit teasing!"

"Oh, was I teasing? Shame on me."

He tipped the can for a final swallow, then rocked forward as if considering matters very solemnly.

"Wouldn't suggest your becoming a high school English teacher like your old man. Not exciting enough, right?"

"It might be OK. I like stories and poems, especially stories about horses and sports and adventures. I'm not a good speller, though. English teachers have to be good spellers, don't they?"

"Yes, of course. Why, English teachers who can't spell are burned at the stake on a regular basis."

"Daddy!"

They wrestled playfully and he let her pin his arm behind his back.

"Be serious, Daddy."

"OK. OK, I will. Just don't bring on the thumbscrews or throw the cooler of beer in the lake. I can't stand too much torture."

"Tell me what I could grow up and be that would please Mom and me both."

"H'm-m-m . . . let's see. So this has to have an answer

before your twelfth birthday?"

"Yes."

"All right. Here it is."

She looked into his mischievous eyes, saw twinkles of warmth, and felt an invisible embrace of love which nearly staggered her.

"Be yourself, Maria. Your own wonderfully unique self."

Speechless for a moment, she leaned forward and kissed his cheek.

"Thanks, Daddy."

"You're welcome, kiddo. But look out, now, here comes your little sis."

Face wrinkled into a scowl, Sophie approached them, her mind set on wriggling up in front of Maria to command her father's attention.

"There really ghosts where we're staying tonight? Maria says there are, but Momma says don't believe all that nonsense. Which is right, Daddy?"

Maria reluctantly backed away from her jealous sister, relinquishing her spot.

"Yes, there are," she exclaimed. "Everybody knows the Blackwinter Inn has ghosts. Tell her, Daddy."

Mindful of the sibling power struggle, Larry maneuvered one daughter onto one knee and the other daughter onto the opposite knee.

"Ghosts, is it? Of course, you're aware I'm an authority on the subject, being a ghostbuster before the movie."

"No, you're not really," Sophie muttered.

But he nodded gravely.

"Yes, oh yes. Why, the things I've heard about Blackwinter Inn . . . oh-h-h my."

He shivered in mock fashion.

Seeing a tinge of fear in Sophie's eyes, Maria had to smother laughter.

"Tell us, Daddy," she prodded. "Sophie wants to hear."

"I won't be scared," said Sophie, jutting out her chin

31

defiantly.

How many times, Larry wondered, have I seen your mother do that?

"OK. Gather close," he murmured.

The two girls scooted nearer.

Larry glanced from one to the other, pleased with their total absorption in his performance.

"Story goes," he began, "that on late autumn days such as this one, the spirits of Blackwinter Inn stir and grow restless and go afoot."

"What's 'go afoot'?" Sophie interrupted.

"Well . . . it's the kind of words ghosts use. I think it means that they start walking around in the walls, making noise. You know, groaning and moaning."

"Are they sick?"

"Sophie! Let Daddy finish!"

He shook his head.

"No. No, not exactly. Not sick. Just . . . very . . . *hungry.*"

Sophie apprehensively pressed a finger into the corner of her mouth.

Larry arched his eyebrows and asked her, "And do you know what they're hungry for?"

Maria giggled; Sophie bit her lip.

"Get closer, and I'll tell you," he whispered.

Bundles of warm, nervous energy, they did as their father requested.

"These spirits . . . the ghosts of Blackwinter Inn . . . wander from room to room, searching for the sustenance they need. Late, late at night — well past midnight — you can hear them: 'We want . . . we want . . . !"

"What, Daddy? What do the ghosts want?" Sophie asked impatiently.

Larry frowned and deepened his voice.

" 'We want . . . *beer and Zingers!*' " he exclaimed.

Maria howled, but Sophie punched him twice and then

32

flitted away, her chin saluting the air.

Alone again, father and eldest daughter stood at the deck railing and surveyed the twilight outline of Blackwinter Inn perched atop the distant island.

"It kinda looks spooky, doesn't it, Daddy?"

"Nah, not spooky. Just interesting. Kiddo, did you know that—so the story goes—Edgar Allan Poe visited that inn back in, oh, I think it was the 1840s. An acquaintance of his knew Mr. Blackwinter and invited Poe to come see the famous hotel. So he did—so the story goes."

"We read one of Poe's poems in English class. Something about a raven. Do you really believe Poe was ever there—where we're going?"

"Oh, I'd like to believe it. He's one of my favorite authors. Wrote a thesis on him long ago. But, no . . . no, he probably wasn't."

"Daddy? It'll be safe to stay over there this weekend, won't it?"

"Now, what do you think, kiddo? Would your daddy let his beautiful daughters spend a couple of nights in a dangerous place? Goodness no."

3

"I hope we're not late."

Kathy Holmes had on her best smile as she bounced up to Gina.

"Late? Well, we should have been better organized by now. Alan, foodstuffs will go over here."

Avoiding Kathy's protracted smile, Gina pointed to a sizeable assemblage of boxes and sacks.

"Hey, have we invited a battalion of soldiers from Fort Benning?" Alan exclaimed, his mouth agape at the amount of supplies. "Or is most of this for Larry?"

He hugged Gina and gave her a peck on the cheek.

"See your picture in the paper nearly every week, lady," he continued. "Still burning things up in the real estate game. That's great."

"You always were a fan of mine," she said. "But you know I'll never forgive you and Dora for letting somebody else sell your house on Jenkins. You lost money, I bet."

Alan raised his hands in mock surrender.

"Learned my lesson. Kath and I won't make the same mistake, will we, Kath?"

"No. No, we won't. Gina, Alan says you really are the best realtor in Goldsmith. And he means it."

Gina rolled her eyes.

"I'll give you some advice right this instant, Kathy. Free advice. All of us can testify that it's almost impossible to tell what Alan *means* and what he doesn't *mean*. Don't get me wrong—he's a sweetheart, but . . . we've known him longer than you have."

Kathy was on the verge of responding when Larry appeared at Gina's shoulder.

"Never mind this woman," he said. "She's trying for last place in the Miss Congeniality category this weekend. I think she's a shoo-in myself. So . . . how the hell are you guys? Let me get a cold one for you while Gina decides which box goes where. Say, Kathy, you look terrific. What do you see in an old, broken-down insurance salesman like Alan?"

As he chattered on, Gina threw up her hands, exasperated.

"I don't need your help," she cried out. "Mike and Sarah will come to my rescue."

Beneath the fuming and fussing, she felt good. She would make Kathy earn her position in the group—*for Dora's sake*. But otherwise she planned to enjoy the weekend and, especially, to examine Blackwinter Inn with a professional eye.

I might, she told herself, be looking at a gold mine.

Chapter III

1

"I'd like something to be resolved. And no more counseling, Sarah. I'm talked out. I've said everything in those sessions I feel like saying."

As the houseboat drifted, Mike Davenport stood at its stern rail next to his wife. Out of the corner of his eye he could see that she was crying. Part of him wanted to reach out and comfort her; part of him said, "You've tried that. Touching isn't enough."

Adrift.

It was an accurate metaphor for their marriage, he thought to himself. Adrift like a derelict vessel. For two years they had been drifting; hoping, he assumed, that they would come upon something—*something*—which would offer a direction to their relationship.

Sarah brushed an escaping tear from her cheek. Then she began to speak in the passionless monotone he had heard so often.

"Why did we only take him out on the boat once? I remember *one* afternoon. One. He loved being here. On the boat. Either at the wheel—I remember you let him steer us to the island—or here, fishing or watching the propeller churn the water. Why only once?"

35

She turned, tears flowing more freely, and continued.

"Why? Was there some reason for denying him something he enjoyed so much?"

"Don't, Sarah," said Mike.

"I'm just asking. I'm just . . . trying to figure out why we were punishing him."

"Damn it, Sarah. We weren't. There were at least three afternoons I can recall when Richard came with us. We didn't *deny* him anything. Stop manufacturing that kind of thing. We never *punished* Richard. We barely ever reprimanded him."

"Then what? What, Mike? What would make a bright, life-loving boy . . . ?"

But she wasn't able to finish. She folded her arms against her breasts and sobbed.

This time he did touch her. He grasped her by the shoulders and leaned down into her face, his tone that of a parent addressing a child.

"Stop it. So help me God, if this is what the weekend's going to be like, I'm docking this boat and going home, and you can stay if you want to. This isn't fair, Sarah. Not fair to me. To you. To us."

She bowed her head and cried softly.

"And it's not fair to Larry and Gina and to Alan and Kathy, either," he added. "They have big plans. They want Blackwinter Inn to become a special place for them. What's it going to be for us, Sarah? Are we going to the island as a step into the future? Or do we call it off right here? I need some kind of an answer."

Not ready to raise her eyes, she shook her head and Mike pushed away.

She gripped the railing and whispered beneath her breath, "I'm sorry."

Turning, she saw that he was sitting in his captain's seat at the wheel. She dried her eyes and stared down into the twilight-silvered water.

He's right. I'm not being fair.

But does he really understand? She wondered.

And was Blackwinter the right setting in which to put the pieces back together?

Lifting her head, she caught a sudden, startling glimpse of the inn dominating the wooded island. It loomed there, holding within it several warm and identity-rich memories . . . and one haunting incident.

One moment of absolute terror.

2

"Ginny Ma, does grandfather eat the same breakfast *every* morning?"

The old woman stopped, seeming to be listening to something far away, and looked off to one side as she always did when she spoke to her grandchild.

"Yes, that's so. Just so. Mr. Blackwinter specifically requests this breakfast, and I comply to the letter."

Why her grandmother consistently referred to her husband as Mr. Blackwinter was one of many puzzles eight-year-old Sarah would not solve until years later when she learned that Virginia Clarke and Ransom Blackwinter had been a "contract" marriage prearranged by their parents.

Breakfast, however, posed sufficient mystery for a girl spending a few summer weeks at the decaying manse propped upon the island like a giant tombstone.

"It's ready," Sarah murmured.

"Best we check ourselves to see that we have it just so."

Sarah, accordingly, pointed at each item on the tray, identifying it in rote fashion: "One hard-boiled egg, lightly salted; four triangles of toast, no butter; two tablespoons of apricot jam; and one cup of coffee, lightened by one teaspoon of milk — coffee not stirred."

"Oh, it's just so. Be off, then. Carry the tray ever so

carefully."

"Ginny Ma," Sarah asked one day. "Will I *ever* see my grandfather? Will he always be way up there in his room with the door shut? Will I never get to hug him like I hug you at bedtime?"

Eyes to the floor, the old woman said, "No. It mustn't be any other way."

"But why?"

"Because that's the fate that life has bestowed upon Mr. Blackwinter. It's just so. He doesn't complain, now, does he? So we mustn't. Run along. Wait on the top stair if you don't see the cart."

Sarah realized that day what a truly remarkable woman her grandmother was, able to tend to the daily affairs of a very large house—the finances, the dealings with two servants—and still devote time and energy to the mystery man to whom she had been wedded. In fact, Ginny Ma seemed almost preternaturally attuned to her husband, by a weird symbiosis of sound and intuition. For example, she and Sarah could be sitting near the huge, stone fireplace, sewing or chatting over afternoon tea—a favorite ritual of the old woman—when suddenly she would freeze all action and speech and announce, "Those are Mr. Blackwinter's bells. I must see what he needs."

Yet, so soft, so nearly inaudible were those tinklings that Sarah almost never heard them, and certainly *never* did she hear them *before* her grandmother did.

Such thoughts and images occupied the girl as, on a humid summer morning, she began her journey to the third floor, balancing the silver tray which needed polishing, one step at a time, not slowing at the second floor which her grandparents kept boarded up—another Blackwinter mystery—and finally reaching the top stair on the lip of the third-floor landing. There she would peer toward the end of the hall to see whether the green cart, an antique knife sharpener's cart, was sentried just outside her grandfather's room.

If it were, she would continue, each step gladdened by the image of the note which awaited her in a gold-embossed envelope on the cart. By the envelope would rest a fine ink pen. And thus grandfather and grandchild would communicate. She cherished each morning's note, despite the fact that the messages were invariably brief and written in a craggy hand, barely decipherable.

They greeted her the same way each time: "Sarah, Sarah, my sweet Sarah."

Most notes offered a pleasantly lyrical view of life:

Sarah, Sarah, my sweet Sarah,
    Yesterday I saw ducks on the lake gliding serenely. I can shut my eyes and see them forever. Did you by chance glimpse the sunset? Joyous pink and a chorus of gold and a single high-pitched silver. Ducks and sunsets. Be thankful, Sarah. Always be thankful.

Other notes spoke of a certain timeless legacy he hoped to leave, fragments of an existence history books would ignore . . . life lived more lovingly:

Sarah, Sarah, my sweet Sarah,
    The daylilies will be here out by the south wall long after I am gone. I watched Sherman tend to them yesterday morning, sweat glistening on his skillful black arms. Nowhere in the universe would a fine gardener be unwelcome. He who brings beauty to the world is immortal.

Occasionally a note would lapse into a curious introspection or melancholy:

Sarah, Sarah, my sweet Sarah,

Last night I wrote a letter to the part of myself I don't care for. I warned him not to occupy so much of my time. I cannot be his friend. Return to that dark cell of my heart or soul, I told him. I cannot embrace shadows; I cannot love all that I am.

But this one particular morning the mystical order of things had been thrown off. No, the green cart stood at its proper post; however, there was no gold-embossed envelope on it. No note.

And one other pulse-quickening difference.

What's going on? Sarah asked herself.

Her body thrummed with a secret tension, a secret excitement.

I should tell Ginny Ma.

Standing as noiselessly as possible, little Sarah listened for the jingle of her grandfather's bells. *Maybe he's sick.*

A crouching silence followed her cautious footfalls up to the cart.

She saw it again, a validation which chilled her.

It.

The tray teetered. A small amount of coffee sloshed over the rim of the cup. Very carefully she set the tray atop the cart. Her arms ached from having carried it so rigidly.

She smoothed her dress nervously.

Was there the slightest bit of sound behind her? Was Ginny Ma calling her?

No. She turned. She blinked her eyes to make very certain she wasn't imagining things. No. It was just so.

The door to grandfather's room stood ajar.

Not much. One inch. Perhaps an inch and a half.

But through that narrow slant of an opening, worlds of knowledge and awareness beckoned — forbidden, yet so . . . so seductive. Virgin territory. There was no way to resist.

Ever so quietly she maneuvered herself so that she could

see through the slant. She held her breath, squinted her eyes. The angle presented to her a slice of dark room, the black outline of a lamp, the arm of a chair. She could not see a bed or the figure of her grandfather.

Grandfather.

The word remained locked in the hard shell of her mouth, not ready to be hatched.

She glanced once over her shoulder and felt a strange sense of relief—she knew she would not, *could not,* turn back. Some invisible point of no return had been passed. Not a physical point, but rather an emotional one.

Her fingers touched the doorknob.

No fire. No ice. No howl of demons.

Sarah, Sarah, my sweet Sarah.

The line singsonged in her thoughts.

She pushed and the door started to swing open.

3

The houseboat's engine roared to life.

Sarah snapped out of the memory so suddenly that she had to hold onto the rail tightly to avoid falling.

In his captain's seat, Mike listened to the metallic hum of the engine, a deep, guttural sound which gradually evened out into a smooth idle. He then reached for the object he had found on the control panel.

His thoughts weighed in against a throng of conflicting possibilities: Who left this? I've never seen it before.

Most unsettling of all was the possibility that someone had been aboard the boat, and yet nothing seemed to be missing. No vandalism.

He raised the object so that he could examine it in detail. It was no more than six inches long—a child's toy—though he noted the care which had been lavished upon the vessel, a steamboat replete with black smokestack and paddle wheel and flagpole, flag missing. Mike recognized it at once as being modeled upon Robert Fulton's *Clermont.*

The chipped paint, the "feel" of the object, the years of handling it had endured told him something else: The toy boat was very old, an antique beyond doubt.

But where did it come from?

"Who left it here?" he whispered.

How many hours had he and Richard spent assembling model boats and planes? Surely, he reasoned, this must be one the boy had forgotten to take ashore the last time . . .

The glass above the control panel spread before him, an opaque curtain created by the onset of evening. A curtain. Like a shower curtain.

He closed his eyes; his jaw stiffened as if he were fighting something.

That night two years ago they had come home from the Bozics' to a dark house.

"Richard? Have you gone to bed? Hey, we're home."

Not downstairs. Not in his bedroom.

Bathroom door open just a bit.

"Richard? Are you not feeling well?"

He switched on the light. And stepped toward the shower curtain.

4

"I'll try," said Sarah.

Mike wheeled around.

"Oh . . . I didn't hear you come this way."

He couldn't tell whether she had seen him slip the toy boat behind his back.

"Sorry. Shouldn't have frightened you. But I have something to say."

The residue of fear and dark images disoriented him momentarily.

42

"Well . . . fine, then . . . what is it?"

She looked at him, felt her need for his understanding.

"Richard's gone," she said, not conscious of how slowly she was speaking. "He won't just magically reappear. We have to have a life together without him. Just . . . just so."

He took her in his arms and they held each other.

And twilight thickened around them.

Chapter IV

1

"I am here."

The shadowy form materialized on the first landing on the bell tower.

"I am here."

In the bank of mirrors, dusty and cracked and fly-specked, which encircled the landing, a reflection emerged, one of singular ugliness. A tall, thin frame clad in ragged garments filled a large rectangle of mirror. The hands of the standing figure were covered by fine, but decades-old, gloves studded with tiny bells. But even in the twilight it was the face which dominated the reflection—a face of hideous splotches and sores, swollen skin, and an eye still and unblinking and grotesquely large.

Shadow studied reflection.

There was a soft jingle as the gloves were removed.

"I am here," said the shadow.

And the figure in the mirror began to transform; the mirror siphoned all available light, and a new face shone forth—a handsome face comprised of strong features, especially the eyes—dark, intelligent eyes.

Pleased, the figure in the mirror stepped forward. It carried a sack of wooden toys.

Over the years the old manse had called upon its resident shadow many times. Once again, the call had been issued. Up the half-dozen spiral steps to the top landing the shadowy figure climbed, pushing open the trapdoor, entering the observation area.

From there, the entire lake and its surroundings could be viewed.

From there, the figure watched people gathering on the distant shore, preparing to embark for their destination.

From a dark chamber of earliest memory, an old woman's words ghosted through the figure's thoughts: *Dragon's voice and demon's eye. You will carry the red death in your touch.*

The figure noticed the white houseboat and recalled the token it had left for Mike Davenport. There would be other tokens — toys of remembrance — for various members of the gathering.

And proper death knells, for a Charleston-style cupola nested atop the tower; it contained a rusting, yet functional, bell. All formalities would be observed.

Six bells for the death of a woman.

Nine bells for the death of a man.

Anger born of vengeance seized the figure.

Hate born of envy held sway.

"Blackwinter Inn is mine."

The bell tower creaked. Dust motes swirled lazily to life.

"I am Joshua."

One final, bright ray of sunlight slanted across the far assemblage.

"I am here," said the figure.

2

"Can you manage this, Kevin?"

The cutting tone of his dad's voice burned the tips of his

45

ears.

"Hurry while there's still light," said Gina, herding the other adults into a knot in front of the trailer.

"Make sure it's in focus. Everything else is set. So don't touch a thing."

Kevin glanced up at his dad and nodded.

Juggling a beer can and a bag of cheese curls, Larry exclaimed, "Let it be known that this is the official photograph of the notorious Holmes, Davenport, and Bozic expedition of November, year of our Lord nineteen-hundred and eighty-eight. Six brave adults and three bored kids prepared to take on the vast, uncharted realm of Blackwinter Inn. I want to see a smile on every face despite the fact that we are now hopelessly in debt."

Having succeeded in evoking laughter, he returned to his wife's side, and suddenly the group fell into the circle visible through the lens as Kevin fingered the focus ring.

Alan and Kathy Holmes. Mike and Sarah Davenport. Larry and Gina Bozic. Smiling broadly. Looking much more like kids than adults. A saturnalian pose. The faces said, This will be a good weekend.

3

They lapsed into a festive clamor, loading supplies onto the houseboat and deciding who would ride in Larry's fishing boat, thus risking life and limb.

Adventure galvanized the group. There was much laughter and kidding around, and when everything appeared settled, they found that they were making their exodus from shore to island in one trip.

"Is everybody on the ark?" Larry called out as he idled the outboard engine. "Where's Noah?"

"Present," someone responded.

And there was more laughter.

Larry had his wife and Alan and Kathy aboard, while his two daughters successfully begged passage over in the houseboat. Kevin, partly to avoid his dad, also sought booking with the Davenport's. His apprehension regarding the weekend had relented somewhat. Perhaps it was the sight of adults smiling and laughing, enjoying themselves more each second as the cares of the real world dissolved. He admitted that it was good to see his dad laughing at Larry Bozic's antics and to see the love in his eyes when he looked at Kathy—good to see that love returned in her eyes.

Maybe.

Maybe it will be OK.

At the rear of the houseboat, Sophie and Maria huddled around Sarah; they, too, seemed to have relaxed into the comfortable spirit of the weekend, chatting about whatever a woman and two girls might chat about. Kevin knew he probably wouldn't be interested—or especially welcome—in their circle, so he wandered through the cabin toward the wheel.

"Hello, Mr. Davenport."

"Oh, hey, Kevin . . . you come up to be my navigator?"

The boy chuckled self-consciously.

"No, sir. Guess not, really. I'll just stand here and watch—if it doesn't bother you."

"No bother at all. Would enjoy the company. Looks like the women have control of the rear of the boat."

"Yes, sir."

Kevin had known Mike Davenport for a long time. Had always liked him because the man obviously enjoyed being around kids. Since the death of Richard, though, Kevin sensed a certain preoccupation in him, as if the man's concentration was glued to some inner television screen on which a drama he couldn't resist were being played out. And matters were further complicated because Richard had been Kevin's friend.

Richard's suicide had hurt Kevin, but not in the sense of

47

loss or the shock of tragedy. No, it was, oddly, the feeling that he had not been let in on a friend's plans. Richard had never spoken of taking his own life—never even alluded to it as far as Kevin could recall. And yet, the slightly older boy had not been happy—not content at heart as many boys are. Kevin knew that Richard had been adopted, and so he assumed the discontent was related to that.

"How's school?"

It was the obligatory adult-to-kid question. But it succeeded in jarring Kevin's thoughts away from memories of Richard.

"All right, I guess. Sometimes . . . I get kinda discouraged, you know."

"Happens to everybody."

"You mean, you get discouraged in your job?"

Davenport smiled.

"Only two or three dozen times a day. So what discourages you about school? What gets you down? Teachers?"

"Sometimes. Yeah, some of them. Mrs. Straker, especially. She's real moody. For some reason she thinks I hate social studies—that's what she teaches—and it makes her want to be hard on me, I guess. I'm not doing well in her class. And some others, too."

"People can get to you. Take my job overseeing the county road system. I can handle it when the equipment breaks down or the effects of weather damage a new stretch of asphalt, but when people come to work late every day or mess up a job assignment, well . . . I'd like to ship them to Siberia or someplace out of my sight."

Pausing, he seemed bemused about something.

"Do you know that I have one employee who has missed a day each week for the past four weeks because he claims he had to attend a funeral. Each time it was his uncle—different one each week, I suppose. What do you do with a guy like that?"

Kevin grinned.

48

"Wait till he runs out of uncles?"

Davenport nodded.

"You're probably right. Must be a finite supply of them."

They were nearing the island; as Blackwinter Inn loomed larger and larger, their conversation waned.

Then Davenport said, "You know something?" He hesitated; his voice gained the thick, slow-rhythmed quality of a man expressing regret. "If I had only had a talk or two like this one with Richard . . . if I had taken a few more minutes a day to ask him how things were going . . . school . . . whatever — it could have made a difference."

Seeing how uncomfortable Kevin looked, he immediately shifted out of that serious tone.

"Kevin, hey, forgive me. I didn't mean to do that. But . . . will you do me a favor? If the discouragement gets worse, tell your folks. They'll listen. They'll try to help, I'm sure."

"All right."

"Good. You change your mind about being navigator? I always have trouble backing this thing into a dock."

"I can help in a second maybe."

The boy stepped away from the wheel. He was feeling panicky. It wasn't simply the overly serious nature of Davenport's earlier comments.

The sensation of floating up out of the cabin grew strong. A flashforward. Something horrible had just occurred.

"I . . . I'm going out by the rail."

"Not seasick, are you?"

"No. No, sir. I'm OK."

But he wasn't.

Panic clutched at his throat.

He drifted above the houseboat for a score of seconds before reentering his body on deck. But he received no picture, no clear image of the source of his sudden terror. He tried to pull himself along the railing only to find that his feet were sticking to the deck. He managed to free himself, but he slipped and nearly crumpled to his knees.

Gaining balance, he scrambled ahead a few yards, out of Davenport's view; then he wheeled around, gasping for air, yet relieved that he could move.

What he saw mesmerized him.

He could feel particles of something like frost forming on the back of his neck. Could feel them spreading up into his scalp.

He was seeing but definitely not believing.

There.

Beyond him.

The perfect outlines of his tennis shoes.

In blood.

Much too much blood.

Chapter V

1

"We're going to need more firewood. We spent too much time setting up that generator the other day — should've cut more wood. Was it supposed to be so cold this weekend?"

Mike shined his flashlight into the pines beyond the rock wall. He couldn't see his breath yet, but the evening temperature was falling, and the moonless night, clear and star-flecked, domed the island and the imposing inn.

Zipping up his jacket, Alan joined Mike on the front porch, then switched on another flashlight.

"Oh, this isn't bad. When we get a roaring fire going, we'll be in good shape. Kevin? Hey, Kevin, come help gather wood."

"Is there only one axe?" Mike asked. "And where's Larry?"

"Never fear, Moe and Curly, the woodsman is here."

Larry pulled on a pair of gloves and flipped up the hood of his parka. Behind him the women and the two Bozic girls were settling into the well-lighted, cavernous, main living room, sorting, separating food from blankets and camping supplies and clothing.

"Yeah, only one axe. You chop and the rest of us will stack and carry," said Alan. "Damn, would you look at this.

Larry's dressed for the arctic."

"And those are my dog-sled huskies tied down by the dock," Larry parried. "I'm ready for winter, friends. While you guys freeze your asses off, yours truly's gon' be warm as toast."

Mike and Alan chuckled.

As they started off the porch, Kevin approached.

"You feeling OK?" Mike asked him.

"Oh . . . yes, sir. I'm fine."

"Just wondered. You seemed a little disoriented or something when we got off the houseboat."

"No, I'm fine. Really."

Alan intruded. "Has he been putting on his weird act? I'll warn you now, Mike, Kevin's developed strange behavior into an art form. He'll be performing all weekend, no doubt."

Mike said nothing; he patted Kevin on the shoulder reassuringly and the foursome began their search for firewood.

Twenty minutes of dragging, chopping, and stacking had each of them winded.

"Y'all realize how out of shape we are?" said Alan, laughing self-deprecatingly. Then he noticed Larry leaning against a pine and staring back at the inn. "Thinking about supper?"

Larry grinned.

"Believe it or not, I wasn't. I'll tell you what, Blackwinter's a real Gothic monster, isn't it? I mean, look at it from here. Brooding. Poe-esque. Our own House of Usher."

Catching his breath a moment, Mike lifted the axe onto his shoulder and glanced up at the inn.

"Spooky thing tonight is that the second and third floors have no electricity. Generator's working overtime just to handle the first floor."

"No telephone, either," said Larry. "God uh mercy, we're flat out isolated, aren't we?"

"Well, there's a CB on the houseboat and a phone in the

trailer. And the two bathrooms on the first floor work, so it's not as primitive as it might seem."

"Still," said Larry, "it's kinda eerie."

"I can't wait to explore the whole place," said Alan. "Especially the wine cellar and the second floor."

"Sarah claims the second floor was boarded up even when her grandparents lived here. That area probably hasn't seen a human being for forty or fifty years. Maybe longer."

As Alan and Larry listened to Mike's comments, Kevin loaded his arms with small logs and began the trek to the inn. Working up a moderate sweat had served as the perfect antidote for hallucinations. And he had made up his mind not to let his dad's observations bother him.

"Hey," said Mike, "we going to stand around while Kevin does all the work?"

"Here you go, Larry. Remember now, these are made of wood. Not good to eat unless you're a beaver."

Alan stacked a few logs on Larry's arms and then speared his face with the flashlight beam.

"Oh-oh, Mike, Larry's deep in thought. I can see it in his eyes."

"Maybe he's about to have a 'Big Mac attack,' " Mike joked.

"Hey, hey, you guys. I do *not* think about food every minute. In fact, I have a serious question to ask both of you."

"Fire away," said Alan.

"OK. It's this: Either one of you think buying this property's a mistake? I mean, what the hell are we gon' do with it?"

"Christ, Larry . . . it's a challenge. We need challenges in our lives," Alan exclaimed.

"Besides that," Mike added, "you need a tax shelter for all that dough you pull down as a high school English teacher."

"Real funny, Mike. You guys know who talked us into

53

this venture, don't you?"

Alan stacked another couple of pieces of wood into Larry's arms. "Wasn't me."

"I thought it was a spontaneous group decision," said Mike.

"No, no. How quickly you forget. The culprit is Gina, my dear, sweet, money-grubbing wife. I'd like to know how she convinced two reasonably intelligent gentlemen like yourselves to do this."

"How did she convince *you?*" asked Mike.

"She has ways . . . little sadistic stuff . . . she threatened to booby-trap the refrigerator. That kind of thing."

"She told me buying the property was *your* idea," Alan quipped.

"Come to think of it, that's true," said Mike.

"He-l-l-l-p!" Larry suddenly whooped into the deep, dark night.

On his way back to the inn, Kevin turned at the sound of laughter. It was a good sound. He hoped the weekend would generate more of it.

2

"Alan's so-o-o excited about this weekend," Kathy exclaimed. "He's trying not to show it, but it's all he's talked about for the last couple of weeks."

"That's Alan for you," Gina responded. "Gets like a wild hare about something, goes nutso over it, and then cools on it overnight. Dora went through this kind of thing a thousand times—Alan has a lot of little boy in him."

Seeing sparks threatening to fly, Sarah handed a cup of coffee to Gina.

"Ladies . . . anyone for coffee? Can't speak for you, but this woman needs some warmth for her innards."

A silent truce was called between Kathy and Gina—for

the moment, anyway. The three women drew up lawn chairs around an old door which had been laid across two sawhorses. They had determined which rooms on the first floor each couple would occupy; sleeping bags had been unrolled, and an Army cot or two had been set up. In one corner of the kitchen, Larry was fiddling with a portable gas grill—hot dogs had been planned for supper.

The chill pervading the high-ceilinged rooms had everyone waiting eagerly for Alan and Mike to set the stack of logs in the huge fireplace ablaze. In the interim, coffee hit the spot.

"Larry, do you want a cup?" Sarah asked.

Having shed his parka, Larry poked his head over the rim of the grill. A smear of grease formed a comma on his cheek. When the women saw it, they laughed.

"Hey, wait till I tell a joke at least."

"Sweetheart, dearest, you *are* a joke," said Gina. "Sarah asked if you want some coffee."

"No. A beer maybe," he replied, ducking back under the grill.

"You've had enough." Gina craned her neck over her shoulder, her attention suddenly drawn elsewhere.

"Larry, have you seen the girls?"

Again his head bobbed up.

"Look . . . I'm either gon' be cook or babysitter. Not both."

"They're probably off exploring," Kathy said.

A slight touch of concern in her tone, Gina asked, "I suppose they can't get into anyplace too dangerous, can they, Sarah? You know the layout better than the rest of us. Usually my kids have pretty good judgment, though occasionally some negative trait from Larry's side of the family rears its ugly head."

"I heard that," Larry muttered from beneath the grill, and again the women had to laugh.

Sarah thought a moment.

55

"No. No, I think they'll be fine."

"Did you actually live here at some point when you were growing up?" asked Kathy.

As the women relaxed and sipped their coffee, warming their hands on the cups, Sarah related how she had spent parts of summers, as well as such holidays as Thanksgiving and Christmas, at Blackwinter.

"Oh, what was Christmas like here?" Kathy asked. "It must have been special."

"It was. Except . . . well, it was, yes. We always had a massive Christmas tree. I remember going out once with my father and Sherman—he was my grandparents' gardener—to cut our own tree. I got to pick it out. We chopped it down and ceremoniously dragged it to the front door. We stood it near the fireplace and decorated it with candles and ribbons because Ginny Ma—my grandmother—loved candles and ribbons—red and green ribbons and bows. And tiny bells. I almost forgot the tiny bells—grandpa's contribution."

"Sounds beautiful," Kathy bubbled.

"Had your grandparents inherited any of the Blackwinter money?" asked Gina. "None of my business, of course—just curious. Was it a lavish holiday as far as you can recall?"

"I was never really aware. We had lots to eat and I had plenty of presents. My grandmother often spoke of helping the poor and— Oh, I do remember one other thing about Christmas—a tradition of sorts. Christmas afternoon, Ginny Ma would have me help clear away wrapping paper and generally clean up the living room. 'The cripples are coming,' she would say."

"Cripples?" Kathy sounded puzzled.

"Yes, they would come from all around the county, and some from as far away as Dadeville and Alex City. Even Goldsmith. There were polio victims, arthritis sufferers, and a few ex-soldiers wounded in combat during World War II or maybe Korea, I'm not sure. Every possible kind of invalid. All ages, too. White and black. Ginny Ma insisted that no one be discriminated against."

Incredulous, Kathy said, "What on earth did you do with them? Did they come for dinner, or did you have special presents for them?"

"In a way we did offer them a special present—hope. You see, even as late as the fifties people believed the mineral springs underneath Blackwinter Inn possessed healing powers and so—"

"They could have made a fortune from it," Gina interrupted. "And it would draw folks today if you advertised right and packaged the product attractively."

"Well, anyway," Sarah continued, "my grandparents had this black cook and maid named Nephredia. Every Christmas, Nephredia, who claimed her childhood lameness had been cured by the mineral water, went down to the wine cellar to a particular spot and bottled several gallons of what she maintained was the most potent water available."

"Did you charge anything for the water?" Gina asked.

Sarah frowned.

"Gina! It was Christmas . . . it was charity. And I got to carry a tray of wine glasses and an ornate crystal carafe, and follow along as Ginny Ma saw to it that everyone who came got a cold, sparkly glass of mineral water."

"What a nice story," Kathy mused.

From across the room, Larry entered the conversation.

"Any of them burn their crutches as they left?"

Sarah smiled.

"No, but I remember one old guy flirted with Ginny Ma afterward, so apparently it raised his spirits or something."

"Maybe the water's an aphrodisiac," said Gina. "Think of the commercial possibilities of that?"

There was soft, pleasant laughter before Kathy asked, "Where was your grandfather during all this? You really haven't mentioned him much."

Sarah took a drink of her coffee and then studied the

steam swirling up from it.

"He was confined to his room . . . and . . . it's not something I like to talk about."

"I'm sorry . . . sorry to bring up something painful."

Kathy glanced at Gina, who, in turn, shrugged.

A faraway cast to her eyes, Sarah said, "In time I'll tell you the whole story. Or most of it. One of those dark family secrets."

Not willing to allow such seriousness to hold sway, Larry quipped, "Gina has one of those. It's called her correct age."

3

"Kevin, would you mind getting the axe," said Mike. "I forgot and left it down where we were cutting wood."

"No, I wouldn't mind."

In fact, he was relieved to escape the company of his dad, the constantly simmering tension between them.

What's he want from me?

The relationship saddened him.

Why does he feel so angry?

Out on the porch, he switched on a flashlight and began to follow the amber spray. The chill reminded him of another day, the aftermath of a violent, summer thunderstorm in Birmingham where he had been visiting his mother.

He fought off the memory, surrendering instead to the dark pines beyond the wall. The cool air cleared his senses, allowing him to take in the rich, autumn aroma of lakeside and the sounds of night birds—a distant owl and possibly a heron. Mentally washed clean, he wondered how the earlier hallucination—the bloody deck of the houseboat—could have occurred. Or why.

Pushing through a thicket, he strained for signs of the

axe. He wigwagged the flashlight beam, scouring the floor of the woods. He heard a rustling and suddenly forgot about the axe. The beam caught a wisp of something white. Or was it a reflection?

The smear of white triggered a return.

He physically struggled against it, and yet he quickly recognized it was futile. Time and space shifted gears. He heard far-off thunder, smelled rain and the ozone trail of lighting.

Here, Ginseng! Here, kitty, kitty!

Everywhere he stepped it was slippery there behind his mother's apartment. She had let out her Siamese before the storm, and now that the rain and wind had passed she couldn't find him.

"Would you look for him, Kevin?"

"Sure," he had said.

High winds had felled small pines; rainwater pooled in the tiny back yard bordered by woods. A few unmelted pieces of marble-sized hail dotted the green grass.

"Here, Ginseng! Here, kitty, kitty!"

And into the fallen pines he made his way until he saw something white.

"Ginseng? Kitty, kitty?"

The animal was probably so frightened it wouldn't come, Kevin reasoned. So he got down on his hands and knees and peered into a thick jumble of pine branches. He heard a faint hissing. Smelled something burning.

But never saw the thin, black, downed power lines.

Until he touched them.

He experienced two sensations at once: First, a heat radiating throughout his body and, second, a physical jolt—it was as if huge hands had taken him by the shoulders and shaken him very hard.

Intuition branded words in his mind.

I've been electrocuted.

Then no other conscious sensations. Instead, he lapsed

into a dreamlike experience unlike any he could have imagined. It was ineffable. Inexpressible. Later, in the hospital, he had tried to explain the experience to the attending physician. But he simply hadn't been able to find words to describe it.

"I've been to a different world," he eventually stammered.

The physician nodded, but Kevin could tell he didn't understand.

The whole experience had unfolded like a weird play. Act one had taken place in the emergency room.

"No pulse," he heard a nurse exclaim.

"We're losing him," said someone else.

A flurry of activity. Endless seconds of muted exchanges — medical terms he was unfamiliar with.

Then: "Christ, we've lost him!"

No. No, I'm alive, Kevin protested.

He tried to move to show them. But his body had been disconnected. That was the only word which seemed to fit the experience. Disconnected from whatever part of him possessed awareness. And yet, the initial frustration and fear soon vanished.

He felt no pain.

In fact, he began to experience a remarkably intense peace.

This is good, he remembered thinking.

Quiet. Serene. Beautiful.

Completely relaxed.

This is what it's like to die.

Easy. Nothing to it.

Then an intrusion of sounds. Very pleasant sounds. Distant wind chimes. Then deeper strains. Orchestral. Magnificent. A fading. Then the totally calming sound of wind soughing high in trees.

He let go.

Slippery slide on a dark playground. Only this slippery slide was different; it was enclosed, tunnel-like. He shot through it at a tremendous speed; air whistled and whooshed. Very, very dark passageway. Not enough room to move within it.

Ahead, dim, but growing brighter, a light. At first, it was like a distant car beam or the rotating light on the front of a train. He was rushing toward it, and it seemed inevitable that he would crash into it. Brighter and brighter, whiter and whiter the light became, dazzling beyond anything he had ever encountered. Yet, it did not blind him.

Within the light, a nebulous form emerged. A figure of light, but somehow *within* the light. The figure of a person, but somehow not a person. And the being of light stood across a boundary line of some kind. Kevin couldn't see it, but he could feel it or sense it.

"Are you ready?" said the being of light.

A peaceful, reassuring voice. Again, like no other voice he had ever heard. In what could not have been longer than a few seconds, something else most peculiar occurred: He saw his lifetime pass before him—moments from his child-hood—some good moments, though the specifics escaped him—some bad moments, incidents he regretted, though, again, specifics seemed almost impossible to grasp.

His Uncle Rayford and Aunt Charlene were there.

And other people he recognized; individuals who had died or been killed—Dennis Locke, a boy he had met at camp—his grandparents—his first grade teacher. And Richard Davenport.

"It's not your time," he heard his uncle exclaim tenderly.

And felt hands literally push him back.

He didn't want to leave, for beyond the forms of people he knew lay a lush green, peaceful valley.

Something snapped. Like elastic. For an instant he was in his body, then out of it. Floating. Looking down at himself on a table. He was alive. He couldn't shake a mild disap-pointment. At least, not until he floated free of the emer-gency room into the hallway and saw his mother.

Saw her crying and couldn't comfort her.

Doctors had feared the left side of his body would be paralyzed. Fortunately their fears were unfounded, though his motor skills had been slightly diminished for several weeks.

NDE. Near-death-experience—that was what a researcher from Atlanta had called it.

"Hundreds and hundreds of people have reported them," he had explained.

"I was dead, wasn't I? It was nice. Not too bad."

"Lots of people have told me that."

Kevin had gone on to spell out the continuation of flashforward and out-of-body experiences.

"When will the weird stuff stop?"

"Perhaps it won't," the researcher had said.

Kevin shook free of the memory.

He knew immediately where the axe was.

He told himself to think of laughter.

But when he turned toward Blackwinter Inn, he couldn't repress a shudder.

4

"You like him. I know you do, Maria."

Sophie was being a royal pest.

Will I be able to stand a whole weekend of this?

"I do not."

"Ye-e-es, you do. I saw you looking at him on the boat. Maria and Kevin. Kevin and Maria."

"Will you stop that!"

"It's the truth. You like the weirdo."

Exasperated, Maria turned on her little sister.

"He's *not* a weirdo, Sophie. Don't be so cruel. He had a bad accident this summer. He almost got killed, they say. Besides that, his folks divorced and now he's got a new mother."

"You're standing up for him, so that means you like him."

"How would it make you feel if Momma and Daddy divorced and Daddy married somebody else and we had a new mother?"

The question caught Sophie by surprise.

She twisted her fingers a moment.

"They won't ever get divorced, will they?"

The two girls were sitting on the bottom step of a long stairway which wound upward for three flights. Where they sat, it was lighted, but as the stairs reached the second floor, shadows increasingly commanded the scene.

Maria shrugged.

"If they fall out of love."

"How do people do that?"

"Must be pretty easy because a lotta people do it. Gretta Swinson, my friend at school, her parents just separated. You do that right before you get divorced. Gretta's real sad about it. She has to choose whether to live with her mother or her father. She can't live with both of them."

Sophie burrowed deep into thought.

"Maria?"

"What?"

"Who would you choose . . . you know, to go live with? Momma or Daddy?"

"We won't have to, Sophie. Momma and Daddy love each other. Of course, they fight, but it doesn't make them fall out of love."

"But Gretta's parents loved each other, too . . . once they did, didn't they?"

It was one of those rare moments in their sisterly relation-

63

ship when Maria was tempted to hug her usual nemesis, to shield Sophie from the world.

"It would be a hard, very hard choice . . . it would break my heart."

"Hey, I know," said Sophie, inspired by childhood insight. "*I* could go live with Momma, and *you* could go live with Daddy. That way both of them would have a kid and nobody would feel lonely and all left out."

"Well . . . maybe."

"I think it's a good idea, Maria. Let's go tell them."

Maria had to grab her escaping sister's arm.

"Are you bonkers? You don't bring up something like that to your parents. It would be . . . upsetting."

"I don't think it would be. You're just jealous because you didn't think of it first."

"Go ahead, then, but I'd say it's a mistake."

Sophie reluctantly shelved her idea. A moment later, she said, "I'm bored. There's nothing to do around here. There's no television or nothing."

"Well . . . you could walk up those stairs and talk to the hungry ghosts."

Her gaze drifting over her shoulder into the shadowy heights, Sophie said, "Daddy was just making a story. Funning with us. There're no hungry ghosts."

"How do you know for sure?"

"I just do. Momma said it was nonsense."

"Momma doesn't know everything. Are you afraid to go see for yourself?"

Pausing for several heartbeats, Sophie sneered, "You're the fraidy cat. I bet *you* wouldn't go up those stairs."

"Sure I would."

"Would not."

"Go borrow a flashlight from Mr. Davenport and I will."

"OK. I'm going to. Just watch me."

And she did.

Maria took the flashlight from her, and Sophie wrinkled

her nose as revoltingly as she could.

"Aren't you going with me?"

"No, because I don't think you'll really do it."

"Here I go."

She started climbing the stairs, amused at the consternation she was creating in Sophie.

In a gasp of breath, the younger sister exclaimed, "I'm telling Momma! I mean it, Maria!"

"Go ahead, tattletale. I'm going to go talk to the ghosts."

"Maria, you're in trouble."

"I don't care."

She could feel Sophie's eyes on her back, could imagine the confused expression on her sister's face. Maria smiled. The beam of light pooled at her feet; she climbed slowly, letting her vision adjust to the combination of illumination and darkness.

The old stairs seemed solid. Hardly a squeak.

At the second-floor landing, Maria paused to study the arched entryway to a large room—the ballroom, she had heard. It was boarded up.

I wonder why?

Below her, a small voice echoed.

"Maria, come down and I won't tell on you."

Again, the older girl smiled.

The adventure thrilled her. It was like walking on the balance beam.

Nearing the third floor, she inched her way more cautiously. New sounds intruded. Secret tickings. Muted reverberations. Yet crouching silence waited like some night animal for a predator to pass. Or was she the prey?

On the top stair, at the lip of the landing, she stopped so suddenly that she almost lost her balance. She had heard something totally unexpected. Was it coming from one of the rooms? Her glance speared three or four doors along the hallway; each was sensibly shut.

Had she only imagined it?

Bells.

Almost inaudible. But definitely bells.

She drew in her breath and considered turning around.

Yet, she couldn't or didn't want to because this reminded her of the challenge of trying a new gymnastics routine or experimenting with a new move.

"You have to extend yourself," she whispered, repeating the line she got from her coach.

Comforted by the flashlight beam, she entered the tunnel of darkness created by the hallway. To her surprise the series of doors and the cool walls were broken by the steep slant of another stairway leading to a pull-down door in the ceiling.

It's the bell tower.

And the temptation to explore it was too much to resist.

5

"How many weeks are we staying?" Alan joked.

Surveying the remaining stack of boxes, sacks, and overnight bags, Mike shook his head.

"Can't decide who's brought more stuff — the women or Larry?"

Alan sought out the cabin of the houseboat to rest a moment.

"Got a twinge in my back. Let's catch a blow."

"Catch a blow?" Mike had followed him. "Is that runner's jargon?"

Alan chuckled.

"Yeah. Yeah, it is. I get used to using it."

"So are you running every day?"

"No. Monday, Wednesday, Friday. And I only run two miles. The others run four."

"There's a fellow down at my office who has this theory about married couples, particularly about husbands who jog."

"Oh, yeah. What's he say?"

"He claims that when a man takes up jogging it's a clear sign his marriage is on the rocks. And he has examples to back it up."

Smiling, Alan nodded.

"Maybe so. Maybe so."

"Doesn't mean you and Kathy are having trouble, does it?"

Alan shook his head.

"What it means is that I'm tired of seeing this spare tire in the bathroom mirror. Kathy makes me feel young mentally, emotionally — so I'd kinda like to feel that way physically."

A brief silence locked into place. Then Alan said, "This stuff won't move itself. Better get going or they'll send out a search party."

"Alan, could I ask you something?"

Mike's sudden transition to a serious tone caused Alan to hesitate. He had started to stand, but instead sat back down.

"You want in our runner's group?"

Waving off the comment, Mike smiled.

"No. I'll suffer through my poor physical condition — I'd probably have a heart attack if I took up running."

"Or prevent one."

"Got me there . . . but . . . well, as I said, I want to ask you about something."

"Spit it out."

Mike sighed resignedly.

"When did you know . . . or . . . was there a point or a moment maybe that signaled to you that . . . that you and Dora . . . that your marriage was over?"

"Christ, Mike . . . what a question?"

"I know. I know. But . . . " He shrugged. "I'd like to hear what you have to say. It would help me."

"You're pretty serious about this?"

"Yes."

Alan leaned back and looked up at the overhead light. It was warm enough in the cabin and cold enough outside to cause the windows to fog over, enclosing the two men in an opaque world.

"I remember one day," he began, "I'd had several difficult auto claims to work on . . . I was dead tired, so I left the office in midafternoon and went home. Told my secretary I'd be in the next day. No more business. Only emergency calls at home. I'd had it. I pulled into our driveway, and it was like . . . like the house wasn't even familiar. Nothing about the yard or the house, nothing about the property looked a *welcome*. You know what I mean?"

"I think so. But maybe that was because you'd been working hard."

"Huh-uh. No. No, and I *knew* it wasn't that. Well, I got out of the car and went inside. Kevin hadn't come home from school yet. Dora was in the kitchen, sitting at the table, making out a grocery list or something. I'd seen her sitting like that hundreds of times. But that afternoon, when I stepped into that kitchen . . . she was — you're going to think I'm exaggerating, but I'm not — she was a *stranger*."

"Stranger? What do you mean?"

"I mean . . . there was no feeling for her . . . on my part. She might as well have been a stranger living in the same house, sitting there at the kitchen table. I never . . . I never shook that feeling after that. She continued to be a stranger to me."

"Had you met Kathy before this?"

"No. No, it wasn't the typical scenario of unfaithful husband falling for younger woman, etcetera. My wife had become a stranger. How can you stay married to a stranger?"

Mike shook his head.

"Maybe . . . maybe you get reacquainted. Maybe you start all over."

"That what you and Sarah are trying to do?"

"Seems that way."

"Richard still the heart of the problem?"

"Heart and soul."

"You've gotten professional help. Didn't solve the problem, I take it."

"Not by a long shot. Oh . . . it helped get some feelings out in the open. The grief. Grief can transport you into some curious realms. Throws you out of orbit. But, you see, we're still in those orbits. Separate orbits. Sarah and me. I thought the tragedy, eventually at least, would bring us closer."

"Instead, it's making strangers out of you, right?"

Mike nodded.

"It's your word. It fits, though."

"Nothing fills the vacuum Richard left?"

"I couldn't have imagined how much he meant to us . . . and yet, we . . . I never told him, Alan. If I had, maybe he wouldn't have taken his own . . ."

His voice broke off, and he tightened his hands into fists.

"Don't blame yourself, Mike. Who can tell what's going on in a boy's mind. Take my Kevin, for example. He's going through a stage now, and I mean, Christ, he's a mystery."

"You might be wrong there."

"What are you saying? I know Kevin. He relishes being an oddball. Part of it's pretty clear—he's blaming me for the divorce, using the accident this summer as a convenient excuse to act weird. He's putting the screws to Kathy, too, though she sticks up for him."

"He just wants somebody to listen to him."

"Listen to him?"

"Yes. Don't make the same mistake I made, Alan. Kevin's reaching out."

"Come on now, Mike, You're running in from left field on this. There's nothing seriously wrong with Kevin. Don't try to draw a parallel between him and . . . it's . . . you're not in a position to judge."

69

"He wants your respect. Why don't you give it to him?"

"Mike . . . God damn it, don't start pushing me on this. I hear enough about it from Dora. Kevin has her wrapped around his little finger. Sounds like he's doing a number on you, too."

"Just stop and realize what you have, Alan. A son. Someone who needs you . . . look . . . " He paused. His voice lost energy and most of its tension. "We've been friends a long time. I don't want to see you go through what Sarah and I have gone through. Give Kevin a chance to talk to you."

"Talk to me?"

Mike could see the anger rising in Alan's face. He hadn't planned on this confrontation, but there seemed no way to escape it.

"You're way out of line, Mike. Don't tell me how I should be handling Kevin. I'll take care of it my own way. I warn you . . . don't do anything to make things tougher on me and Kathy. I'm happy. For once in my life I'm with someone who makes me happy—Kevin will have to accept that. He's the one who has to adjust."

With that, Alan picked up a box and a canvas bag and left the houseboat.

Mike strolled to the wheel.

Beyond the window, an autumn fog lowered itself upon Blackwinter Lake.

6

"What's your secret?"

Gina continued counting plastic plates and calculating the number of utensils and cups needed for supper. But she had heard Sarah's question, had found it amusing, in fact, though her friend had injected some seriousness into it.

"We've stopped drinking city water."

70

Sarah was forced to smile.

"No, really. You and Larry . . . you've got something good going. I don't want Mike and me to go the way of Alan and Dora. Are we just not working hard enough at it?"

"Sarah dear, Larry and I don't work at our marriage. In fact, Larry no longer works at *anything* — except getting *out* of work maybe."

They had remained in the kitchen when Larry, apparently having wrenched the grill into serviceable condition, had hunted down the cooler, seized another Stroh's, and plopped himself onto the stone ledge near the fireplace to "rest up" before he started cooking hot dogs. Hunger led him to add hamburgers to the menu.

"But he's been a busy bee this evening," Sarah countered.

"Ah, but notice . . . all his activities have had something to do with food. The man lives by and for his stomach; where it leads, he follows."

"Come on, Gina, you're being too rough on him. I know you love the guy. Your marriage seems to be able to roll with the punches. Was it always that way? Did it used to have more affection in it?"

Gina stacked the plates and cocked her head to one side. "See those two?"

She pointed into the living room where Kathy had met Alan at the entrance and was helping him set down a box. They kissed and gazed longingly into each other's eyes.

Gina feigned gagging.

"Larry and I have never been like that, thank goodness."

"Never moon-eyed and silly? No romance? I don't believe that. Larry's always seemed like a romantic guy to me. Loves poetry. He's gentle. Bet he wrote you poems when you were first going together."

Gina winked.

"Volumes of poems. Hideous stuff. Yes, he did romantic things. You're right. Larry was romantic. Still is, occasionally. But I'm not. And never have been. And that's why we

71

work so well together."

"Care to explain that."

"Sure. It's simple. I'm the cold, witchy-bitchy type—"

"No, you're not."

"Yes. Yes, I am. And I don't regret it. Can't help it. People of Italian extraction are supposed to be fiery lovers, passionate from the word go—and my Birmingham relatives are like that—but not me. My fire burned in a different direction. I became the materialist. Larry's an exact opposite. What I'm saying is that we have a . . . a pleasant balance. Like a balance sheet, OK? You look at the bottom line. Assets and liabilities equal out. Bottom line is a decent marriage."

Sarah folded her hands together.

"But I envy Alan and Kathy, don't you?"

"No. Not in the least. They'll cool off, and then they'll have to deal with each other on another level. A deeper level. Of course, Kathy could get lucky—Alan could grow up."

Lost in her own wilderness of thought, Sarah said, "Seeing them, I think about the first year Mike and I knew each other. He was churchmouse poor, trying to hold down a forty-hour job and go to college. I used to fix him a midnight snack and drive out to the restaurant where he worked as a busboy. We had everything planned. And everything went according to plan except for having children . . . then when Richard joined us, it was like the old plan had come back into effect. We did something wrong along the way. There's something about the two of us we can't get right. I think it may have contributed to Richard's . . . to whatever he felt."

Pressing a hand onto Sarah's, Gina shook her head.

"No. Don't give up on yourselves yet. Things happen. Things change. Who knows? Here you are, back home at Blackwinter, in a sense. The answer to everything could jump out at you like dollar signs."

"Dollar signs. Honestly, Gina . . . but . . . maybe you're right about this weekend. It does feel good to get away from Goldsmith. And there are several good memories here, especially about the lake. Mike and I used to come up and boat and swim—we spent a few memorable weekends in the trailer, too."

"Oh-huh," Gina exclaimed. "Well then, that's it. Get Mike out on the lake tomorrow; I'll have Larry pack you a picnic lunch."

"Wish our problems could be solved that easily. A boat ride."

"I'm not talking in romantic terms, Sarah. My approach is much more . . . practical, I suppose you'd say. What I'm suggesting is that you and Mike need to get off and see what you have to offer each other—see what you *need* from each other."

Sarah glanced down at her hands.

"You make it sound so matter-of-fact and . . . well, cold, in a way."

Gina shrugged.

"Marriage is a partnership—and like a good business partnership, it's built upon the principle of mutually interfacing needs."

"Mutually interfacing needs? Gina, we're the Davenports, not IBM."

"I think I'm right."

Letting her eyes roam to the far corner of the kitchen ceiling, Sarah said, "It reminds me of the marriage my grandparents had."

"How is that?"

Sarah related what she knew of her grandparents' contract marriage and the evident lack of passion between them over the years.

"I believe Ginny Ma had respect for grandpa, but I realize now that the closeness was never there."

"They had children, so a few times they got close."

Sarah smiled. The twinkle in Gina's eye was infectious.

"Still . . . I wonder if a more passionate love between them wouldn't have taken some of the . . . the gloominess out of Blackwinter."

"I don't see this place as being gloomy at all," Gina responded. "Just look around at the possibilities. That second floor, for example. If we get to examine it tomorrow, chances are we'll find a potential showcase. Proper management, and enough capital, and this inn could return to the splendor it had when it first opened."

Gazing off to one side, Sarah shook her head.

"Perhaps. But I sense that there's a past here—a legacy, whatever—we can't ever quite understand. Something here that will keep those days from returning."

Gina wagged a finger at her.

"Nonsense. That's nonsense."

7

"Cornish hens," said Larry, face aglow, the words tumbling lovingly from his lips.

"On a grill?" Mike asked, slightly amused, slightly incredulous.

"Sounds like sacrilege, doesn't it? But wait'll you taste them. I'll have them swimming in a wine sauce that's orgasmic."

Mike laughed hard.

"Are we going to eat this concoction, or make love to it?"

"Wait, wait, there's more," Larry insisted, grabbing Mike's arm and shaking him. "See that cooler over there? In it, in it, my skeptical friend, is a chocolate icebox cake you would assume was delivered from the gates of chefs' heaven. But ah, no—I made it myself."

Teary-eyed from laughing, Mike flattened a hamburger pattie with his spatula.

"Tomorrow night's the feast, right?"

"If you can just keep your palate in check that long."

The gas grill was covered by weiners and hamburger patties, sizzling, smoking up the kitchen. In the living room two old picnic tables had been placed end to end, and paper plates and cups and utensils — some plastic, some metal — were finding their way there from the kitchen.

Kathy and Gina were pouring out soft drinks from two-liter bottles; Sarah was searching for ketchup, mustard, and relish. Alan was coaxing an uncooperative fire in the fireplace.

"Momma, guess what? Maria's gone way up the stairs. I told her you wouldn't want her to, but she did it anyway; and so I told her she was in trouble."

Sophie stood rigidly, a hand braced against her hip.

"Do you want coke to drink?" said her mother.

"Momma, what about Maria?"

"She'll come down when she's hungry. Now go to the bathroom and wash your hands. We'll be eating shortly."

Gina spun past her obviously miffed daughter, into the kitchen where Mike and Larry were being engulfed in smoke.

"Larry, open the back door and get rid of some of that smoke," she exclaimed, then buzzed away.

Her husband had just popped open another beer, and he nearly dropped the can when he managed to swing the reluctant door back and greet the night.

"Lord uh goodness," he whispered.

He stepped closer to the darkness and switched on the light positioned above the door.

"Mike. Take a look at this."

His companion flipped a couple of patties and then turned so that he was peering over Larry's shoulder.

"My God! Never seen a fog that thick."

They stared into an impenetrable curtain of opaque gray-blackness, the center of which swirled almost menacingly.

In his best Bela Lugosi voice, Larry said, "It is a Transylvanian fog, my friend. And soon you will hear the children of the night calling for their master."

His howl was as wolflike as possible. Mike chuckled and waved some of the smoke out the door.

"Glad I'm not out on our houseboat in this."

"Wouldn't Blackwinter be a perfect setting for a horror movie? Maybe we ought to contact Hollywood."

"Oh, yeah. What's the plot of this movie? And I won't watch it unless it has Jamie Lee Curtis in it."

Larry guzzled a little beer, belched, and then said, "Jamie's name's on the dotted line. No problem. Now, as for plot. Since when does a horror movie have a plot? Buckets of blood and gut-wrenching use of special effects in dismembering folks—who needs plot?"

"Just to be different," said Mike.

"Picky, picky. OK, plot . . . let me see. Hah, I have it. Three adult couples purchase an old, abandoned hotel and decide to spend the weekend there—"

"Hey, I've seen that movie!"

"Seen it? Hell, you're in it! OK, don't interrupt me—I'm on a roll. The couples settle in, but, lo and behold, the first night a thick, *evil* fog—the worst kind, I might add— descends upon the edifice. It frightens them. They cower and lament their existential fate."

"Wh-h-hat?"

"*My* horror movie's gon' have a certain philosophical sophistication. Anyway, here's the plot twist—they discover that the fog is actually made of cheesecake."

"A *gray* cheesecake?"

"You've never seen Gina's, have you?"

Despite himself, Mike laughed at Larry's cornyness, laughed because it felt so good to do so.

"Now, narrative conflict develops in that they must eat their way through this foggy cheesecake. However, some of their number are swallowed whole by this delectable-turned-vicious cheesecake. The hero, a portly fellow, saves the day by eating his way to freedom, ending up in New Jersey."

Smiling, Mike said, "I have to ask this: What created the cheesecake in the first place?"

Larry pressed a finger to his lips and shook his head.

"I haven't the foggiest idea."

Whereupon Mike laughed loudly enough to bring a few companions out to the kitchen to check on him. Seeing Larry there provided a silent explanation for most of them, and, instead of wasting a trip, they filed by the grill and helped themselves before returning to the living room.

"Daddy, you gotta make Maria come down."

Sophie wended her way through the milling adults to tug at Larry's hand.

"Where's she gone, luv, to the moon?"

"No. Won't anybody listen? She went up the stairs where it's real, real dark."

"Oh, well . . . I see. She's gone to feed the hungry ghosts."

"No-o-o! She went because I dared her to."

"My, what a brave sister you have. Tell you what. Let ole dad finish here at the chuck wagon and you and me'll rustle up a posse and round up that outlaw sister. OK?"

"Yeah. That'll be pretty OK to me."

She hugged him and skipped away.

"You've got the touch, don't you?" said Mike.

"Hey, there's nothing to grilling franks and burgers. Wait'll you see my succulent hens. Better yet, wait'll you *taste* them."

"No, I mean what you just did with Sophie."

Larry frowned; his expression of puzzlement was comical—a caricature which came naturally.

"You're a prize-winning father, Larry."

"You almost sound serious."

"I am serious."

77

"Look, if you think this kind of talk can get you an extra Cornish hen . . . you're probably on target, but I'll have to consider other offers as well."

Mike grinned. Then grew somber.

"Do people get a second chance to correct their most horrendous mistakes?"

"You referring to my marriage, Mike?"

Larry studied him and saw that his friend had suffered enough humor.

"Second chance, huh?" he followed up with, before Mike could say something more. "Othello didn't. Neither did Lear. Most of us, though, if we search hard enough for the opportunity . . . heck, yeah, I'm an optimist — I'd say we do."

"You're a good man, Larry."

"Yeah, good and hungry."

8

"Aren't you going to sit with me?"

Alan smiled down at Kathy and kissed her cheek.

"In a second, hon. Fireplace duty at the moment. Make me up a hamburger. Lots of mustard."

He dashed away before she could ask him what he wanted to drink. There was so much commotion she decided not to pursue it until he returned. She let the scene wash over her — a pleasant scene: Alan at the mammoth fireplace, Gina at his shoulder, issuing commands, reminding him that she didn't believe a man could do anything right.

Kathy laughed softly at the two of them. They seemed to enjoy barking at each other, like two dogs not really serious about fighting but in love with the sound of their barks. And there was the comic banter of Mike and Larry a few feet from her at the picnic table: Larry had announced that he could put an entire hamburger in his mouth at once;

Mike had bet a dollar he couldn't.

"This seat taken?"

Surprised, Kathy glanced up.

"Hey, Sarah . . . no, no, please sit."

"Fun group, huh?"

Kathy smiled.

"Yes, it really is. You're all so comfortable together. You seem to know and understand one another."

"Experience. We've had lots and lots of experience."

"Some great times, I'm sure."

Sarah put down her Mello Yellow and laughed into her hands; Kathy watched, starting to laugh herself.

"Sarah, what?"

Controlling herself momentarily, Sarah said, "There was one outing I'll never forget. It was about four years ago, and Alan had gotten this brochure on white-water rafting in north Georgia. Well, he got excited and infected Mike, who loves anything to do with boats and water anyway, then Larry, and, gradually, 'the wives' got pulled into the plan as well."

"You mean you all went in one of those rubber rafts on a fast river?"

Kathy's eyes widened.

Sarah nodded.

"The Chattooga River. You know it's the river where they made that movie, *Deliverance* — Burt Reynolds. You know the one?"

"Sure. Yeah. I saw it. The men got attacked by hill people — yeah, that was a great movie. Scary. And you guys were out in — Oh, my goodness. What happened?"

Sarah started laughing again. She sputtered and eventually righted herself, but all Kathy had heard was the name Larry.

"What about Larry? Tell me," Kathy coaxed.

She had to wait again for Sarah to stifle her laughter.

"Oh-h-h . . . it was so funny. We had a guide, a young

79

woman who could have been a drill sergeant, and she buckled us into the raft. We had helmets and paddles—the works. She took us out where the river wasn't moving very fast and taught us how to steer the raft in one direction or another."

"Sounds so exciting."

Sarah rolled her eyes.

"Well, our guide made one mistake. She had Alan and Dora at the rear of the raft; Mike and I were in the middle, then Gina and Larry. Larry was at the very front—the most important paddler."

"Oh, no."

"Right. And we did fine for a while, though we giggled like grade schoolers when the river got a little faster. Then, all of a sudden, our guide hollered, 'Big drop coming!' But we were confident. Cocky."

"Could you hear her commands over the roar of the water?"

"Some of us could . . . that was the problem. We flew into white-water area between huge rocks and then I remember looking straight ahead and seeing trees. I couldn't see water, so I knew it must be something like a waterfall."

"Sarah . . . you guys!"

"The guide was hollering that we weren't lined up right. In fact, she got frantic, was screaming in Dora's ear so loud that Dora lost her paddle. Actually she was screaming at Larry to go left. On the edge of the drop, Larry turned around and said, 'I can't hear you. Which way?' And then we dropped. No, we *plunged*."

"Heavens! Did you capsize?"

"Sort of. We splashed around, a little shook up if you want to know the truth. For a second or two, we couldn't find Larry. Then, out in the deeper, slow-moving water, we saw this yellow helmet bob up. It was Larry."

"He wasn't hurt, was he?"

"At first it was hard to tell because he was yelling something about being blind. His voice was really muffled. Alan and Mike and the guide swam over to him, and when . . . "

Sarah began laughing once again, forcing Kathy to be patient a few moments longer before hearing the rest of the story.

"When they got to him, they saw that the impact of crashing into the river had knocked the helmet clear around in front of his face. It was so funny. I wish we could've gotten a picture."

Chin propped on her knuckles, Kathy sighed.

"I wonder, you know, whether five or ten years from now we'll look back on this weekend at Blackwinter and laugh about something that happened."

"Having Larry around, there's a good chance of it."

"Hope I don't spoil it."

"*Spoil* it?"

"Sarah, I don't feel like I fit in. Gina reminds me every minute or so that I've stolen Dora's place and . . . that I don't measure up somehow."

"Could be Gina's jealous. You're pretty and you're young, and it makes some of us feel ugly and much older. It'll get better, I promise. You'll carve your own niche, you'll see."

Sarah's smile warmed Kathy.

"All right, Mike's a lily-livered coward, and he cheats when he gambles. No-good snake," Larry exclaimed. "What about you two lean-and-mean-looking cowgals— you itchin' to join our posse? Sophie and I gon' go after that outlaw, Maria, who's hidin' out up in the dark rooms somewhere."

"Not me," said Sarah. "I know those dark rooms. I'll stay here and keep the lily-livered coward company."

"I'll go," said Kathy, surprising herself. "But I don't carry a six-shooter."

"Won't need one, ma'am, won't need one. You see, this outlaw we're after can be coaxed out of hiding with the

81

promise of a chocolate Zinger."

"I'm going to hold the Zinger," said Sophie, "so's daddy won't eat it before we get upstairs."

The adults chuckled. Then Larry, Sophie, and Kathy struck out for the great dark beyond, and Mike and Sarah moved closer to the fireplace to listen to Gina bitch at Alan.

"There's a burger for you over on the table," Kathy called out to Alan as she passed the fireplace. Larry and Sophie, hand in hand, were at her side, singing, trailing giggles.

9

High above, on the first level of the bell tower, Maria shivered involuntarily. A dusty, dark silence hovered behind her; in front of her, the series of mirrors threw back the flashlight beam as a demonic eye, unblinking, stark, and somehow defiant.

Over the spray of light, she examined her reflection, and with her left hand reached up and touched her cheek and smoothed the fear wrinkles, wishing she were prettier. She thought her face had too much of a triangular shape, thought her nose was slightly crooked.

Next, she studied her figure.

I'm getting fat around the waist, she worried. And I'm going to be the last girl to get breasts.

Part of her rallied behind the latter reflection. I don't want breasts anyway. I want to be thin like a pixie. Pixie. I wish I could be a pixie—like Olga Korbut or Nadia or even Mary Lou Retton.

She sighed forlornly.

" 'Mirror, mirror, on the wall . . . ' "

But she chose not to finish the incantation because her attention had been drawn away from the mirror. She'd heard something behind her.

Bells?

Again that soft, oh so soft, tinkle she had heard earlier. Or was she imagining it?

She directed the light at the pull-down door below her. *Footsteps?*

She sucked in her breath. Felt a tightness choke up her throat.

She listened carefully. The silence thrummed.

Redirecting the beam, she noticed another set of stairs, this one leading to another small door which she assumed opened onto the top landing of the tower. She pondered the wisdom of venturing farther.

And something stirred within her — the delicious, seductive magnetism of something slightly forbidden.

Go for it, she told herself, awash in an innocent wickedness.

One step.

Two.

She stopped.

Was there a noise behind her?

She pushed the ceiling door open and pressed herself up onto the landing, waking the dust, sending it swirling into a dance of motes. Getting to her feet, she brushed herself off and then surveyed her surroundings. The landing, perhaps ten feet in diameter, was rounded in glass which, in daylight, would offer a panoramic view of Blackwinter Lake.

"This is neat," Marie whispered.

And she vowed that she would try to spend as much time as possible there over the next two days.

It will be my place.

A perfect hideout. She could escape her mom and Sophie and enjoy being in her own world, pretending it had been created just for her. The pleasant thought buoyed her.

Until she speared the floor with her light.

And saw the outlines of footprints in the dust.

She sucked her bottom lip, determining for certain, as she glanced around, that *she* hadn't made the prints. Questions rose in her mind in a whirlwind of alarm: Who's been here? How long ago? Why have I been so foolish to come up here alone?

Then, unmistakably, she heard someone on the first landing.

She nearly dropped the flashlight, thus giving away her presence, then switched off the beam, hoping whoever was below hadn't noticed it. The immediate surrender to darkness startled her. She crouched down.

Should I scream for help?

It seemed the best course, and yet something caused her to hesitate—the light from another flashlight was bleeding through the floor. Someone was coming up the steps.

Someone was pushing the door open.

And it all happened so quickly.

"Who's there?" she gasped.

Then she screamed—not a loud scream, more like a shriek.

And the door angled shut.

"It's me."

At first, she couldn't recognize the voice, but it did not sound threatening.

The door slowly swung open.

A light scoured the room.

Maria held her flashlight up, prepared to smash the intruder.

"It's me, Kevin. Who's here?"

His voice quavered, signaling to Maria that he was every bit as frightened as she was.

"Kevin?"

She had scooted as far away from the opening as she could.

"Maria? Is that you?"

He brought the light around, centering it on her face.

"What are you doing here?" he asked.

Fending off the bright beam, she stood up and brushed at

her knees.

"Just exploring."

He let out a sigh of relief.

"You really kinda scared me," he admitted.

And they both laughed nervously.

Kevin pressed his way through the opening and looked around.

"Quite a place. Has a bell up there, too."

"I hadn't seen that," said Maria. "I came here to get away from my little sister."

"Well, you succeeded."

There was an embarrassing pause in their conversation; the awkwardness of being young held sway.

Finally, Maria said, "Were you here earlier?"

"No."

"Somebody was," she said, unable to repress a note of fear. "Look."

She sprayed her light across the floor a yard or so from her.

"Hmmm, footprints. Wonder where they came from? Unless . . . could be that when my dad and Mr. Davenport were out once during the week, setting up the generator, they made them. Maybe they wanted to see the view of the lake from here, you know."

Maria relaxed a notch, reassured by Kevin's explanation.

"Does it bother you to be up this high?" she asked.

Instantly she regretted the question. Would Kevin be offended?

His expression didn't register that he was.

"No, not really," he said. "And I'd guess you're not bothered. I've seen you working out on a balance beam in the gym at school. You're pretty good."

Her cheeks flushed.

"Oh, thanks. I'm shaky on my pivots. Sometimes my hands start acting clumsy — it's like they forget where they're supposed to be."

85

Kevin slowly scanned the room again.

"This does bother me some," he admitted. "My head gets disconnected from my body every so often . . . because of the accident. I guess you heard about it, didn't you?"

"Sure. It musta been super scary. Kids were sayin' you really died somehow and that you can do . . . "

"Weird stuff?"

"Well . . . yeah."

"Some say the accident made me mentally unstable."

He grinned; then, realizing the comment may have unsettled Maria, quickly added, "But I'm not. I mean, the doctors haven't found anything like that. Just headaches and . . . some things I can't explain. And neither can they."

Maria began to feel more bold.

"My friend, Gretta, she heard that you can read minds and hypnotize people."

Kevin laughed, a hearty laugh, released as if he had kept it in a cage for too long. Maria laughed a bit also, sharing the unexpected mirth.

"I've heard wilder stuff than that," said Kevin. "It's been going around that I can make our opponents in football lose and that Coach Turnham's going to have me standing along the sidelines with the team all season. We'll be league champs."

Maria shook her head, laughter continuing to linger near.

"Kids are as bad as grownups about starting rumors."

Another curious silence drifted down upon their exchange. Kevin's eyes met hers and he said, "If I show you something, will you promise not to tell anyone?"

She felt a tiny surge of excitement course through her.

"Sure. Yes, I promise. I'm good at keeping promises."

"You see, like I said, some things I can't explain have been going on. Like, well, like feeling sometimes that I've been boomeranged into the future and can see, maybe, what's going to happen. I don't have good proof or anything, but two or three times I think I've seen into the

86

future."

"Gosh, that would be strange."

Kevin nodded.

"And I can—if I really concentrate, you know, focus my will on something—I can make it stop. Like my watch. I can make my watch stop running. I did it on the drive to the lake this afternoon. And it's not a crummy watch either."

He could tell that Maria was trapped between doubt and a willingness to suspend her disbelief.

"OK," he said, "I'll try to show you."

Maria tensed. "Oh, that's all right. You don't have to unless you really want to."

Kevin scratched the back of his head.

"What could I . . . ? Oh, I got it."

"This won't make your head hurt, will it?"

He brushed her comment aside.

"OK, here's what I want you to do. Hold your flashlight so it's pointing toward the belfry."

"Like this?"

"Yeah, that'll do it, I think."

The splash of light illuminated the undergirding of the belfry and cupola. Maria held the flashlight as steady as she could, though she was conscious that it quivered ever so slightly.

Kevin slowed his breathing.

And stared at the light. There was a thread of pain, and some invisible force tugged on it. He swallowed.

And began to float.

And to witness a scene unfold: It was Maria. She was walking dangerously high atop the roofline of the inn . . . as if she were on a balance beam. Then the scene dissolved to blackness.

And so did the bell tower.

Maria gasped.

"You did it!"

Kevin staggered, blinked, and Maria's flashlight came

87

back on. He pressed a thumb and forefinger onto his eyelids.

"Guess I could be the life of parties doing that, huh?"

"Kevin, it's true. You have supernatural powers."

"Nothing really special. I think it'll go away in time. I don't want to show it to anyone else . . . maybe a doctor. I feel like a freak doing it."

"I'm glad you showed me," said Maria.

A moment later, a voice intruded. "Come on out, we have you surrounded."

Kevin and Maria exchanged glances of surprise.

"It's Daddy," she whispered, somewhat relieved.

"Oh, yeah, we're probably missing supper."

"Kevin . . . I've got one question."

"Yeah?"

"When you said you could see into the future sometimes . . . well, have you seen anything about this weekend?"

Kevin felt the muscles in his neck stiffen.

Below them, Larry continued his babbling.

"I'm not sure," said Kevin. "Maybe." For a moment, images of the paddle wheeler, the mysterious stranger, the blood on the deck of the houseboat, and Maria walking along the roofline held his attention. "We ought to be careful. But, Maria, I thought about telling my dad . . . it wouldn't do any good. It has to be *our* secret. Yours and mine."

Chapter VI

1

"I bet you were kissing."

"We were not!"

"I bet you were."

"Sophie, you're a twerp!"

"No, I'm not!" she exclaimed. "What's a twerp?"

"A twerp is a little sister who bugs her older sister all the time and says dumb things and teases and is spoiled and a brat."

"You were up there in the dark by yourself with Kevin. Daddy and Kathy and me caught you."

"Don't call her Kathy—she's Mrs. Holmes."

"She told me I could call her Kathy."

"It's not polite."

"What were you doing in the dark?"

"It wasn't dark. We had flashlights on, and it's none of your business what we were doing."

"Must have been kissing."

"We were talking."

"What about?"

"Will you leave me alone!"

Maria scooted away from her sister's incessant questions, seeking out the front porch where the adults had gathered.

She looked for Kevin, but could not see him at first. There was no need to, though, for she continued to bask in the warm afterglow of their conversation in the tower.

And the exercise of Kevin's wild talent — the extinguishing of the flashlight beam — now seemed even more miraculous. And one more memory, something Kevin said: *It has to be our secret. Yours and mine.*

She considered that she was being silly, but it did not matter. She held fast to Kevin's words and felt older and more mature. Middle East terrorists couldn't pry the secret from her.

The weekend at Blackwinter Inn had been transformed from clouds of boredom to a rainbow of promise.

"It's incredible," Mike exclaimed as he and the other adults gazed at the star-filled sky. "Not thirty minutes ago, a thick fog blotted out any sign of stars."

"So beautiful," whispered Kathy, pressing herself close to Alan.

"Yes, you are," he whispered back.

"But it's pretty damn chilly," said Gina. "Let's go in and warm ourselves around *my* fire."

"*Your* fire?" Alan responded. "Larry, your wife's out of control. Get her leash, please."

"I'm opposed to violence," Larry answered. "Especially violence inflicted upon my own portly person — which is what would happen if I tried to put a leash on Gina."

"Good boy," Gina muttered.

There was laughter, and it continued as they went inside and drew near the blazing fire. Then Mike and Larry and the girls went to get glasses and cups for beer and wine and soft drinks.

The cavernous room gained a coziness usually reserved for a smaller and more intimate one. When drinks had been poured, Alan glanced across at Sarah.

"Hey, quiet one. You look as if you've taken flight into another world."

Suddenly everyone was staring at her and she felt self-conscious.

"Oh, I was just thinking . . . something from the past." She hesitated, her eyes fixed upon the flames.

"The last time I saw a fire like this was also on a November evening—around Thanksgiving. Ginny Ma and my parents and I were sitting like this and . . . the most curious thing happened. A boy, about Kevin's age, I suppose, just walked into the room. He said he was looking for work. Was probably a runaway. My father talked to him and Ginny Ma fed him and then he seemed to just disappear as mysteriously as he'd appeared. It was almost like . . . like the fire had drawn him, a moth in the night."

"My, you're waxing poetic," said Larry, and Sarah instantly blushed, embarrassed, not wanting to be in the focal point of attention.

"Speaking of poetry," Mike put in, "I nominate Larry to offer a toast for the weekend."

"You'll be sorry," said Gina.

"Got you covered, Michael," Larry shot back, lifting his beer glass as if it were a scepter. Then he captured center stage. He gestured, seerlike, with a sweep of the arm—a man plumbing the depths of the future, albeit comically.

"My friends, the watchword for this weekend is 'mystery.' "

There ensued some murmurs and a chuckle or two.

"Yes, 'mystery,' for we have assembled and dissembled here at the historic Blackwinter Inn to explore and deplore its history and hidden secrets so that in days to come it may provide us with both pleasure and big bucks."

Everyone brightened to Larry's histrionics.

He continued.

"As the mediocre philosopher, Seneca, once said, 'Our universe is a sorry little affair unless it has in it something for every age to investigate.' For us, it is Blackwinter Inn. May we dance among its shadows."

"Hear, hear!" someone called out.

"Amen!" someone else exclaimed.

Larry nodded his glass toward each adult and each child, and then muttered, "Friends, it doesn't get any better than this."

Whereupon he was booed lustily. But the lighthearted mood had seized them. The roaring fire on a chill November evening. The company of good friends. What, indeed, could have been better?

"Time to talk business," Gina declared.

"Oh, Lord, here we go." Larry moaned.

Gina feigned surprise and disappointment at the general lack of enthusiasm for her idea.

"Hey, folks, isn't this why we invested in Blackwinter?" she continued. "We need to discuss and tentatively agree upon the direction our investment should take."

"Let's talk about it tomorrow," Larry suggested.

"Hush, love of my life, you've spoken your mind—Larry wants to convert Blackwinter into a brewery."

He smiled broadly and chugged on his beer.

"You know," said Alan, "a brewery's not far afield from what I've been thinking about."

"I was joking," Gina exclaimed.

"Well, I'm not."

And so Alan stood, glass of wine in hand, and addressed his friends.

"A brewery's probably out of the question," he began, "but this isn't."

To punctuate his point, he held out his wine glass.

"Nectar of the grape."

"Are you serious?" someone asked.

"Yes. Yes, I am. I've learned that the land around this part of the county has excellent potential for growing grapes. Old Jacob Blackwinter grew them over a hundred and fifty years ago. Why do you suppose he built such a large wine cellar if having vineyards wasn't feasible? We ought to at least look into the possibilities."

"How about the commercial potential of the mineral water?"

The question was Kathy's; Gina quickly responded.

"Dear, you pleasantly surprise me. Maybe you're not just a hothouse flower as I first surmised. That's a good idea—mineral water is becoming popular again."

Kathy forced a smile, uncertain of the sincerity of Gina's compliment.

"If you ask me," Mike chimed in, "we're dismissing the real potential of this place by concentrating too much on the inn. What about the lake? Boating and fishing possibilities? If we put some money into building docks and developing water recreational facilities, that would draw people—especially once we've refurbished the inn."

"But the inn is the key," said Gina. "I say we go all out and try to attract additional investors by putting together a master plan to completely redo the interior. The first floor won't need that much work—tomorrow, we'll see what kind of shape the second and third floors are in."

"And the wine cellar, too," said Alan.

"Hang on to your wallets and purses," Larry exclaimed. "Gina has that look in her eyes—an entrepreneurial glaze."

"Someone give my husband another beer so he'll be quiet."

It was Gina's turn to stand and hold court; she pushed Alan aside, and for the next fifteen or twenty minutes waxed enthusiastic about the creation of a "new" Blackwinter Inn—a splendidly rejuvenated hotel with an elegant ballroom, fine dining, choice wines, salubrious mineral water, and boating and fishing opportunities unparalleled in the state of Alabama.

She even received a round of applause when she finished.

"I'm feeling generous," Larry then announced. "Since my

wife has detailed the grand rebirth of Blackwinter, the very least I can do is fund the enterprise. Thus, I offer a blank check!"

"Marvelous!" Mike cheered.

"Of course, that's the problem with all of Larry's checks," said Gina. "They are blank because he has no money."

There was more talk. And more laughter.

The bond of friendship among them strengthened despite the overly ambitious plans. Silently most asked themselves where they could get the money to make this dream a reality.

Conversation had waned when Kathy turned toward Sarah.

"What do you think? What would you like to see us do to Blackwinter?"

Sarah delivered a bombshell.

"Part of me would like to see us destroy it."

2

Out of the swing of the adult conversation, Kevin had been thumbing through an issue of *Fantasy and Science Fiction* he had brought along to fend off boredom; he hadn't noticed that Maria's eyes strayed his way occasionally, and he hadn't concentrated on the lofty projections for Blackwinter Inn. He did, however, catch Sarah Davenport's comment. Immediately, he searched her expression and was pleased to see that she was serious.

No one spoke for several loud ticks.

"Come on, Sarah, we're not that far in debt yet," said Alan, adding an uneasy chuckle.

Sarah looked at Mike.

Kevin saw her lips shape the words "I'm sorry."

"Why, Sarah?" Kathy asked, as Mike rose and stood near the fireplace so that he wasn't facing his wife. "It's a beautiful old building and our plans for it . . . What's wrong?"

Even Larry sat speechless, the seriousness of the moment having stolen all his one-liners.

"Something . . . something awful happened to my grandfather in this . . . this building. And I—"

She broke off, excused herself, and left the room.

Taken aback, they all watched her leave. Then Kathy said, "Mike, shouldn't you go see about her?"

He turned and gestured that such a move was unnecessary.

"No. It's . . . it's all right. She'll be fine. Too many ghosts out of the past haunting her all at once. I'm sorry this has dampened the mood of things."

He hesitated, tried an awkward smile, then said, "Hey, we can't waste this fire. Anybody interested in roasting marshmallows?"

"Me, me!" Sophie cried, her patience worn thin by the adult exchanges.

"Me, too! Me, too!" Larry exclaimed, imitating Sophie's high-pitched voice.

"We have to have roasting sticks," Mike advised. "Larry, you're in charge of that crew. Here's a flashlight and my pocketknife."

Smiling delightedly, Larry recruited Maria and Kevin to help him, and by the time the smaller logs had burned down, creating deep orange coals, they had returned, huffing and puffing and chilled. The marshmallows were passed around and various theories of roasting were bandied about.

Sarah rejoined the group, choosing to sit next to Kathy who sympathized with her. All serious conversation fled the scene, replaced easily and readily by meaningless, yet good-spirited chitchat. Everyone grew comfortable and warm.

The timeless reverie of an eager fire drew them into a knot of companionship, and the flames generated high flushes on their faces. There were scattered comments and soft laughter, most related to Larry's antics—such as his swallowing four hot marshmallows in one gulp.

Because they had slipped into a serene and calming realm, the sudden appearance of a stranger in their midst was all the more surprising and unexpected.

"Hello."

The young man's voice broke upon them from the front door.

An old-fashioned, billed cap in hand, he walked slowly to the rim of the semicircle they had formed.

"The door was open a little and no one seems to have heard me knock, so I came on in."

It was Mike who rose to greet the young man.

"What can we do for you?"

"Well, sir, I found a fishing boat drifting away from the landing and knew it belonged to someone here. I retrieved it and tied it down, but I thought I should inform you of my action."

"Nice work, Larry," said Alan. "Didn't secure your boat? You're a real sailor."

Tipping his stick toward the young man, Larry said, "Thanks. Listen, you're welcome to a marshmallow as a reward."

There were some nervous chuckles. The young man smiled.

"You have a good fire," he said.

"Come on in and join us," Mike exclaimed. "We've got plenty of marshmallows and firewood."

The young man approached, showing no sign of timidity. To everyone else in the room, he was apparently only a curiosity. His flannel shirt and cap, his baggy trousers held in check by suspenders—it was attire right out of the nineteenth century.

To Kevin, however, the stranger was something more. A wave of apprehension rushed over him as the young man took the marshmallow stick which Mike offered.

96

"Who are you?"

Everyone turned at the intensity of Kevin's question.

Alan frowned at his son, but the stranger seemed unshaken by the verbal challenge.

"My name's Joshua Butera, and I live back up in the woods with my father, Silas."

"I didn't realize anyone lived around the lake," said Mike. "Does your dad farm, or is he a pulpwooder?"

Joshua positioned his marshmallow above the coals; he gave every indication of feeling perfectly at home among them.

"No, he used to be a drum—I mean, a salesman. Now he tinkers around with wood. He carves toys and he sharpens knives. He's lived near here for many years and knows the history of this area. He has many stories about Blackwinter Inn."

"You're looking at the new owners of the inn and the island," said Mike. "We're spending the weekend, hoping to come up with some good ideas as to what we should do with the property."

The young man surveyed the room as he ate a marshmallow. He nodded, and then said, "It's my favorite place. I enjoy exploring the inn and the island. I apologize if I've been trespassing." His eyes roamed to Sarah. "Silas knew you were coming—he knew your grandfather. You're Sarah Blackwinter, aren't you?"

A ripple of surprise registered in everyone's expression.

Sarah stared at the young man, and Kevin sensed that she shared some of the apprehension he had just experienced.

"Yes, I am. Or was," she stammered. "Sarah Davenport now. This is my husband, Mike."

Mike, in turn, introduced the other adults, but not the kids.

"We weren't aware that we were under surveillance," said Larry. "Heck, I'd have worn a clean shirt had I known."

Joshua grinned.

"We don't mean any harm. It's a result of our coming to believe that Blackwinter is our adopted place. We feel . . . protective."

Her curiosity repressed long enough, Sophie edged forward and said, "You sure have goofy-looking clothes. Why are you dressed like that?"

"Sophie!" Gina cried. "That's not polite!"

Joshua glanced down at his shirt and baggy trousers. He shrugged and gave Sophie a smile.

"They're about the only clothes I've got. Hey, I have a present for you."

"A present for me?" She giggled.

From a deep front pocket, he pulled out an object and handed it to Sophie. Everyone in the room leaned forward, intrigued.

"Silas made it," Joshua explained. "It's a Queen Anne-type doll like the ones made in England a long time ago."

"Sophie . . . have you forgotten your manners? What do you say?" Gina prodded.

"Oh, thank you."

It was Gina and Mike who took particular interest in the doll.

"It's wooden," said Gina, examining the doll as Sophie held it. "It has real hair sown into some kind of linen base on top of the head. And look at the Regency dress and the leather shoes—it appears to be so . . . so authentic. Like a valuable antique. Your father *made* this?"

"Yes, ma'am. He can make about any kind of toy out of wood."

"A boat?" asked Mike. "Excuse me. I have something I want you to see." And he left the room before Joshua could respond.

While others gathered closer to Sophie to view the doll, Kevin held back; he felt empty. There was a blurring of the scene. And suddenly he couldn't see Sophie's face. He fought the sensation as Mike returned.

"By any chance did your father make this?"

He showed Joshua the wooden steamship he had found earlier in the houseboat.

"Yes," said the young man. "I must apologize again. Another case of trespassing. I left that on your houseboat because I knew how much you like boats. I like them, too."

"How could you have known that?"

It was Sarah's question, and it carried a tone of fear and suspicion.

"Easy enough to figure, I guess," said Mike, coming to Joshua's defense. "We have a houseboat. Anyway, I accept your gift. And if you're going to be around this weekend, maybe you'd like to cruise the lake with us."

"I would truly enjoy that," said Joshua.

Then he reached into his pocket again.

"Maria, please don't think I'm leaving you out."

"You know my name?" She brightened with surprise.

Kevin could feel something building in his chest as he watched; his attention had shifted to Maria—a milky gray cloud seemed to have enveloped her.

Joshua handed her a wooden horse mounted by a figure Kevin couldn't recognize at first.

"It's a circus rider in a ballerina's costume," Joshua explained. "But you can imagine it to be a gymnast."

"Gee, it's very nice," said Maria. "Thank you. But I don't understand how—?"

Kevin lunged forward.

No longer concentrating on Maria, he trained his eyes upon Sophie, who was admiring her wooden doll. However, he was not seeing the same girl as everyone else.

Joshua reeled back as if expecting to be struck.

Kevin reached for Sophie.

"Don't hold on to that!"

Sophie froze.

And Kevin cringed as he saw her face swell, her cheeks blossom with angry red splotches boiling up into sores.

Blood began a steady flow from her nose and mouth and ears.

"There's something wrong! Can't anyone see!" Kevin shouted.

Alan caught his son and roughly pushed him away.

"What the hell's going on? Have you lost your mind?"

Sophie shrieked and dropped the doll, ran to her mother's arms.

Straining against his father's hold, Kevin looked at the girl again, but the grotesque transformation had dissolved, evaporated, and disappeared like a steamed-over window having suddenly cleared.

There was no scarlet mask. No blood. Only an innocent and very frightened little girl.

The stunned gathering murmured as Alan guided Kevin from the room.

3

Kathy had changed into her nightgown and was brushing her blond hair as Alan, buried in the sleeping bag, gazed stony-eyed at the ceiling. The barren, first-floor room seemed to dwarf them.

"Where is Kevin going to sleep?" she asked.

"Out by the fireplace, I suppose," Alan muttered.

Switching off the light, Kathy groped her way to the edge of the sleeping bag, a double one they had purchased especially for the weekend, and slid in next to her husband.

"Did he give any kind of explanation? I'm just so worried about him, Alan."

"Don't be."

"Why would he make a scene like that? He scared poor little Sophie half to death, and I feel he must have had some reason. What he did was so irrational. What did he say, Alan?"

She listened to his breathing. Could feel the tension in his body.

He sighed deeply.

"He believes there's something wrong with that doll the boy gave to Sophie. Said something ridiculous about the girl's face changing—made some connection between the doll and something awful happening to Sophie. He thinks the boy is dangerous somehow."

"Joshua . . . he said his name is Joshua. He *is* rather curious . . . but why would Kevin . . . ? It has to be the accident, Alan. Hallucinations. Disorientation. Mood swings. Please promise me you'll take him to see a doctor next week. Birmingham. Take him to Birmingham—not to a local doctor. I'll call around and see who's good. He ought to see a neurologist and a psychiatrist."

She waited for Alan to respond. He made a small sound in the back of his throat, but spoke no words.

"Alan? Please . . . promise me you will."

"Kath, don't you see a pattern in this?"

His voice had a hollow, angry tone.

"I see a young man who needs our help."

"No! He needs to grow up and help himself. Can't you see? This episode tonight . . . he was jealous of that boy, and as long as we let him, he'll keep using the accident this summer as an excuse for outrageous displays and unacceptable behavior. We can't let him get away with it. Most of all, we can't let him spoil the weekend . . . not only for us but for the others as well."

She snuggled against him, shivering more from a nameless fear than from the chill in the room.

"I feel sorry for him, Alan . . . and I feel . . . *responsible* somehow. I've played a part in disrupting his life."

"I don't agree, Kath."

His anger had relented, to be replaced by a quiet frustration.

"Maybe tomorrow will be better," she whispered.

"I'm still looking forward to it," said Alan. "But if I have to, I'll take Kevin home — Blackwinter's too important to me to allow a self-centered young man to ruin our experience with it."

Then he added, "I've tried to be a good father to him, and I'll be the first to admit that I could have done a better job."

"You *are* a good father, Alan. You'll always be a good father. Kevin loves you. He respects you as his father and . . ."

She started to say more, started to fill the darkness with revelation, a revelation she hoped would change the tone of Alan's weekend, completely. But she decided it was not the right moment.

She rested her head against his shoulder.

Yes, she would wait for the right moment to share the good news that in a matter of months he would have a second chance at fatherhood.

She listened to the beat of his heart, a secure rhythm, and in that moment she wanted desperately to make him happy, to heal the wounds that he and his son had inflicted upon one another.

"Kath?"

His voice startled her.

"What?"

"What else were you about to say?" he murmured.

"Oh . . . nothing."

"You sure?"

She shifted over on top of him and kissed his chin and his nose and his lips.

"Just that I think you're a delicious man and I love you and I loved you even before I met you. Even before I was born."

She giggled, hoping he wouldn't press her further.

"Hmm . . . sounds as twilight zoney as our mysterious visitor this evening. But you're not fooling me. I want you to spill it — go ahead, tell me I'm all wrong about Kevin."

"No, I wasn't going to say anything more about that."

"What, then?"

"Well . . . I . . . I'm feeling more at home with everyone. Gina's going to be tough to win over. Sarah . . . she has reached out to me. But she's troubled. It's obvious that the inn bothers her."

"Bad memories, apparently. Sarah's always been hard for me to figure. Losing Richard . . . she's more and more likely to crawl into her private shell."

"I like her."

He squeezed her and angled his mouth up to bite her ear.

"And I like *you* . . . every inch of you."

He locked his legs over her bottom, and when they kissed, it was full and long and eager, a prelude to a rush of warmth within the looming darkness.

4

"You'll be right here in the next room. See, that door leads to Momma and Daddy's room."

Larry smoothed Sophie's dark hair and smiled at her. He and Gina had fixed pallets on the floor for their daughters, but Sophie had cried out in fear when they'd turned out the light.

"Daddy, why did Kevin yell at me about my doll? Why did he? It made me real scared."

"It's that boy, Joshua," said Maria. "He's spooky. He knew my name, and he knew I like horses and gymnastics. How could he have known that?"

Holding one hand up in mock submission, Larry said, "Hey, little ladies . . . I'm really not sure how he knew, or why Kevin did and said what he did. The excitement of the weekend affected him perhaps. Thing is, now we need to settle down and forget about it and get some sleep."

"Will it be all right to sleep by my new doll?" Sophie

asked timidly.

"I'm not putting that wooden horse near me," Maria declared. "Maybe Kevin knows something about Joshua that we don't."

"Oh, I seriously doubt there's anything wrong with those toys or the boy, either. You heard what he said: He and his father sorta watch over this old place. They've made it their business to find out who we are and what we're up to. Innocent enough."

"I'm laying my doll right here on my pillow," Sophie announced, glancing defiantly at her sister.

"I wouldn't," said Maria. "Could be it has some kind of voodoo hex on it."

Sophie turned to Larry for affirmation of that charge; he shook his head.

"No. Maria, let's put an end to that talk. Sophie, there's no voodoo hex or anything like that. You two get in your beds 'cause I'm gon' turn off the light. Give me a big hug first."

One at a time, the girls did.

"Good night, little ladies," he said. "Sleep tight . . . and don't let the hungry ghosts bite."

"Da-a-ad-eee!" Sophie sang out as he plunged the room into blackness.

"Hush, Sophie," said Maria. "He's just joking with you."

Their pallets were only a few feet apart, so they could whisper and not be heard by their parents.

"Maria?"

The blackness held the word aloft like a balloon.

"What?"

Sophie hesitated.

"I don't think Joshua's bad. Do you? He gave us both a toy. If he's bad, he wouldn't have, would he?"

"You can't ever tell."

"Maria?"

"Sophie, I don't want to talk. Go to sleep," Maria

104

snapped.

"But I need to ask you something."

"What is it?"

"Will you hold my hand till I fall asleep?"

"You're being a baby. You know that, don't you?"

Sophie was silent.

Feeling a painful stitch of guilt, Maria reached out in the darkness, walking her fingers along, eventually bumping into Sophie's tiny hand. She gripped it, though it was warm and sticky with sweat.

"Good night, Maria."

"Good night, Dopey-Sophie."

"Don't call me that."

"Sorry. Good night."

She squeezed her little sister's hand. Within ten minutes she could hear the steady, easily recognizable breathing— Sophie was dead-to-the-world asleep.

Maria patted the tiny hand; then, in a gesture she couldn't resist, she pulled the hand to her lips and kissed it.

"Sweet dreams, Sophie," she whispered.

But for Maria sleep did not come—at least, not readily.

What does Kevin know?

She considered a dark possibility. What if the accident really had upset Kevin's mental faculties? What if he were going, minute by minute, hour by hour, insane? That could explain his behavior.

She didn't want to believe it.

But neither did she trust Joshua, the dark-eyed bringer of gifts.

In the adjacent room, Gina stared into the shadowy reaches as Larry speculated about the evening.

"You notice how Mike was drawn so immediately to Joshua? Sad business in a way. He'll always be looking for a replacement for Richard. Sarah, on the other hand, didn't warm to the boy. And Kevin . . . poor Kevin . . . he's really having a rough time, isn't he?"

"Do you have any idea what they may be worth?"

Larry could tell by her empty, distant, distracted tone that she hadn't heard a word he had said.

"The Davenports? Or Kevin?" he replied, knowing full well she was not referring to people.

She rolled off her cot and, when she had flooded the room with light, pawed through her purse for a cigarette.

"Those wooden toys," she muttered.

She sat on the edge of the cot, her body seeming to derive much needed sustenance from each inhalation. Larry watched her blow a plume of smoke.

"Thought you were gon' quit."

"Tomorrow," she said. "I'll quit tomorrow. This helps me think."

She wagged the cigarette at him.

"An expensive, nasty, unhealthy habit," Larry observed.

"Spoken by a man who guzzles beer and Zingers. Don't rag at me about nasty, unhealthy habits."

He twisted onto his back.

"Damn, I'm hungry. Think I'll go raid the kitchen."

"I have a perfect idea, Larry," she exclaimed. "Listen to this."

He grunted.

"Those wooden toys, Larry . . . don't you see? We could sell them in a gift shop here at the inn. For that matter, we could convert several of these first-floor rooms into shops. A crafts shop, for example."

"Blackwinter gon' have a bar?" he asked.

"Yes, of course. The 'Larry Bozic Memorial Bar.' "

He gave her a toothy grin, and she continued.

"And we'll sell the mineral water. Wine, too, if the wine cellar is still functional. Gold mine, dearest," she said, her dark eyes bulging and gleaming. "Blackwinter can be a gold mine."

Larry furrowed his brow.

"I've been thinking about something, too. Something Sarah said."

Disregarding her husband, Gina attacked her purse again, scattering items until she came upon a notepad and a pen. She began to write as rapidly as possible, smoke curling from her nose as if she were some machine cranking at full bore.

Larry squirmed on his cot.

"She said that something awful happened to her grandfather when he lived here. Gina, do you remember her saying that?"

"I suppose I do. Why? Sarah was not herself tonight."

Gina slowed her furious writing pace only slightly.

"What exactly did happen to him? I can't recall anything specific. I'm sure Sarah or Mike must have mentioned it in the past."

Gina stopped writing.

"A sickness. Some kind of disease—like yellow fever—that's what I heard."

"Yellow fever? Jesus . . . in the twentieth century?"

"It was some rare disease. That's all I remember hearing."

And with that remark, Gina started writing again, faster, leaving Larry to ponder the implications of her information.

"I'm gon' get a leftover hot dog—thinking about all this makes me hungry. You want something?"

But she was too involved with the notepad to respond.

5

"I'm going to have to excuse myself. If you two want to stay up and talk, feel free, but I've had too big a day already."

Sarah rose. So did Mike and Joshua. Mike touched her

elbow.

"I won't be much longer," he said. "Josh has so much Blackwinter history at his fingertips it's difficult for me to let him go—I'm learning volumes."

When Sarah turned to say good night to Joshua, his dark eyes and a smile greeted her, and there was something in his confident manner which reminded her of Richard.

"Oh, I almost forgot," he exclaimed. "I have something for you."

A bit uneasy, Sarah glanced at Mike, who grinned and said, "And it's not even your birthday."

Joshua held out something toward Sarah, something small and virtually buried in his palm.

"My father puts these on our Christmas tree."

She stared at the object, but did not take it from him at first.

"What is it?" said Mike. "Oh, I see. A wooden wreath surrounding a bell. Yeah, a neat Christmas ornament."

Joshua raised the object and gently shook it.

The delicate tinkle of the bell was precisely as Sarah recalled; she blinked her eyes to ward off a sudden onslaught of dizziness.

"Where did you get this?" she asked, managing a note of reserve.

"My father made it. If it's inappropriate, please say so—I thought you would like it."

"Of course she does," Mike said. "She has always liked bells."

After another moment of hesitation, Sarah took the object.

"Yes, it is very pretty. Thank you, Joshua."

"Does it remind you of anything?" he asked.

Her eyes met his and she reluctantly nodded.

"Grandfather."

"Well," said Mike after a lengthy pause, "I'm certainly glad Larry failed to tie up his boat—or we might never have met you, Josh."

His eyes still riveted on Sarah, the boy said, "I had planned to meet you. If not tonight, then tomorrow. I had to know whether Blackwinter would be in good hands. And, once again, I trust you will forgive my trespasses. I must be going. My father will miss me if I stay longer."

"You'll be back tomorrow, won't you?" Mike asked.

"Yes, provided your generous offer regarding the boat ride stands."

"Wear your sailing gear."

Joshua smiled at Sarah.

"Thank you for your hospitality this evening. Good night."

"Good night," Sarah murmured.

"I'll see you to the door," Mike said. "I assume you have a boat to get you from the island to the shore."

"I'm accustomed to finding my way around the area," said Joshua. "But I do appreciate your concern."

"Do you need to tend to the fire?" Sarah asked her husband as they readied for bed.

"No. Kevin said he would. He's sleeping out by the fireplace. I spoke to him about the fire right before I left."

"Mike?"

"Hmm?"

"Joshua . . . I feel like . . . I've seen him before."

She stood, holding the wooden wreath and bell in a tight fist, trembling slightly as if buffeted by a strong breeze.

"Maybe you have, especially since he and his father live near here."

"No . . . he . . . it's a little unsettling that he seems to know Blackwinter so well . . . and my background . . . . The familiarity . . . isn't it rather unsettling to you?"

"No, I wouldn't use that word. I do find it . . . *uncanny*—but it's mostly his resemblance to Richard. He has

Richard's mannerisms, Richard's intelligence. Could that be why you feel you've seen him before?"

She shrugged.

"He is a lot like Richard. You're right."

"Sarah, are you OK? Everyone's kinda puzzled by things you've been saying and the way you've been acting."

"I'm sorry, Mike. I feel like . . . like I should go home tomorrow. Would you really mind if I did?"

He gently gripped her shoulders.

"Yes, I would. You and I *need* this time at Blackwinter. We'll go cruising on the lake tomorrow and relax, get away from the others. We need to, Sarah. Stay. I want you to."

She put her arms around him, and he hugged her.

And when she loosened her fist, the tiny bell jingled.

She barely heard it over the anxious beating of her heart.

6

"You keepin' the homefires burnin', Kevin?"

Having lost himself in the reverie of the flame, the boy jerked awake.

"Oh . . . Mr. Bozic . . . hey, I thought everybody was asleep."

"*This* never sleeps."

Larry patted his stomach and sat down on the ledge of the fireplace. He was carrying a half-eaten hot dog. "Say, you want a snack?"

"No, sir. Thanks. I haven't been very hungry this evening."

Finishing off the hot dog in two bites, Larry chewed noisily as he gazed into the dying fire. When he had swallowed the final bite, he said, "Winking embers and coals . . . good setting for a ghost story, huh?"

Kevin grinned.

"Yes, sir."

"I can just imagine ole Edgar Allan Poe settled in by this fire, nursing a strong drink, his mind tripping off into Gothic realms. Did you know that he may have visited Blackwinter Inn?"

"No, sir. Poe? Really?"

There was a flicker of excitement in the boy's voice, and, accordingly, Larry followed up.

"Wouldn't be hard to believe that this place inspired him — gave him the idea for a short story."

Kevin glanced around and edged closer to the fire.

"It's a creepy old building. I don't much like it — oh, I'm sorry . . . I mean . . . it's probably a good, you know, a good investment and all that. Everybody has big ideas about it. I hope they work, but . . . "

"But your intuition is giving you some — what do they say these days? — negative feedback."

"Yes, sir. Lots of it."

He looked at Larry, seeming to ask for understanding.

"That negative feedback include our visitor tonight?"

Kevin's jaw flinched. He fidgeted with his hands.

"Do you think I'm crazy, Mr. Bozic?"

"Whoa . . . hold on. I think you deserve a chance to explain your actions this evening. At the outset, I've got to admit that that young man was most peculiar. You evidently saw even more than the rest of us did."

Kevin shifted restlessly on the ledge, and when he eventually spoke he appeared to spit out his words as if they tasted bitter.

"He's evil."

Larry raised his eyebrows.

"Evil? Interesting word, though it likely means different things to different people. What do you mean by 'He's evil'?"

At first Kevin shrugged; Larry could tell that the boy regretted saying anything.

"What I mean is, I think he's going to hurt people . . .

some of us. I mean . . . he's not . . . human."

"I see."

"I can't explain it. And maybe the accident this summer really screwed up my head. Maybe I am going crazy. My dad thinks so. But I saw . . ."

Larry didn't press him.

The fire sloughed off into muted pops and crackles. The room collected darkness. In the waning glow, Kevin's face halved into slanted shadow and an expression of consternation, and his jaw tightened and his eyes registered fear.

"Mr. Bozic, I'm sorry I brought all this out. It sounds nutso to you, I bet."

"Well, my reaction to Joshua was not as strong as yours, and, hey listen, I don't think you're crazy. It wouldn't hurt for all of us to keep an eye on that young man — just to be on the safe side."

He pushed up from the ledge and stretched.

"I'm going to hit the sack. Don't dwell on things too much, Kevin. You're too young to be infected with worry."

"Mr. Bozic? I just want to say . . . thanks . . . thanks for hearing me out . . . and for not telling me I'm crazy."

Larry winked at him.

"Hey, you can't be crazy because *I'm* the resident kook for this group and I'm not ready to resign my position yet."

He left Kevin with a grin on his lips.

But on the way back to his room, Larry felt something he was very unaccustomed to feeling.

Fear.

The few remaining logs collapsed upon themselves, hissing, spiraling sparks, yet continuing to radiate heat. His face turned toward the heat and dwindling light, Kevin invited sleep, invited oblivion. But neither came.

In the resonant burning of the coals, he saw a visage which planted daggers of terror in his chest.

112

Am I imagining this?

He pushed to his feet and tried to calm himself.

Behind him, reflections of the dying fire flickered in the front windows, giving the impression of tiny conflagrations erupting around the inn.

Kevin felt alone.

And suddenly he knew he was being watched.

Slowly he turned, and the figure of Joshua materialized outside a window, standing, it appeared, in the burning coals. The two young men stared at each other.

Kevin experienced the stab of a chill.

Then a branding of anger.

He ran to the front door, but found Joshua was no longer at the window; he glimpsed movement as the stranger beat a path for the rear of the inn. Determination fired in the pit of Kevin's stomach.

"Stop!" he called out. "I see you! I've caught you!"

But Joshua continued to flee.

Kevin scampered after him, staying within twenty yards of him until they reached the solid rock foundation upon which the back wall of the inn perched. The wall rose fifteen to twenty feet as it blended with the slope of the island. Dead wisteria vines covered most of the wall, and there was no visible door leading to the cellar beneath the inn.

And yet Joshua disappeared.

Kevin rushed to the section of the wall where he had last seen him. Through the leafless vines, he pressed his fingers onto the rock. He pushed at it, finding no entry.

Where did he go?

Winded, confused, Kevin stood back from the wall.

Then, again, he searched along its surface.

I saw him.

After another minute of digging at the vines and brushing his fingers over the lower part of the wall, he decided to give up. He was cold. He had lost his nemesis. But where?

How?

Saw him as clear as day.

Should I wake everyone? he asked himself.

He knew he couldn't. Couldn't face his dad without some proof that Joshua was, indeed, dangerous.

Best idea would be to go back inside and try to go to sleep, he admitted reluctantly.

Light flickered to his left, perfectly timed to counter his decision.

He crouched and duckwalked another thirty feet along the looming wall; the light, a torch, was showing through the squares in an iron grate. The light held steady.

Kevin began to work on the grate, tugging at it, pushing, lifting, prying. Minutes passed before he succeeded in pulling it away from the wall far enough so that he could let himself through the opening.

Fortunately there was only a drop of perhaps four feet to the floor of the cellar. He sought out the light from the torch, and it began to move again . . . as if it had been waiting for him.

When his eyes had adjusted to the immediate darkness and to the shadows ahead, he could once again see the figure of Joshua.

"Hold it there!" Kevin cried.

Neither of them moved.

Their eyes locked.

They were standing in the largest room of the wine cellar, beneath an arched ceiling; huge, old wine barrels surrounded them, and beyond Joshua the room funneled into a narrow passage and the wall around the passage sweated trickles of mineral water.

It was cold and dank. Joshua's torch added tendrils of smoke to the cavernous room, but Kevin noticed little about the scene. A confrontation was under way. Invisible lines of force emanating from Joshua had him paralyzed.

Joshua smiled.

114

"Has our chase ended?"

Kevin rocked forward on the balls of his feet. He strained, clenching his hands into hard fists. His tongue went numb.

"Not so brave as you were earlier—is that correct, my friend?" Joshua taunted.

His entire body trembling, Kevin forced himself to concentrate, to slow his breathing and relax.

"You offer a challenge?" said Joshua. "Go ahead. You don't have a prayer, for my power has increased over the years. The mineral springs are my source. And there is more. I have the demon's eye, the dragon's voice—and the touch of the red death. But more . . . I have *companions.*"

Kevin could feel himself meeting Joshua's powers, momentarily equaling but not surpassing them.

Stop time, he shouted within.

He began to float free, and the invisible, yet tremendously strong, lines of force relented by degrees.

Joshua appeared surprised.

"My friend, I see you have some powers of your own," he stammered, then retreated a few steps.

"No matter," he continued. "Blackwinter is mine. I am here. It is my place of birth. My home. No one else will ever possess it unless I wish them to."

Weightless. Kevin could sense the lines of force dissolving.

But when he snapped back to his body, he saw that Joshua had disappeared again. Within the narrow passage leading deep into the cellar, Kevin could see a splash of torchlight.

His head throbbed. He wasn't certain he was physically able to go on.

But he believed he must.

He found that he had to bend over to enter the passage and move along its cool, wet, constricted confines. Twenty yards he burrowed into it before it dropped sharply and to his right.

The glow of torchlight drew him to the ledge of an opening, a rock pit ten feet or so in diameter into which mineral springs, originating from several different spots, flowed, creating a dark pool.

In that pool stood Joshua.

He had secured his torch in a fissure in the rock formation surrounding the pool.

"Welcome, friend," he exclaimed. "But prepare yourself. I am not what I seem."

Looking down upon the strange young man, Kevin responded.

"I have seen the ugly side of you. I know that you're evil . . . that you mean to hurt the people who've come here this weekend. But I'm going to stop you—stop time and then send you back to wherever you came from."

"My origin is the red death, my friend. Allow me to show you."

And the first stage of his transformation unfolded.

The grotesque, scarlet mask. Blood and sores. And the demon's eye, large, liquid, vulturelike.

"There's more, friend," roared the voice of a dragon.

As Kevin viewed the next stage of the preternatural scene, he felt every nerve come alive. The torchlight focused his attention on Joshua's eye as it began to bulge from its socket.

Blood rimmed the rapidly enlarging eyeball. There was a nervous pop as the ball broke free of the socket and oozed down across Joshua's cheek; yellow brain matter pressed forward, escaping from the opening.

Then a black, clawed hand.

Bone and flesh tore—it was the sound of cloth ripping— Joshua's red death mask split down the middle and a dark demon crawled free and the shell of the young man's body fell away and sank into the pool.

The demon fixed its stare upon Kevin.

The creature itself was a nightmarish mixture of reptile and carnivore, all claws and fangs and predatory intent, and even as Kevin watched, it constantly shifted its shape, taking on new and more terrifying countenances second by second.

And then the final transformation occurred.

Its belly distended, the demon writhed up out of the pool and shrieked; birthing cries echoed deep within the cellar.

Kevin held his ears, and when the demon raked a razor-sharp claw over its stomach, the boy screamed at the sight of what emerged. He turned and ran, praying that the dark fury of noise and movement was not chasing after him. Breathless, he raced through the shadowy passage into more blackness, frantically searching until he located the opening through which he had entered.

He clambered free.

Behind him the cellar chorused with the most frightening sounds he had ever heard. Beyond the opening, he collapsed, his heart pounding so hard he felt that it would burst.

Images swirled through his thoughts.

The visage of the red death had horrified him, as had the demon. But what the demon had given birth to was worse.

Much worse.

Chapter VII

1

"It was horrible," Gina murmured, holding her head in her hands, laughing against her will.

"Have some coffee," said Sarah. She was cold, but felt cheered by the blisteringly bright, morning sunshine slanting across the lake beyond the windows.

"I dreamed that we were exploring somewhere in the inn—upstairs, I'm not sure where—and I found this chest, a heavy, wooden chest—like a pirate's chest." Gina paused to sip at the coffee Sarah had poured. Over at the gas grill, Larry was frying bacon and eggs, and humming to himself. Gina laughed, apparently remembering more of the dream scenario.

"And as I tore at the chest I could *smell* money in it."

"You could *smell* money in it?" Sarah flashed a mock smile.

"That sounds pretty bizarre, doesn't it? But it's true. I could smell it."

Bunkered behind the grill, Larry asked, "What did it smell like—George Washington's dirty socks?"

Gina ignored him. She thought a moment.

"Rich. It had a . . . rich aroma—mixture of things: Pipe tobacco and fresh ground coffee and the aftershave I gave my dad one Christmas . . . and like varnished wood . . . and like the inside of a bank. It was an absolutely marvelous smell, and it was driving me wild and I was clawing at the chest."

She raised her hands and curled her fingers and raked at the air.

Sarah giggled.

"Gina!"

"I was."

"So that's how my shoulder got scratched," said Larry. "I thought we had made passionate love in the night and the shock of it all had blanked my memory. Should have known better."

"Did you get the chest open?" Sarah asked, still giving way to a broad smile.

"Yes, finally. My fingers were bloody, and I was so angry because I had yelled for the rest of you to come help me and no one would—in fact, most of you were smirking and making fun of me—and I screamed every profanity at you I could think of."

"I was having my own dream," said Larry, "or I would have helped, sweetheart."

"No, you were *in* my dream . . . the end of it at least."

"So what was in the chest?" said Sarah.

Gina arched her eyebrows.

"Gold coins! Hundreds of them!"

Puzzled, Sarah shook her head.

"Then what was so horrible about the dream?"

"Wait. There's more. I got the chest open and stared at the coins, drooling and trembling. I was speechless. I jammed my hands into them and the feeling—oh, it was ecstasy." She laughed hard before gaining control and adding, "It was like I was having an orgasm."

Sarah put her hand over her mouth and rocked back and forth, laughing, giggling. And Larry mumbled, "Dearest, why didn't you tell me that would be a turn-on. Now I can throw away my black bikini briefs and pile gold coins on the bed instead."

"After this dream, I don't want to be around gold coins ever again," Gina exclaimed. "You see, what happened was this. I hollered for everyone to come look at what I'd discovered. No one came except Larry . . . Well, he picked up one of the coins and said, 'Don't you know what these are?' 'Of course,' I said, 'they're gold coins. It's the treasure of Blackwinter Inn.' "

"The treasure of Blackwinter Inn," Sarah echoed. "Sounds symbolic. Is that Freudian?"

"No," said Larry. "It's vintage Gina."

"All right, let me finish the dream—here's the awful part. Larry took one of the coins and started *unwrapping* it. I couldn't believe my eyes. He peeled gold foil off the coin and there was chocolate underneath it . . . and he *ate* the coin."

Sarah and Larry both laughed.

"But—but wait!" Gina exclaimed. "When *I* tried to peel the foil away, the coins were real. Larry called the kids over, and Maria and Sophie began eating the coins, too. And I had to fight them because when I held the coins they continued to be real gold . . . so right before I woke up, I was snatching the coins away from everybody so they wouldn't all be eaten. Horrible—just a horrible dream."

After a final round of good-natured laughter, Larry said, "It's some kind of warning from your subconscious that your love of money can't *feed* you."

"Or it means I have a glutton for a husband."

Gina stuck out her tongue at him.

"I can't remember whether I dreamed," said Sarah. "I tossed and turned a lot. It's never been easy for me to sleep at Blackwinter."

"Where's Mike?" asked Larry. "He could be helping me burn the bacon."

"Down by the lake doing heaven knows what with the

houseboat. He would live and die in that thing if he could. Wants to take Joshua out on it today—I suppose I'm invited, but I hesitate to ask."

"Joshua's a little different, isn't he?" said Gina. "I need to meet his father and talk some business about those wooden toys—what a product!"

"The kid is from the strange side of somewhere," said Larry. "And speaking of strange, I kept hearing music all night—like waltz music—and the chiming of a grandfather clock. Anyone else hear it?"

"Not me," Gina muttered. "Twice, though, I was awakened by the mating groans and moans from the room next door. Alan and Kathy had their sleeping bag crying for mercy. It's probably worn out this morning—*something's* bound to be worn out this morning."

Sarah laughed softly, and Larry blew his wife a sarcastic kiss.

Maria and Sophie, bleary-eyed and yawning, filed into the kitchen. The three adults greeted them, and Larry announced the breakfast menu.

Within the next half hour, Mike ventured up from the houseboat and Alan and Kathy rose and made their way to the kitchen, hanging onto one another like newlyweds.

Kevin, not really hungry, sneaked through for a slice of toast and jelly, then he escaped the raucous noise of the adults and the other kids, stealing up to the bell tower for peace and quiet.

He needed to be by himself.

He needed to think.

And decide what must be done.

2

The view was magnificent.

From the top landing of the bell tower Kevin surveyed island and lake and shore in a breathtaking three-hundred-sixty-degree sweep.

How can there be evil in such a beautiful place?

He began to doubt the experience in the wine cellar. Had his dislike of Joshua phantomed demonic creations? Was it a case of seeing evil where there was none?

The pool. The transformation.

The final scene. The sounds.

He shivered at the rush of images. It was almost as if he could imagine being trapped by those creatures — trapped and realizing his powers were not strong enough.

What next?

Somehow he had to prove to the adults that Joshua posed a threat. That would be difficult — especially since he couldn't be totally certain himself.

He closed his eyes and heard Joshua's voice.

"Blackwinter is mine. I am here. It is my place of birth. My home. No one else will ever possess it unless I wish them to."

But Sarah Davenport's grandparents had lived here, Kevin reasoned. Was Joshua bluffing? Had the transformations involved some elaborate trick?

The accident. That could explain it. Some kind of brain damage had brought on a tendency for vivid hallucinations — no one could change into the shape of a demon. Or worse. There was no scientific or rational context for such a thing.

But it had been real. Nightmarish, yet real. He knew it. Forget the arguments against the supernatural.

With difficulty, he swallowed his last bite of toast and drank in the pristine scenery. Far below and to his left the wall of pines opened and there, along the shore, were Maria and Sophie, walking, stopping occasionally to toss a rock or a stick into the water and watch the resultant circles widen to infinity.

122

Out in the lake some twenty yards, a lone fisherman, a stranger, was casting for bass, no doubt unaware that anyone had purchased Blackwinter Inn and the island. But it was a pleasant scene — quiet, serene — a calender-photo clarity.

His eye followed the line of the girls' meandering.

And suddenly his breath caught in his throat.

Perched on a granite boulder, looking for all the world like a satyr from the pages of mythology, was Joshua.

3

"Why don't you like it?" said Sophie, holding the wooden horse up, examining it closely, comparing it to the doll in her other hand.

"I think it's dumb — it's a dumb toy," Maria responded. She gathered a handful of rocks and tossed them into the lake, careful not to throw them where they would interfere with the fisherman, an elderly man wearing a straw hat.

"You don't like it just because Kevin doesn't. I know that. You love Kevin. Might as well say it."

"Oh, Sophie, you're getting nerdier every day."

"Tell me why you don't like the horse and ballerina if it's not 'cause you love Kevin. Go ahead and tell me."

"Perhaps she's outgrowing horses and ballerinas."

Both girls were startled by the approach of Joshua.

Flushed with embarrassment and anger, Maria tightened her lips together and would not meet his eyes.

But Sophie greeted him, smiling, eager to talk.

"She loves Kevin, and Kevin doesn't like these toys, and he doesn't like you, either."

"Do *you* like me?" Joshua asked, hunkering down to one knee near her.

"Sure. You brought me this doll."

"I'm glad you like me and like the doll I gave you. I'm

very sorry that Maria doesn't like the gift I gave her. She likes horses. I'm sure of that. And she likes gymnastics. You know what, Sophie?"

The little girl slid her tongue into the corner of her mouth and balanced herself nervously on one foot.

"What?"

"Secretly, deep inside, Maria likes her toy — I'd wager she does, wouldn't you?"

Sophie nodded.

"She does. Yeah, she really does." She giggled.

Maria had turned her back on the two of them, but suddenly wheeled around defiantly.

"Sophie, be quiet! You're not supposed to be talking to strangers — Mom told you about that."

"But I'm not a stranger, am I, Sophie?"

Like a puppet, Sophie shook her head.

"You're more like a friend. Like my boyfriend. Like Maria has Kevin for a boyfriend and I have you for a boyfriend."

Joshua brightened.

"Why, you're absolutely right. I'm going to be a very close friend."

He looked into Sophie's eyes and smiled.

"Know what I think? I think that if you were to take the horse and ballerina toy over to Maria, she would admit that she likes it. Why don't you do that? Take it over to your sister."

"OK, I can do that."

Smirking triumphantly, she did.

Maria surprised herself by accepting it; she felt so angry the backs of her knees threatened to buckle. She glared at Joshua and her sister.

"I'll show you," she exclaimed, "how I feel about this dumb toy."

She grasped it and tried to break it in two, but couldn't. Frustrated, cheeks burning at the sound of laughter from her challengers, she lifted the wooden toy and hurled it out into the lake. It splashed and the fisherman glanced disapprovingly her way.

Joshua's eyes narrowed.

"A most inappropriate gesture, young lady. I don't easily forget it when someone has insulted me that way."

"Keep away from me and my sister—and keep off our island," said Maria, barely controlling her fury.

She began walking toward the inn, taking long and hurried strides.

Joshua scrambled in front of her.

"This is *not* your island," he muttered through clenched teeth. "You'll realize that soon enough."

"Get out of my way!"

Continuing to block her path, Joshua exclaimed, "This is *my* island! Do you understand that? Blackwinter belongs to me!"

Anger and hatred contorted his face; the mask hiding the red death threatened to sip off.

"Leave her alone!"

Maria turned to find Kevin, slightly out of breath, looking straight at Joshua.

"You and Sophie better go on back to the inn," Kevin murmured.

"No," said Sophie. "I bet there's gonna be a fight and I wanna see it."

"Come on, dopey. Right now."

Maria fetched her sister by the arm and pulled her toward the inn.

When the two girls were nearly out of sight, Joshua smiled and said, "Ah, the knight in shining armor, is it? I would have thought that your observance of my companions would have kept you at a sensible distance from me. I seem to have underestimated your courage . . . or your stupidity."

Kevin clenched and unclenched his fists. He had never

been any good at fighting; in fact, he had generally avoided fights whenever possible, but this situation dictated the possibility of action.

"How much courage does it take to pick on girls?"

Kevin's remark stung Joshua. It was evident in the sudden flash of rage which flamed across his expression. The dark-eyed young man said nothing at first; he strolled to the shore, hands in his pockets. The old fisherman captured his attention; he seemed to study man and boat for half a minute; then, purpose renewed and revitalized, he gestured toward Kevin.

"You may prove to be a worthy adversary yet, my friend."

"I'm not your friend. I don't understand who you are . . . or your powers. But I believe you're evil, and I won't let you hurt anyone here if I can stop you."

"A rather large *if*, I would say. And you forget, Master Kevin, that Mike and Sarah Davenport think quite highly of me. Also, would your own dear father side with you?"

Kevin's throat burned.

"I'll prove to them that you're evil."

"*Evil?* Such a strong word. I am merely reclaiming that which is mine — how can that be evil?"

"You have supernatural powers. I've seen them. But I don't know where they come from, and I don't care. I do care about the people on this island."

"But what you fail to understand, Master Kevin, is that your puny abilities are no match for me. My companions terrified you last night, and they obey my commands. For your own safety, don't force me to unleash their fury upon you. If you wish to be helpful, I would suggest that by the end of the day you convince the adults to give up their foolish idea of claiming Blackwinter as their own. Sunset — you'll have until sunset to get everyone to leave. After sunset . . . well, you've received images of what is in store, haven't you?"

Kevin could feel himself swaying as he stood; he fought

off an attack of dizziness and concentrated on his response.

"I'm not afraid. They won't leave—so I'll have to fight you."

Surprised that he held his ground, Joshua hesitated. Again he let his gaze drift out to the fisherman, now even farther from the shore.

"You're not prepared to do so, Master Kevin. It may well be that I can help ready you."

He turned and smiled; Kevin steadied himself.

"I don't need your help—I don't need anything from you."

"Allow me, however, to test your mettle," Joshua exclaimed.

The stillness of the autumn morning framed the scene.

Kevin wanted to run; he had no idea what Joshua had planned, but he knew he couldn't retreat. He had gone too far. Strength of will—he had to have it.

"See the fisherman?" said Joshua.

Momentarily confused, Kevin kept his eyes on Joshua.

"He will be your test."

By degrees, Kevin slowly shifted his attention to the man in the boat. He watched the silvery tip of the fishing rod flick outward, saw glints of sun vibrate through the air. The man's straw hat reminded him of the type men in a barbershop quartet wear.

"What are you going to do?" he muttered, struggling against a rising tide of fear.

Joshua chuckled.

"I'm going to stir up the water a little."

He raised his hand, and Kevin thought he saw a swirl of shadows leap from Joshua's fingers, move along the ground and into the lake. Amazed at the sight, Kevin followed the shadows as they raced beneath the surface, tiny ripples breaking out as if birds were skimming low atop the water.

And the shadows were heading straight for the fisherman.

Kevin ran to the edge of the lake.

"Hey! Hey, mister . . . you in the boat! Look out!"

When the old man finally heard Kevin, he waved and said something the boy couldn't make out.

"Look out! Something's coming toward your boat!"

The shadowy swirl churned the surface as it closed to within ten or fifteen yards of the boat; the water bubbled as if it were boiling.

"God, he doesn't see," Kevin whispered to himself, in shock.

He started to yell one last time, but it was too late; the old man shouldered around as the shadowy mass slammed into his boat. It bobbed and spun, and the man dropped his rod and grabbed the sides of his small craft. His expression was that of a frightened child on an amusement ride.

A black swarm of tiny creatures began clambering into the boat; too surprised even to scream, the old man brushed at them frantically. But in a matter of seconds they poured over his face and into his mouth and pulled him down. And almost as quickly the bottom of the boat ripped apart.

Kevin plunged into the lake as the boat was sinking.

God, I've got to try to save him!

The lake water, November cold, took away his breath. He groaned aloud as its chill blanketed his face and chest and clutched at his genitals. He thrust his head up and gasped for air.

Beyond him he saw the nose of the boat disappear; saw the old man's arm, black except where bloodied flesh showed through, thrashing the water; saw the straw hat float innocently away; saw bubbles dance and whirl. The only comparable image in his mind was that of a shark attack.

Some autonomous mechanism within him took over. He swam against the wall of cold. His body, heavy, sodden, wanted to sink, but he wrestled with it, determined to reach the man.

He had splashed his way another five to ten yards, gaining strength, adjusting to the severe chill, when he began to feel something pinching softly at his arms.

He pulled up and treaded water, whipping his head from side to side. He swatted at the dark objects beginning to materialize near him, but they would not scatter; instead, they encircled him.

Just beyond him, the old man broke the surface one last time, a strangled gurgle escaping into the clear, autumn air. And then Kevin focused on the dark ring, and what he saw caused him to shriek in fear.

There were hundreds of spidery creatures, clinging to one another, swarming and yet keeping their distance from him as if waiting for the right opportunity to attack. Kevin suddenly looked back to the shore and realization swept through him — Joshua stood poised there, eyes glazed in a resolute fury.

I've got to concentrate, he warned himself. *Float free. Stop time.*

He hiccuped and shivered, actions generated more by terror than the cold water. But gradually he gained control of his will — the spider creatures drew no closer.

Out of body, Kevin rose above the lake. He could see the dark swarm, and he could also see himself treading water and the old man sinking into the chill depths.

I have to try to save him!

He cried out in pain as he snapped back into his body. The spider things parted as he swam furiously through them and angled down toward the bottom of the lake.

Too murky to allow him adequate vision, the water tumbled and billowed detritus from its floor, particles of mud and sand and vegetation stirred by the old man's frantic struggle.

Kevin went deeper. He swung his arms in arcs out from his body, hoping to make contact with the drowning man, recognizing all the while that he might be too late. Two summers ago he'd completed a lifesaving course, but could not recall much except the bare essentials of pulling the victim from the water and administering emergency resuscitation.

His lungs stitched fire; he needed air and so he jetted to the surface, bobbed free, and glanced around for signs of the old man. On shore there was no sign of Joshua, in the lake, no sign of the spider swarm.

Kevin took an expansive breath and, a second or two later, touched bottom.

And the old man's body.

It seemed almost too light as the boy locked his elbow under an armpit and began towing him to the ceiling of the water. The body felt leathery and lifeless.

My God, he's dead. I can't save him.

It was like tugging on a wet and empty sleeping bag.

But Kevin continued, disregarding the odds, reacting instinctively. Exhaustion clawed at him as he labored toward shore. He considered yelling for help, but chose to conserve what little energy remained.

One arduous stroke at a time, he struggled until he reached shallow water and his feet hit the slippery lake bottom. He fell once and lost his hold on the old man's body, then recovered and lugged himself and his apparently lifeless burden to the lip of the shore.

Facedown, the old man looked shriveled and shrunken.

Catching his breath a moment, Kevin straddled the body, mentally rehearsing vital lifesaving procedure, hoping against hope that he could revive the bundle of skin and bones.

He lifted the body farther into the shore and carefully turned it over.

A skeletal face lurched up at him, bearing a rictus smile. All the flesh had dissolved. Or had been eaten away.

Kevin jerked back in horror.

But something held him.

A skeletal arm and hand.

The fingers taloned like those of a predatory bird.

5

He had no way of knowing how long he fought to get away as the skeletal creature which had once been a man slithered from the shore, seeking to pull Kevin with it into the cold depths of the lake.

Screams caught in the boy's throat; his tongue seemed paralyzed. His thoughts reeled.

Can't someone hear the splashing? Won't somebody save me?

He was losing strength.

The thing succeeded in dragging him into deeper water.

Concentrate, he told himself. *Damn it, concentrate. Float free. Stop time.*

You can do it.

He closed his eyes.

Don't panic!

Skeletal fingers locked around his wrists like handcuffs.

Now! he shouted within.

His world grayed; his mind registered a static snow of blankness.

And he had started to drift up from his body when he opened his eyes to find the skeletal face a few inches from his own. As he stared at the hideousness of that face, the skull bloated and swelled to twice its size.

Skeletal jaws opened wide.

The spider things gushed out like vomit.

Kevin screamed.

131

He felt himself reenter his body, a hard jolt, like a door slamming.

The spider things poured from the skeleton's eye sockets.

And in the final blink of consciousness before Kevin gave up and sank beneath the swirling mass of shadows, he watched, horrified, as the skull split apart and a horde of the creatures boiled out into the lake and swam toward him.

Like a net, they covered and bound him.

6

"Did you see how this happened, Maria?" Alan asked.

Curiously, there was skepticism in his tone as if he thought Kevin had somehow staged the episode.

Maria stared down at Kevin, who was trying to sit up, but Kathy had wrapped a blanket around him and was insisting that he not move because she believed he was in shock.

Also gathered near were Mike and Sarah, Larry and Gina and Sophie. There was hushed anticipation and a nervous air of puzzlement.

"I heard him call out — he screamed," said Maria, "and so I ran straight down here."

"Kevin," Kathy murmured, "don't move, please. We'll carry you to the inn. Don't move on your own."

But he twisted free of her hold; he focused on Maria, though for an instant he couldn't recognize her.

"He was drowning, I think," Maria continued.

"So how did he get to shore?" Alan prodded. "By himself? Did you help him?"

She shook her head and then pointed along the shoreline.

"*He* pulled him out — it was Joshua — Joshua saved him."

All eyes turned to the figure slumped against a pine, clothing and hair wet; he appeared very tired as if he had just completed some exhausting task.

Thoughts clearing rapidly, Kevin scrambled to his knees

and reached for his dad's arm.

"No! No, that's not how it was!"

Then his eyes met Maria's.

"You didn't see everything—you don't understand what went on, Maria."

Kathy caught him by the shoulders.

"Kevin, don't . . . . Alan, please . . . we need to get him inside and build a fire. The combination of chill and shock could be dangerous. Please."

Looking at Kevin, Alan gestured for Kathy to wait a moment.

"Let's . . . let's hear the rest of this. What are you saying, Kevin?"

The boy began to shiver uncontrollably; he suddenly realized it was likely no one would believe his story. He watched as Joshua made his way to the edge of the group and huddled near Mike and Sarah. Mike clasped the strange young man on the shoulder as if congratulating him on his valor.

"He killed someone, Dad! I saw it!" Kevin exclaimed, glancing from Joshua to Alan. And he could feel his heart shrinking as the look in his dad's eyes changed from curiosity to disappointment to something bordering on hatred.

"What the hell are you talking about? Maria says he saved your life!"

Kevin squeezed his forehead; pain and exhaustion were bearing down on him. He feared he might faint.

"Before . . . before I . . . There was a man fishing out on the lake in a boat. Maria and Sophie saw him."

Maria indicated that she had.

Words spilling from his lips, some coherent, some not, Kevin kept talking.

"Joshua came along and was picking on the girls, so I told him to leave and then . . . he did something . . . he has some kind of powers . . . the man in the boat—Joshua made the boat sink and the man was drowning, and then I

133

swam out to save the man and Joshua—The man's body . . . a skeleton . . . and it was *alive* . . . Joshua . . . he made . . . "

Kevin stopped.

A gentle breeze danced off the lake.

He shivered hard.

Tears welled up in his eyes.

For what seemed an eternity no one spoke.

Suddenly Maria, crying, ran toward the inn.

Larry stepped forward and quietly said, "Here, Kathy, I'll help you take him inside."

Kevin felt numb. He rested most of his weight on Larry's shoulder.

Behind him, he could faintly hear his dad say, "I'm sorry, Joshua . . . Thank you for what you did. . . . Kevin's not . . . I'm sorry about what was said."

Chapter VIII

1

"My mind's made up, Kath. I'm *not* taking him home, not going to let him spoil the whole weekend—not giving in to him."

Alan paced the kitchen restlessly.

Kathy stared at her hands, wondering how the plan for a wonderful excursion had gone so awry. In her mind, images of fabric coming unthreaded dominated, and the prospects of an idyllic scene in which she shared her "news" with her husband had grown dimmer.

"He needs our help," she murmured. "There's something very seriously wrong, Alan. Mentally, emotionally—something's been triggered. Kevin's not doing this on purpose. He needs to see a doctor. Why are you resisting that?"

"Because I *know* my son, Kath," he exclaimed.

She couldn't recognize his face suddenly. The sensitive, intelligent, loving, mature-seeming man she had married was not the same man who was gesturing wildly, his expression contorted.

"I'm not going to let him win this one," Alan continued. "I never dreamed he would take it this far, but he has and I'm *not* giving in."

The kitchen lapsed into silence, though the tension was

135

nearly palpable.

"I just hope he doesn't catch his death of cold," said Kathy. "Larry's got a fire started. Kevin changed out of his wet clothes and doesn't appear to be in shock, but . . . it's your decision on what should be done."

"I've warned him—no more outbursts this weekend."

Alan paced some more, mentally biting off words, and Kathy could feel his hurt and something more: He was disappointed that she was defending Kevin.

"Alan, I wish that boy . . . Joshua . . . I wish Joshua wouldn't come around anymore this weekend. He and Kevin obviously don't get along. Kevin's projecting his paranoia onto him—it's just not a good situation."

"So are you suggesting I tell Joshua to stay away? Kath, he apparently saved Kevin from drowning, and he's with Mike and Sarah right now. They like him . . . I can't believe you'd . . ."

He sighed and ran his fingers through his hair.

"I should have had him spend the weekend with his mother in Birmingham. But I thought that maybe, just maybe, we could have some time together—the three of us—break down some barriers, have a good time—be a family."

She went to him and roped her arms around his waist and pressed her face against his back.

"I love you, Alan. I'm only trying to help. It hurts to see this rift between you and Kevin. He's not himself—you said so yourself. Won't you at least agree to let me take him to see someone next week? A thorough checkup? For me? Would you agree to it for me?"

He turned to hold her.

She could feel his body trembling, the afterthrall of anger and confusion.

"All right. If you think it might do some good."

There was reluctance in his tone.

He loved his son. She knew that. She knew also that he

would love the new child, too. Wasn't that enough?

"Thank you," she said.

He kissed her and whispered in her ear.

"I need you, Kath. I'm feeling like . . . like life's walling me up . . . things are closing in on me . . . out of control. I need you."

She gently pushed away and smiled up at him.

"I know you do." She kissed his chin and then said, "So tell me—what's on the agenda today?"

"Well, Mike and Sarah are going boating. Larry and Gina have some exploration of the wine cellar and upper floors planned. Let's join 'em—keep Larry out of trouble."

She nodded.

"Sounds good. I'll check on Kevin and be ready to go in a minute."

2

Maria tiptoed near the fireplace.

A blanket draped over his shoulders, Kevin stared, zombielike, into the flames. He wasn't aware he had company.

"Kevin?"

He wheeled around so suddenly that she jumped.

"Oh," he exclaimed. "Oh, I didn't hear you."

He tried to smile, but only one side of his mouth would cooperate.

"Is it OK if I sit here with you?" she asked timidly.

"Fine. Yeah, fine with me . . . if you don't mind being around a crazy person."

He shook his head and shivered, continuing to experience a chill from having been in the cold lake so long.

"I don't think you're crazy."

She hesitated, then added, "I told my dad that I thought Joshua was bad . . . that he doesn't want us on the island or at the inn . . . and that I didn't like him or trust him."

Kevin turned to face her.

"Do you believe me?" he asked.

She frowned and looked away.

"I-I want to," she whispered.

"It's the truth—what I said down by the lake. He killed that fisherman, that old man in the boat. He did something . . . he made things—some kind of creatures—swim out to the boat . . . and it's all so . . . incredible. But I saw it. I tried to save the man. I pulled him to the shore and . . ."

His voice trailed off.

"No one could ever believe me," he finished.

"I will. I'll be on your side," she said.

This time his smile worked on both sides of his mouth. He shrugged.

"But what can I do? I mean, they're not going to believe what I'm saying about Joshua until they see him do something. If I can't stop him before tonight . . . then we're all in danger. Real danger."

He regretted that he sounded so hopeless.

Maria traced her fingertips over the stone surface of the ledge.

"Can you stop him by doing, you know . . . what you did to the flashlight up in the tower? Making the light go out?"

"I'm not sure. Maybe. Maybe I ought to find a way back to Goldsmith and get the police."

"Or you could call them from the Davenport's trailer," she suggested.

"Hey, yeah." Kevin brightened.

Almost as quickly, a sobering realization struck him.

"They'd never believe me, Maria. No more than our folks will."

"But wait," she said. "What if we found the fisherman's body? Could you prove to them that Joshua made him drown?"

"The body . . . yeah, that's the thing. Maybe I couldn't prove anything, but my dad would have to believe some of

138

my story."

Kathy pressed forward, her head cocked to one side. "What is this about your dad having to believe your story?"

Puzzled, she smiled at the two of them.

"Oh, it's . . . nothing. We were just talking," Kevin stammered.

She put her hand across his forehead.

"Are you feeling any better?"

"Yes, ma'am. A little."

"Maria your nurse?"

The girl blushed and Kevin smiled.

"Sort of."

"Well, why don't you keep close to the fire. You've had a shock and a bad chill. Your father and I are going exploring with the others. You could join us later if you're feeling up to it."

"Exploring? Where?" Kevin asked.

"Your father's very interested in the wine cellar."

Kevin searched her face; images of a demon rising out of a pool played across his thoughts.

"It's not safe down there," he exclaimed.

Kathy touched his shoulder. "I appreciate your concern, but we'll be real careful."

She smiled and waved goodbye.

When Kathy was out of sight, Maria said, "Kevin, is there something wrong with the cellar? Something bad in it?"

He hesitated, his eyes fixed upon the deep center of the fire.

"Everything," he muttered. "Everything."

3

"Are you cold?"

"No, sir."

"My things are a tad big, but at least they're warm and

139

dry."

Mike watched Joshua slip into a pair of jeans and don a long-sleeved sweatshirt bearing a logo and the words, "Grateful Dead."

"This is a very kind gesture," said the boy. "But why do you have these words on your shirt?"

"You mean 'Grateful Dead'? You've never heard of them?" Mike exclaimed, surprised.

"Them?"

"Yeah . . . they're a rock band. Classic. Immortal, some would say. The Dead. Your generation hasn't gotten to know them, I guess. I paid fifty bucks out on the west coast in the seventies to see one of their concerts. Worth every penny."

"Oh, yes, sir."

"When I was a little older than you, I hitchhiked out to California. Wanted to see the counterculture—L.A., San Francisco, Berkeley—all the places I'd read about in the sixties. Strange area if you were an Alabama boy who hadn't seen much."

"I've seen New Orleans," said Joshua.

"What'd you think of it?"

"It wasn't very friendly to me."

"Big towns can be like that."

Joshua nodded.

"I like Alabama. I like the woods and the lake and Black-winter."

The boy glanced around the high-ceilinged room.

"I'm with you there," said Mike, patting him on the shoulder. "Listen, Sarah's packing a picnic lunch, and we were wondering if you'd like to sail around the lake in our houseboat with us?"

Joshua's face became animated.

"I would thoroughly enjoy that. But . . . am I welcome? Am I seen as a troublemaker?"

Mike frowned.

"Oh, you mean the episode with Kevin? Hey, no . . . appears to me we have a lot to thank *you* for. I can't imagine what Kevin was talking about. No one sees you as being at fault . . . I mean, other than Kevin . . . and, well, he's had a very difficult year."

"I'm sorry," said Joshua. "I'd very much like to be his friend. He's suspicious of me without cause. I assure you, without cause."

"Hey, look, I believe you. As I said, Kevin's gone through a tough period. His parents divorced, and then this past summer he had a near fatal accident—the combination has left him . . . emotionally unstable, I suppose you'd say. He seems confused and may be using you as a scapegoat, lashing out because he's feeling so . . . so hurt inside."

"I understand. He feels he's been wronged. I understand that feeling. If I can demonstrate my friendship toward him, could that change his view of me?"

"Be worth a try. Anyway, don't worry about it. Why don't we locate Sarah and hustle off to the houseboat—we're wasting a beautiful day."

Larry was offering some advice on the sandwiches when they reached the kitchen, but Sarah was shooing him away, laughing at some comical remark he had made.

"You'd better find your explorer troop," she exclaimed. "Alan and Kathy just left. They think you and Gina are in the wine cellar."

"I was feeling weak," Larry returned, jamming a large, open bag of potato chips under his arm. Then he stuffed his mouth so full that, as he exited, he could only spew soggy crumbs at Mike and Joshua.

Mike laughed and turned his attention to a basket Sarah was loading. He rubbed his hands together greedily.

"Today's the day the teddy bears have their picnic. You make plenty for three?"

"I did. Hello, Joshua. Hope you like ham loaf."

"Yes, ma'am. I wouldn't want to think I've put you to

extra trouble."

She shook her head.

"No, it's pretty simple grub."

She smiled, but Mike could detect that she hadn't completely warmed to Joshua yet.

Reaching for the handle of a cooler, Mike said, "All set?"

But Joshua didn't move.

"What are these little packages?"

Mike and Sarah exchanged glances.

"They're packets of sugar," Mike explained. "I compulsively steal them from McDonald's and other fast-food places. Haven't you ever seen them before?"

"No, sir."

Like some inquisitive animal, the boy tore open one of the packets and sprinkled the contents onto his tongue.

"You're right. It is sugar."

Sarah arched her eyebrows at Mike, then stepped through the back door into the late-morning sunshine.

Mike watched as Joshua tore open a second packet and disposed of it in the same manner as he had the first one.

Memory spiraled the man to a hitchhiking summer years ago.

"Seeing you do that," said Mike, "reminds me of a guy I met in Oklahoma once."

Joshua swallowed and licked his lips.

"A good friend?"

Mike rubbed his chin and half smiled.

"Not the type of individual you'd claim as a friend. Not likely anyway."

Mojesky.

He hadn't thought of him in years, but Joshua's innocent act of eating sugar right out of the packet had triggered recall of a terrifying incident from the past.

Mojesky.

The dimpled young man with the infectious laugh and winning manner. And something more. Whatever hap-

142

pened to him? Was he ever caught? Was he still out there on the road somewhere—doing "odd jobs," as he called them?

Mike shuddered at the thought.

"I can carry this for you."

Joshua took the cooler from him, and suddenly another memory image erupted: The eager, helpful ways of Richard.

"All right. Thanks."

Mojesky and Richard. The images were polar opposites—light and dark—day and night.

Mike grasped Sarah's hand and she smiled weakly.

The three of them piled onto the houseboat, and when Mike readied himself at the wheel, he felt pleased that Joshua so obviously enjoyed the boat and appeared to enjoy being with them.

The polite and eager-to-please young man offered a casual remark about their having the lake to themselves; his words provoked a question from Sarah.

"Joshua, earlier this morning, Kevin said he saw a fisherman on the lake. Did you see one?"

"No, ma'am. He must have been mistaken."

Mike glanced at his wife, and she returned the look, not bothering to mask her doubts.

"I'm just wondering," she said, "why he would make up such a story."

"Josh and I have talked about it some," said Mike. "My theory is that Kevin's very confused—completely out of sync with himself. He was probably out in the lake and got into trouble—an undercurrent, maybe—and then when Josh pulled him to the shore, he was too ashamed and embarrassed to tell the truth. So he fabricated the business of the fisherman. As for the rest of his jibberish—well, it could be time to admit to his having some serious mental imbalance. Just last night I suggested to Alan that he try to get closer to Kevin. The boy's crying out for help. Find out what's going on. Now it looks like professional help is needed."

Sarah seemed to accept his explanation.

"Regardless," she responded, "I'm certainly glad Joshua was nearby—we can't forget about that." She turned to Joshua. "You were heroic."

"No, ma'am. Anyone else would have done the same."

"Kevin should have shown some gratitude," Mike added. "What's Shakespeare's line about a thankless child? How something or other it is to have a thankless child?"

" 'Sharper than a serpent's tooth,' " said Joshua, filling in the missing quotation.

"Yeah, that's it. 'Serpent's tooth.' Listen to this, Sarah. We have our own literary scholar on board—don't need Larry."

Mike started the engine, and Joshua and Sarah went to the side to lean against the rail and soak up the sunshine and bask under the high-domed blue sky. He watched them, secretly hoping they would get along, hoping especially that Sarah would drop her suspicions, the exact nature of which puzzled him.

'Serpent's tooth.'

The phrase wrested his thoughts and attention away from Joshua and Sarah.

Coincidence?

Of course, it had to be.

Mojesky again.

The years fell aside, and as the silken surface of Black-winter Lake stirred with the advance of the houseboat, Mike found himself reliving a warm summer night in June of 1973. He was eighteen and a thousand miles from home on a journey to discover America, or at least California. But mostly, he admitted, a journey to discover himself.

A salesman had given him a lift all the way from Tulsa to Guymon, Oklahoma, the man's hometown, and thus the young traveler lingered a spell around a truckstop there before resuming his thumbing routine. His plan called for him to be in New Mexico by nightfall. He was coming up short.

A mile or so out of Guymon, on a lonely stretch of Highway 54 as twilight set in, he won another ride. At the moment the rattletrap Chevrolet panel truck lurched to a stop, Mike thanked Lady Luck for smiling on him—later, he would change his mind, deciding she was no lady if indeed she had sent a curious piece of humanity known as "Mojesky" his way.

You had to see Mojesky's smile, the remarkable resemblance to a young Kirk Douglas, to appreciate the experience. Mike hit it off immediately with him, and the godforsaken miles between Guymon and the Oklahoma-Texas line passed quickly, given impetus by the nonstop chatter of Mojesky telling the wide-eyed kid from Alabama about living on the road—the towns, the women, the drugs, the heady excitement of being free, totally, cosmically free.

"I envy you," Mike had told him, "but how do you get money?"

The flash of that Mojesky smile, the dimple coming alive—Mike felt as if he were watching and listening to a circus performer or a carnival act.

"Odd jobs," Mojesky exclaimed, laughing. "Me and my buddy do odd jobs."

"Buddy?"

Mike had glanced over the seat into the shadows of the rear section, expecting to find someone sleeping, someone he hadn't noticed when he got in. But the seatless area appeared to contain only boxes of books, mostly paperbacks spilling out in profusion.

Turning back toward Mojesky, he heard a distinct click, saw something flash, and met Mojesky's eager smile.

"This is my buddy."

The point of the enormous switchblade seemed to hover in the air a couple of inches from Mike's chin.

"Oh, I thought you meant another person," he muttered,

swallowing with difficulty. "It's a knife."

Mojesky frowned.

"Fuck, no!"

The glint of anger sucked at Mike's breath. The point of the blade pushed a hungry inch closer to his chin.

Mojesky, eyes straying occasionally to the empty highway, explained.

"This is no ordinary knife. *This* . . . this is Serpent's Tooth."

"Serpent's Tooth?" Mike had echoed, wondering how his companion could create terror so instantly.

"Sure. You see, I read a lot."

Mojesky motioned over his shoulder, and, in doing so, drew the blade away from Mike's chin.

"Yeah, you got a bunch of books back there," Mike agreed, breathing out in relief.

"Mostly, I read fantasy books . . . I like medieval stories . . . Arthurian legends—shit like that. In all of those stories, the heroes give names to their weapons. You ever notice that?"

Mike nodded.

He kept his attentions fixed upon the switchblade, its glistening handle and blade. Was the handle made of pearl? How long was the blade—ten, twelve inches?

"Like Excalibur," Mojesky continued. "So I figure a bad ass like myself from New Jersey should have hisself a weapon fuckin' bad enough to have a name. So I got Serpent's Tooth here—in west Philly one night—off this black dude who jumped me. He ended up dead, so I figured Serpent's Tooth here needed a home. He was kind of an orphan like me—know what I mean?"

Again, Mike nodded. He tried to think how far the next town was—tried to calculate a way, a time, to escape from the unnerving situation.

"Had the name put on the handle—see it?"

In silver letters, the words "Serpent's Tooth" winked at

Mike in the shadows.

"You say you're from Alabama, Mike? You read any Tolkien down there?"

The sudden shift in topic, away from the switchblade came as a pleasant surprise.

"Yeah . . . yeah, at least, I have. A few of my friends, too."

"So who's your favorite character in the whole fuckin' trilogy?"

Mike shrugged, and for an instant, he couldn't recall any of the books, let alone the characters. Finally one filtered into his thoughts.

"I guess maybe . . . maybe Frodo."

Mojesky howled as if in pain.

Mike kept an eye on the switchblade as if it were a live snake coiled to strike.

"Frodo's a fuckin' nerd," Mojesky cried. "And Gandalf's full of shit — just my opinion, of course."

Mojesky flashed that smile, partly a little boy's mischievous smile, partly a grown-up psychotic's smile.

"Nah, my favorite character is Bombadil. Tom Bombadil — is he a bad ass or what?"

"He lives in the Old Forest, doesn't he?" Mike had managed to respond.

"*Lives* in it! Jesus drives a Corvette — he's *the Master!* You see, Bombadil's totally cool."

"How so?" Mike timidly asked.

"Look at the fucker. Can't you see? Shacked up there in the forest with some gal — he plays it cool. Didn't get caught up in that shit about the Ring and Sauron and Mount Doom — no, not him. He's cool. He's *Master.* That's me, too, because you see this whole big, motherfuckin' country is Middle-earth, and it's for 'takers,' for 'masters' like Bombadil. And *me.* No laws of Middle-earth apply to us."

Mike felt his throat constricting.

"You're in luck, Mike," Mojesky continued. "I'm needin'

147

some work. There's a gas station comin' up. Odd job."

Kirk Douglas smile, dimple and all.

The dusty, weary, empty station had two pumps and one attendant, a greasy-faced kid with the name "Joe" stitched in script above a shirt pocket.

"Top it off with regular, wouldya pal?" Mojesky ordered him.

Mike felt sick. He tried to think.

Should he warn the attendant? Or save himself?

"I gotta go to the rest room," he told Mojeseky, who was standing by a gas pump, stretching and yawning.

In the rest room, Mike belittled himself for being such a coward. He pressed his ear to the door and listened. He wasn't certain what Mojesky had in mind, but he feared the worst.

He waited ten minutes.

He heard the panel truck start up and drive off.

He waited another five minutes, so nervous and upset that he barricaded himself in one of the stalls and dry-retched.

Cautiously he left the rest room and reentered the station from the rear, sneaking through a dark and cluttered lube bay. He could see out onto the highway.

No traffic.

A narrow hallway connected the lube bay with the cash-register area. He entered the hallway, again listening intently. A radio was playing country music, though the volume was low.

There was no sign of the attendant. But the scene delivered most of what he had expected: The cash register drawer was open; Mojesky's panel truck was gone; and below the register, on the floor, two drops of dark blood shimmered. Like buttons.

Mike braced himself in the doorway.

He felt dizzy.

The black cord leading to a phone on the counter had

been severed.

Fear numbed him.

The buttons of blood reclaimed his attention.

Until he heard a distinctive click and felt the point of a knifeblade in the small of his back.

"Don't turn around," Mojesky whispered. "This is where our paths part, Mike. Me and Serpent's Tooth, we got a lot more of Middle-earth to see. We travel better alone. Now . . . you do what you got to do. But just remember this: I'm the Master. And I'm so cool, I'm gonna let you live."

Mojesky slipped out the back; Mike never saw where he had parked his vehicle—never saw the body of the attendant, but it was safe to assume that "Joe" was taking a ride with "the Master," probably to be dumped along the end of the world, otherwise known as Highway 54.

Mike did the right thing. He flagged down an eventual motorist and told the entire bizarre story to Oklahoma law enforcement officials. They held him in Guymon for two days, asking him to recount the incident again and again.

When they let him go, he seriously considered returning to Alabama and ditching his plans to see the USA. A remnant of courage kept him on the road, but he traveled in fear, expecting every turn in the highway, every restaurant and rest area, to harbor a black panel truck—and its psychotic driver.

Mojesky.

Serpent's Tooth.

Mike shook off the memory, his darkest except for the finding of Richard's body.

Joshua and Richard. Joshua and Mojesky.

His mind played with images.

Out on the deck, Sarah was pointing toward the shore, toward a jutting finger of sand. He couldn't hear what she was saying, but he could read her lips: Driftwood.

He smiled and slowed the boat.

She entered the cabin area, a warm pleading in her eyes.

"There's a beautiful pile of driftwood on the sand. How close can we get?"

Mike shook his head.

"Not that close. I'll take Larry's fishing boat and pick it up for you tomorrow."

Disappointment clouded her face.

"Can you hold steady a short while?" said Joshua.

And before either of them could say anything, the young man had scrambled over the rail into the lake. He waded through the waist-deep water toward the spit of sand, and as he did, Mike knew precisely what Sarah was thinking. The scene was a carbon copy of a shining afternoon when Richard had retrieved some driftwood for her on the other side of the lake.

She had a collection of it stacked in the garage and planned one day to do something with it. Mike doubted that she ever would. No matter. The curiously formed wood interested her—that was enough.

"This remind you of anything?" said Mike, gesturing at the figure of Joshua.

For a couple of heartbeats, Sarah remained silent.

"Have I been wrong to be suspicious of him?" she asked.

Mike shrugged.

"Seems like a fine young man to me."

In his thoughts, he pushed aside the image of Mojesky's smile, letting the image of Richard take its place.

"He's so much like him in ways," Sarah continued. "It's . . . it's haunting."

Mike put an arm around her shoulder.

"Glad the sun is shining like it is," he said. "Twice in the lake in one day—hope he doesn't catch cold."

Joshua returned with the driftwood. Mike gave the wheel to Sarah and went out on deck to help him aboard.

"Got it!" Joshua exclaimed, holding up several large pieces of wood.

"I think you've won Sarah's heart," said Mike.

Joshua chuckled.

Back inside the cabin, he presented the driftwood to her and she thanked him.

"What are you going to do with it?" he asked.

Mike couldn't resist an opportunity to interrupt.

"There's a special spot in our garage—the 'driftwood corner.' These pieces will have plenty of company."

Sarah jabbed at him with her elbow.

"Oh, be quiet. I *do* have plans for it. I simply need inspiration."

Mike hefted one of the pieces.

"Here's a good walking stick."

"Or a husband beater," Sarah quipped.

Then Mike noticed that Joshua was examining the piece.

"Could your father carve a head onto this?"

Joshua's eyes twinkled.

"Yes, sir. He could. I believe I could too . . . if my knife hasn't lost its edge."

From the front pocket of his trousers he pulled out an ebony-handled knife and unfolded its long blade.

Mike thought again of Mojesky, and as he watched Joshua study the piece of driftwood, he could see Mojesky knocking back packets of sugar as he drove through the Oklahoma night, boasting of his exploits on the road.

Serpent's Tooth. Odd jobs.

Mike glanced at Sarah, but she appeared to feel no discomfort.

"I'll take this out on the deck," said Joshua, "if you don't mind. I believe I detect a shape at the end and that I could set free."

"Set free?" Sarah echoed.

"Yes, ma'am. My father claims every piece of wood has designs and figures, potential shapes begging to be set free."

"Such a beautiful way to approach it," Sarah murmured.

Joshua excused himself and, knife and driftwood in hand, went to the front deck and promptly sat down and

151

busied himself applying blade to wood.

Sarah stood with Mike at the wheel. For a considerable span of seconds they looked on, saying nothing. Mike eased the houseboat out into deeper water. And the sun enclosed Blackwinter Lake in a glorious dome of bright light.

4

The better part of an hour, Mike stood at the wheel, his mind switching images, magicianlike. One moment the figure on deck carving the driftwood was, unquestionably, Joshua, but the very next moment some curious time-slip occurred, the air would blur into an opaque sea, and the face of Richard would appear where Joshua's had been.

It was a heart in the throat experience.

Behind Mike, Sarah busied herself setting up a cardtable and preparing for lunch.

"Are you hungry?" she asked.

"You're right," he said, not paying attention to her question. "There *is* a ghost on deck."

She looped an arm through his elbow and rested her cheek against his shoulder.

"Ginny Ma used to tell me that if you lost something you loved dearly, God would provide a replacement. She rationalized the death of Grandpa that way."

"What was his replacement?" Mike asked.

"His ghost," she murmured.

Mike chuckled.

"Ah, come on. I never met your grandmother, but she's always sounded pretty down-to-earth to me. Did she really believe in ghosts?"

"In Grandpa's. Yes. She claimed his ghost haunted his room, and I believed her. I was only in that room once when he was alive . . . and I never went back to meet his ghost."

"Something must have given you a big scare in that

room."

"It did. I'd rather not even think about it."

"Then don't. Let's eat lunch instead. This looks like a good spot to drop anchor."

A cavernous, blue sky greeted them as Mike suggested they eat out on the deck. They placed canvas-backed chairs around the card table, and Joshua set aside his carving materials to help Sarah bring sandwiches, potato chips, and soft drinks out into the roaring sunshine.

The houseboat was positioned so that they had a magnificent view of Blackwinter Inn nestled high on the island, monarch of all it surveyed.

"It's a great feeling to own your very own castle," Mike observed when they had settled in at the table.

"I've always liked to pretend it's mine," said Joshua. "Like I was Jacob Blackwinter himself, a wealthy man giving elegant balls and serving guests fine food and wine—wine from my personal wine cellar."

"Speaking of which," said Mike, "the others are probably down there right now, exploring. Alan's all excited about it."

"I hope they're careful," said Joshua.

Puzzled, Mike and Sarah exchanged glances.

"What I should say," Joshua quickly added, "is that the mineral springs can make the surface of the cellar very slippery. My father knows the cellar well. Years ago, he showed me the physical layout of it."

"Do you live alone with your father?" Sarah asked.

"He's the only person who has ever been kind to me. I've had no brothers and sisters in Alabama, and I never knew my mother. But, these days . . . I fear what may happen because my father's health is failing."

Mike leaned forward, suddenly more interested.

"You must have some relatives around, don't you?"

"No, sir. None that I know of."

"What would you do? That is, if something happened to

153

your father?"

"I've thought about it. I'd like very much to live in a town like Goldsmith—I know that's where you're from—perhaps to go to college there."

Sarah felt a new surge of curiosity about the young man.

"You seem educated beyond your years—as if you'd received an old-fashioned education. The schools up here are apparently much better than I thought," she replied.

"Oh, I haven't attended formal school," he exclaimed. "My father has served as my mentor, and I've taught myself as well. Over the years—if you try—you can learn a considerable amount."

He hesitated and smiled toward Mike. "Missed learning about The Grateful Dead, however."

Then he looked down at the front of the sweatshirt and shook his head.

Mike laughed.

"Not the most essential bit of information. Better off knowing math and science."

"Yes, sir. And history. And architecture—one of my favorite subjects. I've studied the architecture of Blackwinter Inn—it's a merging of Victorian, Queen Anne, and Gothic."

His gaze drifted to the inn.

"I would sacrifice anything to live at Blackwinter forever."

Both Mike and Sarah chuckled at this overly dramatic statement.

"Tell you what," Mike said, "if and when we get the place back on its feet as a hotel, we'll offer you a job—won't we, Sarah?"

"Sounds as if we could use him in the advertising and public relations department. He's obviously sold on this place."

Joshua smiled.

The three of them devoured lunch and then pushed away

154

from the table to bask in the sun.

Sarah broke the reverie.

"We almost forgot about your carving, Joshua. May we see what you were working on so diligently?"

"Yes," said Mike, "I'm eager to see it."

Joshua reached toward his feet.

"It's in a very rough state—truly not a piece worthy to be shown to others."

"My, you're being modest," said Sarah. "Isn't he, Mike?"

"Extremely so. Please. We understand that it's not finished."

"As long as you don't have high expectations . . . "

He lifted the stick of driftwood and offered it to Sarah.

She examined it; soon a smile creased her lips.

"Mike . . . what a remarkable effort."

"A unicorn," he exclaimed, gently taking the driftwood from his wife and surveying the carved head more closely.

"Good. At least you recognize it," said Joshua. "Unicorns are among my favorite mythological beasts—they're magical."

"Did you see the detail on the horn and the mane?" Mike asked Sarah.

She nodded.

"Joshua, you're very talented," she said.

"Thank you. But, as I said, it's rough. Couldn't get the shape of the eye the way I wanted it to be."

"Wait till Gina sees this," said Mike. "She'll take Joshua back home with her and set him up in his own wood-carving shop."

Pleased at the attention he was receiving, Joshua smiled broadly.

A breeze shimmered the lake.

The sun was warm. An Indian-summer day had emerged from the chill of morning.

The three of them continued to examine the driftwood and its transformation into a walking stick topped off by the head of a unicorn.

On the shore, Kevin located the houseboat and the tiny figures on deck.

"Maria? There they are. See them?"

Chapter IX

1

She squinted into the green sheen of water and sun.

"No, where?"

"There."

He pointed toward the southwest, and she traced the line of his arm and hand.

"Is he with them?" Maria asked. "Do you see Joshua?"

"I'm pretty sure he is. They think he's a hero — they think he saved me from drowning."

Despite the warmth of the sun, Kevin shivered and then coughed several times.

"Maybe we ought to go back inside," Maria suggested. "Your cough sounds bad."

He shook his head.

"I'm OK. I've got to do something — afraid something's going to happen to the Davenports."

"But would they believe you if you tried to warn them?"

"Not likely. And the others — my dad and Kathy and your folks down in the wine cellar — it's not safe there either. I saw something. . . ."

She waited for him to finish. His body trembled violently.

"Kevin?"

"This is a nightmare, Maria."

He knelt to one knee.

The innocent scene of houseboat on lake, a small rectangle of white occupying space as if dangling in an abyss, spread before him, a challenge to the darkness he knew existed at Blackwinter.

Maria tried to console him.

"If they can see, you know, that Joshua is mean and dangerous—"

"More than mean and dangerous," Kevin exclaimed. "You don't understand—Joshua is *evil*. Before this weekend I never thought that word meant anything. Just a word you hear in church, or something some fantasy writer dreamed up. But it's *real*, Maria. And I know . . . I can *feel* that Joshua's evil."

Silence joined them like a third person.

"The body," Maria eventually murmured. "The fisherman's body—or his boat. If we could find them, they would have to listen to your story."

Kevin got to his feet.

"You're right," he said.

Then he scanned the sky.

"It must be about noon," he added. "We don't have much time."

"Kevin?"

He turned and saw something wild and disoriented in her eyes.

"What?"

"Are you . . . are you scared?"

He sighed heavily; watched a hawk wheel through the air high above the lake; and felt the brush of a breeze.

"Yeah. Yeah, I guess I am. Real scared."

2

"The thousand injuries of Fortunato I had borne as I best

158

could."

Larry's voice echoed in the womblike opening at the entrance to the wine cellar.

"Is that from Shakespeare?" said Alan, rolling his eyes and grimacing.

"Oh, I know what it is," Kathy stammered, delighted with herself suddenly. "It's Poe. From one of his stories, I think."

"Give the lady a Kewpie doll," Larry exclaimed.

"And give this lady some light," Gina grumbled, inching her way down the shadowy steps.

"Sorry," said Alan. "These overhead lights are the only ones working. Stay close to Larry's flashlight or mine."

"Which story?" Kathy asked, as the foursome edged into the center of the main room. To their left, huge wine barrels lined the wall like legless and trunkless elephants; to their right, wine racks, eight to ten feet in height, stood gathering dust and cobwebs.

In a Bela Lugosi voice, Larry droned, " 'The Cask of Amontillado.' "

"I read that once," said Alan. "Wasn't Poe a few bricks short of a load, you know . . . up here?"

He tapped the side of his head.

"That's why Larry's so attracted to him," said Gina.

Larry assumed center stage and lifted his flashlight over his head so that the beam bathed the solid rock ceiling.

"Nemo me impune lacessit."

"I love it when he talks dirty," Gina quipped.

Alan and Kathy laughed.

"OK," said Alan, "don't keep us in suspense. I feel like I'm on 'Jeopardy.' I don't even recognize that language."

"It's Latin," said Kathy. "But I haven't a clue as to what he said."

"Fellow explorers," Larry announced, "those ringing words are the motto of the ancient and bloodworthy Montresors. The translation is as follows: 'No one provokes me with impunity,' or, in modern vernacular: " 'I'm a real bad ass so don't mess with me or I'll rearrange your face.' "

More laughter.

And someone asked, "Is that Poe, too."

"Right again."

Alan and Gina wandered over near the wine barrels while Larry and Kathy continued to banter about the short stories of Poe.

Rapping his knuckles against one of the barrels, Alan said, "They're empty, but they appear to be in good shape."

Gina clasped her hands together like a young girl receiving a doll she had dreamed of for months.

"Think of the possibilities, you guys! Alan, how difficult would it be to rig up more extensive lighting down here?"

He glanced around.

"Shouldn't be difficult at all. And you wouldn't have to worry about air conditioning. It's almost chilly."

Rubbing her upper arms, Kathy joined them.

"I hear water dripping."

"The mineral springs," said Gina. "Larry, shine your light toward the back of the cellar."

A wall of rock, glistened by thin finger-rivulets of water, loomed in the distance. A fine mist rose at the wall like a gauzy curtain.

"The water's supposed to be very healthy, isn't that right?" said Kathy.

Hands on her hips, Gina smiled. "Healthy and lucrative."

Suddenly, behind them, they heard a small, plaintive voice.

"Oh, that's Sophie," said Gina. "I almost forgot that we left her at the top of the steps. She was too scared to come down. I think it's claustrophobia."

"This place gets to me, too," said Larry. "Makes me hungry. And I'm ready to take a look at the second floor."

Flashlight beam pushing away the shadows, Alan had been drawn to the wine racks.

"Why don't you and Gina go on?" he said. "We'll be

People crowded by. Her mother tried on one of the necklaces.

Kathy wandered a few feet away, the sight of a legion of dolls too much to resist. She glanced back at her mother and could imagine a nearly invisible cord, a silver thread, connecting them.

She dared to go a few feet more.

Dolls and stuffed animals chorused for her attention.

A look back. Silver thread still in place.

She skipped down the aisle.

More people jammed by her.

A herd of shiny, red tricycles sent out their invitations to touch — and perhaps to climb onto their seats and ring the bells on their handlebars and race to freedom.

In the next aisle, a miniature doll's house, a stunningly diminutive replica of a Victorian mansion. There was a cutaway section to show rooms and Lilliputian furniture, and Kathy delighted herself by walking her fingers from living room to kitchen and . . . She turned.

The silver thread had dissolved.

Panic clutched at her throat.

"Mother," she whispered, barely able to squeeze out the word through her fear.

Jewelry counter.

She ran, bouncing off shoppers as if she were a silver ball trapped in a pinball machine. Lights flashed; noises crashed.

Mother!

Here. Right here at the jewelry counter.

There she is.

Relief coursed through her.

She grabbed at her mother's wrist.

A woman she had never seen before turned and smiled down at her.

"Are you trying to find your mother?"

The tears seemed to form deep in her chest.

163

Memory flagged momentarily.

Where am I?

She had entered a narrow passageway where she had to duck her head in order to make her way.

The sudden and unexpected adventure of it thrilled her. And she marveled at the thought of how frightened she would have been at age six—that little girl in the department store would have been scared to death.

The serpentine passage wound deeper; she followed, breathing in the chill air and considering whether to go back after Alan and have him share the experience with her.

All was silent except for the rasp of her footsteps on the rock floor.

Memory flickered.

The lost little girl tore away from the strange woman.

"Mother!" she cried out.

Heads turned, but she recognized no face.

Tears flooded her throat.

"Mother!"

She began to run, again slamming into people as specters of abandonment rose viciously and taunted her.

"Mother!"

A woman caught her arm.

"Little girl, little girl."

Kathy wheeled and the smiling face, unfamiliar, leaned close.

"Are you lost?"

Kathy's lower lip quivered.

"Yes."

"OK, honey . . . It's going to be fine. We'll get on the public address system and locate her."

And she did.

Only one other image remained in Kathy's memory: the deliciously secure feeling of hugging her mother's legs and feeling her mother's hand brush the top of her head lovingly.

The passage opened out.

A gasp escaped from her lips.

She heard water dripping beyond the boundary of rock ahead.

Cautiously, ever so cautiously, she inched toward the edge of what she soon recognized to be a pit.

She stared down into a pool of water, the surface of which seemed to swallow her beam of light.

Amazed and giddied at the sight of the pool, she nevertheless felt a stirring of apprehension. A realization pressed its way into her thoughts: someone or some *thing* has been here. She looked around for signs of an animal's den.

There was nothing.

Only rock and the pool and the rivulets of mineral springs and the chill, dank air.

She turned.

She saw openings for two different passageways.

Slightly disoriented, she stepped forward.

Again, the sensation . . . the awareness of a presence.

She spun quickly, half expecting something to be emerging from the pool.

"Alan," she murmured.

Neither opening held familiarity.

Little-girl panic was giving way to genuine adult fear.

"Alan!" she called out. "Alan!"

After a few seconds, she could hear him.

"Kath, stay where you are, but shine your light so I can see."

"Alan, hurry!"

"Told you not to get lost."

He was closer, emerging finally, repressing laughter.

She didn't care.

She rushed to him and hugged him, and she longed for his hand to caress her head.

The plywood shrieked and protested.

Larry and Gina persisted, and when they had won the battle, they stood at the dark, yawning mouth of the ballroom and said nothing. Larry, astounded that his wife had been rendered speechless, let the beam of his flashlight roam through the cathedral-silence of the large room.

"There's canvas or something covering the side windows—I can see specks of light coming through."

He handed her the flashlight.

The cloth covering, mostly rotted, tore away easily.

Through six tall, arched windows sunshine poured into the room.

"Larry . . . my God, my God!"

Despite the dust, the emptiness, the disrepair, the ballroom retained shadows of its magnificence.

Larry whistled between his teeth.

"Some kind of fantastic, huh?"

"I had no idea," Gina muttered, "that it would be so large and so . . . it must have been . . . spectacular."

Sauntering into the center of the ballroom, Larry lost himself in a private vision. A line branded his thoughts:

Blood was its Avatar and its seal—the redness and the horror of blood.

Gina, with Sophie in tow, slipped past him, headed for the far end.

"More rooms," she exclaimed. "Through here there're more rooms, Larry."

She had to call him several more times, impatiently.

When Larry shined the light through the ballroom archway, he expected to see a long hall with rooms off to both sides. But what he and Gina found instead was quite different.

"It's like a maze," he whispered.

Twenty or thirty feet into the hallway they came upon the

first room, signaled by a wall and a sharp right turn.

"Why would there be a window looking into the hallway?" Gina asked.

Larry played the light upon a tall and narrow Gothic window — except for a few pointed shards, all the glass had been broken out.

"I think there had once been stained glass here," he said. "See this?"

He tapped at a jagged tooth of blue glass.

The room itself was no more than a cubicle, empty and dust laden.

"What would these rooms have been used for?" Gina murmured.

"You got me."

"Let's look at the others."

There were seven rooms in all, every other one angling off to the left or right, and each in turn protected by a jutting wall containing a tall and narrow Gothic window housing only remnants of colored glass — each window a different color.

The second: Purple.

The third: Green.

The fourth: Orange.

The fifth: White.

The sixth: Violet.

"Say something, Larry. I don't like it when you're this quiet."

"Bizarre," he whispered as he entered the seventh room and saw indications that the colored glass panes had once been scarlet.

"The decorating possibilities are unbelievable," said Gina. "Each area could be turned into an elegant little sitting room — or perhaps a gallery. What do you think, Larry?"

"I think this is incredible."

His beam of light had captured the outline of something

on the far wall.

"Gina, what does that look like to you?"

A large, heavy piece of furniture had obviously once been situated against the wall. Now only its outline survived.

"A clock — a big, grandfather's clock."

"No . . . no, I mean *all* of this."

He gestured with his hands, his voice continuing to quaver.

"I see what I want it to be — I see a gold mine."

Behind them, Sophie suddenly cried out.

"Momma!"

"We're coming, honey," Gina returned.

They found Sophie planted in the center of the ballroom clutching the wooden doll Joshua had given her. She was trembling and on the edge of tears.

Gina hunkered down to her.

"What is it, sweetie?"

"I don't feel good."

Gina pressed the back of her hand gently against the girl's cheek.

"Well, you are a little flushed. Come on, let's go downstairs."

Larry patted Sophie on the shoulder.

"Too much excitement this morning. I'd say this lady needs a nap this afternoon."

Gina nodded agreement, and after stopping to take one more look at the ballroom, they filed down the stairs to where Alan and Kathy were waiting.

6

"Kathy's a real Clara Barton," Larry exclaimed. "Even impressed Gina — and that's not easy to do, believe me."

"Sophie feeling better, is she?" said Alan.

"Yeah, she's asleep. Kinda scary when a kid's temperature goes up like that. Can't ever remember Sophie having a nosebleed."

"Lot of flu going around Goldsmith these days. Probably nothing to worry about."

They were sitting in lawn chairs on the long and commanding porch. At an angle to their right, they could take in the Davenports' houseboat, a pearl afloat on the sapphire lake.

"This morning upset her," said Larry. "You know, the incident with Kevin."

When Alan didn't respond, Larry asked, "Is he all right? Kevin, I mean . . . he seemed very distraught."

Alan waved it off.

"A phase . . . I hope to God he gets over it soon. That boy is trying my patience. Sorry the rest of you have to suffer through his behavior."

"He and Maria appear to have struck up a friendship."

"I'll apologize beforehand if he's a bad influence on her," said Alan, and Larry could tell by his companion's discomfort that he wanted to change the subject.

"Ever see anything like that ballroom?"

Larry popped the top on a Stroh's and took a long drink. His mind had been toying with an idea which had him bubbling inside. While Gina and Kathy tended to Sophie, he had taken Alan upstairs to see the ballroom and the curious apartments.

Alan shook his head.

"Beats all, doesn't it? But it would cost a fortune to refurbish it — we couldn't do it unless we could get some grant money. Historical restoration — that kind of thing."

"Mike would know about that," said Larry.

Alan nursed his beer, pausing to glance out at the houseboat.

"Mike has more pressing matters on his mind these days."

Larry responded with a puzzled expression.

"He and Sarah are having trouble," Alan continued.

"I figured as much," said Larry. "Odd, isn't it, that they should be attracted so immediately to Joshua. You know, he must remind them of Richard."

As Alan was about to say something more, Gina and Kathy came out onto the porch.

"Sophie still asleep?" Larry asked.

"Like a baby," said Gina, going to the porch railing, stretching, drinking in the view of the lake. Larry went to her.

"Madam, will you promenade with me?"

He bowed to her, and she punched him in the chest.

"We're going to take a walk," Gina called to Alan and Kathy, who watched them stroll away.

"Don't you kids get into any trouble," Alan exclaimed.

"I can take care of myself around wild women," Larry shouted back, playfully shifting into a karate stance.

"Larry can't stand to be serious very long, can he?" said Kathy.

Alan pulled her down onto his lap. "But you . . . you're *always* serious."

He traced a finger over a wrinkle in her brow. The gesture forced a smile from her.

"Not always. Just now, though . . . "

She hesitated as if waiting for Gina and Larry to be further out of earshot.

". . . I'm concerned about Sophie."

"Some kind of flu, isn't it?"

Kathy shook her head.

"Could be it's just that . . . the fever and the nosebleed and . . . the splotches. I want to keep an eye on her."

"As long as you keep an eye on me, too," he murmured.

She snuggled against him and gazed out at the lake.

"Mr. Blackwinter built a paradise."

"Now it's *our* paradise," said Alan, ". . . but with no serpent."

Chapter X

1

"Joshua knows we're watching."

Kevin sat on a bed of pinestraw needles which covered a curl of red clay rising above the shore, his eyes never leaving the houseboat. He had taken off his jacket and tied the arms around his neck.

"How can you tell that?" Maria asked.

She had followed him along the shore, had removed her sandals and rolled up her jeans to her knees so that she could wade in the lake, but when Kevin had sought a better vantage point, she'd joined him.

"Can't explain it," he muttered.

And he could feel himself beginning to lapse into a trance, could imagine himself skimming over the surface of the lake like some fish-hunting bird, could feel the deck beneath his feet, could hear idle conversation; could see—

"Blood!" he exclaimed.

Maria sat down and angled her head so that she was staring into his face.

"*What* did you say?"

He blinked his eyes rapidly; his breathing had accelerated until he had to gasp for air.

"They're in trouble!"

He pushed himself to his feet and looked around.

"Hey, what are you going to do?"

"I'm going to warn them."

"How?"

But he had sprinted down the slope and was heading toward Larry Bozic's fishing boat.

"You'll see."

"Kevin?"

He stopped beside the boat and waited for her to catch up.

"Help me push off," he said.

He waded into the water and tugged on the boat.

"Kevin, no."

For an instant, he froze. A look of consternation swept across his face.

"Maria, I have to. Don't you see that? I have to."

She stood back and hugged herself as if suddenly very cold.

"They won't believe you. They won't. Don't go out there."

He climbed into the boat and leaned over the outboard.

"They've got to believe me. I've seen blood . . . I know what's going to happen."

Grabbing the starter cord, he glanced up at her, a quiet desperation in his expression. Twice he yanked hard, but the motor wouldn't kick over. Four times more he tried. Frustrated, he found a paddle in the bottom of the boat and began to shove off.

"Kevin, please!"

He stabbed the surface hard and the splash broke upon the afternoon stillness. Seconds later he had maneuvered the boat twenty yards from shore, straight on line with the houseboat.

In his thoughts, a demon rose from the shell of Joshua's body.

172

It was a demon he would have to do battle with.

He paddled faster.

The sun spread diamonds on the lake surface. And, suddenly, the light nearly blinded him.

He slowed his paddling.

The boat glided until it rested dead in the water.

A cold blast of realization staggered his thoughts and his resolve.

They won't.

Maria's right.

They won't believe me.

For a period of minutes he slumped over.

A curious peace washed through him.

He looked out toward the houseboat; no vessel could have appeared more free of danger, more secure.

He turned.

Maria was standing at the shore.

She's the only one who doesn't think I'm crazy.

And the next wave of emotion brought fresh resolve.

The body.

The fisherman's body.

We have to recover it.

Images of a grotesque, skeletal face ballooned in his thoughts, but he brushed them aside.

Joshua's evil.

He had to explain it to Maria. Paddling hard, he reached the shore in a few minutes, scrambled out of the boat, and tied it down.

"Why did you come back?" she asked him.

"Because of the body . . . you've been right all along . . . we have to recover it. Joshua's evil . . . somehow he used his evil to make me see the fisherman's body as a demon . . . as an awful thing from a horror movie. The real body's in the lake on the other side of the island, and we've got to find it."

Maria studied his face.

173

A frown creased her forehead.

"The real body?"

Kevin reached for her hand.

"It's too fantastic and strange to explain. Just come on and help me . . . please."

A spot of warmth radiated upward from the pit of her stomach.

"Sure. You know I'm on your side."

Suddenly he halted in his tracks.

"Maria, it's not a matter of *sides*. We're all in danger if I can't convince someone else that Joshua's evil," he exclaimed.

He heard the harshness in his tone, then quickly added, "I didn't mean to jump on you like that . . . but there isn't much time . . . and I feel pretty damn helpless if you want to know the truth."

She grinned.

The gesture threw him off balance.

They chased around to the opposite side of the island, the site of the incident with the fisherman and Joshua.

Kevin pointed to an area a few yards from the shore.

"I dragged the body in to about there."

He glanced at Maria, and she appeared to be deep in thought.

"What is it?" he asked.

"I was thinking . . . if you used your will . . . if you concentrated real hard . . . could you *see* the body . . . you know, get a picture in your mind of where it is?"

For a moment Kevin looked doubtful.

"Maybe . . . . I guess I could try."

She stepped back as if giving him room to exercise his wild talent.

He slipped off his shoes and waded a few yards into the lake, the cold water sucking at his calves and then his knees, reminding him of the skeletal thing which had threatened to pull him under.

174

Dipping his hands into the water, he idly splashed around, clearing his mind, setting up the first stage of his concentration. Maria walked farther down the shoreline, pausing once or twice to glance his way.

He closed his eyes and envisioned the fisherman and his boat.

Then his throat tightened a notch as he also envisioned a swarm of shadow things moving like miniature sharks about to feed.

He forced both images from his thoughts.

The body.

Where is the fisherman's body?

In. Out. In. Out.

He controlled his breathing.

Stop time.

He relaxed his hands. They rested atop the water like hyacinth blossoms.

He let go.

And he fell, or seemed to fall, through a massive cloud of grayness.

He opened his eyes and discovered that he was a spectator, an eavesdropper on a conversation between an elderly couple. They were in a boat not more than a half-dozen yards beyond him. Moonlight streamed across them.

Strangers.

And he was invisible to them, yet he could see them and hear them, and a star-flecked night had replaced an autumn day.

2

"Ransom, you're not one to keep secrets . . . even little Sarah was suspicious the last time she was here. Your notes to her must have been more than ordinarily peculiar. You have always shared what troubled you . . . why has that changed?"

Only one side of the man's face was visible to Kevin, a face shadow-splotched and encrusted with sores that could be seen even in the moonlight.

"Ginny . . . oh you have endured much, haven't you? A marriage lacking passion. You deserve peaceful years as the end approaches."

"Whatever do you mean?" the woman exclaimed. "I won't listen to childishness or gibberish."

It struck Kevin as odd that the woman looked off to one side as she spoke.

"Certainly it cannot be gibberish," the old man replied, "to tell you that one of the few joys I feel comes from these moments — these minutes of release from that prison upstairs, these midnight boat rides with which you are willing to indulge me."

"I'm . . . aware of what they mean to you."

"Ginny . . . does Blackwinter truly give you peace?"

She started to respond, but the old man raised a hand to gently cut her off.

"Wait . . . please . . . I need to finish. My . . . my affliction — this scarlet death which pulls me closer to the grave each day — is, I am convinced, a product of Blackwinter — of a presence, in the structure itself somehow, which is so vengeful, so evil that it will never cease to plague future inhabitants."

Staring off into the water, the woman shook her head. But the man continued.

"Would it not be best, once I am gone, for you to move away from this . . . this dark legacy — whatever it may be?"

The woman raised her head, and, there in the moonlight, Kevin could see her smile.

"Wasn't it you, Mr. Ransom Blackwinter, who long ago explained to me that by resisting something we make it evil? You seem to believe that if I were to leave here I

176

would be leaving darkness to find light. But I believe that if I stay, the dark presence you speak of will be weakened."

Quite suddenly the scene began to fade.

Images became unfocused.

Kevin could see that the old couple were continuing to speak, but he could no longer hear them.

He woke to full consciousness, his mind buzzing with questions about the scene and the two conversing.

At the same time, he felt disappointed.

He had not located the fisherman's body.

His powers had given him some moments from the past, but nothing more.

3

The bird had injured its wing.

A sparrow, she believed.

It had fallen into the lake, crashed into it, in fact, and now was limping upon the surface, flailing its wings in futility, chirping a survival chirp.

"Oh, here. Don't move," said Maria.

She forgot about Kevin and his meditation. All of her emotions and thoughts shifted to the floundering bird.

It continued to beat the water, managing to stay afloat, semicircling until it rested against a partially submerged pine bough.

"I'll help you," she murmured.

From out of her memory came the voice of her father.

Hurt hawk . . . it has too much natural pride to allow us to save it.

But Maria had disagreed. And Sophie, too young then to do more than mimic her older sister, chanted the same refrain.

"We'll keep him in the garage until he can fly again,"

Maria had maintained.

Larry Bozic had reluctantly assented.

"But that hawk would prefer a bullet in its heart to this shame," he said.

And for several days Maria had hated him for saying that. Could he be right? she wondered. She and Sophie dutifully prepared a large cardboard box for the hawk — the wounded bird that they had found in the vacant field across from their home. They filled the box with grass clippings and any other vegetation they felt might make a hurt hawk feel at home.

They fed it pieces of bread, and would save a last bite of hamburger or a nibble or two of macaroni or whatever had been served at dinner.

"Could we tape his wing and make it better?" Sophie had asked one day.

"No, dopey. The bone's broke. He was shot and the bone's broke and he needs to stay in this box till he gets well."

"Daddy says he won't."

"Daddy doesn't know everything."

"He doesn't?"

"Not about hawks."

"Should we give him medicine . . . like momma gives us medicine?"

"He's a wild bird, Sophie, not a human person. He just needs to rest."

And so for a week they tended to the broken bird, and each day Maria would consider the misery in that savage god's eyes.

But she persisted.

The bird, occasionally feeling a surge of energy, a spark of the old instinctual drive, would flop about the box, sometimes even managing to escape to the floor of the garage.

Maria urged her parents to be very careful to keep the

garage door closed so that the hawk would not venture out before well enough to fly. Passing cars, she reasoned, would threaten the bird more than any other predator could.

One day, regardless, it happened.

She was coming home from school, and before she reached the front yard she could hear shrill cries and the eager barking of dogs. They had circled him, like a pack of wolves, one Golden Retriever and two Labs, snarling, dashing close, yet staying safely beyond the perimeter of his talons and beak.

The hawk stood his ground.

He stared them down.

He shouted them down.

Maria felt proud of him, and believed that once she had chased the dogs away, she would return the bird to his box and he would remain there, lesson learned, and not stray.

But the blood of wildness pumped through the hawk's veins.

Maria could not fully understand or appreciate that.

The worlds of little girl and hurt hawk could not become one.

The inevitable, the final proof, occurred one Saturday afternoon when the garage door had, again, been left open.

She heard the commotion.

Chest burning in fear, she ran out into the yard, Sophie trailing, more excited than frightened.

This time there were four dogs. One too many.

She screamed at them, her anguished protest rising over the agonizing shrieks of the terrified hawk. He battled furiously, sacrificing feathers as he struggled valiantly to beat away his attackers. And even as he perished, he tore at the mouth of the dog which tried to carry him away.

Father and daughters buried him in the vacant field.

"Daddy . . . it's like he . . . like he committed suicide," she said after they had shoveled the final scoop of dirt, obliterating the perfect feathers, the proud head, and the broken wing, the bone gleaming white at the point where the fangs of the dogs had ripped away flesh.

"No," her father explained. "Being in that box was death. When he faced those dogs, he was alive—really alive. They ended his physical life, but they never touched his wild spirit. It took flight. And it will always be in flight."

She wanted desperately to accept that poetic projection of the hurt hawk, but as she watched the sparrow out of its element, her only desire was to save it.

4

The bird spun itself farther out into the lake.

Maria reached down and rolled up the cuffs of her jeans, silently calculating how deep the water might be. The sparrow was approximately thirty feet from the shore, spinning, seemingly treading water in a brushy area of pine boughs and other fallen limbs.

"Please hold still," she said, her heart clamoring for the helpless bird.

The water rose to slightly above her knees; she had to walk cautiously because the lake bottom was slippery. She concentrated, her tongue seeking out the corner of her mouth. It felt good to be rescuing the soft-winged creature, and because it was a sparrow, rather than a hawk, she believed it would respond to her nurturing and not choose virtual self-destruction as had the hawk.

The bird twittered frantically.

The dark lake water around it swirled.

"Darn it," Maria whispered, "I bet there are turtles after you."

But she could advance only a step at a time—a very deliberate, tentative step—and with each step the bird, frightened as much of her as of the water, edged a bit farther beyond her grasp.

"Please . . . I'm trying to help you . . . . Don't keep doing that."

As Maria continued on her rescue mission, Kevin took a deep breath and attempted to shake off the dark webs of the vision he had experienced. But some of the words uttered by the old man clung to the walls of his thoughts.

. . . this scarlet death . . . a presence . . . so vengeful, so evil that it will never cease to plague future inhabitants.

Joshua.

Of course. They had been talking about Joshua. Sarah Davenport's grandparents. A horridly complete picture was forming—a legacy of evil inseparable from Blackwinter Inn.

He felt suddenly faint, and the bright sunshine of the day seemed not to penetrate the shadows, the twilight that had surrounded him. He turned and nearly fell as he stumbled to the shore, raising a splash which caused Maria to shift her attention away from the bird to him.

"Kevin?"

She motioned for him to come to her.

"I need your help."

She pointed.

"It's hurt. Can't fly. I'm afraid a turtle's going to get it. Or maybe a snake."

On shore, Kevin steadied himself.

Crystal clarity and light returned. But what it allowed him to see caused him to cry out as if in pain.

"Maria! God, please don't move!"

There she was, locked in place like some innocent and enchanted princess in a dark fairy tale, and the lake pulsed with underwater shadows—dragons and demons.

181

Can't she see them?

He ran toward her.

His thoughts leaped forward.

He could imagine . . . something . . . gleaming . . . bone-white fingers reaching up from the water . . . catching her . . . pulling her down.

"Maria!"

But the bird's renewed fluttering tugged at her. She waded closer to the brush pile where the bird took refuge, momentarily contented.

"Kevin . . . I'm going to save this bird."

"Oh, God, please stop, Maria!"

And the intensity of his voice touched a nerve.

"Kevin . . . what is it?"

He slowed as he entered the water and began to wade toward her.

"Maria, there's something in the brush."

Her eyes darted to the small, thin, needleless limbs which harbored the injured sparrow.

"I don't see anything."

But her face had blanched; fear seemed to circle her eyes like a mask.

"I'll come get you," he said. "Stay there."

"Kevin?" her voice quavered.

She tried to move her right leg.

"Stay there."

The bird had grown quiet.

"Kevin . . . I can't move. I think something's . . ."

Don't scream, she told herself.

"Here," he said, "take hold of my hand."

He extended his arm as far as he could; he kept his eyes on the brush pile and the lazy, menacing swirl of the water within it.

"Kevin . . . it has my leg. . . ."

"Here. It's OK."

Their fingers touched.

182

She squirmed toward him, but something held one cuff of her jeans.

"Kevin!"

He kicked viciously at the water several times, and she lurched free.

He struggled, pushing Maria toward the shore.

"Move!"

He kicked several times more as Maria scrambled away, terrified, on the verge of calling out for the adults to help them.

Suddenly Kevin muttered, "Oh, God . . . it's not . . ."

And he laughed. A nervous, tension-relieving laugh.

"Kevin?"

He stopped laughing and shook his head.

"I'm sorry . . . didn't mean to scare you . . . look."

From the brush pile he lifted a rectangular fish trap, its wire mesh broken and twisted free.

Maria closed her eyes and forced a smile.

"Oh, no . . . I thought . . ."

"So did I," said Kevin. "So did I."

He dragged the trap onto the shore.

"You OK?" he asked.

"Yeah . . . but the sparrow . . ."

He followed her glance out to the brush pile.

"I can get it," said Kevin, relief continuing to whirlpool in his chest.

"It's hurt," she said. "We could put it in a box and keep it till it could fly again." Even as she spoke, she repressed the memory of the hawk.

"Hand me that limb by your foot," he said.

It was a dead limb, five feet long or so, and when Maria extended it to him, he felt satisfied with the heft of it. It would provide balance for him as he inched along the slippery bottom of the lake.

"Thanks for doing this, Kevin," she called as he waded out farther.

183

"No problem. I'm a sucker for injured birds and animals, too."

He probed with the limb, finding the most solid footing, and then he sought out the location of the bird.

"I don't see any blood on him," he called over his shoulder.

"One wing acts like it's broken," Maria returned.

Kevin focused on the sparrow nestled against a network of limbs.

"Stay there, fella . . . I'm coming to get you. We'll help you. Something bad's going to happen to you if you can't fly."

The bird ruffled its feathers, frightened of his approach. It opened its beak as if to cry out, then dropped back into the water.

"You're going to drown yourself, fella."

"Kevin, it's getting away."

"Too slippery for me to go faster."

The bird flapped wildly, at moments sinking far enough in the water to wet its wings.

Kevin followed, the cold lake creeping up his thighs.

A furious round of fluttering and flapping—then, surprisingly, the bird gathered momentum and took flight, not a smooth, confident one, but it managed to wing in an arc toward shore, settling low in a cedar tree.

Maria clapped excitedly.

"You saved it!"

Kevin turned to face her, smiled and shrugged.

"I guess it was just resting."

Smile met smile, and Maria said, "Thanks."

Kevin planted the limb he was using as a walking stick, but hesitated before taking a step.

The water around him was generating a methodical swirl.

He glanced at the shore, found Maria's face; and suddenly her smile dissolved and she screamed, "Kevin, look

184

out!"

Something wrenched the limb from his hand, nearly causing him to fall. He twisted halfway around in time to see white, skeletal fingers clawing at him.

"God!" he exclaimed, reeling back as if punched.

He pumped his legs hard, and Maria rushed into the shallow water to grab for his hand.

He could hear the skeletal thing a few feet behind, churning the water; a menacing, yet whisper-soft clamor like a flock of birds taking flight.

"Kevin!"

He belly-flopped forward, landing partly in the water and partly on shore. Maria frantically tugged at one of his arms, and he crawled as fast as he could to safety.

They looked back.

The water swirled lazily before acquiring stillness once again.

The skeletal thing had disappeared.

Breathing heavily, Kevin said, "You saw it, didn't you? You saw it."

Maria, terrified speechless for a moment, could only nod.

She waited for him to catch his breath.

"I'll tell my dad what I saw," she said. "I'll go tell him and he'll believe me."

She pushed herself up, but he caught her hand.

"No. No . . . no, he won't. Not unless he sees it."

Trembling, she sat down beside him.

"Kevin . . . it's horrible . . . how could it . . . ?"

He looked at her calmly.

"Joshua."

For several minutes they stared at the water, testing their suspensions of disbelief.

A hundred yards out on the lake, the houseboat, engine purring mutedly, nosed into view.

Discouraged, chilled, and feeling the pull of exhaustion, Kevin said, "I'm going inside. At least I know where Joshua is . . . . I've got to think some more about what to do."

"Kevin? If Joshua . . . if he can turn the fisherman's body into a monster . . . what else . . . what other evil . . . what other monsters are waiting for us?"

Chapter XI

1

"Mother, mark my words, one of these days he's going to pull you under."

The frail-looking elderly woman clawed her way around her daughter, tossing colorful pillows, scattering magazines and newspapers, and three or four sleeping cats, from a well-worn sofa.

"Bing Crosby, have you seen my hat? Can't go fishin' without it—that's all there is to it," she exclaimed, but the big orange tom only stretched and yawned and seemed, all in all, unperturbed by the intrusion upon his sleep.

"Mother! Look at these! Bills! Credit card bills! Most of them Uncle Ray's!"

The woman followed on her mother's heels, flapping a handful of slips of paper.

"How'd it get back here?" said the old woman. "Tsk, tsk, tsk—was that your work, Bob Hope?"

The gray Maltese tom merely sat on his haunches and methodically licked at a paw.

Florence Jolene Harper, known to friend and foe alike as FloJo, dragged the white sailor's cap from beneath the sofa and brushed at the dust and cobwebs matted upon it.

She was eighty-four years old and weighed approximately eighty-four pounds, a coincidence she was proudly aware of and cultivated with some glee, explaining to anyone who would listen that next year she would have to gain a pound to maintain a "cosmic balance."

Her daughter, Connie was fifty-six, heavyset, and guilt-ridden—as some daughters are when their mothers grow independent and, perhaps, irresponsible.

"Mother, the whole point of setting you up in this cabin on the lake was to free you from having to tend to things. Uncle Ray's a burden—Uncle Ray should be institutionalized."

Before those words filtered out of her daughter's mouth, FloJo had paid little mind, but she slammed on the brakes as if some hesitant creature were trying to cross the road in front of her when that word "institutionalized" entered the room.

"He is not!" she yelled. "Not! Not! Not!"

Even the pack of cats moved out upon hearing that explosion.

Connie threw up her hands and plopped down on the sofa.

It groaned. A black-over-white tom named Frank Sinatra, slow to exit, squalled as she nearly landed on its tail.

"Scat! Out of my way," Connie cried.

FloJo, anger stiffening her like a rod, marched through the kitchen to the back porch, gathered her fishing equipment, and returned to the living room.

"It's much too nice a day to waste inside, wrangling over mundane matters such as bills. I'm going fishin'. As for my baby brother Ray, he has been my guest for the past six months and we are doing famously. My family members love him, and I believe he loves them. I have looked after, and will continue to look after, whatever medical needs he has. If you will excuse me, I—"

"Mother!"

FloJo paused to tuck a gray ringlet of hair beneath the

188

edge of the turned-down sailor's cap, then bent over to tighten the laces on her Reebok's.

"Daughter, you're welcome to spend the afternoon—there's frozen pizza in the fridge, but there will be fresh bass or crappie if you're able to stay till evening. Oh, did you see the way the family perked up at the mention of bass and crappie? Yes, you freeloaders—sing for your supper? I doubt you will."

The cats kept a sensible distance.

"Mother." Connie lowered her voice. Exasperation beaded sweat on her fulsome jowls.

"Mother, Uncle Ray's the issue here. I'm concerned that you won't—that he's too much trouble for you."

"Miss Connie Pie, I have four passions in my life now that James is dead and my nestlings have flown off on their own—I have my family of stray cats, I have old movies on the Nostalgia Channel, I have fishin', and I have my brother Ray, whom I have protected and looked after for many, many years."

Undaunted, Connie battled back.

"There's a new facility in Goldsmith, Mother—it's called Placid Towers—just for senior citizens who need extra care. I thought we could drive down and see it this afternoon, you and me and Uncle Ray. I've checked it out, and I can promise you it's a first-rate facility."

"A fancy prison—don't have to see it to know that."

"No, Mother. It has a full-time staff of professionals. They would monitor Uncle Ray—his health, his every need."

"Monitor, hell. Handcuff him's what you mean."

"Well, Mother, they wouldn't allow him to order every crackpot thing advertised on TV. Like you do. He's ordered several hundred dollars worth of junk."

FloJo smiled.

"Like Opus—in *Bloom Country*—Baby Ray ordered Nat King Cole's golden treasury of hits—not available in stores—because he knew how I love Nat Cole's voice."

"And I suppose you wanted exercise equipment and phony diamond rings and oriental plastic containers and pairs and pairs of sunglasses?"

"They are all amazing bargains," FloJo returned, mimicking television announcers she had heard.

"Mother, Uncle Ray can't pay for this mess of stuff he's ordered. Don't you understand that? He's going to pull you down."

"Thermos," said FloJo, tired of talking with her daughter, ". . . hmm . . . coffee or iced tea? Better make it coffee . . . wind comes up on the lake it'll likely be cool."

"Mother?"

"Excuse me, Connie . . . have to fill my thermos."

Her daughter followed her to the kitchen.

"What about it, Mother?"

"The coffee? Oh, don't worry—it's decaffeinated."

Connie gritted her teeth.

"Uncle Ray! Placid Towers!"

"Out of the question, dear."

Hands on hips, Connie strained to calm herself.

"Why don't we let Uncle Ray decide that?"

"No point in it," said FloJo.

"Where is he?"

The old woman paused. Having poured her coffee, and stirred in two spoons of sugar and a smidgen of cream, she twisted the lid onto the thermos.

"He's . . . asleep."

She had been praying her daughter wouldn't ask. Truth of the matter was that FloJo had no idea where her baby brother was—except, well, she guessed he was out on the lake, but she couldn't tell Connie that or the woman would develop heart failure on the spot.

Furthermore, FloJo was beginning to worry. Ray had apparently slipped away early—she'd noticed that his straw hat was missing. If he boated too far, would he remember

190

the way home?

"Wake him up. This is important."

"We shouldn't."

"And just why not?"

"He . . . has been feeling poorly."

Fear widened Connie's eyes.

"Isn't his heart, is it?"

FloJo shook her head.

"Long and short of it is . . . his old body's tired."

Connie sighed heavily.

Then she crept to the back bedroom door.

"It's locked," said FloJo. "Ray wants it shut and locked when he's sleeping so the family don't bother him. Bing Crosby's real bad about jumpin' up on the bed."

"Mother, you've got to promise me something: Next weekend you and Uncle Ray are driving to Goldsmith with me to see that facility. I'm not taking no for an answer, Mother."

Connie glanced at her watch.

"I've got to get on back . . . do I have your promise about next weekend?"

FloJo nodded vigorously.

" 'Course, dear. Baby Ray be feelin' some better by then."

Studying the closed bedroom door for a moment longer, Connie sighed again—a gesture of defeat.

"You try my patience, Mother . . . I'm serious. Something has to be done about you and Uncle Ray."

"Don't worry your head. We can take care of our ownselves."

Connie looked doubtful.

FloJo escorted her out to her car. They said nothing to each other until an energetic, black tomcat leaped into the front seat.

"Honestly," said FloJo, "that animal would drive off with the devil himself. Eddie Murphy, you get out of there.

191

Kitty, kitty."

Connie frowned as FloJo had to lift the reluctant cat from the seat.

Before she pulled away, the vanquished daughter lowered her window.

"Mother, please . . . look after Uncle Ray . . . this situation's getting out of hand."

"Don't you worry, daughter," FloJo assured her. "I've been takin' care of my Baby Ray for longer than you been breathin'."

"And, Mother . . . I wish—I really *wish*—you wouldn't try to take the fishing boat out by yourself. Why don't you at least wait till Uncle Ray wakes up so he can go with you?"

"Pshaw, girl. Bein' in that boat's safer than walkin'. Nat King Cole rides along. He's my watchcat."

Connie gripped the steering wheel, started to speak, but held back, realizing she was overmatched by a remarkably independent woman.

They waved goodbye.

FloJo impatiently waited for the car to disappear from view. She looked down at a circle of cats which transcribed themselves around her.

"So-o-ooo, family, where's that scamp of a brother?"

Mewing syncopated. A few of the cats brushed against her legs, tails dancing in anticipation of further attention. However, the old woman had no time or energy for them.

Hand bridging her eyes, she swept the surface of Jackson Lake.

"Oh, Ray . . . where are you? You been gone too long."

She hustled her fishing tackle and tackle box and thermos and extra sweater down to the docks. Spry for her age, she descended upon the ladder and balanced herself in the small and teetery, aluminum fishing boat. Her brother had taken a matching boat hours ago.

"He's never been gone this long," she muttered to herself. "Never."

Fear blew a cold wind through her.

A shudder prowled along her shoulders.

"Oh, I'm being silly. Give him fifteen minutes and he'll show — won't have caught no fish. I'll look out and see that ole straw hat of his shinin' and a bobbin' — won't let him know I was worried."

She turned to face the wide expanse of lake, her eyes drawn to a pine-clad finger of land to her left which jutted out fifty yards or more into the dark water. Beyond that finger, in a shallow cove, was Ray's favorite fishing hole.

Maybe he got lucky, she thought to herself. Maybe he's catchin' fish.

It seemed unlikely. She had fished many times with her younger brother, and often after they had begun casting for bass, she had discovered that the end of his line contained a leader but no lure. She would harangue him for the oversight; he would smile and tip his straw hat.

"Thanks, Floey," he would say.

Where is he?

Doors slammed on images from the past; she clawed at the tie-down rope. Noise up on the dock slowed her. A half-dozen cats were peering at her over the edge.

She had to chuckle.

"You gents my send-off party?"

Each appeared to want to jump into the boat.

She raised a finger of protest.

"Only one. Who's it gon' be?"

Of course, she knew. She merely desired to create a pretense of fairness, for her choice of companion was ever the same.

"Nat King Cole, you merry ole soul, you been good this mornin'?"

The silken black tom pressed through the crowd of cats, steadied himself to jump, and a blink later landed in the bottom of the boat with barely so much as a thud.

"Next time one of you others gon' get to go — you got to be good first," she said.

Taking his customary place at the prow, Nat King Cole pivoted his head, glancing to FloJo as if to say, "Come on, let's get this show on the road, old lady."

She smiled at him.

"You a handsome thing and you know it."

Then she pull-started the tiny horsepower motor; it purred to life like a giant cat. She worked the rudder stick, maneuvering out into the bright afternoon sun. From her jacket pocket, she extracted a pair of sunglasses.

"You forget your shades, Nat?"

The cat appeared to frown at her; feline indifference reasserted itself, and the tom assumed a position not unlike a statue or the figurehead of a ship, his ears twitching in the blow-by breeze, tail coiled like a sleeping snake.

Gradually Flo-Jo's attention strayed from the cat to the business of handling the boat and scanning the lake for signs of her brother. Steering to her left, she sideglanced the cabin, remembering how happy she and James had been when he retired and they purchased the place. At his death, she'd almost lost it, but Connie and her husband, Lloyd, had come to the rescue, making certain the abode of memories remained hers.

But loneliness had stung her.

Ray had played the role of companion, another stray joining the ranks of the family of cats she had collected from the county humane society. He had worked for years with the postal service; they carried him as long as possible, aware of his dwindling mental faculties, shuttling him into less and less demanding positions until they could not justify his employment one more day.

"Lord knows he's not never hardly any trouble," she murmured to herself. "Never hardly."

As she approached the spit of land, a miniature peninsula to itself, she mentally crossed her fingers. Wind soughed in the pines. Waves lapped gently on the shore, then gained strength as her boat animated the water.

"Let me see that ole straw hat," she prayed.

The boat slewed to the right and the cove opened to her. The empty cove.

It's a big lake, she reminded herself, swallowing back the painful scald of disappointment.

"Hang on, Nat . . . we're gon' explorin'."

For the better part of an hour, they did. The backwater, the marina—nearly every inch of Jackson Lake. But no sign of Ray.

At the massive state highway bridge separating Jackson Lake from Blackwinter Lake, FloJo paused to survey the impressive structure, tall enough to allow a paddle wheeler to pass beneath it.

You gone this far, Ray?

The black tom twisted around, shaping his mouth into a silent cry.

"Don't rush me, Nat. I got to think a spell. Don't like the feel of things."

Afternoon continued apace.

She tried to judge the number of hours before sunset. The rapid approach of autumn's early darkness often surprised her.

"Somethin' tells me our baby brother's crossed the line," she whispered.

Then, more loudly, "Keep your eyes peeled for Ray, wouldja, Nat?"

As the boat gathered speed, the cat braced himself, and the dauntless pair glided into Blackwinter Lake.

Chapter XII

1

Sunlight slanted across the rear deck of the houseboat, bright, yet bereft of its warmth because of a cool north breeze. Still, Mike Davenport, feet propped on the rail, felt good, basking there like a well-fed animal.

Why are you feeling so contented? he asked himself.

And no immediate answer popped into his mind.

The gentle rock and swell of the boat deepened the contentment, a lullabye for the emotions. Somehow the conflict he had been experiencing not twenty-four hours ago had been resolved. Or forgotten.

Had it even existed?

He and Sarah. Their marriage. They would make it. They would forge ahead. Blackwinter had been the catalyst, the *têmenos* or place of isolation where they could empty out the past and fill themselves with the future.

Mike leaned back and angled his upper body so that he could view the magnificent edifice. It's so damned solid, he thought to himself. Secure. Like a rock. But part of him admitted that it wasn't just Blackwinter that had affected him — and Sarah. Good friends had played a role. But those same friends had always been available.

He mused, losing himself in the tripartite beauty of lake

and island and inn.

He barely noticed when Sarah bustled out onto the deck, two steaming cups of coffee in hand.

"Thought you might enjoy a cup," she said. "That wind is chilly."

"Thanks. Yeah, I'd love some."

He took the cup as she carried a deck chair next to him.

"Where's Joshua?" she asked.

"Front deck—carving on the driftwood again."

Sarah chuckled.

"Knocking himself out to please us," she said. "A good strategy—it's working."

"I've been trying to tell you he's a good kid."

"Oh, Mike . . . I never said he wasn't good. I like him. I really do. At first . . . well, there was something—can't put my finger on it—something unnerving about the way he knew so much about Blackwinter, about me and my family."

Mike reached for her hand. At his touch she smiled; he squeezed her hand and shifted his body toward her.

"Being out here this afternoon—with you and Josh—I feel kind of like we have a new family. Like we've been given a second chance on some things."

"He's not Richard," she said.

There was no defiance in her tone. Rather, a matter-of-factness, a desire to keep reality in perspective.

"I realize that, but . . . well, you heard Josh. His father's declining health—the boy wants a future. With no parents, no relatives to help him . . . we have something to offer him it seems to me."

Sarah glanced out at the lake.

"Mike . . . are you hoping that if Joshua becomes a part of our future it would bring you and me together again . . . bring back the closeness we used to have?"

"Would there be anything wrong with that?"

She shook her head. Then forced another smile.

"No . . . no, of course not. It's just so odd, or ironic . . . or something."

She looked away, a flood of mixed emotions rushing through her.

"Sarah?"

Their eyes met.

"We can be happy again," he said. "I believe that."

He saw the tears threaten, saw her mouth quiver.

She touched his face, kissed him softly.

"I do love you, Mike. But there's a little girl inside me who's very . . . confused and frightened."

"I'll love her too," he said. "And take care of her."

"No . . . she has to find her own way."

He wasn't certain he understood, but he nodded.

"Blackwinter . . . and Joshua . . . they wake up that little girl and I have to relive so many—"

She stopped.

He held her.

"It's going to be all right," he whispered. "Everything's going to be all right."

2

"Hearts."

Sarah giggled.

Confusion swept across Joshua's face. He glanced at Mike.

"I have to play a heart?"

"You got it. Sarah is a nasty Crazy-Eights player—I believe she cheats somehow."

Joshua studied his cards.

Shadows lengthened outward from the island, but the houseboat rested in the muted light of sunset, a minirainbow of colors: pink, orange, and blue-green.

"Beautiful sunset," Sarah murmured.

"It's been a perfect day," Mike added.

Joshua scratched his head and began to draw.

"Is it true that cards—decks of cards—are the tools of the Devil?"

Sarah burst out laughing; Joshua continued to draw cards from the stack in the center of the table.

"Not of the Devil—just of card sharks. Next game, I'll sit on that side of Sarah," said Mike. "She can drive you nutty. Always has more eights than anyone else."

"I'll have to grow another hand," said Joshua, "in order to hold all of these."

The cards spilled away from him comically.

"You're a good sport," said Mike.

He played. And then Sarah announced, "One card."

Joshua looked helpless.

"We've got to stop her from going out," said Mike. "Too bad neither of us has supernatural powers or we could see what her last card is."

"Yes," said Joshua. "Yes, unfortunate. I must not be a lucky player."

Moments later, the inevitable occurred.

"I'm out."

Sarah offered smiles all around.

"We might as well give up, Josh. We don't have a prayer against her."

The boy reached into his pocket.

"I have something for you . . . for winning the game."

He handed her a small piece of driftwood. She held it for several seconds, shaking her head slowly in obvious admiration.

Mike shifted forward.

"Let me take a look—what is it?"

"A gargoyle or a demon," said Sarah. "Very impressive. Thanks, Joshua."

She squeezed his forearm.

He glanced away as if embarrassed, and then rifled

through his trouser pockets and placed his carving knife on the table.

"I'm telling you," said Mike, "Gina could set you up in business—who knows, with your talent and Gina as a business manager, you might one day have enough money to buy Blackwinter Inn for your own."

Joshua sat quietly. He fidgeted with the knife, opening out and reclosing the blade until Mike's attention was drawn from the driftwood figurine.

"How sharp is it?"

"I would like for it to be sharper," Joshua replied.

Mike carefully dragged a fingertips down the blade.

"Whoa . . . plenty sharp enough, and it's . . . "

Serpent's Tooth.

The words seemed to come from nowhere. The memory of Mojesky's knife.

He looked up.

In Joshua's smile he saw the lines of Mojesky's smile— not the *same* smile . . . but close. Close enough.

He folded up the blade and pushed the knife toward the boy.

"If y'all will excuse me, I need another cup of coffee. Want a cup, Josh? Sarah?"

They shook their heads, and he made his way to the cabin.

Joshua turned to gaze into the bright orange ball of sunset.

"Years ago I would see ducks on the lake gliding serenely," he said.

Sarah propped her chin on her hand, musing at the image.

Then Joshua looked at her and said, "I can shut my eyes and see them forever."

He closed his eyes and something of a smile touched his mouth.

Sarah suddenly felt her heart accelerate.

Joshua's words . . . they echoed from somewhere. From someone.

Her throat prickled.

And the boy continued.

"Joyous pink and a chorus of gold and a single high-pitched silver. Ducks and sunsets."

He opened his eyes, but they seemed no longer the dark, intelligent eyes she was growing accustomed to. Now they appeared hooded, reptilian.

Demonic.

"Don't . . . say things like that," she muttered softly. "I mean . . . "

She felt hollow.

An inexplicable fear wrapped itself around her.

"Be thankful, Sarah."

She stared at him.

"How could you know . . . ?"

"Always be thankful."

"Dont' say—"

"Sarah, Sarah, my sweet Sarah."

With a violent push away from the table, she stood up. "Stop this!"

Light nimbused above the young man's head, but out on the lake, darkness steadily claimed the day.

"Sarah, Sarah, my sweet Sarah . . . what did you see behind that door?"

She moved hurriedly along the rail, hand pressed to her mouth, wanting to believe that the scene was not occurring.

Mike returned with his coffee. Joshua pressed by him.

"If you're looking for the head," said Mike, "it's at the rear of the cabin."

"Thank you," said Joshua.

Noticing Sarah at the rail, Mike went to her.

"Twilight's so peaceful out here. Hey, is this spot taken?"

Her face had been turned away from him, and it took

him by surprise when she wheeled and sought out his arms.

"Oh, Mike! Oh, God . . . I'm so scared!"

"Whoa! Hey . . . just a second. Let me set down my coffee. What is this?"

She trembled so hard that he had to hold her shoulders.

"Sarah? Sarah, for God's sake!"

"Mike! Mike . . . start up the boat and get us to shore! Now! Please!"

"What on earth for? What happened?"

She calmed herself, but her face glistened with tears.

"It's Joshua!"

"What about him? What?"

As best she could, she recounted the curious and frightening exchange.

"Are you sure he wasn't joking . . . playing a little game. They couldn't have been your grandfather's actual words . . . they couldn't have been. I can't understand why he would — I'll go talk to him."

"No, Mike. Please. Please . . . just start the boat and take us back to the island."

"I want to hear his explanation, Sarah. He may not be aware of just how much he scared you."

"Please," she murmured.

But he tore away from her, moving stiffly toward the cabin.

"Josh?"

At the railing, she could follow the sounds of his search. She glanced around apprehensively, every shadow seeming to harbor a threat.

"Oh, dear God . . . help us."

In the cabin, Mike called out, "Josh!"

But got no answer.

The door to the head was closed.

"Josh . . . we need to talk."

He knocked and listened. Heard nothing.

Memory caught him, throwing him emotionally off balance: a replay of the moment when he had pushed through the bathroom door at home only to find Richard . . . the total unreality of the suicide aftermath.

His hand slowed as it approached the doorknob.

"Joshua?" he muttered.

Pain stabbed at his temples.

"Joshua?"

Deep breath.

The door swung open.

The tiny room was empty.

After searching the opposite deck, he returned to Sarah.

He had switched on the cabin lights as well as the lights above the wheel and all of the deck lights.

"I can't find him anywhere."

"But where could he have gone? Where could he be hiding?"

Mike shook his head.

"He may . . . I still think he may be playing a game with us—there's probably an explanation. There has to be."

"I don't want an explanation," said Sarah. "I want to be back on the island with the others . . . with our friends."

"OK. It's all right. We've been out long enough anyway. Larry's probably started preparing his gourmet feast—we'll go. It's all right."

His voice sounded reassuring, but Sarah stayed near him.

Mike positioned himself at the wheel, then glanced around.

"Josh? You can come out now. We're heading in."

Silence held firm.

When Sarah's eyes met his, Mike shrugged.

He worked the instrument panel. Flicked the ignition switch.

The click was hollow and resounding.

"Hmm . . . . That's funny."

He tried it again and again. Same results.

The he dug out a flashlight and went on deck where he lifted the swing-up door to the engine compartment.

"Mike, what's wrong with the boat?"

"I really don't know. Appears the motor's dead. Getting nothing. No connection. No juice. Nothing."

He sprayed the inboard motor with light. Worked his fingers here and there.

"Sarah . . . get me that toolbox in the cabin, would you?"

"Mike?"

"Go on," he said. "I think maybe I can get it started."

"Mike, what's happening to us?"

"Nothing," he exclaimed. "Nothing we can't handle."

3

"He's never gone this far," FloJo whispered.

She switched off the small motor and glided closer to the shore, hoping for a glimpse of a docked boat. She had concocted a dozen possible scenarios in which her brother Ray could have decided to seek out land rather than continued navigating the lake.

"Nat King Cole—you see him? You got better eyes than me this time a day."

Twilight had thickened on Blackwinter Lake. At a considerable distance ahead and to her right the dark island-mound on which Blackwinter Inn rested loomed.

The black tom, perhaps hungry, evidently impatient, left the prow for the comfort and warmth of FloJo's lap.

"Gon' be nippy this evening. Hope Ray wore his jacket."

She turned on her powerbeam, an oversized flashlight she often used when fishing at night. She speared the shoreline, the ranks of pines, but captured no indications that her brother was nearby.

"Could he uh gone to that island, Nat? Could he uh run out of gas . . . or what? This is makin' me heartsick . . . not knowin' where he is."

The cat pressed against her stomach, purring, positioning himself as if creating a warm nest to sleep in.

A twinkle of light suddenly caught FloJo's attention.

Straight ahead several hundred yards floated a rectangle of blackness checkered with illumination.

"Oh, see that!"

She lifted the cat and framed his head so that he was looking directly where she wanted.

"Could be it's somebody who's seen him."

Her spirits rekindled, she started the motor again, reviewing mentally which words of reprimand she would use when she finally tracked down her wayward brother.

Chapter XIII

1

Kevin prodded the fire, coaxing the kindling to catch and send flames into the larger logs. To the boy the blaze was an appropriate image, what with conflict raging within him. He needed to act. Needed to do something. Needed to fire up his volition.

Because we're all in danger.

Beyond the front windows he could see the clutch of twilight.

Would Joshua follow through on his threat? Would there be violence after sunset?

"Why so glum, Kevin?"

It was Larry Bozic's question.

The boy looked up as his dad and Larry entered the room, cans of beer in hand, and plopped down by the fireplace.

"No, I'm not glum. I'm just . . . I've been thinking."

"How'd you get your pants' legs wet?" his dad asked.

"Oh, I was playing around by the lake, and I guess I sorta stumbled into it."

"Sure Joshua didn't push you?"

He didn't like his dad's tone—the sarcasm, the bite of the words.

"No, sir. Joshua's out on the houseboat with the Davenports and . . ."

There was much more he wanted to say, but his dad's expression issued a warning.

"Mike and Sarah need to be coming on in," said Larry. "Or they'll miss my grilled cornish hens — wait'll you taste them, Kevin — heavenly stuff."

Kevin smiled weakly.

"I'm getting hungry," said his dad. "Remind me to go down in the cellar for a bottle of Blackwinter wine to go with our feast."

"Hey, good idea," said Larry. "A cask of Blackwinter from our private cellars."

"That another Poe story?"

Larry saw that Alan was egging him on, so he took a long sip of his beer, belched, and got more comfortable.

"I'm going to share a very wild notion with you two," he said. "About Poe and this place. You're going to swear this is a cock-and-bull idea, but I can't get it out of my head."

"Larry," said Alan, barely repressing a chuckle, "why would we ever think you were feeding us a line? We take what you say as gospel."

Warming his back at the fire, Kevin found himself relaxing at the rhythm of their exchange. It was hard to be morose around Larry Bozic. Thus, for a few minutes Kevin let dark images of Joshua slip away.

"I think Poe must have been here," Larry began. "I'm serious. There have been stories — I always thought they were apocryphal — that Poe visited Blackwinter Inn early in the 1840s. I think he did, and that's not all."

He paused to size up the reaction of his listeners.

Alan glanced at Kevin.

"Watch out, son. It may start to get deep. . . . What is it? Poe's ghost skulking about?"

Kevin allowed himself half a chuckle, anticipating where Larry would take the story.

"This is better than his ghost. Potentially, it's scholarly dynamite."

"Scholarly dynamite? Larry, don't give us English-teacher rhetoric—OK?"

"No. No . . . this is the real poop. I'm talking about the ballroom and all those little odd-shaped apartments upstairs."

"So, what about them?"

Larry turned to Kevin.

"Have you read Poe's 'The Masque of the Red Death' ?"

The boy thought a moment.

"No sir . . . don't remember a story called that."

"Is that the one where the guy buries his sister alive?" asked Alan.

Larry shook his head.

" 'The Fall of the House of Usher'—no, in the one I'm talking about, a wealthy man, Prince Prospero, throws a big costume party for some of his friends. He has this castle isolated in the country, and much of his reason for inviting his friends is that there's a plague devastating the land—something called the 'Red Death.' So, you see, he was trying to protect his friends from the plague, but, ironically, he ends up trapping them *in* with the Red Death—who shows up as sort of an allegorical figure that crashes the party."

"Don't see a connection, Larry," said Alan. "But then, I never could see half the things my English teachers found in stories and poems."

"Well, the parallels are pretty clear—let me give you a few more details: In the story, there are seven apartments or rooms, each decorated in a different color—each with a stained glass window of that same color. The first, I think, was blue. The last one was decorated in black. The last room also had a gigantic ebony clock."

Over the rim of his can of beer, Alan considered the energy in Larry's expression.

"Like those rooms beyond the ballroom . . . that what you're suggesting?"

"Exactly. It's an uncanny similarity, don't you see?"

Alan appeared summarily unimpressed.

"I think it would make a better story to have seen Poe's ghost—we could use that in our promotional material for the inn."

Larry threw up his hands.

"Damn, don't you see the significance for students of American literature? Blackwinter Inn may have been the inspiration for one of Poe's short stories."

"What happened?" Kevin asked, his curiosity pricked. "I mean, in the story, when the Red Death got in the castle?"

In comical fashion, Larry gestured in a throat-cutting motion.

"They all got offed. The story has a great final paragraph. I think I can still quote it. Goes something like this: 'And now was acknowledged the presence of the Red Death. He had come like a thief in the night. And one by one dropped the revellers in the blood-bedewed halls of their revel, and died each in the despairing posture of his fall. And the life of the ebony clock went out with that of the last of the gay. And the flames of the tripods expired. And Darkness and Decay and the Red Death held illimitable dominion over all.' "

Alan raised his can of beer.

"An *A* for the professor."

Kevin shifted uncomfortably.

"Was there really such a thing as the 'Red Death' ?"

"Fictional creation," said Larry. "But from Poe's description of it, you would see similarities between the Red Death and yellow fever, which wreaked some havoc in this part of the state at various times in the nineteenth century."

"A bad fever? Is that what the Red Death would do to somebody?"

"That and worse. Much worse. Turned your skin all red. Made sores. Finally you'd begin bleeding from your nose and mouth—a horrible affliction if you look closely at Poe's account of it."

Larry and Alan found themselves gazing at Kevin's reaction, his slackened jaw, his stony expression.

In the boy's mind, images of Sophie rose, and he saw again the transformation of her face from cherubic innocence to a grotesque mask, disease-wracked, splotchy, spotted with sores.

And the blood.

"Kevin? Hey, it's just a story," said Larry.

He and Alan both chuckled.

"Everybody good and hungry?" Larry continued. "My stomach's growling—but then, Gina would say it always is."

"I'm getting there," said Alan. "But I still think we ought to make up a tale about Poe's ghost. Could attract tourists."

"You saying you aren't convinced by my theory?"

"Red Death? Sounds farfetched to me."

The two of them, embracing a buzz from their beers, stumbled a step or two as they headed for the kitchen, leaving Kevin alone at the fireplace.

The image of Sophie's face has been supplanted by one of Joshua's demonic countenance.

"Touch of the Red Death," Kevin whispered. "Joshua has it. It's real."

No, he knew he couldn't be absolutely certain of that. But the sight, beyond the front windows, of darkness tightening its grip on the day jolted him.

He wandered through the kitchen, where Kathy smiled at him, and Larry and Alan and Gina chatted, their conversation interspersed with the comfortable sound of adult laughter. But Kevin did not stop to join them; he was looking for Maria and, perhaps even more so, for Sophie.

The door to their room was open, yet he knocked anyway and entered cautiously to find Sophie resting on a pallet, Maria at her side. Sophie had the wooden doll Joshua had given her pressed close to her body.

The girl's face appeared flushed.

"Hi, Kevin," said Maria.

"Is she sick?" he asked.

Sophie shook her head, but Maria countered.

"Has a fever."

"She shouldn't be holding onto that doll."

Sophie frowned, and Maria stood up.

"Why not? What's wrong with it?"

"You can't take my doll away," Sophie insisted, hugging it even more tightly.

Realizing there was no point in frightening the girl unnecessarily, Kevin relented.

"Could we go outside and talk, Maria? It's important."

"Sure. Yeah, OK."

Maria turned to Sophie.

"Remember, momma said for you to stay here and rest."

Sophie smirked, but did not object. She was more concerned with keeping her doll securely in hand.

Maria followed Kevin out onto the porch and then down to Larry Bozic's fishing boat, quizzing him along the way; but he said nothing until they reached the shore.

"Listen to me," he said, his voice tremulous. "I've got a feeling Joshua's going to make good on his threat. I'm not sure about this, but I think he's given Sophie a real bad sickness—you need to go back and be with her. My stepmom, she's been a nurse. If Sophie starts getting a lot sicker, you tell her as well as your mom."

"What's he done to Sophie?"

"I don't know for sure. Just help me push off in the boat and then get back to her. I'm going out to the houseboat."

"I wish you had a gun . . . or some weapon," she said.

211

"I know you can do some things with your mind, but will they stop Joshua?"

Light filtering down from the inn allowed her to survey his shadow-strewn face.

He was scared.

"If not," he said, "well, it's got to be. It's just got to be."

2

Sarah hesitated.

She watched Mike busy his hands in the bowels of the engine compartment. She knew, above all, that she should remain calm. Put things in perspective.

Mike was probably right: Joshua, keyed in to the light-hearted mood the card game established, was playing a joke, trying to have fun with the situation.

Sarah, Sarah, my sweet Sarah.

"Oh, God," she whispered.

And for an instant couldn't move.

How could he know Grandpa's very words?

The puzzle of it dizzied her.

Her heart rose in her throat like some cancerous growth.

"Sarah? The toolbox. Please."

Mike's voice startled her.

She blinked to awareness.

"I'm going for it. I am. Sorry. I am . . . going for it."

But it was an excruciating effort to move one step at a time; her feet seemed to weigh hundreds of pounds.

Why am I so scared?

The cabin door was open slightly.

Light slanted through.

She took a deep breath and chided herself for being silly. Mike needed the toolbox. Joshua would grow weary of hiding. *Poor boy: He seems so out of place, out of time.*

Sarah, Sarah, my sweet Sarah.

She closed her eyes tightly.

"I'm OK," she whispered. "Everything's going to be all right."

She heard the echo of Mike's words in her own.

I love him.

And she told herself she would believe him. Trust him.

She stared at the cabin door.

Stepped toward it.

Then abruptly stopped.

She heard something vaguely familiar.

And when she fully recognized the sound, she felt the air in her lungs being sucked out. It was like the sensation of icy water showering down a naked back.

She had heard the clear, unmistakable tinkling of her grandfather's bells.

Sarah, Sarah, my sweet Sarah.

Beyond the door, the tinkling became more animated. Then slowed. Then ceased.

"Ginny Ma."

The name barely escaped her lips.

She steadied herself.

She reached for the doorknob.

Touched it.

Time for the tricks of memory to end.

She steeled herself, pushed and the door started to swing open farther.

Her eyes strained to take in everything at once: the windows, high and to her left; the tiny restroom straight ahead; a small table and three chairs in the center of the room; a bed to her right.

And a figure sitting on the bed facing away from her.

She gasped. And her chest heaved and sour saliva filled her mouth.

She fought off an urge to call for Mike. And when a second or two had passed, she focused on the figure.

213

"Joshua? Joshua . . . I'm sorry. You frightened me . . . but I should have seen that you were only—"

The figure began to turn.

The room swam, details assuming an underwater lack of clarity. It was like looking into a huge, goldfish bowl. And the familiar cabin had transformed into her grandfather's room.

Her eyes fastened upon the figure.

"Sarah," a voice echoed from the past. "My sweet Sarah, you shouldn't have come in here. Don't look upon me, Sarah."

"Grandpa?"

"Go away, Sarah. Please go away."

"Grandpa . . . I want to hug you."

The figure said nothing, pausing as if to consider something grave.

"It's the only thing I want," Sarah murmured, her voice the voice of a girl once again.

She started around the bed.

"I like all of your pictures, Grandpa."

Dozens of the old photos materialized, sepia-toned portraits of men and women in late nineteenth-century fashions, old buildings, a locomotive, a man and a woman in a boat on what appeared to be Blackwinter Lake—these and more.

And there were books. Old books. They lined one wall, their spines cracked and split; yet, the dusty tomes retained an aura of solidity.

"Have you read every one of these books?" she asked.

"Not every word," the figure answered.

"Grandpa . . . I heard your bells. They're such nice bells."

She continued to edge around the bed, though she could not see the figure's face.

"Sweet Sarah . . . promise me something? Swear to me you'll do as I ask."

214

"I will, Grandpa."

"Keep your eyes on the floor."

"On the floor, Grandpa?"

"Yes, sweet Sarah. If you'll do that, then I can hug you."

"I can, Grandpa. I can do that."

"Come ahead, then."

And the figure extended a hand, but did not turn toward her.

She concentrated on the hardwood floor. The warmth of the moment, the impending joy, caused her to tiptoe softly as if a footfall might crush the illusion.

"Grandpa, you know what?"

"No, sweet Sarah. What?"

"Inside me . . . well, there's this tiny person that has wings and when she's happy you know what happens?"

The figure chuckled weakly.

"Oh, I'm afraid I don't."

"When she's happy her whole body lights up like a Christmas tree light. Or a candle."

"Is she happy right this moment?"

"Yes, Grandpa. Her light's pretty bright."

"Your eyes still on the floor, sweet Sarah?"

"Yes, sir. And I'm 'bout to you."

She could smell good grandfatherly smells — pipe tobacco, shaving lotion, old leather.

The figure touched her arm, and in one gentle, continuous motion, he curled her body next to his.

"I love you, Grandpa. Oh, wait'll I tell Ginny Ma what I did."

"No, goodness, Sarah. Don't. It could upset her. Why not let's you and me have this visit as our secret. Mrs. Blackwinter . . . she just might not understand."

"OK, Grandpa," she replied reluctantly.

She wanted to lift her head, wanted to search his eyes — they would be kind eyes, for that's how she imagined they

215

would be, and they would twinkle and throw off glints of love and compassion.

She hugged him hard. His old body felt insubstantial as if filled with straw.

"Run along now before Mrs. Blackwinter misses you. And, remember . . . eyes to the floor."

"Eyes to the floor," she whispered.

"You're my Sarah."

"It's all bright inside me, Grandpa. Bright as it can be."

"Goodbye, my Sarah."

"Goodbye, Grandpa."

Tiptoeing away, buoyed like a cork floating upon water, she carried her joy to the door. But there was too much energy, too much good feeling to contain in such a small body.

At the door, Sarah wheeled.

"Oh, Grandpa! I love you!"

She ran to him.

Surprised, he turned at her approach.

She stumbled into him, her momentum throwing her within inches of his face.

Illusion and memory merged.

Sarah the child, Sarah the woman.

Her grandfather's horrifying mask of flesh — a face touched by the Red Death, and yet not her grandfather, but Joshua.

Demon's eye, hideous, unblinking, staring into the secret cell of her heart.

Sarah began to scream.

3

She staggered and collapsed to her knees.

The scream tore away from her throat as if someone were wrenching it violently from her. The rush of sound scalded her lungs and parched her throat. Her mouth burned.

The small cabin exploded with the suddenness and intensity of the scream; terror resonated and echoed louder and still louder until Sarah had to hold her ears to keep her eardrums from bursting.

Her eyes teared and her upper body jerked and heaved.

Stunned and frightened, Mike clambered into the cabin.

"Sarah! Dear God, Sarah!"

As if beyond her control, aftershock screams and whimpers continued to escape from her. Mike fell to his knees and pressed her to him, but her body trembled with such force that it took all of his strength to prevent them from toppling to the floor.

"Sarah, Sarah," he murmured over and over.

He kissed her forehead and caressed and smoothed her face and gently rocked her.

Eventually some of the shock wore off and he looked down at her, questioning with his eyes. She blinked as if unable to recognize him.

"Ginny Ma, I'm sorry . . . you told me not to . . . but I wanted . . ."

He rocked her some more.

"What is it, Sarah? Dear God, what happened?"

As he held her, he glanced around.

"Is Joshua here? Did he scare you? Try to hurt you?"

Through her tears, she said, "He did this to my grandpa."

It was the voice of Sarah the child, and Mike's reaction was to shake her, his fear generating anger rather than compassion.

"Get up, Sarah. Stand up. Stand up and come with me. We'll start the boat and get out of here."

But her legs would not hold her. He guided her to one of

the chairs at the small table.

Rage building inside, Mike pushed away from her chair. "God damn it, Joshua! Where are you?"

And when the echo of his shouting had dissolved, he watched as Sarah raised her hand and pointed at one of the windows bleeding in darkness through the ineffectual deck lights.

"There," she whispered calmly.

He looked up.

The dark, intelligent eyes held a hint of a smile.

Mojesky's smile.

Then the window seemed to cloud. The Red-Death face emerged—demon's eye, large and liquid, staring, staring. Then the face of Joshua reemerged, Mojesky's smile intact.

The boy lifted his hands into view.

And unfolded the blade of his carving knife.

Mike hesitated.

Sarah, in shock beyond further screaming, clung weakly to his arm—it was the touch of a child.

"I've got to stand up to him this time," said Mike.

He pulled away from Sarah and ran toward the cabin door.

And suddenly every light was extinguished.

"God damn!" he exclaimed.

He jolted through the cabin door and slammed into a jutting corner of the wheel area, determined to reach the deck and wrestle the knife away from Joshua.

"Joshua!"

He fumbled his way onto the deck.

"Joshua!"

But the image dominating his thoughts was that of Mojesky.

Dear God, I can't let this happen again.

He strained to see the deck railing, to seek out a block of humanity within a sea of shadows.

"Joshua. Joshua, give me the knife and stop this."

His hands were shaking as he groped along the dark deck. Mist and fog curled up from the lake and chilled his face. He found the rail and pulled himself, grasp over grasp, faster and faster until he had reached the rear of the deck.

And found the back door to the cabin open.

4

The mist drew across the bow of the boat like a gauzy curtain.

In the distance, in the direction of the scream, the mist had thickened into a fog which blunted her powerbeam.

"My soul, Nat . . . never heard a scream like that one."

Having abandoned his position at the prow, the cat lazed in her lap, annoyed that the wet mist was beading on his whiskers and fur.

"Gone too far," FloJo murmured. "Me and Baby Ray . . . we gone too far this time."

The scream.

The fog had curiously amplified, instead of muffling, it, transforming it into something unearthly. It rang in her ears and lodged in her thoughts; it bred horrific images. A scream like that meant death.

She should turn around. She knew that.

"Can't leave, Nat, till we find out 'bout Ray. We can't."

The source of the scream, she estimated, had to be within two hundred yards, perhaps only a hundred. She thought she could make out faint lights.

Her boat's small motor purred at idle.

She shifted to a very slow trolling speed and aimed the boat toward the scream.

"Ray's got himself in trouble, Nat. I can feel it's what he's gone and done."

219

Was it a woman's scream?

She guessed it was. Or a wild animal in anguish. Or . . .

"This fog's gettin' thick as soup," she muttered.

He's going to pull you under.

Daughter Connie's words filtered through an internal fog.

"Baby brother, Ray, where are you?"

The cold mist seeped into her skin.

But there was no turning back.

"Nat, I've watched after him too long . . . too long to give up on him. He's out there. Somewhere. I'm not 'bout to leave till I find him."

5

"Damn you, thing," Kevin exclaimed.

The outboard on Larry's boat wouldn't start even after Maria had helped him push away from the shore. So he had paddled another ten or fifteen yards out and then tried it again.

"Damn you."

He was hunkered over the outboard when the scream wafted across the lake through the fog and rising mist.

Kevin sat down hard.

He held his breath.

Terror flooded through him in such a torrent that he felt himself begin to float free of his body. But he caught himself and listened—and knew that if he didn't hurry, it would be too late.

He looked out at the houseboat and angled his small craft accordingly.

Moments later, he stopped paddling.

The lights burning on the houseboat had suddenly winked off.

Chapter XIV

1

Gina laughed and buried her face in her hands.

Kathy, laughing too, realized there was much more to the story.

"All I said was raisin pie," she protested, glancing from Gina to the men in the room.

"Did I hear someone say, 'raisin pie'?" said Larry. "Sweet raisin pie?"

He lowered his pronged fork and made choking gestures.

"Hang on Kath," said Alan, "we're going to hear a courting story."

"Courting story?"

"Yeah. Larry and Gina have a couple dozen—grin and bear it."

They had been sitting at the kitchen table, Gina and Kathy, talking pleasantly, absently, about their most memorable dates from high school and college. Kathy had told of bringing a boy or two home for dinner and of the fuss her grandmother always made on such occasions, particularly her ritualistic baking of a raisin pie to test their politeness.

"Granny was a pip. I mean, she loved to play tricks, and

what she would do was put extra sugar in the raisin pie—
deliberately—and then watch the poor guy who had been
invited to dinner to see whether he would say something
polite about the pie. I could have murdered her."

The mention of raisin pie had turned the conversation.

But Kathy hadn't minded; it seemed to her that Gina
had lowered some barriers and seemed to be accepting her
into the closed circle, thus allowing her to replace Dora.

"It was my birthday," Gina announced. "Larry and I
were juniors at Goldsmith College and I had declared to
him that on the night of my twentieth birthday we would
be virgins no longer."

She paused for the inevitable snickering from the others.

Larry pressed his fork into one of the cornish hens.

"I believe she had discussed this matter with both her
accountant and her banker, not to mention her priest," he
added, grinning at the memory.

"Well," Gina continued, "I got all dolled up and went to
his trailer, and Larry had shipped his roomate, Eugene,
off to the bowling alley—or somewhere—with express di-
rections *not* to return until morning."

"Cost me thirty bucks," said Larry.

"But it was worth it, right?" said Kathy.

"Listen to the rest of the story," Larry muttered.

Gina shook her head.

"Larry had roasted a duck for dinner—can you imagine? And I—I had baked a sweet raisin pie. Now, you tell
me—what's an Italian girl from Birmingham know about
baking a Southern pie?"

"Don't try to answer that," Larry interjected.

"Anyway, we had this terrific dinner—except that the
trailer was so warm that I was sweating on my upper lip. I
tried to act cool and coy when Larry handed me a couple
of presents."

She began to laugh again, slapping the table to control
herself.

222

Larry looked sheepish.

"You see," he said, "I thought Gina was a rosary-carrying, bead-counting Catholic, so . . . Well, you tell them, babe."

"He bought me this beautifully bound volume of *Sayings of the Saints*—my name on it in gold-embossed letters—*and*—wait, there's more—and a huge bottle of 'Tigress' perfume."

The room vibrated with laughter, too much laughter, in fact, to allow them to hear a scream out on the lake.

"I can explain," Larry sputtered. "The book of Catholic nonsense was to show her I acknowledged her spiritual needs, but the Tigress, ah, that . . . that was to remind her she had *other* needs . . . and so did I."

"And everything was going so well," said Gina. "Larry was so gallant and such a good cook, and we had moved from the table to the couch and it wasn't long before I was eager to move to the bedroom—but Larry, dear sweet man, insisted he try a piece of my raisin pie first."

"Never in the history of romance," Larry exclaimed, "has a man ever committed such an egregious error."

"What on earth happened?" Kathy asked, barely containing her laughter.

"He cut a large piece of that pie," said Gina, "and he ate every bite of it. And said it was real good. A noble liar."

"I shall long remember," said Larry, "the taste of that pie—it was beyond words."

"I'm not certain," Gina explained, "but I think I used baking soda instead of baking powder. Well, somehow Larry maintained his amorous charade. We made it into bed before he got sick."

Larry waved his pronged fork like a conductor's baton.

"The word 'sick' does *not* sufficiently or accurately convey meaning or impression of what I experienced that night."

"The poor dear threw up over everything. Me. The bed.

The bathroom. The hallways. My book of *Sayings*. Our passion. Everything."

"The figure of Death crouched at my shoulder by midnight," Larry explained.

Kathy and Alan laughed at the story, Alan breaking up despite having heard the incident recounted several times over the years.

"After that, Larry never allowed me to bake anything again. To this day I have to have special permission to enter the kitchen. I'm in charge of our finances; he's in charge of meals."

"Every once in a while she threatens to bake another sweet raisin pie. I beg her not to as I fight off waves of nausea."

"Oh, I'm sorry Mike and Sarah are missing this," said Kathy.

"They've heard it," said Alan.

"We'd better give them a holler shortly," Larry advised. "These hens are reaching perfection."

"Set out an extra plate for Joshua—they've probably adopted him by now," said Gina. "Hope they've secured rights to his wood carvings."

Conversation gradually waned.

Kathy strolled to the back door of the kitchen and tried to peer out.

"You guys . . . there's a heavy fog on the lake. . . . Do you think they might have trouble coming in?"

2

"Why does Kevin keep acting so weird?"

Maria frowned.

"He doesn't, dopey. Why do you ask that every five minutes?"

She jumped two of her green marbles and watched

224

Sophie finger one of her yellow ones, unsure of what move to make.

"You're worried about him."

"I am not."

"Yes, you are, Maria. And I'm going to tell Daddy if Kevin says any more bad things about my new doll."

"Sophie, why don't you line up your marbles so you can jump several at a time? You can't win at Chinese checkers that way. You're not even good competition. Try harder."

"I have a headache," Sophie exclaimed. "And I feel hot."

"Dopey, take that cover off."

"No . . . then I get cold. Cold and hot at the same time."

Suddenly Maria reached out and scooped up all her green marbles.

"Hey!" Sophie protested. "I was gonna win. Why'd you do that? That's not fair."

The marbles spilled through Maria's fingers, scattering loudly across the hardwood floor. She tightened her fist, and her hand trembled.

"Sophie, listen to me."

Her sister's mouth formed a small *o* of surprise.

"Listen to me."

Having gained Sophie's attention, Maria looked away, uncertain how to share what dominated her concern.

"Maria . . . I'll play better . . . I will . . . I can try harder."

"Stop talking. Don't talk. Can't you see I'm upset?"

"But I said I'd play better. We can start all over."

"No, Sophie. Listen. . . ." Maria's jaw stiffened and she searched for her most adult voice. "I'm scared," she admitted.

"Like . . . of the dark are you scared?" Sophie whispered, glancing around apprehensively.

"No!" Maria shrieked.

225

And Sophie reached back and grabbed her doll for comfort.

"Don't yell at me."

Maria stared at the doll.

"You don't understand what trouble we're in. Kevin and I know. We know about Joshua . . . and you have to grow up and understand, too."

Sophie, startled, puzzled, cowered in the covers.

Maria snatched at her doll.

"This is not a good thing for you to have. It's from Joshua, and he's done something to you . . . and Kevin thinks you're going to get real sick and I have to watch you."

Holding onto the doll with all her strength, Sophie began to cry and scream.

"Maria!"

"I bet it's this doll," said Maria through clenched teeth. "This is what's making you sick."

She wrested the doll from her little sister who, in turn, threw the covers aside and sprinted to the kitchen, crying out as if mortally wounded.

"Donchoo run to Momma," Maria called after her.

But the escape was clean and loud, and Maria had hardly had time to contemplate the magnitude of her error when she heard the stomp of her angered mother.

"*What* is going on here?"

Maria instinctively raised her hands in front of her face, anticipating violence of some sort.

"I didn't do anything," she protested.

"Young lady, I've had my fill of you lately. You're not so big that I can't put you over my knee and warm your bottom."

"Momma, donchoo see?"

"I see a missy who's gotten too big for her britches — spoiled, self-centered, and childish. You know Sophie hasn't been feeling good. Why would you upset her and make her cry? Why? Tell me."

"Momma . . . we're all in trouble."

"No, ma'am . . . *you* are the only one in trouble. I want you to march right into the bathroom with Sophie and help her wash up for dinner. And I don't want to hear so much as a squeak from either of you."

"Momma . . . Sophie's going to be real sick . . . Kevin knows, and he . . ."

But she could read the fierceness in her mother's eyes, a fierceness which closed the woman's ears to the bizarre reality of the emerging moments.

"Now I better hadn't hear of you pestering your sister the rest of the weekend. In fact, if I were you, I'd make myself as invisible as possible."

If only I could, thought Maria.

Sophie stole quietly back into the room as her mother, trailing wisps of anger, stormed out.

Maria, thoughts in a dark swirl, felt crystals of ice form around her heart. She wanted to cry. Wanted to do something to help ward off the threat Kevin believed to be imminent.

Is he wrong about Joshua?

Doubts lingered, and yet, she reminded herself, hadn't she seen proof?

"I left my doll," said Sophie.

Sighing, resolving to abide by her mother's wishes, Maria watched her sister sink down upon the pallet.

"You heard Momma. We have to wash up for dinner."

Sophie hugged the wooden doll and began to rock back and forth.

"Come on," said Maria, "before Momma gets mad again."

"My face," Sophie stammered. "It's hot."

Maria hunkered down and felt it; fear stirred, and her breath caught in her throat.

"Stay right here," Maria insisted, trying to keep her

227

voice calm.

"I feel real bad, Maria."

Sophie lay on her side and closed her eyes.

The fear within Maria escalated to terror.

"Oh, please God," she murmured, her memory racing to recall a simple prayer that might comfort both of them. Her mind went blank.

Intuitively she reached out and took the wooden doll from her sister's weak and fragile hold.

And then she hurried to the kitchen.

3

"Sarah? Say something so I'll know where you are."

Mike entered the darkness of the cabin and bumped into the table and chairs. He fumbled his hands along the edge of the table to regain his balance.

He touched an arm.

"God . . . Sarah?"

For an instant, a fleeting second, he couldn't be certain. "Sarah?"

He squeezed the arm and leaned down.

Sarah moaned.

"Ginny Ma? I'll never do it again, Ginny Ma."

Mike pulled her close and pressed his fingertips onto her face.

"Sarah? Sarah . . . it's me. I'm going to look for some matches. For some light."

He groped his way to the cabinets beyond the table and rifled past paper cups, canned goods, napkins, a box of crackers, plastic forks and spoons, finally tracing the raspy, striking surface of a matchbox.

He held the box, pausing a moment to allow a mixture of emotions to level out: his anger toward Joshua—and fear, as well. *My God, what is wrong with the boy? What set him off?* And Sarah. She had been so deeply frightened that she had retreated to some childhood shelter—or was it to the cage of some dark incident he could never understand?

The match hissed.

His fingers trembled as he waited for the small flame to take hold.

"Grab onto my arm," he said to his wife.

She obeyed, but in the muted light of the match, he saw her eyes, pupils dilated, wild, childlike.

"It's OK," he whispered, regretting how stupid the comment sounded.

He moved forward, stopping once to blow out the flame as it ate its way close to his finger.

He struck a second match and pressed toward the wheel.

"Joshua? This has gone far enough," he called out.

He could not . . . could not completely convince himself that the young man meant to do them harm.

There would be some explanation. There had to be.

He glanced around.

Everything near the wheel and captain's seat seemed to be in order. The switches. The dials. A well-thumbed operator's manual. A gas can on the floor.

Then he noticed the CB radio, its cord yanked loose from the unit.

He blew out the second match and lighted a third, mindful of his distance from the gas can. He considered going back to the cabinet to see whether they had any candles. And he wondered how they could have been so foolish not to have had a flashlight aboard.

"I have to help Grandpa," Sarah suddenly exclaimed, and slid away from him before he could catch her.

"Sarah, damn it, stay beside me. I need your help to get the engine started."

But she appeared not to hear him, so determined was she to return to the cabin. As he started after her, two things occurred simultaneously: First, the match burned down, and, second, he saw movement out on the deck heard the scrape of feet.

"Joshua!" he exclaimed.

Anger and confusion rekindled, he scrambled out onto the deck. The box of matches dropped from his hand, hit the deck, and skidded along.

"Joshua! Stop right there!"

He didn't bother to look for the matches, choosing instead to keep the chase alive. But the surface of the deck, covered with a sheen of night moisture, gave him no footing.

"Joshua!"

His left foot suddenly splayed to one side; his ankle buckled; his knee slammed hard against the deck.

"God damn it," he cried, rolling, hitting his shoulder as if to punctuate the fall.

It was a curious moment in which his anger relented, and despite the severe pain in his ankle and lesser pain in his knee and shoulder, he had to chuckle at himself—at his clumsiness, at the absurdity of chasing after a boy who might only be playing a trick on them.

"Damn, Mike . . . you're really something," he chided himself, placing most of his weight on the deck rail. He tested the ankle. Neon jangles of pain flashed out from it.

"Sarah? Sarah, I need you. I've hurt my ankle."

He listened, but the houseboat was perfectly silent.

Fog droplets swarmed at his face like tiny, summer insects.

He felt helpless and very foolish.

"Joshua? Someone . . . give me a hand."

He slid along the railing, clomping like a peg-legged pirate.

"God, what is this?" he whispered.

The unnerving silence, the darkness, the totally unexpected behavior of Joshua . . . and, echoing through his thoughts, Sarah's scream.

My God, what did she see?

He pushed on.

And by the time he once again reached the back door of the cabin, he had lowered himself to the deck and was crawling.

"Sarah? Sarah, help me."

The pain had sponged all the saliva from his mouth.

But sweat ran in rivulets from his forehead into the corners of his eyes. He blinked, swiped his wrist across his face, and paused to catch his breath.

And he laughed derisively.

"Sarah . . . helluva clumsy thing . . . I've sprained the shit out of my ankle."

He struggled to his feet again.

"This is all Josh's fault. When I catch him, I'm gon' kick his butt."

The words filtered into the darkness.

He felt cold.

"Sarah?"

He waited for a response.

"Joshua?"

He stumbled toward the bed.

Sarah was lying on it. He could smell her perfume.

He collapsed down next to her; he knew how upset she must be—this always happened when she got terribly upset—he would find her lying on the bed or couch, not asleep but quiet, dealing inwardly with some unanticipated blow to her emotions.

"Sarah?"

He hesitated before extending his hand toward her.

"I'm sorry about all this."

Her arm felt cool.

"Let me rest my ankle a second, and I'll find you a blanket."

He pressed his face against her shoulder and listened for

231

the soft swell of her breathing.

"Sarah?"

His fingers touched the clammy surface of her cheek. Then slid down to the warm blood seeping from her throat.

4

The old woman recalled a jingle from her childhood — a three-line saying which powerfully generated memory. Had Ray created it himself? No, he must have heard it from one of his older friends. Regardless, the simple lines never failed to excite her, bathing her in fear and delight.

Floey, I'm under the bed!
Floey, I'm on the edge!
Floey, I've got you!

It was his favorite trick, she recalled. Scaring the hell outta big sister.

Knowing her fear of "things lurking under the bed," he would often sneak away during the evening and secret himself beneath her old half-tester, and when she had snuggled under the covers and relaxed, he would start his ghostly, Halloween chant.

And she would scream, beating off his clutching fingers, angered by his laughter, embarrassed once again that he had fooled her. Only after he had orchestrated his practical joke a half dozen times or so did she fail to be genuinely frightened.

Baby Ray, you uh mess!

She smiled to herself, recalling her squeals of fear-lined delight.

How the sound contrasted with the scream from the throat of the fog.

"Nat King Cole, what do you see?"

But the cat had curled within itself, averting the mist and fog.

"Baby Ray's got himself in a fix."

She reasoned that, of course, it could be he was merely helping someone else or, perhaps, he was miles away — had put to shore in any one of a million places and was, at that very moment, trudging back to the house.

Something ahead drew her eyes.

She switched off the powerbeam.

A hundred yards beyond her, deep into the fog, the suggestion of a light flickered. And a voice. Yes, she was certain of it.

A man shouting.

The fog muffled the sound. And the night swallowed it.

Was it Ray's voice?

She couldn't tell.

"Floey's comin' for you, baby brother," she muttered.

She switched on the powerbeam again and adjusted her course.

Panic flashed through her.

If Connie finds out about this . . .

Her heart shrank; that would be the last straw.

She could easily anticipate her daughter's words.

"Mother, what more indication do we need? Uncle Ray is *not* responsible for his actions. And *you* . . . you are to blame for letting him take that boat out. What were you thinking? To top it off, you got the crazy idea to go out after him in the dark and the fog. Mother, I'm amazed at you. Both of you need to be placed under professional care — I can't stand to have to worry about you anymore."

She could fight her daughter. Insist upon independence. Or beg for one more chance.

Or . . .

There was a possible way out.

Find Ray. Haul him home. Never let daughter Connie

233

hear of what happened.

Never.

"That'll be what we do, Nat," she said softly.

But over the purr of the cat and the small motor, she heard, off in the distance, a man cry out in anguish — the pitch one a man might use as he dropped into the fiery pit of Hell.

5

Kevin heard it, too.

And he knew.

Mr. Davenport.

Terror enclosed Kevin like a hard plastic bubble.

He paddled faster, his imagination struggling to envision what horrifying events were taking place on the houseboat.

He called up the faces of Mike and Sarah Davenport. These were people he had known over the years — his parents' friends. They had always given him a Christmas gift and, on his birthday, a card and a five-dollar bill.

How could something terrible have come into their lives?

Within forty yards of the houseboat, he slowed. Far to his left, he saw a faint glow of light. Someone else was on the lake.

Who could it be?

The paddling had winded him — his thoughts had no clarity — reason slipped away.

He entertained one final thought of turning back for help: to get his dad and Mr. Bozic.

Rejected it.

The fog tore in patches, washing at his face as if directed by cold hands. He leaned forward to catch his breath. And to think.

The cry of anguish. My God!

It rang out again.

No time to think and plan.

Mike and Sarah Davenport needed someone.

Images of Joshua's supernatural transformation flooded the boy's mind.

Darkness filled his consciousness.

And a demon's eye from that darkness rose.

Chapter XV

1

He wouldn't allow himself to accept the reality.

He curled himself against her back as he had at night in bed a thousand times over the years.

They had always slept that way.

Sarah's dead.

No, the voice that insisted upon speaking to him was not one he would willingly hear. *Sarah's dead.* If, he sadly reasoned, he could avoid hearing those words, saying them, or even *thinking* them distinctly—then they could not be true.

His Sarah could not be dead.

But her body was losing its warmth rapidly.

Like a man in a trance, Mike got up from the bed.

It was anger. Or rage. Pure rage which controlled him.

In the darkness of the cabin, he laid his hands on one of the chairs and broke off one of its legs as a weapon.

"Joshua!" he cried.

He slammed into the wheel area and out onto the deck.

"Joshua!"

The liquid sloshed onto his pants and jacket. Then more of it onto his neck and face. He swung out wildly.

"Joshua?"

The pungent aroma of the gasoline filled his nostrils, burned his skin. He coughed and staggered forward.

"Where are you? God damn you, let me see you!"

He whirled around. Then back.

A block of darkness near him seemed to move.

He swung at it, connecting only with the chill, night air.

"Joshua," he murmured, the gas fumes making him dizzy and blistering his skin.

"Where are you?"

He swung again, slipped, and fell to the deck.

Grasping the rail, he pulled himself to his feet.

A match flared.

And behind the small flame, he saw the fog-shrouded face of Joshua.

And Mojesky's smile.

Before the face began to change.

And the small flame flicked through the air toward him.

2

Kevin switched on his flashlight, but there was no need.

One end of the houseboat erupted in fire, its glow spreading an amber light through the fog. It was a surrealistic scene: the fog, the muted light, the source of the burning.

Then the cry.

In a reflexive move, Kevin stood up.

He couldn't believe his eyes.

The flames surrounded the dark figure of a man, spinning, writhing as he stood on the deck. Kevin clenched his teeth and wanted to look away, but the horrific event was a magnet. The fire burned eagerly at the man's legs, arms, hands, chest, and head.

Mike Davenport—God, it's Mr. Davenport.

And in a final, pain-crazed survival effort, the man crashed at the deck rail until it gave and he tumbled into the cold lake.

The splash hammered at Kevin's ears.

His knees buckled.

He screamed. And felt himself lifting.

As before, he fought the sensation.

Save him! God, you've got to try to save him!

But for a span of time—Kevin had no idea how long—his arms were too weak to paddle. He watched helplessly as a funnel of mist and steam rose where Davenport had sunk.

Then fear seemed to jump-start the boy, powering him through the shock, and he began to paddle.

He realized that every stroke was probably futile. Burned to death. Drowned. Did the actual cause matter? The man could not have survived, coldest reason told him.

Still he struggled forward, and in a matter of seconds he reached the spot where he believed Davenport had disappeared. Steam mixed with mist and fog remained thick in that area, but the surface was relatively calm—there was no sign of a body.

Kevin dipped the paddle to feel around, hoping to make contact with something.

"God, no," he exclaimed.

It was as if words had been strangled by the shock of the occurrence and suddenly had been revived; he cried out again and again. His eyes teared, and his chest and stomach ached.

But his mind cleared for an instant.

And he remembered Sarah Davenport.

Hands trembling, he clutched his flashlight. The beam

discovered the broken railing and the deck ladder descending into the water. A small flame or two burned on deck, and Kevin soberly recognized what must have happened.

He smelled the gasoline fumes.

"Mrs. Davenport?" he yelled.

But the boat lay silent.

Where is Joshua? he wondered.

What is he planning next?

"What should I do," he whispered.

An argument waged within: Go back and get help, one part of him demanded; take your stand against Joshua—here, now, the other insisted.

As he considered his next move, the fishing boat started to swirl.

The lake gurgled softly.

Kevin shined the light in a gentle arc out from the boat.

He felt his throat constrict.

His hands tingled.

The swirling ceased for a few seconds. He grabbed the paddle and stroked madly to close the thirty feet or so between the fishing boat and the houseboat.

Then he heard them. The spider creatures. Churning the water. Rasping against the sides of the boat.

The boy groaned with the agony of exertion.

Ten feet more.

Paddling faster. Beating at the creatures.

Water began to seep into the bottom of the boat.

The paddle was jerked away from him.

He put the flashlight in his left hand, stood up, and leaped forward.

Behind him, the bottom of the boat tore, and he could hear the lake suck it under, could hear the spider creatures clawing at it as it sank.

The cold water took his breath away.

He battled forward, extending his hand, feeling wildly for the deck ladder.

They were at his back.

He could hear them.

Pain flared in his calf.

He reached out.

His fingers curled around a rung, then slipped free.

He screamed, feeling a fresh round of pain.

He swallowed water and the chill of it burned his mouth.

He reached out again. This time his fingers held. He pulled.

His upper body slapped against the deck, and with an effort that seemed to exhaust the last ounce of his energy, he swung his legs away from the attacking creatures.

He gripped the flashlight in a death-lock, but his hands were too cold and numb to switch it on.

He lay there, each breath a razor cut to his lungs.

His only desire was to find warmth.

And rest.

And sleep.

And wake to find that everything had been a dream.

Only a horrible dream.

3

FloJo opened her mouth to scream or cry out, but no sound issued forth. The left side of her body lost all feeling. She pressed a hand to her heart, terrified that it might have stopped beating.

The sight of the burning man plunging into the lake had totally stunned her. Paralyzed with fear, she had then watched as a lone figure had struggled onto the deck.

Ray?

Oh, was it Ray?

Nearly forty yards away from the houseboat, she could not tell who it could have been.

She managed to turn off the small motor and to let her boat drift.

"Nat, what are we gon' do?"

Sobs choked her words.

The cat, agitated and cold and wet, was under her legs, meowing his alarmed meow.

"What are we gon' do?"

Don't show 'em you're scared.

The inner voice was not hers.

It belonged to her father: Jonathan Copley Storpink. And she recalled vividly the night he had leaned down to her and whispered those words.

She had witnessed a burning that night, too.

The year was 1911.

A warm April evening.

The light from the flames had awakened her—that, and her mother's excited voice downstairs. She rolled out of bed and went to her window. She looked down upon something strange, strange and somehow frightening, though she could not understand why.

She scampered down the stairs.

Her parents were huddled at the front screen.

"Why are we burnin' that cross?" she asked.

There it was, six-feet high, planted in the middle of their yard.

A fiery cross.

"We're not, Florence. Of course not. It's the Klan," her mother exclaimed, obviously very upset by something.

Her father swept her into his arms.

"Little one, you should be asleep. No reason for you to be up."

"Why's it there? What's the Klan?"

He hunkered down and situated her on his knee.

In his eyes, she could see a reflection of the eagerly

241

burning cross, and she could feel her body stiffening with fear.

"This is the way stupid men act, little one—men who hate others because deep inside they hate themselves."

"I don't understand that. Why do they hate us?"

"Just me, little one. Not you. Or your mother. Or baby Ray. Just me."

She stared out again at the cross; shreds of burlap were falling away, sparking tiny fires in the new, spring grass.

"But why? What did you do to them?"

"At the county school where I teach, well, there are only white children. Just up the road from the school is the Dowdell family."

"The nigger family?"

"Honey, remember we talked about not using that word. It's a bad word—it degrades a whole people. Say 'Negro' instead."

"The Negro family—what did *they* do?"

"You know Henry and Shem Dowdell, the two older boys?"

"Yes, sir."

"Well, they came to me one day last week and wanted me to teach them to read. And so I said I would. But some white men in town got very upset when they heard about it. They don't believe Negroes should be given a chance to learn to read."

"And that's why they burned a cross? Crosses are for Jesus."

Then, before her father could respond, she added, "Are they gon' burn our house, too?"

"No, no, little one. They're much too cowardly to do that. In fact, they're so cowardly they hide under white sheets and usually only come out at night. They practice fear and hatred."

"Mother's scared," she said, hoping her father could reassure her further.

"She is, yes. But we must help her. We mustn't be scared."

"I think I am . . . I am some scared," she admitted.

"Don't show 'em you're scared," he told her.

The flames began their gradual burn down.

"Are we gon' burn 'em back?"

Her father shook his head.

"No, little one. If we did that, we would become as stupid and hateful as they are."

"Should we get some water and put it out?"

He smiled.

"Why don't we let it burn. As a symbol."

"A symbol? Is that like a thimble?"

He smiled again. Then got serious.

"A symbol is something which stands for something very important in our lives—in this case, our willingness to help others learn regardless of the color of their skin."

"Could we burn a cross just for ourselves next week?"

He laughed his deep, resonant laugh.

"Little one—it's a complex world out there, isn't it? It's hard for a little girl to understand. Hard for grown-up men and women, too."

She nodded solemnly. Then brightened.

"I'll tell everyone at school about our cross."

"Well . . . not all of them will understand. Some will call you names and try to make you afraid."

He carried her up to bed. Baby Ray, an infant at the time, slept through all the excitement.

In the morning, FloJo had scrambled out of bed to view the charred cross. Looking at it in its ruined state, she wondered how it had ever frightened her.

But this was different.

And she longed to hear her father's comforting voice and to feel his strong and protective touch.

"Hey, punkin'. You doin' OK?"

Larry leaned down, winked at his daughter, and pinched her flushed cheek.

"I'm not, Daddy. I feel sick. And Maria said—"

"Never mind what Maria said," Gina interrupted. "You lie still. Kathy here's been a nurse. She can make you feel better."

Kathy smiled and touched Sophie's forehead.

"Is your throat sore, honey?"

"No."

Kathy felt the girl's throat and neck.

"Would you like to take a couple of aspirin for me?"

Sophie hesitated.

"I guess maybe so."

"I have some children's aspirin in my purse," said Gina.

And she left the room to get them, leaving Larry, Kathy, and Alan huddled near the sick child. Kathy stood up and moved several feet away. Maria, fighting back a rising, indefinable fear, watched and listened from a corner.

"Larry, I'm kind of worried," said Kathy.

He shrugged nervously.

"Just flu or something like that, isn't it?"

Kathy shook her head slowly.

"I don't think so. Those red splotches on her face—I've never seen anything quite like them. If she gets worse, we really ought to let a doctor examine her."

A mask of worry slipped onto Larry's face.

"Are you sure?"

"No, not really certain. I'm afraid maybe it's scarlet fever, though the symptoms don't match up exactly."

"Scarlet fever? Lord God, isn't that pretty serious stuff?" said Larry, growing visibly more concerned each moment.

"I shouldn't speculate. I'm sorry. I could be way off base on this."

Kathy glanced at Alan, and he said, "I'm sure she'll be fine. Excitement of the weekend — you know how kids can get upset easily. Aspirin and rest — she'll probably be fine."

Kathy hugged at Larry's arm.

"I'll keep a close eye on her."

"Thanks," he said as Gina reentered the room.

"Here we go, sweetie," she purred, offering the aspirin and a glass of water.

Maria stood in the corner holding her breath, her stomach tied in knots. She had never felt so frustrated and helpless in her life.

"Larry, please go on and tend to your dinner," said Kathy. "Gina and I will sit with her."

Before he left the room, Larry bent over and kissed Sophie's fingers.

"Punkin', you close your eyes and rest and you'll be just peachy."

"Daddy, Maria said . . ."

But he raised a finger to his lips and shushed her.

"I'm gon' leave two angels to watch over you," he whispered. Then he and Alan exited, heading for the kitchen.

Maria started to follow them, but lingered at Kathy's shoulder, peering down at her little sister.

"Is she really, really going to be fine?"

Twisting around, Kathy reached out and squeezed Maria's arm.

"I believe so. Think good thoughts about her — that will help."

Maria nodded.

"OK."

Then she caught the expression on her mother's face; a

residue of anger remained there.

"You could help your father with dinner," said Gina.

"Yes, ma'am," said Maria.

She went to the kitchen, her thoughts ranging through a wilderness.

She felt lost.

In the doorway to the kitchen, she heard an exchange between her father and Alan.

"Kids—I'd rather be sick myself than have to see them suffer," said Larry.

"Know what you mean," said Alan. "Hey, I just remembered something. Your gourmet meal wouldn't be complete without wine. I'll go to the cellar and get a bottle or two."

"Good idea. It'll lift our spirits."

Seconds later, alone with her father, Maria relaxed at the sound of his babble. They worked together, preparing a salad and other complements to the main fare.

Maria guarded her concerns for as long as possible.

Finally she said, "Daddy, Kevin's gone out to check on the Davenports . . . he thinks they're in danger . . . that Joshua—"

"You like Kevin a lot, don't you?"

Instantly embarrassed, she became flustered.

"Daddy!"

"So naturally if he's sort of imagining something, you might want to go along with it."

"He's not *imagining* this."

Her throat pricked hotly.

"Maybe not," he said. "Anyway, they should be coming in or they'll miss out on our terrific eats. The houseboat is probably docking this minute—you could go see."

Still feeling defensive, Maria sighed heavily and walked into the foggy, night air, hoping that near the shore she would glimpse the approach of the houseboat and find that Kevin had been mistaken about everything.

246

Spearing the lake with his light, Kevin scanned for any signs of the fishing boat or the spider creatures. There were none.

Clothing soaked, emotions jarred, he began to shiver. His body shook so uncontrollably that he was forced to clutch the rail to stand up. One leg stung with a stitchinglike fire.

"Welcome aboard, friend."

The voice startled him.

He could see his breath in the spray of the flashlight beam.

He could also see the figure of Joshua thirty feet away.

"I salute your bravery," said Joshua, raising the shimmering blade of a knife in mock salute. "But it appears you are too late. Mr. Davenport is . . . no longer on board. And Mrs. Davenport is . . . perhaps I should say indisposed."

Kevin aimed the beam at Joshua's chest, creating a yellow-orange aura at the edges of the young man, producing an eerie, unsettling image.

Take your stand against him. Here. Now.

Kevin tried to concentrate.

If he could use his powers and destroy Joshua—here, now—then those at the inn would be spared further terror.

Here.

Now.

But the severe chill rattled his teeth and punched out his breath.

He could not concentrate.

"Is there a problem, friend?"

Joshua's words were transformed by the fog and the

night into haunting strains.

"Don't move," Kevin stammered.

Half a foot at a time, he pulled himself along the rail, his shoes constantly losing contact with the deck.

"Are you angry at me, friend? Mr. Davenport got angry and out of control. Perhaps you saw him fall from the boat. A tragic accident. Most unfortunate."

"Demon!" Kevin shouted. "God, I know what you are. I know what you did."

"No, I'm your friend. I want to help you. But I can't as long as you remain at Blackwinter. Go back to the inn — I'll help you — get the others away from here. Blackwinter belongs to me."

"No," Kevin muttered.

"You've been injured, friend. Look down."

Kevin hesitated. He did not trust Joshua.

Slowly he angled the beam to his feet. And there he saw bloody footprints and a blood-soaked pants' leg and shoe, and he thought of the earlier vision he had experienced.

My blood. Not the Davenports'.

"You need my help. You're hurt. You're cold."

"No," said Kevin.

He reached down to feel his wound, for his leg had numbed. His blood warmed his fingertips.

"Come into the cabin. You need warmth. I can give you warmth."

And Joshua disappeared into the darkness at the opposite end of the boat.

Kevin followed, dragging the bleeding leg, moving slowly, carefully, along the rail. He knew he had to gather as much strength physically and mentally as possible or he would not be able to challenge Joshua.

His hands were growing numb from the cold; his wet clothing was plastered against him like sheets of ice. He shivered and coughed; he felt dizzy and disoriented. But

248

he was also fiercely determined.

It took several minutes for him to negotiate to the rear of the cabin.

The door stood open.

He limped through it and began to shine his light all around.

Like being underwater.

That was the visual sensation which greeted him. The cabin had filled with fog, thus muting the beam of the flashlight so that it seemed as if he were deep-sea diving, exploring some ancient vessel sunk centuries ago.

Everything the beam illuminated appeared to rise up through murky water: a table, chairs, a bed.

Someone lying on the bed.

God, oh God.

He stumbled toward the bed and put out a hand and touched the cold, stiffening foot of Sarah Davenport.

But what he experienced was not horror but a surprising relief.

Both were dead. Mike and Sarah. It was a nearly perverse relief, but relief all the same because now one would not have to suffer alone, to grieve over the death of the other.

Kevin slumped against the end of the bed.

Exhaustion held sway. Tiny lights flashed in his brain. He fought an all-encompassing drowsiness.

Get up, he told himself. *Get up and go after him.*

He staggered to the front of the cabin, and when he saw the wheel and the controls, the sight struck a nerve of hope. But once at the wheel, he began to smell the cloying odor of gasoline fumes, fresh waves of them curling in from all sides.

Then a running spine of light and flames.

"God, oh God," he exclaimed.

And soon the fire ringed the deck and he was surrounded.

And trapped.

FloJo saw a ring of crosses flame alive through the fog. She stroked her throat fearfully.

"My Lord. Oh, Nat . . . my Lord."

But, in reality, there were no crosses—she had imagined them.

The outline of the houseboat burned clearly like a brand in the night, and it seemed to send out a warning: *Stay away. Stay away.*

"My Lord, Nat."

Inside the houseboat, Kevin looked on in confusion and terror as the flames vaulted higher. He searched wildly for a break, an opening in the barrier of fire.

He crawled closer to the flames and glimpsed a possible escape route, a spot to his right at which the trail of gasoline had thinned out.

Two or three steps and a leap over the railing and he would be free.

He readied himself.

He clenched his teeth, thinking about another plunge into the cold water—his genitals shrank at the anticipated sensation.

Deep breath.

Hands curled into fists. He pressed onto the balls of his feet.

Yet, he could not move.

Something held him there.

A force.

It was as if he had been bound to the deck by invisible chains.

He flailed his arms and cried out. One word ghosted to mind.

Joshua.

He knew.

As heat from the flames radiated against his body, he envisioned his death. Images of Mike Davenport flitted through his thoughts.

"Joshua!" he shouted, determined to battle his apparent fate.

He remembered the beam of light he had seen earlier as he had approached the houseboat.

"Help! Help me! Somebody out there help me!"

He was losing strength.

Calm. Calm down. Stay calm.

Concentrate.

The heat and smell forced him back from the deck.

He closed his eyes.

Fear and the approach of death took control.

He relaxed despite the terror.

Lost himself.

Began to float free.

He suddenly looked down and saw himself trapped by the flames.

Dying would be so easy.

The pain would shut off quickly.

Friends were waiting beyond the night in a place so incomprehensibly peaceful he never wanted to return to the pathetic shell crumpled, cowering, there below him.

But he had to.

For his dad and Kathy. For the Bozics.

And especially Maria.

And for himself. Because the fight with Joshua was not over.

Not by a long ways.

He cried out as he snapped back into his body.

Stop time.

Move.

For an instant, the flames flickered lower.

Two steps. Three.

He jumped.

The lake rose to meet him.

The cold attacked from all sides.

He recovered, bobbed his head, splashed, gasped for air, coughed, and began to tread water.

Then another jolt of fear: *How long before the fire reached the houseboat's fuel tanks?*

He had to put more distance between himself and the boat.

He thrashed at the water, but had no energy.

He knew he couldn't last.

In a matter of seconds, the night would push him under and Blackwinter Lake would embrace him forever.

7

He heard something approaching.

God, oh God.

They're coming.

Images of the fishing boat being ripped apart dominated his thoughts.

Bobbing frantically, he suddenly saw a light.

It's happening again.

Brighter and brighter. Only he wasn't rushing toward it, *it* seemed to be rushing toward *him*.

He watched, and as before a figure emerged within the light.

Cross the boundary, Kevin thought.

He heard a voice.

But it was not the peaceful, reassuring voice he had heard after the summer accident.

"Reach, hold my hand! Reach, hold it!"

Confused, Kevin stared at the beam of light.

A scratchy, fear-lined voice—an old woman's voice—

issued from it.

"Reach here!"

A boat maneuvered near him; he glanced over his shoulder at the flames, and he remembered that the houseboat could blow at any second.

He gathered strength, and when the old woman's hand became visible to him, he grasped it — and found, surprisingly, that she was able to pull and lift him enough to allow him to clutch at the edge of the boat.

He teetered there.

The old woman put down her powerbeam and heaved him up, the boat threatening to capsize.

He squirmed and inched his way forward until his upper body was in the boat.

"Roll onto your back," she exclaimed.

He did, but something moved beneath him and he shrieked, imagining that Joshua had sent his creatures.

"It's gist old Nat," said the woman. "Nat King Cole's his rightful name."

Kevin heard the cat squall a protest and then worm out from under him.

The fog closed around them.

"Head away from the houseboat — the fuel tanks — goin' to explode," he exclaimed, nearly breathless.

"Lord, hang on."

She wound the small motor full tilt and slewed the boat around, on a dead arrow point toward shore.

They didn't make it far.

The explosion began like a distant drum roll.

A huge screen of red-orange light materialized behind them.

Heat gushed and debris began to rain down.

They covered their heads; the old woman tried to protect the cat as well.

Seconds later, Kevin braved a look back: Flames and smoke mushroomed from the houseboat.

"God, oh God," he whispered.

The old woman stole a glance.

"My Lord," she said.

It was another twenty or thirty yards before they escaped the perimeter of fiery embers witching down out of the night and through the fog.

"They'll see us from the inn," said Kevin. "Someone will see us." He paused. "Thanks. You saved me—saved my life."

"I was so scared," the old woman cackled. "Didn't rightly know what else to do."

8

FloJo continued to direct her fishing boat toward the shore, but the going was slow because of the heavy fog. Behind her, the Davenports' houseboat spirited flames into the sky as it burned. Smoke mingled with the fog to produce an eerie, surrealistic backdrop.

FloJo and Kevin introduced themselves, a bond forming immediately between them. Kevin told her about the weekend, about the Davenports, and described the psychopathic activities of Joshua.

"My Lord, it's awful. Gist awful," she murmured. "Then you're sayin' that Mrs. Davenport was still on the boat?"

"Yes, ma'am. She'd been murdered, I believe."

FloJo mumbled something incoherent.

Kevin was sitting up, though he was so cold that he shivered violently, his breath puffing out as thickly as the fog. He watched as FloJo aimed her powerbeam at the shore.

"Be we still headin' the right way?" she asked. Then added, "This is the worst thing I've ever . . . my ole heart can't hardly take this."

Suddenly she appeared to choke as if starting to cry—a tearless cry—and she slumped over.

"Ma'am? Hey, what's . . . ?"

His leg shot pain as he moved to see about her. He put a hand on her frail shoulder.

"Hey, you got to hold on till we get . . . "

Then the boat began to angle off course. He released her and reached for the rudder stick. The huge black cat slunk out of the way.

Kevin jerked on the stick and the motor sputtered and shut off.

"Damn," he muttered.

FloJo recovered some. He heard her mumble something about crosses.

"Ma'am . . . how do you start this motor?"

She came more fully alert and worked with the starter for a moment. Then said, "It's all outta gas. I came too far."

"Maybe we'll drift to shore . . . seems like we are," said Kevin.

Silence fell around them.

Kevin blew into his hands; his fingers felt as if he had on gloves made of ice. He stole another glance at the burning houseboat, and as he did FloJo grasped his arm. The gesture took him by surprise.

"Have you seen him?" she asked.

The back of Kevin's neck tingled.

Something in the tone of her voice—something vacant and ghostly—tapped at his nerve endings.

"Him?"

She held the powerbeam close to her so that the spray of light glinted in her dark eyes.

"My brother, Ray."

Puzzled, Kevin said, "I don't know . . . don't think so."

"He went out fishin'. This mornin'. I feel like he came

this way."

Like a reel of film, images flickered in Kevin's thoughts.

"Oh, God," he murmured.

The old woman's face stiffened.

"You've seen him, then, haven't you?" she exclaimed, tightening her grip on his arm.

Kevin stared at her.

"I saw . . . somebody . . . . He was wearing . . . "

"A straw hat?"

"Well . . . yeah."

"Which way did he go? That was Ray. I'd say it was."

"I don't . . . I don't really know what happened. . . ."

It wasn't exactly a lie, he told himself. Not exactly.

"Oh . . . I see," she said.

"Joshua . . . he's the one . . . he's a demon."

They were drifting. Kevin had no idea what to say. No words of consolation.

"Baby Ray . . . that's what I called him," she said. "He sure loved bein' out on a lake. Never much caught any fish, you know. But . . . well . . . "

She sighed.

Then said, "Daughter Connie's right. I didn't take good care of him. Even when he was a little fella, you had to watch him like a hawk . . . had to be responsible for him. He was never right in the head, if you know what I mean."

Kevin nodded.

He saw that they had edged into shallow water. And he was about to say something to FloJo when, through the fog, they heard a voice.

"It's Maria," said Kevin, relieved. "I told you someone would see us."

"Don't show 'em you're scared," the old woman replied distractedly.

Her comment made no sense to Kevin: *Oh, God, her*

256

mind's going.

"Let me have the light," he said. "I'm going to pull us to the shore."

He splashed into the icy water, felt his feet touch the slippery bottom.

"Maria!" he called out. "We're here!"

"Kevin?"

"Maria, we need help."

"I'll get my dad!" she shouted.

Buoyed by the sound of her voice, by the prospect of reaching shore, Kevin wheeled around.

"We're going to make it," he said.

He sprayed the light at the small boat, illuminating FloJo and the amber dots that were Nat King Cole's eyes.

The old woman was looking down into the lake.

Kevin followed the angle of her frozen stare.

He blinked once. Twice.

God, oh God.

But the skeletal hand which had emerged from the lake to grip the old woman's wrist was no illusion.

Chapter XVI

1

A skull rose from the dark water.

FloJo jerked back, emitting a shriek; but she could not escape the grasp of the skeletal thing.

Kevin tried to rush to her aid. His feet slipped with each attempt to gain traction, and for a score of seconds, he could only look on in horror as the skull opened its mouth and spider creatures flooded forth, gushing as well from the vacant eye sockets.

FloJo fought furiously, screaming and beating at the hand which held her.

Determined to help, Kevin dived forward, closing in on the attacker, swinging the powerbeam with all his strength.

To no avail.

There was a splash and a churning of water. FloJo's head bobbed once and Kevin caught a glimpse of her face in the spray of light as she began to scream a final, terrified scream.

The spider creatures covered her chin and mouth, seeking out her eyes.

One violent pull and she disappeared beneath the surface.

Some survival mechanism deep within took control of Kevin.

There was no chance to save the old woman.

Save yourself. Move.

Powerbeam still in hand, he thrashed his way toward the shore where Maria and her father watched, shining a light his direction to help guide him to safety.

Although Maria was crying out Kevin's name, her father seemed to have been stunned into silence. They waded forward as Kevin neared.

Maria's voice echoed into the night and the fog.

FloJo's fishing boat floated away.

The spot where she had been pulled under grew calm. Out on the lake, the houseboat continued to burn.

2

The flames in the fireplace gathered momentum.

Kevin, wrapped in a blanket, huddled as close to it as he could without being burned by the radiation of heat.

Kathy had brought a pillow and insisted that he lie down. She elevated his feet and studied his eyes.

A mixture of sounds filled the air.

Gina, frightened, angered, bewildered, was demanding that Larry do something, call the police, call someone.

Crying against her father's shoulder, Maria trembled; Larry tried to console her, at the same time countering his wife's frantic requests.

"We have no boat. No phone. For God's sake, Gina, what do you expect me to do?"

Kevin's head spun; the clatter of voices, the anger, the fear, the crying—he wanted to shout out for silence.

Stop time.

"Lie still," Kathy whispered. "You've had a bad shock. Don't try to say anything."

She stood up.

Suddenly all of the exchanges broke off.

Maria sobbed quietly.

Larry patted her gently, and the three adults looked at one another. No one spoke for half a minute — seemingly an eternity.

"What can we do?" said Gina, eventually breaking the silence.

Larry glanced at her; perhaps for the first time ever, he heard a confusion, a fear in the voice of this usually indomitable woman.

"Dear God, was the explosion an accident? What happened?" she persisted.

"Mike and Sarah," said Kathy tonelessly, ". . . it just can't be true."

"Kevin claims it was Joshua," said Larry. "But the old woman . . . what I saw . . ."

He shook his head.

"Alan's still down in the wine cellar. I'll go get him . . . maybe he'll have an idea about what we can do," said Kathy.

"No," said Larry. "No, let me go after him. You stay here."

Gina strolled near the fireplace.

"If Joshua did this . . . the fire on the houseboat . . . then he's dead, too, and we don't have to fear whatever else he might do."

With Gina's words, Kevin stirred.

"No," he muttered. "Joshua's not dead. Not dead."

Larry pulled away from Maria.

"Let's all try to keep a level head. I'll get Alan . . . we'll think things out. Everyone stay put. We can handle this if we keep a level head about things."

"I heard thunder and crying. Where's Maria?"

Kathy smiled at Sophie and wiped the girl's forehead and cheeks with a cool rag.

"She's in by the fireplace. What *I* want to know is—how are *you* feeling?"

Gina, cigarette in hand, hunkered down to the pallet.

"How's my sweetie?"

"I feel . . . funny," said Sophie. "I keep hearing things. Music. Comin' from upstairs. Like it's a big party."

Kathy exchanged glances with Gina.

"Well, honey, it could be your sickness has made your ears ring."

The little girl shook her head.

"When I close my eyes, I can see them—people dancing."

Then she turned to Gina.

"Momma . . . you said you'd stop ever doing that again. Smoking. You said you'd stop."

"I know, sweetie, I know. You see . . . momma's . . . nervous and kind of upset, but I'll stop."

She crushed out the cigarette and then arched her eyebrows in an exaggerated fashion.

"There. See that? I've stopped. Just for you."

Sophie smiled.

Kathy leaned forward and pressed her fingertips along the surface of a dark splotch on the girl's face.

"I'm gettin' sicker, aren't I? Maria said I would."

"It's too early to tell, honey," said Kathy.

Visibly agitated, Gina stood.

"How about if I brew up some fresh coffee? Maybe some hot chocolate for Sophie?"

"Well," said Kathy, "I think it would be better if she didn't have anything just now. Kevin could use a hot drink, though, I'm sure."

Gina nodded, seemingly eager to leave the room.

"I'll get Maria to help me," she said.

Sophie's eyes followed her mother.

"What's wrong with Momma?"

"She's . . . she's a little worried about you . . . and adjusting to being here kind of isolated and . . . Nothing for you to be concerned about. Your job is to get well."

"Has Joshua done something?"

Kathy hesitated.

"I think we've talked enough. You need rest. How about closing those eyes for me?"

Sophie grinned.

Surveying the girl's face, her thick eyelashes and eyebrows, Kathy marveled at the beauty Sophie would possess as a woman. She watched as the delicate eyelids fluttered softly.

"He's upstairs," Sophie murmured.

It seemed a trancelike voice.

Kathy felt her throat prickle.

"Higher. He's going up higher," Sophie continued, eyelids still closed.

"Sophie?" Kathy whispered.

"Going to the tower. He's in the tower."

Kathy leaned away, embarrassed that the innocent child's words were frightening her.

"He's going to ring the bell. Listen."

"Sophie? Sophie, please don't do this."

4

"I want to know exactly what you saw," said Gina, as she handed the cup of hot chocolate to Kevin.

"I've told you most of it," he responded.

"But what you've told me can't be. It can't be. You've let your imagination run away with you."

262

"Momma . . . it's the truth. And Daddy saw what happened to the old woman."

"No!" Gina shrieked. "No, I refuse to believe there's something . . . something supernatural. There has to be another explanation."

"I . . . I'm sorry . . . it's the only explanation I have. Joshua's a demon, a monster of some kind . . . and he's not dead, and if we don't get out of here, we're in a lot of danger."

Gina, unsatisfied with Kevin's comment, wheeled out of the room.

"Don't mind her," said Maria.

"No, I understand," Kevin responded. "Why should any of them believe me?"

"Daddy saw. . . . He has to believe now."

"Whether they believe it or not . . . it makes no difference. We've got to get away from here."

"But how?"

"FloJo's boat. You know, the old woman. If we could find her boat . . . It's probably drifting near shore."

They mused in silence.

The fire popped and crackled. It should have been a cheerful fire to them, but it did nothing to comfort them or allay their fears.

Kevin examined the bandage Kathy had applied to his leg wound.

"It stopped bleeding finally."

Maria wasn't listening to him.

"What will he do next? Joshua. What will he do?"

There was another round of silence.

And then they heard it. High above them, drifting down.

The tolling of a bell.

Nine tolls.

Then more silence.

Then six more tolls.

Larry heard the tolling, and it caused a chill to spread from his groin to his throat.

The wine cellar had a bad feel to it. He had called out Alan's name several times and gotten no response. The tolling seemed to punctuate his worst fears.

"God bless it, Alan, where are you?"

He shook off the rising chill.

And as he searched along the wine racks, his thoughts returned to images of the old woman in the boat . . . something had pulled her into the lake.

"Alan? Are you down here?"

He began to consider that there might be some secret passage from the cellar up to the first floor. Maybe Alan was upstairs at that moment.

He searched as far as the light allowed.

"Alan? We've got problems, buddy. Where are you?"

Problems.

A ludicrous understatement, he chided himself. Damn it to hell, Larry, you have more than problems.

He thought of Mike and Sarah and the burning houseboat. Thought about the good times they'd experienced together.

God, they're gone.

The realization hit him—hit him as if he hadn't accepted it before.

"Alan!"

God, what on earth is going on?

He thought of Sophie and Maria and Gina.

Can't let anything happen to them.

He glanced around.

Every shadow threatened to metamorphose into something monstrous.

"Alan," he whispered.

Something had entered the cellar. He could feel its presence.

Blood was its Avatar and its seal—the redness and the horror of blood.

The line from Poe's fiction flared painfully in his mind—like the fiery stitch of a wound reopening.

He began to move toward the entrance stairs, but he would not, could not, turn his back to the shadows.

6

"It's like he's . . . like he's playing some kind of weird game with us," said Maria. "He's murdered people, and now he's ringing bells and playing . . . scaring us like a bully."

"As soon as I've dried off some more, I'm going to find the old woman's boat," said Kevin. "It's our best—maybe our *only*—chance."

"But you can't. Your leg. Wait and let my dad and your dad go for it."

Kevin stared into the flames.

"We could probably do it in two trips. Three at most," he mused.

"Would it be too far for somebody to swim it? I mean, if we can't find her boat, could someone swim it?"

Kevin shook his head.

"I couldn't. And I know my dad's not a great swimmer."

"Mine either," said Maria.

"That water's so cold—I 'bout drowned in it. Besides, Joshua has some 'companions' that like the water. None of us would make it."

"Wait a minute—surely someone will be looking for

the old woman. Someone will call the police when they find her missing."

Maria grew excited as she entertained the thought.

Kevin shrugged doubtfully.

"I don't know. We can hope that's true, I guess."

Edging closer to the fire, Maria said, "I'm really starting to get scared. Are you?"

He slid along the stone ledge, up next to her, then lifted his blanket, and draped it over her shoulders.

"Yeah. I am."

He reached out, seeking her hand. He fumbled for it clumsily. Then found it and squeezed it warmly.

They shared their fear, moments isolated from all the horror.

The sound of someone approaching broke their reverie.

"Daddy?"

Larry entered the fireplace area, his face slack, eyes twitching nervously. He forced the start of a smile and then sat down by them.

"Look," he said, directing his comment at Kevin, "I can't seem to locate your dad. I'm pretty sure he went to the cellar—told me he was going after a couple of bottles of wine for dinner, but . . . I'm not getting any answer when I call out for him."

"Daddy, are you sure?" Maria interjected.

"Yes, baby . . . unless there's another way out of the cellar. I take it you haven't seen him."

"No, but he's down there," Kevin replied. "I think I know what happened. This is Joshua's plan . . . this is how he's going to try to get to me."

"I'll go back down with you," said Larry. "I wanted to check on Sophie again first."

"I need to go by myself," said Kevin, defiance in his tone.

Then he looked from Maria to her father.

"There's something you could do while I go after my dad. You could go out and search for the old woman's boat. It's probably drifting along the shore. We have two flashlights; I'll take one and you take the other. That boat—it's probably our only way out of here."

Larry nodded. He seemed relieved.

"OK. OK, this sounds good. Maria and I will tell Gina and Kathy what we're planning. You get your dad, and when we find that boat, we'll make our way to the Davenports' trailer and call the authorities."

He sighed heavily, again, a gesture of relief.

"We'll let the police sort all this out. Everything's gon' be fine."

But he didn't believe his own words, and he saw doubt in the eyes of Maria and Kevin.

"Take the powerbeam," said Kevin. "You'll be able to see better with it."

As they rose to leave, Maria touched Kevin's arm.

"Please be careful."

"You, too."

Kevin turned away. The wound to his calf burned and his chest and head ached. But it was not time to think of himself, of his discomfort.

He was frightened for his dad, knowing that an inhuman creature had taken over Blackwinter Inn.

A demon.

And that demon would not be satisfied until the old inn had returned to its vacant state.

Steeling himself to the danger, Kevin walked to the entrance of the cellar.

I'm coming for you, Dad.

7

"Is this where Kevin came ashore?" Larry asked his

daughter.

"I think so. Lots of footprints here."

She pointed at the sand illuminated by the powerbeam.

Out on the lake, the houseboat, tipped over onto its side, continued to burn, though the flames hugged low to the cabin area and smoke nearly blunted out all visibility of it.

The fog rolled in as thickly as before.

"I can't see very far out there, can you?"

Larry squinted into the spray of light as he lifted and redirected the powerbeam.

"Let's go farther this way," said Maria, moving tentatively along the water's edge.

"Watch for brush piles," said Larry. "A boat would likely drift in and get caught up on one of them."

"Daddy?"

"Maria, can you tell if there's any kind of undercurrent?"

"Daddy, listen."

"Turning colder," Larry muttered.

"Daddy, listen!" Maria exclaimed.

Both of them stopped walking.

Silence mingled with the fog.

Then they heard something—at first it seemed to be a chill night breeze soughing high in the pines.

But there was no breeze.

"Daddy?"

"Lord God," said Larry, "what's out there?"

8

"Wet this rag with cold water—ice water, the colder the better."

Kathy pressed the washcloth into Gina's hands and

pushed her toward the door.

"How long has she been like that?" Gina exclaimed.

"Just go. Please go," said Kathy.

Reluctantly, Gina obeyed, eying her daughter all the while.

Kathy had never seen anything like it — the surface skin irritations, red, erupting into sores even as she watched. And the girl's expression — blank, locked into place as if controlled by something deep within . . . something foreign. Alien.

She grasped the girl's hand and thrust her face up as close as possible.

"Sophie. Sophie, please."

Every muscle in the little girl's body appeared as taut and inflexible as steel.

"Lie back down. Please."

Something glinted in Sophie's eyes.

Her tiny mouth twitched.

"He's coming."

She was staring straight ahead, and despite the fact that Kathy had aligned herself directly in the path of the girl's vision, the staring continued as if Kathy offered no barrier whatsoever.

"Sophie honey."

"Can't you hear him?"

"Sophie, no. Please relax and lie back down."

"You won't know him when you see him."

The eerie, toneless quality of Sophie's words filled Kathy with terror.

Don't panic, she told herself. Do not panic.

"Honey, it's OK. I'll cool off your head and you'll be OK."

But, oh God, Kathy knew that wasn't true. And she felt helpless to stop what was taking place.

When Gina returned with the cold rag, Kathy grabbed it from her.

"Help me push her down," she exclaimed.

"Dear God, what's wrong . . . what's happened to my baby?"

Gina threw her arms around Sophie, hugging her, trying to rock her as if the girl had just awakened from a nightmare and needed consoling.

"Gina . . . Gina, let go. I need to cool off her face."

Gradually the woman released her hold on her daughter, and Kathy pressed the cold rag onto Sophie's forehead and cheeks.

"Dear God, she's burning up," Gina whimpered.

"Ice," said Kathy, straining to remain calm. "We have to pack her in ice—submerse her in ice water. Go to the kitchen and get as much ice out of the coolers as you can."

Gina stared at her.

"Go on!" Kathy cried.

When Gina had scrambled away frantically to do what she'd been told, Kathy began to try to remove the girl's nightgown.

"Honey, we need to take this off. Your fever. We have to break your fever."

But the girl stiffened, her body rocking back and forth.

Despite applying all her strength, Kathy could not stop the frenzied rocking.

"He's coming for me," Sophie murmured.

Suddenly Kathy stood up.

"Over there," said Sophie, and the rocking slowed.

She pointed a small finger into a shadowy, far corner.

Kathy was trembling, her mind a dark screen. She followed the line of the girl's finger.

The air appeared to stir.

Sophie held out her hands as if about to receive something.

A form materialized. The figure of a young man, his

270

face hideously misshapen.

Kathy felt a scream rising within her, but it was as if she were too terrified for the sound to emerge.

"He's here," Sophie whispered.

"He's here."

Chapter XVII

1

Kathy felt the cool breeze of inner calm stir within. Eyes fixed upon the Joshua creature, she heard her heart beat, a thrumming behind her ears. Yet, her fear had peaked, and, like a color tinting from a darker shade to a lighter one, fear became resolve.

Time breathed slowly.

She felt strong.

The Joshua creature stood rigidly, its very being continuing to materialize, nearing completion. It gave no sign of attack, but its presence spoke no other language except the language of threat.

Behind her, Kathy sensed that Sophie remained in her pose of surrender, that the little girl would freely, willingly, give herself to the creature, a curiously perverse gesture.

"No, Sophie," Kathy muttered.

She could hear the girl's breathing, deeper, raspier, like that of a woman experiencing desire; and she could feel heat radiating from the small body.

"No, Sophie."

The large, vulturelike eye nesting in the creature's hideous face bulged, and Kathy felt some of her resolve flag.

The room gained degrees of darkness.

She clenched her fists.

You can't have her.

You cannot have this precious child.

Blood glistened below the creature's nose and at the corners of its mouth, shifting its terrifying countenance to a higher, more intense level; yet, the young man wrapped in the guise of a monster made no move to attack.

Her plan was working.

She had asserted her will, drawing upon something deeper, something in the darkest, most remote cavern of herself which she never dreamed existed. She felt a jolt of triumph, she nearly smiled.

"He can't have you, Sophie. Can't have you."

Kathy wanted to laugh, wanted to shout for joy. Alan would be proud of her. So would Kevin. And Gina would thank her and be forever grateful. Would fully accept her. The moment of transcendent happiness and strength held until she thought of Mike and Sarah.

She gritted her teeth.

Don't think of them now.

Don't lose control.

Joshua hovered there not twenty feet beyond her, nearly immobile, in a rare, grim silence like a grotesque tapestry—some allegorical figure from a medieval nightmare.

A fire glimmered in the demon's eye.

"You can't be real," Kathy whispered.

And felt her muscles weaken, her blood pulse faster; her concentration wane. A noise, a repulsive gurgle, issued from Sophie—it reminded Kathy of a patient she had once attended, an elderly man whose lungs had filled with his own fluids which threatened to drown him.

"Kathy!"

She wheeled around as Gina entered the room carrying

an ice bucket.

"Stay back!" Kathy exclaimed.

The scene was turning. Kathy sensed it. Knew she had lost control. She was thankful Gina did not scream, that the woman fixed her stare upon the creature and appeared to be locked in the grip of her own disbelief.

The air in the room heated up a score of degrees.

Kathy heard again the throaty gurgle.

Sophie, eyes twinkling with maniacal glee, reached toward Gina and plunged a hand into the bucket of ice.

Instantly, plumes of steam rose and filled the shadows.

An eager hiss echoed.

Sophie giggled, but not a little girl's giggle—rather the seductive, sensuous giggle of a woman at the height of her passion. And the girl-transforming-into-woman laughed as Gina's disbelief crumbled and she screamed, dropping the bucket of water.

The dark, childthing pushed Kathy aside.

Joshua waited.

There was about that demonic figure a perfect patience. This deathless resident of the old inn, guarding it as a dragon might guard its hoard of gold, had passed the years largely in silence, allowing only a selected few to live at Blackwinter. Time had deepened the creature's anger, its hatred—perhaps its envy, for it could not belong to the world of man.

Now it existed, emboldened by an insatiable need to destroy.

Life but for life.

"Sophie, don't do it," said Kathy.

She caught a piece of the girl's nightgown, but with preternatural quickness, the child raked clawlike fingers across the woman's forearm.

"Baby, no!" Gina screamed, making a move to stop her child.

Like a serpent coiling to strike, Sophie pitched back,

her body ticking with a controlled violence which sent chills down Kathy's spine.

Gina froze.

"My baby," she whispered. "Dear God."

But both women could see that little resemblance to Sophie remained in the nightmarish face of the childthing.

Kathy clasped Gina's hand.

"Help me concentrate," she said. "We can stop him from taking her."

"No," said the childthing.

The voice was warm and mature.

"He has come for me. To die in him. The touch of the Red Death."

The words caught in Kathy's mental filter: *To die in him. The touch of the Red Death.*

"No, please," Gina whimpered. "You're my baby."

The childthing turned its attentions fully upon Gina.

"Come die in him with me. Come feel the touch of the Red Death."

"Sophie . . . sweetie, no. Stay with your momma."

Gina stumbled forward, hands reaching out like hungry, desperate mouths.

The childthing's face torched anger.

"I belong to him. I have no mother."

Kathy stepped forward and looped an arm through Gina's elbow.

"Help me concentrate . . . we can stop this . . . he can't overcome our wills. Please, Gina. Concentrate."

The woman turned, her eyes pools of confusion and despair. She spoke slowly, distractedly.

"What . . . happened . . . to . . . my . . . baby?"

Kathy shook her head.

"Don't think about it. Help me. Help me concentrate."

The childthing laughed, a husky, womanly laugh.

"*You* . . . wouldn't you like to die in him, too?"

Blood beginning to trickle from its nose and mouth, the shell of Sophie approached Kathy.

"The touch of the Red Death . . . no more pain. Die in him."

Within the shadows, the Joshua creature writhed as if suddenly impatient, and lurking just beneath the mask of the Red Death, a demonic countenance, all hellish and reptilian, an ancient predator from mankind's darkest memories.

The childthing's voice suddenly singsonged.

"Come into the light. Come into the light. Come into the light."

It beckoned to the two women, then wheeled with the reckless abandon of a child running from the reprimand of a parent—and ran into the embrace of the Joshua creature.

Gina screamed, and it was the sound of all her energy escaping, of some vital part of her dying forever. She struggled to move, almost instantly collapsing, afterthralls of her scream shaking her; Kathy held her by the shoulders and looked up as the shadows swallowed the childthing.

Then a light ghosted free.

Kathy saw that it came from Sophie's body as if it were some essence of vitality or innocence that could find no other form but a pure and transcendent light.

Kathy stared in awe.

The room warmed with a furnace blast of heat.

And an odor which could only be burning flesh mingled with blood. Kathy's muscles relaxed; she had no feeling in her hands, was barely conscious of Gina slipping away from her, clambering to her feet.

"My baby," Gina muttered.

The Joshua creature released the childthing and it dropped heavily to the floor.

Gina scrambled forward.

The Joshua creature drew her into its embrace. The shadows pitched to a solid, nearly palpable blackness. But a light winked, the flash of an electric bulb before it burns out completely.

The helpless form of Gina seemed to move in some indefinable pattern as if locked in an awkward waltz. Then she swooned and fell as if she had merely fainted.

Kathy stood up, a realization hammering at her senses: *I am alone. I must face this thing alone.*

She closed her eyes and steadied herself, but when she blinked into the shadows the Joshua creature had disappeared, leaving the bodies of Sophie and Gina. Kathy approached them cautiously, suspicious of any sound or movement.

Sweat bathed her face.

She lowered herself next to Gina's body and managed to roll the woman onto her back. Even in the shadows, she could see the blood—so much blood—and the facial sores—the touch of the Red Death.

Stunned for a timeless whirl of seconds, Kathy remained there, glancing occasionally from Gina's body to Sophie's.

Do something, Kathy, an inner voice demanded.

Do something now.

She pushed to her feet, fighting dizziness, and went to the kitchen. She called out for Alan, received no response, then busied herself finding ice and washcloths.

I am alone.

As she returned to the bodies, those words beat a dull, self-negating rhythm in her thoughts. This time she hunkered near Sophie. She had started to clean the girl's face when the tolling of the tower bell broke free and clear, echoing throughout the inn—six tolls. Silence. Six more.

Kathy sobbed quietly as she dabbed at the drying rivulets of blood.

She knew they were dead. Had denied it at first. But

277

knew.

She touched Sophie's throat for confirmation.

No pulse. The same was true for Gina.

Kathy hung her head, cried into her hands.

"I'm sorry," she murmured.

The bodies had darkened and drawn up into fetal positions; they resembled mummies and smelled sour and bitingly pungent. Kathy stared at them, calming herself as best she could. She leaned over Sophie and brushed at a delicate curl on the girl's forehead.

Fingers of a tiny hand suddenly clamped upon Kathy's wrist.

She gasped and started to jerk away.

The grip loosened.

The lips of the childthing that was Sophie moved.

"Dear God," Kathy moaned.

Frightened, she reached hesitantly again toward the girl's throat, lightly stroking the rapidly cooling skin.

No pulse.

"Dead," Kathy whispered. "I know you're dead."

The childthing's eyes opened, ovals of muted light, lusterless as far distant stars.

"He wants you," it said.

"Oh, dear God, no," said Kathy, scrambling away.

"He wants you," the childthing repeated, stirring slightly, yet bound, it appeared, to the same position. "He wants *both* of you."

In the doorway, Kathy slumped against the jamb; the room seemed to splinter into a million shards of light and darkness. She was losing consciousness, but could do nothing to hold onto reality.

And in the span of seconds before a realm of forgetting welcomed her, she could hear—more intensely than ever before—subtle sounds in the room: the skittering of insects, the melting of a stray cube of ice, and every intimate sound of her autonomous bodily functions.

And one more.

The presence of a sound reaching forward to her from a previous century.

A voice.

The clamor of pain. Panting. Breath after excruciating breath.

Somewhere in Blackwinter Inn, a woman was giving birth.

2

They heard the tolling, and, momentarily, it wrested their attention from the lake.

"Lord, God . . . that bell again," said Larry, a shiver dancing across his shoulders.

"It's Joshua," said Maria. "I think I know . . ."

But she cut off her words as if, perhaps, not wanting to face the horrible conclusions materializing in her thoughts.

"Could it have drifted this far?" asked Larry, shifting his concern to the boat they hoped to locate. "We're a long ways from where we started."

Maria looked in the direction from which they had come, her thoughts more tangled than any brush pile possibly lurking in the dark lake. The fog had grown colder, was flecked with traces of ice which stung her nose and cheeks. She stuffed her hands deeper into her jacket.

"I can't tell . . . we haven't come to the boat ramp yet."

Larry played the powerbeam into the thick curtain of fog, angling it back and forth like an airport searchlight. He squatted, aiming the beam lower as if anticipating that he could see beneath the curtain.

Maria studied the shadows smeared on his face like war paint. She could feel the tension in her father's body—he was out of his element here: out in the night, searching the unknown, physically confronting the darkness. No, this was not his place; his place was at home in his den, relaxing in his rocker recliner, cold mug of beer nearby, book resting in his lap. Always a book. For she never envisioned her father as somehow complete without a book in hand—like some bodily appendage. Sometimes, of course, settled there in his rocker recliner, a comfortable buzz from the beer dulling his senses, eyes weary, he would nod off.

To Maria, it was the most irresistible image of her father she could entertain: asleep, book opened but unattended, his head lolled back, mouth agape. Whenever she saw him like that, she would be tempted to rush forward and hug him and declare: I love you. I love you just as you are. Please don't ever change.

"There's no wind," he said, dissolving her reverie. "A wind would help break up the fog."

"Daddy, maybe we ought to keep—"

He gestured for her to shush. She was about to suggest that they keep moving, keep following the lazy curve of the shore, when her father stood up.

"Quiet!" he exclaimed.

Maria's heart was beating high in her throat; the tension of the moment created a curious static in her ears so that at first she didn't hear what her father heard.

"There it is again," he whispered.

Feeling herself starting to tremble, Maria closed her eyes tightly, straining to concentrate as much as possible. There was the minuscule lapping of the lake against the shore—nothing more.

"I believe it came from that way," said Larry, spearing the beam to his right.

Suddenly they both heard it.

Like a cry in response to the light. But not quite a sound one would equate with human sounds.

"It could be a heron, Daddy . . . one of those big birds we see up here sometimes," Maria offered.

"Wait," he said, gesturing again for her to listen.

Maria balanced first on one foot, then the other. She heard something, but couldn't determine what.

"It's a boat," said her father. "Someone's out there in a boat."

Growing more excited, he put a cupped hand to one side of his mouth.

"Hey, out there! Hey, we've had some trouble! Come ashore! We need some help!"

They waited.

No response.

"Daddy, nobody's going to be on the lake without a light."

He turned toward her, a mixture of disappointment and embarrassment in his expression.

"I guess you're right. But I could've sworn I heard . . ."

Then, once again, the curiously inhuman cry.

Immediately Larry shined the light in the apparent direction of its source.

The cry was followed by a pausing, halting voice, though no distinguishable words.

"It *is* somebody," Maria exclaimed, feeling an injection of hope, a hope she hadn't permitted herself to embrace.

"Who's there?" Larry called out.

"Help us! Please, help us!" Marie added.

Larry sprayed the lake with a semicircular sweep of light.

"Where's it coming from?"

"Farther out," said Maria.

The two of them fell silent.

Seconds ticked by. Frustrating, helpless-seeming seconds.

Then it appeared that their patience was rewarded.

They heard a splash. A very small splash, yet a distinct one.

And another sound. A new one.

A pathetic mewing, a muted cry of distress.

Something was drawing toward the shore.

3

There was a frightened intensity in Maria's voice as she tugged at her father, fearful that he was edging too close to the water.

"Daddy, it could be something sent by Joshua."

Larry hesitated. He shrugged, a nervous, confused gesture.

"Whatever it is, it's not very big . . . listen to it."

The high-pitched mewing continued.

"Daddy, this way . . . shine your light this way."

Moving to his left, Larry wigwagged the powerbeam.

"You see anything, honey?"

Squinting into the oval of light, Maria stomped her feet to generate warmth.

"Keep it there . . . I know I heard something."

Larry inched next to her and put one arm around her shoulder.

"Gettin' colder," he mumbled.

Maria's teeth chattered, but she kept her eyes on the lake.

"Daddy . . . could the Davenports . . . ?"

"No," he replied. "I just don't think there would be any way they could have survived, honey."

The mewing never flagged as it changed course suddenly, veering to their left.

Larry traced it with the beam.

"There!" Maria exclaimed. "See it?"

They scuttled along the shore to meet the approach of some living thing.

"Yeah . . . yeah, it's some kind of animal."

"A cat. Daddy, it's a cat."

The animal, its black fur glistening in the yellow light, paddled furiously, its mouth locked open in a constant cry. Wet and sodden, it crawled onto the shore.

"Lord, God . . . poor thing," Larry muttered.

"Kitty. Here, kitty, Don't run. I won't hurt you."

But, at first, the cat kept out of her reach, choosing to shake off its wetness and begin to lick itself dry.

"Where in the world did it come from?" asked Larry.

"The old woman . . . it was hers, I bet."

"We oughta bundle it up and take it in by the fire. Warm ourselves up, too."

"But, Daddy . . . what about the boat? How are we going to get off the island? Joshua . . . We can't stay on the island."

"Honey, I know. I know. This fog . . . until it lifts we're just stumbling around like blind folks."

Maria petted and soothed the cat, and soon it was purring and butting its head against her jacket.

"We'll come back and keep trying, won't we, Daddy?"

He hugged her and reached out to stroke the cat's head.

"Sure, honey. I promise."

They turned to leave.

"Kevin's found Alan by now," Larry added, mustering a tone of reassurance. "We'll sit down and decide what to do. Don't worry, honey."

It was a moment in which the shock, the horror, the cold — all the desperate features of the night — coalesced, and the resultant burden was too much for Maria. She leaned against her father, fighting gamely not to cry.

"Go ahead," he said. "No use holding it in."

"Daddy . . . I don't want to be a baby."

"Hey, truth is, I feel like crying myself."

She started to laugh; he hugged her again; the tears came.

And when, after a minute or so, she had stopped, she kissed her father on the chin. The night lapsed into a calm around them, allowing them to hear a garbled call from upon the lake.

"Good God, something's still out there," Larry murmured.

"Daddy, don't shine the light."

He followed her suggestion, aiming the beam at his feet.

As before, they waited.

Through the fog, riding over it eerily, the not-quite-human call broke upon them. By degrees, they discerned a pattern, an insistent repetition.

"What is it saying?" Larry whispered to his daughter.

Maria continued to pet the cat, though it was beginning to squirm.

Suddenly the cat leaped from her arms.

"Daddy? Daddy, don't you see?"

"No, honey, I don't."

"Whatever's out there is calling the cat."

Larry coughed nervously into his fist.

"Hey . . . whoever you are . . . bring your boat in."

The cat sat on its haunches at the edge of the lake, obviously having recognized the voice wafting from the darkness.

Twice more the voice echoed toward shore, seemingly several yards closer the second time.

Maria slipped her hand into her father's.

"We could see them now . . . they sound like they're not far away."

Larry nodded.

He swung the beam up and directed it outward. The fog caught it, pushed it back. Then the prow of a small fishing boat slid into view.

"Daddy!"

He lifted the beam a few feet higher; Maria did not scream, but her fingers squeezed harder than her father could have believed they could.

Two figures were in the boat.

Skeletal, their flesh mostly stripped away.

The figures turned into the full illumination of the powerbeam.

"Oh, Lord God!" Larry exclaimed.

The powerbeam fell to the ground. And he pressed his daughter's face into his chest, could feel her scream rising, driving into him, and knew that for as long as he lived, he would not forget what he saw when the faces of the two figures stared into his own.

4

This was the memory.

Kevin and his dad planned a surprise. His mother's birthday was approaching, and Kevin knew exactly what would please her, though the details behind her particular wish remained nebulous to him—something about a creek near the homeplace where she had grown up.

"It's gotta be a willow, Dad. A weeper willow."

And his dad had smiled. "You mean a 'weeping' willow?"

"Yeah, 'at's it."

So off they went to the Garden of Eden nursery.

Kevin, six years younger at the time, felt such a rush of happiness that he virtually tiptoed among the starter oaks and maples and fruit trees until they came upon a stately five-foot specimen anchored to a large root ball.

"But dad, it's not hangin' over and weepin'," Kevin had protested.

"It will," his dad assured him. "It won't weep until it grows up some."

Kevin reflected upon that comment, then said, "Grown-up people don't cry—but grown-up trees do?"

"Well, when you're talking about willow trees, that's a fact."

"OK, let's get this one."

And they did, plopping it into the trunk of the car, from which it eagerly protruded, whipping in the wind; and Kevin and his dad sang all the way home.

"Where should we plant it?" his dad queried once they reached the back yard.

"I know. I know."

Kevin ran to an open area beyond his swing set, beyond the dog's house.

"Right here."

"Looks like a fine choice. You ready to dig?"

"Sure."

That was the heart of it. The beginning of the best aspect of the memory.

Breaking ground.

Oh, there was disparity in the digging—Kevin's one bare shovelful for every four that his dad contributed. But they were doing it together, sweating, getting their hands dirty, projecting optimistically about how much the tree would grow in one year.

Eventually a sizeable hole was formed. They dumped in a little sand, a little peat, some potting soil, and the readiness was all.

"But, Dad, it's got a sack wrapped around its feet."

"Burlap—it'll decay in time—we'll drop the whole tree in. Help me position it."

They set it just right, filled dirt around the root ball, watered it, spread pinestraw at its base—and stood back and beamed.

"We did it," Kevin had exclaimed. "We made a tree

come to life."

Kevin's mother had been shopping all afternoon. She had no more than entered the front door when he whisked her away to the back yard, exhorting her to keep her eyes closed.

Kevin and his dad sang a halting version of "Happy Birthday to You" and led her into the middle of the yard. Kevin had never seen his mother cry about anything, but when she opened her eyes . . .

The distant echo of his mother's tears mingled with other sounds there in the wine cellar. Kevin had been calling out for his dad, and he had heard the muted tolling of the tower bell.

Flashlight in hand, he had probed deeper into the cool, dank cellar, keenly aware that Joshua controlled Blackwinter Inn. He feared what the tolling might portend. He feared what might have happened to his dad.

"Dad!" he cried out again.

His flashlight illuminated trickles of the chalybeate spring as it meandered along the cellar floor, cutting rivulets in the stone. He dipped his fingers into the water. It was chilled, but not as cold as the lake.

Over the gentle purling of the spring, he suddenly heard another sound.

A voice, perhaps.

"Dad?"

He spun around, flashing the light nearly in a full circle.

He listened. Thought he heard a scream from upstairs.

Or from within the walls of the cellar.

He closed his eyes to concentrate.

Time seemed to spiral backward.

A woman cried out in pain.

Kevin tensed.

Then he heard snoring. And there, propped against a wall nearby, was the faint outline of a man, a man sleeping in a fog of whiskey fumes.

The hallucination was so real that Kevin nearly lost his concentration. But it held, and several feet to the other side of him two other figures materialized: a woman partially covered by a blanket, locked in the thralls of giving birth; and a second woman looming at her side, apparently midwiving the birth.

"Portisha!"

The voice of the woman with child hammered at Kevin's senses.

"Portisha, will it be healthy?"

No one can see me, Kevin realized as he moved closer to observe the scene. Closer. He cringed at the woman's pathetic wailing. And then, in the torchlight, he saw her face.

5

He felt cold and naked.

It was as if some preternatural light from an unknown source had showered down upon him. He trembled, recalling the sores, the bleeding—the woman's grotesque mask. In a trance, he had listened and watched from the side as the midwife tended to the dying woman.

He had heard the midwife speak of demon's eye and dragon's voice and the touch of the Red Death. He had seen the child. He had held his breath and listened to his heart thunder when the old midwife directed her murderous intentions upon the child—Joshua, the child.

And he had experienced a curious relief when the drummer had stepped forward to stop her and to claim the child for his own. Then all had melted into the stone underfoot—those wandering moments from the past had performed their brief play, a pageant of birth and death, and had passed by and returned to the stone and the miracle spring which held their lasting impressions.

"Dad," Kevin murmured, needing security, envying that moment in which the drummer had so selflessly volunteered to take care of the newborn infant.

"He's not here."

Kevin swung the flashlight in an eager circle.

A figure appeared to walk out of one of the walls.

"Joshua," said Kevin, immediately recognizing his nemesis. "Where is he? Where's my dad? What have you done to him?"

"Taken care of him," said Joshua.

He drew himself into the spray of the flashlight.

Kevin's face tightened with anger.

"You've killed him, you bastard!"

Joshua frowned and waved off the outburst, and, in doing so, blunted Kevin's desire for revenge.

"No . . . no, you misunderstand me, friend."

Trembling, shaken by a mixture of confusion and fear, Kevin forced himself to stare into the dark eyes of the mysterious young man.

"I heard the bell . . . it means death. You can't deny that."

"Ah, but not the death of your dear father." Joshua hesitated, and something of genuine humanity crossed his expression. "There is, in me, a special fondness for fathers."

"Where is he, damn you!"

"If you will indulge me, friend, I'll share with you my origins. Then and only then will you understand my actions. For you see, murdering your father . . . walling him up, or strangling him, or touching him with the touch of the Red Death would be inappropriate. It would not force you to suffer sufficiently. What I have done, you will see, amounts to a more intimate revenge."

"I'll fight you . . . I don't care what happens to me."

"Hear me out," Joshua gently pleaded. "I have something planned for you."

And Kevin found himself curiously mesmerized by Joshua's account of living in New Orleans with the drummer and his family over a hundred years ago and of the young man's eventual return to Blackwinter Inn.

The belled gloves. The glittery ballroom. And the murder.

"They buried me there . . . in the far corner of this cellar. The spring — that's the dark secret, friend."

Joshua stooped down and let a rivulet of the spring trickle across his fingers.

"Eternal life. Eternal darkness. Demon's eye. Those who buried me would not have dreamed that, ironically, they made it possible for my spirit to claim Blackwinter as my own . . . forever."

"What does this have to do with my dad?"

"I sent him back."

"Sent him back?"

"In time . . . to the hour of my death."

"You're lying! Liar!"

Kevin made a move to rush at Joshua, but the young man disappeared as mysteriously, completely, as he had appeared.

The air in the cellar thickened; the choking smoke curling free of several torches began to fill the cavernous room. Kevin saw things as through a diaphanous, gray-black veil. Heard sounds as if over a faulty telephone connection.

Above him, waltz music.

And at the entrance to the cellar, the shouts of men. A blur of movement. Faces ballooned; he recognized Joshua, saw the anger in the expressions of the men who were dragging him roughly into the torchlit room.

Frightened, Kevin stood aside.

The clamor swelled.

He sought out a distant corner of the cellar, but the sight of someone numbed his senses. His skin, his muscles, his nerves — all that was flesh and blood — seemed to drape upon the scaffolding of his bones, lifeless, as alien to him as if suddenly he had looked into a mirror and had seen a stranger's face reflected there.

Near the stairway stood his dad.

The man appeared thoroughly baffled.

Lost.

Even across the length of the cellar, Kevin could detect the anguish and shock in the man's expression.

Joshua had not been voicing idle threats. Somehow he had accomplished it, had transported Alan Holmes into the nineteenth century, into the early years of Blackwinter Inn.

Angry words range out. The scuffle, Joshua at its center, continued, but Kevin stayed clear of it, his design only to reach his dad and explain.

Cold realization pinned him to the stone beneath his feet.

He's done it to me, too.

Trapped in time.

Terrified by that recognition, Kevin crouched against a wall of stone. The spring whispered near him. He forgot about his dad for the moment and the ugly scene developing around Joshua.

Save yourself, the frightened child within cried.

Save yourself.

Before it's too late.

Chapter XVIII

1

He burrowed deep within himself, out of reach of Joshua, of space and time. He could hear the moan of an inner wind as it blew through him, a wind animated by his secret rage, his secret fear.

He wanted to slingshot himself forward in time, falling into reality where he chose, and that choice would be some innocent day in his life, perhaps the day of the willow planting, perhaps some other.

Stop time.

But he didn't know how.

I don't want to grow up.

That was the crux: There in his secret cell, sharing himself with no one else, he would not have to face the world outside—the evil of Joshua, the responsibility of finding his dad and of helping the others at Blackwinter Inn.

I don't care about the others.

It was a lie, of course, but the kind of lie a boy can tell himself. He did care. About his dad and the others.

What can I do?

No one's ever taught me about evil.

Deep within himself, he searched for scraps of infor-

292

mation—words of his parents, or his minister, or a teacher—something that a boy could use to confront evil. He discovered nothing.

Deliver me from evil.

It was a desperately quiet plea.

He thought of all the books he had read—fairy tales and fantasies—most certainly one or more had contained sage advice on defeating evil and the wicked at heart.

Wicked.

The word cut through his thoughts like a gleaming saber.

By the pricking of my thumb/Something wicked this way comes.

Deep within himself, he smiled.

Of course. Ray Bradbury. Of course.

Jim and Will. Two boys who had confronted the evil which dies not, but lies in wait. To return and return and ever return.

Something Wicked This Way Comes.

He had read that book a dozen times. Two dozen.

Near the end of it, what had Will's father said? He couldn't remember the exact words—something about . . . laughing . . . yes, laughing evil out of existence.

It was worth a try.

He summoned all the comic images he could think of. He conjured up the voices of Bill Cosby and Eddie Murphy, clips from movies like *Beetle Juice* and *Big*. He mustered a weak chuckle. Nothing more.

Deep within himself, they accumulated. Those ever-falling, ever-swirling autumn leaves from Bradbury's stories ushered in a chill wind. They numbed him.

He felt himself letting go.

Hidden in his secret cell, he slept.

He woke to the thrum of an empty, dark, and silent cellar.

The throng of men around Joshua had disappeared, as had Joshua himself and the drummer. And the mysterious figure who had so resembled Kevin's dad.

Hours had passed, though Kevin wasn't sure how many. He switched on his flashlight and rose from his hiding place.

"Dad?"

He knew he would receive no response, and yet he continued to refuse to acknowledge that Joshua had succeeded in transporting the man into another century.

It's impossible.

But so was much that had occurred at Blackwinter Inn and out on the lake.

"Dad, it's me, Kevin. Where are you?"

He trudged up the cellar steps, conscious of how cold the old inn had become. He smelled the smoke of the fireplace and quickened his pace.

"Who's here?" he called out.

Ahead, in the shadowy room, startled voices jangled.

When he came upon the sources of the voices, he slowed, relieved and yet deflated by what he saw: Huddled close to the dwindling fire were Maria and Kathy, wrapped in blankets which even covered their heads. They reminded Kevin of nuns.

At the sight of him, both struggled to their feet; neither appeared to believe he was real.

"Kevin?" said Kathy, her hands extending from the blanket, hanging in the air as if not connected to her arms. Hers was the countenance of someone witnessing a miracle.

But Maria rushed to him, not crying, though trembling with fear and excitement. She nearly knocked him over.

"Don't leave us again," she exclaimed. "Please, please, don't leave us again."

Kathy helped him over to the fire, Maria continuing to cling to him. He glanced at Kathy, her face illuminated by the glow, and he could see and feel something being rejuvenated there—a kind of hope—and it pleased him that he might have played a part in that change.

"Sit right here. It's the warmest place."

She poked at the fire; sparks erupted; flames took hold of a slumbering log. The warmth was delicious, providing enough of a rise in his body temperature for him to relax and, for a handful of seconds, forget all the terror, all the horror.

"I can gather us some more wood," he said.

"This will burn a while," said Kathy. "Are you hungry?"

And suddenly he realized he was.

"Have you and Maria had something?"

Kathy smiled weakly toward Maria.

"We're bearing up OK. I'll go fix you some food."

As Kevin watched her leave the room, it occurred to him that she was hiding something, being strong, probably a carryover from her nurse's training. And he respected her for her strength even as it, for reasons he couldn't pinpoint, frightened him.

He turned to Maria, who had her head on his shoulder.

"Where's your dad?" he whispered.

There was an edge of tears in her voice as she started to speak. She hesitated. A log in the fire dislodged and crackled, flaming up.

"He's . . . in the other room with Momma and Sophie."

Maria's doing it, too, he reasoned.

Following Kathy's lead. She's struggling with the

295

weight of Blackwinter Inn on her shoulders.

"The boat, Maria? Did you . . . ?"

She shook her head.

"It's out there, but we couldn't . . . we couldn't get it. There was . . . We tried, Kevin."

"OK, don't worry. We'll think of something. Is Sophie any better?"

But before Maria could respond, Kathy approached with a plate.

"It's one of Larry's grilled hens—it's cold, but it's going to taste good if you're empty. Larry had planned such a nice dinner, and now . . ."

Just as eagerly as his hunger had arisen, so it suddenly flagged. He raised the meat to his lips, took one bite, and swallowed it with difficulty. He felt their eyes upon him.

His appetite dissolved completely.

Kathy tried to smile.

He could tell that whatever dominated her thoughts was about to be given words.

"Your dad, Kevin . . . he loved you. It was hard for him to show it."

Kevin felt an invisible hand clutching at his throat; he knew what Kathy assumed, but couldn't imagine how to explain the truth.

"He's not dead. My dad. I mean . . . Joshua . . . I saw my dad. He's not dead."

Maria slid over next to Kathy and hugged her. Kathy shut her eyes and clasped her hands together as if offering a prayer of thanksgiving.

"Oh, thank God!" she exclaimed. "Thank God. When I didn't see him with you, I thought . . . it was too much to hope for. You'd been gone so long. I went down there several hours ago to look for you. And when I couldn't find either of you, I thought both of you were . . . oh, thank God!"

The words flooded from her mouth, reminding Kevin darkly of the spider creatures pouring from the skeletal things out on the lake.

"Has Alan gone for help? That's it, isn't it?" Kathy rambled on. "Why didn't you say something immediately?"

Kevin could only stare at her, at the excited flush in her cheeks, at the eager glints of light in her eyes, spawned there by the flames. It was Maria who first intuited that Kathy's reading of things was inaccurate.

She pressed her hand atop Kathy's.

"Wait," she said. "Give Kevin a chance to explain."

But, at first, he could think of nothing to say.

Kathy tried to comfort him with her expression. He could tell she was embarrassed that she had apparently misconstrued events. Maria held the woman's hand reassuringly. Some curious metamorphosis seemed to occur, a shifting of identities in which, for a fleeting instant, Maria was the older of the two, the adult, and Kathy was the girl.

"He's not dead," Kevin repeated, the words escaping him in a dull stammer. "He's not . . . I can't . . . it's hard to make you understand because I don't understand myself."

They encouraged him.

With the fire a third companion, he began a halting account of what had transpired, or what he *thought* had transpired in the cellar. Some of the things he had experienced required a vocabulary he didn't possess. During his explanation, Kathy stopped him occasionally for clarification. And when he had concluded his narrative, he shrugged.

"I know it's impossible. But Joshua . . . he has powers . . . I could be imagining a lot of it."

He glanced down at his hands.

"I got scared," he added. "I thought Joshua had

297

trapped me, too."

It was a sudden and forceful rush of guilt; part of him wanted to cry; part insisted on being strong. Tough.

"There's still hope," Kathy murmured.

She sighed heavily.

"We have to help Larry," she said, her voice breaking slightly, a rasp that drew further sympathy from Kevin.

He looked at Maria.

"What's wrong with him? Is it Sophie?"

Kathy started to get up.

"No," said Maria. "I'll take him."

She took Kevin's hand and gently led him away from the fire; he was surprised by the chill of her touch, all the more reluctant to leave the warmth of the coals.

"Hey, you going to be OK?" he asked her.

Even in the shadows, he could see her eyes tear. He spoke again.

"I guess that's a pretty stupid question, huh? None of us will ever be the same after this. But we gotta believe that we'll make it outta here."

She half nodded, averting her eyes from him.

At the entrance to the kitchen, something darted under the table.

Kevin froze.

Images of the spider creatures branded his thoughts. Reflexively, he tried to hold Maria back, but she was hunkering down, looking under the table before he could stop her.

"What was that?" he exclaimed.

"The cat. The one we found by the lake."

Having released herself from Kevin's hold, she duck-walked toward the table.

"Kitty. Here, kitty, kitty."

Kevin squatted at her shoulder.

"Oh, hey, it's Nat King Cole."

Wrinkles of puzzlement on her brow, Maria glanced around at him.

He smiled, gesturing at the cat.

"It's FloJo's cat. The old woman who . . . who saved me. It's her cat."

Skittish, not trusting anyone, the animal took a while to slink out to them.

Maria lifted the cat into her arms and pressed her cheek against its fur.

Kevin scratched the top of its head, and within no time at all, the cat was purring. It was a restful, peaceful sound, so in contrast, Kevin thought, to the sounds of terror he had experienced since sunset.

Maria was crying.

"Hey, don't get tears on him. Cats hate water," he teased.

She shook her head, her mouth set rigidly in a stone grimace. She struggled, then broke through the barrier of a dark memory.

"They were calling for it . . . out in the boat."

"They?"

Maria squeezed the cat more firmly. It cried and clambered free, jumping awkwardly, yet landing on its feet.

"They? What do you mean by 'they'?" Kevin persisted.

In a haunting monotone, she told him of the voice in the night, the boat, and the gruesome skeletal figures.

"God, I'm sorry you had to see that, Maria."

He reached out to touch her cheek, and they embraced; all the while Kevin was recalling the spunk of the woman who referred to herself as "FloJo."

"I wouldn't have made it without her," he murmured.

They relaxed their embrace.

And Maria said, "I can't go back in there. I thought I could, but I can't."

She was staring at a hallway which led into three rooms.

"Go be with Kathy," said Kevin. "She needs somebody. You can comfort each other. I'll talk to your mom and dad . . . we'll decide what to do next."

Tears rolled down Maria's cheeks.

"Kevin . . . nothing could be done . . . Kathy told me all about it."

He let her pull away, unsure what she was alluding to.

Apprehension renewed, he walked cautiously to the opening of a dimly lit room peopled with shadows.

"Mr. Bozic?"

His eyes gradually adjusted to the lighting.

No one responded to him, but a scene began to materialize: to his right, a body on the floor covered with a blanket; to his left, Larry Bozic on his knees beside another body, also covered.

Kevin could hear the man mumbling something indecipherable in the tone used for a bedtime story, and for some reason that made the hair on the back of the boy's neck stir and stand up.

Trespassing.

That was what he felt he was doing as he started across the room. Trespassing or invading someone's sacred space. A family gathering. He didn't belong there. And then the full force of reality slammed into his chest.

His eyes shifted to the body on his right.

Oh, God . . . Mrs. Bozic?

The man on his knees slowly turned.

"Who is it?"

Kevin's tongue seemed to thicken.

"It—it's me, Kevin. I-I couldn't find my dad. Not exactly. And I'm sorry . . . God, I'm really sorry about . . ."

"Come over here, would you, Kevin?"

He had never heard Larry Bozic speak in such a tone, such a disembodied voice.

But he obeyed.

And as he approached and bent down on one knee beside the man, he whispered, "I'm really sorry."

"Kevin? It is you, isn't it?" said Larry.

There was enough light in the room to allow Kevin to survey the man's expression, the network of wrinkles on his brow, the puffiness beneath his eyes, the curious hollowness of his cheeks. In fact, the hollowness gave Larry Bozic's face a likeness to a partially deflated football.

The man moved his hands very slowly and gently, touching the blanket which covered his daughter as a pianist would touch the keys.

"Yes, sir. It's me. Maria and Kathy, they're out by the fire. And, like I said, I haven't found my dad. Not yet. Not quite."

"Did you see what happened to my baby?" said Larry.

Kevin felt his chest balloon with cold air.

"No, sir. Not exactly. Joshua's to blame. I'm pretty sure of that."

"See this."

And the man lifted the blanket.

Kevin gritted his teeth. Took a quick look. Glanced away.

Took a longer look before he twisted aside and shut his eyes.

Nausea gripped him.

The sweat beading on his forehead was ice cold.

As he started to push away, Larry grabbed his arm and held him.

"Wait, son. Wait. I have to talk to someone about this."

In that moment of rising horror, Kevin could think only one thought:

He's gone.

The old Larry Bozic. Larry Bozic, the life of any get-together. Jokester. Prankster. Beer drinker. Hail-fellow well met. Man of laughter.

He's gone.

"I have to talk. Please. Please hear me out," the man continued. "Someone has to."

Reluctantly Kevin surrendered to his hold.

"We . . . we have to decide what to do," said Kevin, hoping they could return to the front room and the fireplace and the spectacle of life rather than death.

"No. This first. Listen to me. I don't know what to believe."

Kevin stared at the floor.

The man talked softly and with conviction as if the words had been released from some inner prison, having been denied voice for years and years.

"I've never believed in the supernatural. I thought it was just something fictional, you know, something primitive man created to explain a world that seemed mysterious to him. But I've seen things . . . and Kathy has, too. And Maria. And you. I don't know what I believe anymore."

Kevin cleared his throat, but could find no words to respond. He could only listen.

"My wife. My baby. I brought them to Blackwinter because it was a good place. And my friends. Mike and Sarah — Lord God."

"It's all Joshua," said Kevin.

Larry looked into the boy's face.

"But who is he?"

"He's a demon."

"Is he Satan? Does he come from the devil? It's not something I've ever believed in. Never."

Kevin shrugged.

"He's evil. And he can't be laughed away."

There was silence.

Eventually Kevin stood and watched as Larry stroked the blanket covering his daughter, then rose. Together, man and boy left the room.

3

Kathy and Maria joined them on another search along the shore for the fishing boat, but it was a futile effort. The cold fog had redoubled itself, and Kevin could see that Larry and Maria could muster no real enthusiasm for a possible confrontation with the occupants of that boat—if, indeed, those occupants continued to drift upon the night lake.

When the hapless foursome returned to the inn, Kevin and Maria built up the fire while Kathy fixed hot drinks and Larry sat alone, like a derelict vessel on a strange sea of thought.

"The fog should start clearing at dawn," said Kevin. "I think we should stay right here and wait out the night." .

"I agree," said Kathy. "Except . . . the only thing is . . . well, won't Joshua try to attack us? How could we stop him if he did?"

"Kevin can protect us," said Maria. "He can . . . he has powers of his own. I've seen what he can do."

"No," Kevin responded. "I mean . . . I can't be sure of them. We're in a lot of danger staying. We just have to hope that Joshua's satisfied. It's his. Blackwinter Inn is his. It's what he wanted. That should be enough to satisfy him, so maybe he'll leave us alone. And in the morning we'll get the boat and go, or maybe somebody will find us. By then, somebody may be looking for the

303

old woman, for FloJo."

Hearing his own words, Kevin was almost convinced. Yes, there was hope. Wait things out.

Minutes passed, in which they lapsed into a darkly expectant reverie by the fire. Every sound instantly alerted them to the possibility that Joshua—in one form or another—had returned.

Maria sat near her father.

Kathy stared into the flames.

Kevin petted Nat King Cole, the cat having left the kitchen and rejoined them.

Deep into their reverie, Larry suddenly directed a question at Kevin.

"Where do they come from? Joshua's powers? Where?"

All the humor had drained from Larry's face. His eyes bore down on Kevin—eyes that were sad and serious and, most of all, perplexed.

Kevin could feel that Kathy and Maria were looking at him, too; the magnetic force of their expectation seemed to weaken him, to sap his energy. He concentrated on the cat, stroking behind its ears, comforted by its steady purring.

"What I know is what he told me," Kevin began, and searched his way through a repetition of Joshua's explanation, discovering new meanings to various parts of the narrative. Yet, everything resolved itself to a single focus.

"The spring," said Kevin. "If Joshua's telling the truth, it's that spring down in the cellar. It brought him back to life. It gave him powers—to change shapes and . . . and to live forever. It's like he wants revenge on most everybody who has anything to do with Blackwinter."

"The spring?" Larry echoed. "A supernatural spring?"

Kevin nodded.

"At first, you know, I didn't believe it, but what else could explain what has happened and what he can do?"

"It restored his life?" Larry muttered, obviously wrestling with the impossible notion.

"They killed him and buried him where the spring ran over his body—and he came back to life."

"What about the disease?" asked Kathy.

"You mean the 'Red Death'?"

"Yes, does that come from the spring, too?"

"No, or at least I don't think so. His mother . . . Joshua's mother had it and passed it on to him."

Kathy frowned.

"What I have trouble understanding is how Sophie apparently was infected with it and lived for hours, while Gina was struck by it and died instantly."

Kevin suddenly thought of the vision of the elderly couple on the lake.

"Mrs. Davenport's grandfather—I think he had it for a long, long time. Maybe some people die of it right away and others have it and don't die for a while because they're stronger or something."

Maria pitched up, away from her father.

"But Kevin can protect us from the sickness and from Joshua," she exclaimed. "Tell them, Kevin. Tell them we're not helpless."

"Is there . . . is there something you can do?" Kathy's eyes were fixed on the boy.

Downplaying his abilities, Kevin recounted his near-death experience and its aftereffects, especially the manner in which his will had been strengthened and the capacity he now had to occasionally glimpse the future as well as the past.

"Joshua's more powerful than I am. I think we're at his mercy," he added.

"I feel like our plan to wait is the best idea," said Kathy. "We're bound to be able to find that fishing boat when the fog clears."

Maria started to speak, then turned and gazed at the fire.

Larry quietly fidgeted with his hands, apparently lost in thought.

"I have one other idea," Kevin heard himself say. It wasn't a well-conceived idea, he admitted that. But he felt it was time to mention it.

Kathy encouraged him.

"Well," he said, "it's a pretty desperate idea, but maybe it would work. I've been thinking we could set the whole building on fire and all go down by the shore and maybe somebody would see the flames. There's a fire tower on Jackson Lake—they'd see the fire maybe."

Kevin leaned back, surprised that the idea sounded reasonably good.

Kathy pondered it a moment, glanced at Maria and Larry, and then said, "But what about Alan? What about your dad?"

Something hot and sharp stabbed at Kevin's chest.

She was right. Until they knew for certain where his dad was, destroying the inn would be out of the question.

"Yeah, OK," he murmured. "I forgot."

"We can wait it out," said Kathy, generating as much optimism as she could.

The talking waned; everyone appeared exhausted, a psychological reaction more than a physical one.

"If y'all want to sleep a little," said Kevin, "I can keep a watch. I'm not sleepy."

Kathy smiled.

"Thanks. We could use it, couldn't we, Maria?"

The girl managed a weak smile.

"I wish Daddy would sleep," she said.

Larry mumbled something more about the spring;

Maria hugged him.

Kevin felt sorry for the man—he had lost his wife and daughter. Maria, her sister. And Kathy . . . possibly a husband.

But, thankfully, reality was obliterated somewhat by the radiating warmth of the fire; Kathy and Maria closed their eyes and within fifteen or twenty minutes, it was evident to Kevin that they were asleep.

Larry held Maria against his shoulder; his expression was blank, reminding Kevin of a zombie from a horror movie.

Continuing to hold and pet the cat, Kevin mused upon potential rescue scenarios; but mostly he thought about the figure in the cellar—the one he had seen when he had found himself in some incredible hallucination of past events.

His eyelids grew heavy.

The cat purred.

The fire enveloped the scene in an amber glow.

Suddenly Kevin blinked awake.

He felt an electrical shock of fear. He had been asleep.

How long? How long was I asleep? God, I have to stay awake.

He glanced around.

And his heart rose into his throat.

Kathy was sleeping. So was Maria.

But Larry had disappeared.

4

Flashlight in hand, Kevin ran to the front door, believing that the man had gone down to the lake to look again for the fishing boat. The boy's nerves came alive like ants being stirred from their mound.

God, where is he?

He called out for him, but the fog easily crushed his words. Through torn places in the curtain of moisture and darkness, he forced the beam.

No trace of Larry Bozic.

He raced back to the inn and was met by Maria.

"Kevin, stop him! Please, stop him!"

Near the fireplace Kathy had awakened and was clutching Larry's arm.

God, what is he doing?

"Larry? Larry, no."

Kathy continued to tug at the man's arm.

"Put her down, Larry," she persisted. "There's no use. Please."

In Larry Bozic's arms rested the corpse of his daughter, Sophie.

Kevin approached, and Kathy said, "Talk to him. He's in such grief."

Like a plodding robot, Larry marched away from the fireplace toward the entrance to the cellar.

"What's he trying to do?" Kevin asked Kathy.

"The spring. He said something about the spring."

Kevin scrambled forward and planted himself in the man's path.

"Why are you doing this?" he exclaimed, staring into a gray, ghostly face.

Larry hesitated a moment and repositioned his hold on his daughter. The blanket which had been covering her body fell away. He surveyed her disease-ravaged flesh.

"It's my only hope. You said the spring brought Joshua back to life. It can do the same for Sophie and Gina."

Kevin felt the backs of his knees weaken.

"Oh, damn," he whispered to himself as the man pushed on toward the cellar entrance.

308

Kathy and Maria watched from a distance, though Kathy made a move to help, only to be gestured away by Kevin.

Slowly, methodically, Larry continued.

Kevin kept pace with him.

"It won't work," the boy insisted. "Joshua came back to life, but as an evil thing. Is that what you want for Sophie? She'll become a demon just like Joshua. Is that what you want?"

Time seemed to balance on the scene as Larry paused.

Kevin heard every sound that the old inn was producing—every secret tick, every note of sentience.

"Don't take her to the spring," he murmured.

Larry turned and, in an apologetic voice, said, "It's my only hope."

And then he began to descend the steps into the cellar.

Chapter XIX

1

Kevin heard every one of the man's footsteps pound at his temples. It was a helpless feeling, watching him carry off the shrunken, darkened corpse of Sophie, and fearing the transformation that might occur.

At the top of the stairs, Kathy and Maria huddled near Kevin.

"Please try again to stop him," Maria whispered. "Please."

Kevin couldn't keep an edge of anger from framing his words.

"His mind's made up," he exclaimed. "I told him what could happen. I warned him."

"It's the grief," Kathy stated quietly. "He has to find some way of dealing with the grief. This is his way."

"We have to try and stop him." said Maria.

She was fighting tears, and nothing Kathy or Kevin could say or do would console her.

Larry had walked deep into the cellar, crossing into the shadows created by the massive wine barrels.

"It's dangerous," said Kevin. "Joshua's there. He's back in there deciding what he's going to do next."

Suddenly Maria tore away from them.

"Maria!" Kathy called out.

But the girl ran, her footsteps echoing out from the stone floor.

Kevin's body stiffened.

"God, no. They'll both be killed," he exclaimed.

He scrambled down the stairs. Then slowed.

Kathy caught up with him.

"What is it?" she murmured.

"I . . . I don't know. I'm not sure."

Beyond them, at the rear of the cellar where the spring formed tiny rivulets through the stone, Maria was kneeling beside her father who had lowered the corpse of Sophie to the floor.

The shadows had been brushed aside by a curious white light which nimbused Maria and her father like a soft spotlight or a halo. It appeared that Maria was talking to her father, but neither Kathy nor Kevin could discern her words.

"I think I've seen that light," Kathy observed. "Upstairs . . . Sophie . . . some illumination from within her. It's so strange."

Kevin discovered that as he was listening to Kathy, holding his breath, thoughts swirled like dust devils. The merest suggestion of a solution to all their problems was emerging. Yet, it remained too undeveloped for him to articulate.

They waited.

And watched.

And hoped.

Several minutes slipped away.

The scene of Maria and Larry and the corpse of Sophie at the spring hadn't changed.

"We'll lose them," Kevin mumbled. "Like we lost the Davenports and Sophie and Mrs. Bozic and FloJo . . . and my dad."

"No," said Kathy. "No, don't let yourself believe

that."

"Joshua has control," Kevin added, though even as he spoke, that nebulous solution, its faintest outline, was materializing. It was approaching inexorably—like the dawn.

"Oh, dear God, look!" Kathy exclaimed, her voice ringing with surprise and joy.

Shadow and light. Movement.

Larry had staggered to his feet.

They were returning.

And the solution, once as distant as another galaxy, streamed nearer.

"He's changed his mind," said Kevin, hoping wildly that he was correct.

"Dear God. Thank goodness," said Kathy.

Maria led her father forward, and when they had reached Kathy and Kevin, Larry glanced down at the corpse of his daughter and said, "I don't want her to become a monster."

No other words seemed necessary.

The foursome climbed the stairs leading out of the cellar; Larry returned his daughter's body to the room from which he had taken it. Kathy followed and covered the body with a blanket.

At the fireplace, Kevin and Maria embraced.

"You did a brave and good thing," he told her.

"I had to," she replied. "It wasn't a matter of being brave or good."

And in Kevin's thoughts the solution gathered clarity.

He waited for Larry and Kathy to join them. He stoked the fire and then turned to address them; something resembling hope beamed out from his expression.

"I think I have a way. A way to stop Joshua forever."

There was an understandable degree of doubt in their eyes, but they saw a revival in Kevin's spirit—it presaged the forming of a new bond among them.

"It's going to sound like a far-fetched possibility. You probably won't think it will work, but I think it will."

Exasperated, Kathy exclaimed, "Tell us what it is! Don't keep us in suspense!"

Kevin hunkered down, his back to the fire.

"The answer is the spring. I realize it now. It's been the answer all along."

"Kevin, no. What do you mean?" said Maria, apprehension evident in her tone.

Before Kevin could continue, he heard it.

His eyes automatically met Kathy's.

She hears it, too.

Maria pressed herself to attention.

"Kevin?"

And Larry cocked his head to one side. Some of his former vitality had returned, but a disquieting confusion and anxiety loomed always close by.

The pool.

As if it were a psychic vision, Kevin could see it.

Joshua in the pool in the bowels of the cellar.

The transformation had begun.

"Kathy? Kevin? What's going on?"

Maria stood up, clenching and unclenching her fists.

"Quiet!" Kevin yelled.

He could imagine the scene that was unfolding at the pool. Joshua into demon. Demon into thousands of clawed, night creatures which skittered along like spiders and delivered death to whatever they confronted.

"We have to get out of here," he exclaimed, straining to keep his voice as calm as possible.

"From the cellar," said Kathy. "They're coming from the cellar, aren't they?"

Kevin nodded.

And Maria appeared to understand.

"Those things in the lake . . . Joshua's sending them to—"

313

"Help your dad to the front door," said Kevin, cutting her off. "Come on, let's move."

A weapon. If we only had a weapon.

His thoughts scattered as if blown by an inner wind.

Where can we go to get away from them?

There's no place to hide.

"Grab the flashlight," he called out to Kathy.

If nothing more, it could be used as a weapon, he reasoned: But what good will it do against those creatures?

He could feel the panic rising in him as his three companions hurried to the front door.

"Kevin, there's the axe," said Maria, pointing to the tool they had chopped wood with the night before.

Kevin hefted it, and it felt solid and substantial in his grip.

Behind him, the approach of the creatures continued; they were moving slowly, but the clicking sounds their claws made on the stone floor of the cellar was loud and unnerving.

Suddenly Kathy screamed.

At the door, she turned; the flashlight beam angled off wildly.

"They're out there, Kevin!"

He stared at her in disbelief.

Oh, God. Help us.

He took the flashlight from her and aimed it out beyond the porch.

The light sent them into a frenzy. Hundreds of them.

"Upstairs!" he shouted. "Hurry!"

The ensuing seconds passed in a surrealistic collage, a blur of movement and sound—and a sense, a *feel,* of one mass of those creatures surrounding the inn, another crawling up from the cellar.

Kevin pushed and prodded; Kathy helped Maria pull her father up the dark stairs. But the man struggled against them, bound, as if in a straitjacket, by his own fear and bewilderment. And something more.

Insane? Kevin wondered. Has he cracked up completely? My God, who could blame him?

They reached the first landing; Kevin, flashlight in one hand and axe in the other, wheeled around to check on the advance of the creatures. He couldn't see them, but he could hear them, their inexorable clawing, scratching movement up the cellar stairs.

Kathy and Maria had stopped and were hunkered down next to Larry.

"God, you have to keep going," Kevin exclaimed.

"Daddy, please, come on."

They were tugging at the man; he was on his knees, a hand clamped onto the railing.

"We can't budge him," said Kathy, her voice lined with fear.

Kevin pressed close to Larry Bozic, shining the flashlight in his face.

"We have to keep going. Don't you understand that?" he cried.

"No," said Larry. "I've gone far enough. Far enough."

Kevin glanced up at Kathy and Maria.

"You two go on up to the bell tower."

They hesitated.

"I won't leave without Daddy," said Maria.

Frightened, angered, Kevin laid the axe down and clutched at Larry's shoulder.

"You're putting everybody in danger," he shouted into the man's face. "Can't you see that?"

Skittering, clicking—a rushing, terrifying clamor below them.

The spider creatures were at the bottom of the stairs.

"See them!"

Kevin forced Larry's head around so that his attention was directed at the stairs; the flashlight beam captured the first wave of the creatures. They shrieked at the light, held back momentarily, but then began again their methodical advance.

"See them!" Kevin exclaimed.

And he could detect in Larry's eyes a glinting of recognition. And horror.

The man stirred; his lips moved and a strangled gurgle issued from his throat.

"Come on!" Kevin shouted.

Larry relaxed his hold on the railing.

Kevin handed the flashlight to Kathy as Maria helped her father get to his feet.

"Get up to the tower," the boy commanded.

He watched as they scrambled behind the path of light. Then he turned and kicked frantically at two of the creatures; scores of their companions followed. Desperately Kevin beat at them with the dull head of the axe, smashing several. But his actions seemed only to excite the rolling mass of them.

They continued up the stairs like a dark carpet spreading step by step.

Kevin stumbled halfway up the next flight; the stairwell had lapsed into a realm of shadows as Kathy and Maria and Larry climbed still higher with the flashlight.

The creatures animated those shadows, never slowing.

It would be suicide to stand and battle them. Kevin knew that, but in the clutch of terror and of anger triggered by an inner survival mechanism, he turned, raised the axe above his head, and buried the blade in one of the creatures two steps below him. Wood splintered and the blade split open the creature, pinned it against the stair.

Kevin jerked at the axe handle, but the blade had been buried too deeply; he couldn't force it loose.

"Kevin! Hurry, for God's sake," Kathy called out from above.

She and Maria and Larry had made it to the top landing, and Maria was near the small door leading to the tower.

One of the creatures scrambled up the axe handle before Kevin could let go; it scraped a claw across his hand, drawing blood. He shrieked in pain and fell backward, slamming his buttocks against a stair and whiplashing his neck.

He could hear them, feel them coming; pain flared throughout his body, and yet fear drove him, a catalyst for surmounting the discomfort. He pushed himself to his feet. Ahead of him, Maria and Larry had slipped through the opening onto the first landing of the tower.

Kathy was waiting for him.

"Kevin!"

"Go on!" he called back.

But his thoughts raced beyond him.

What next?

Was the tower such a good idea? he wondered.

We'll be trapped.

He sprinted for the tower steps. It occurred to him suddenly, frighteningly, that he had become the leader of their pathetic little group—with Larry still suffering from shock and grief, Kathy and Maria had turned to him.

At the tower steps, Kathy reached out, and even as he caught her hand, he was thinking:

Why me?

Why should I be the one?

Dad. God, I need you, dad.

I can't do this.

317

But there was no time for self-doubt.

He shoved Kathy through the opening; then, instinctively, he twisted around at the clamor below him. A half a dozen of the creatures were at his feet. He kicked viciously. Two managed to slice at his ankles.

He cried out but felt Kathy and Maria tugging at him.

He struggled, frog-kicking his legs.

And made it.

"Shut the door!" he shouted.

Once inside the dark pocket of a room he tried to catch his breath.

Kathy focused the light on the door. And beyond it, the creatures scratched and tore at the wood, and as they massed against it, the door threatened to cave in.

"Kevin!" Kathy screamed.

He rolled over and sat upon the door.

"Give me some room," he exclaimed.

Kathy, flashlight in hand, gestured for Maria to join her father in the corner. The creatures continued to pulse forward, their predatory intent too strong to ward off.

"God, you have to concentrate," Kevin whispered intensely to himself.

But the noise, the terrifying clatter of the creatures, made it all but impossible for him to draw upon the supranormal power of his will.

Concentrate.

Do it.

Stop time.

Float free.

Kathy huddled with Maria and Larry; Kevin forced himself not to look at them—the fear in their faces would destroy his concentration.

"Hold the light away," he said.

Reflexively Kathy pooled it at her feet so that Kevin

was plunged immediately into shadow.

He pressed down with all his might, but he had assumed an awkward sitting position; he doubted he could hold off the crush of the demonic creatures.

Stop time.

Float free.

Cold drops of sweat beaded on his forehead.

He could feel the anticipation of his companions.

They're depending on me.

His jaw tightened. Spasms rippled through his body. He closed his eyes.

Then the first sensation of an incredible lightness of being.

He drifted a few inches above himself and felt the pressure of the creatures relent slightly; their clawing and tearing eased up.

It's working. God, it's working.

Time stopped.

He became a silhouette of stone in the shadows.

How long he remained that way he couldn't determine.

Drifting.

Floating.

The clawing of the creatures became a mere susurrus, a muted rustling.

The strength of his will had made them retreat.

For the moment, he and his companions were safe. But as he floated, a peace came over Kevin. A spectacularly bright light beyond a tunnel of darkness drew him like a powerful magnet.

He fought its pull.

And when he snapped back into his body, he groaned. All around him the sound of glass breaking set his nerves on fire.

He blinked his eyes.

On her hands and knees, Maria scrambled toward

him.

"You did it!" she was exclaiming as he tried to focus on her. Shards of glass continued intermittently to crash to the floor.

She hugged his neck; the warmth of her touch amid the horror nearly overwhelmed him.

Kathy, a thunderstruck expression on her face, quietly scanned the room with the flashlight beam and uncovered a curious sight: the panels of mirrors which had covered each wall had been destroyed, apparently by the exercise of Kevin's will.

On two of the walls were windows looking out upon the roofline of the inn.

But Kevin's attention had shifted elsewhere.

He made his way over to Maria's father.

"They're gone," he said to the man. "For now, they're gone. For now, we're safe."

And the man nodded and seemed to understand.

3

"Are they really gone?"

Maria searched Kevin's expression for the truth.

"God, I hope so," he replied. "But . . . I doubt that Joshua will give up until he's driven us off or until we're all . . ."

He hesitated, shifting his position on the floor. The four of them had moved from the lower landing of the bell tower to the upper landing. Once again, a small, rectangular door separated the landings. Above the landing was a cupola and bell, and circling the room were panels of glass, which, during the day, afforded a viewer an impressive panorama of the island and lake.

"Daddy's still in bad shape. He's never . . ." She stopped to swallow back tears. Kevin held her.

"There's nothing we can do, Maria, but try to survive."

He glanced to one side where Larry was leaning against a wall, slumped over, locked in a parody of sleep. But Kevin's concern had gravitated to Kathy, who appeared to be in a great deal of discomfort as she sat, legs splayed out in front of her, across the room.

"Hey, are you all right?" he asked her.

Through the shadows created by the oval of the flashlight beam, she returned a weak smile.

"A little punk. I wish I had some water. I'm so thirsty."

She pressed her fingertips onto her stomach and added, "*Both* of us are thirsty, I imagine."

The comment slipped readily past Kevin; Maria, however, became suddenly animated.

"Did you say, 'both of us'?"

Kathy shook her head and allowed a tired smile to inch across her face.

"I had pictured some romantic setting with Alan," she said. "Some quiet and tender moment to break the news to him—not this."

Maria moved over to her and embraced her.

"Is this for real?" the girl asked.

Kathy nodded.

Puzzled, Kevin said, "What are you talking about?"

Maria looked at him and smirked.

"Kevin, are you dense?"

He shrugged.

Maria and Kathy exchanged smiles.

"She's going to have a baby," said Maria.

Kevin's mouth fell open.

"No, it can't be," he exclaimed.

"Yes, it can," said Kathy matter-of-factly, a touch of a smile lingering at one corner of her mouth.

"I think it's great. Don't you, Kevin?" said Maria.

The incongruity of it all hit him full force.

Strange patterns of lines and colors and shapes filled his thoughts. And the image of a baby. A little brother? But mostly he thought of his dad, and for a disconcerting run of seconds, he couldn't call up his dad's face. He couldn't think of words, either.

"It's . . . a surprise," he managed to comment finally.

"Your dad and I want this baby very much," said Kathy.

Something in her tone, something about the distant sparkle in her eyes swept away all of Kevin's confusion and doubt and, perhaps, jealousy.

"I'm . . . I'm glad. I really am."

And he went to her and they embraced.

It was a good moment, one seemingly isolated from reality.

"Daddy, did you hear the news?"

Maria edged over close to her father.

"Kathy's going to have a baby."

By degrees, as Maria repeated the words, recognition glimmered.

"That's good," Larry eventually murmured. "Good news."

Then Maria led him across the room.

Kevin studied the man.

Is he pulling out of it?

It was virtually impossible to tell.

But Kathy's revelation appeared to reforge a bond among them. And even as Kevin continued to listen for the return of the creatures, he thought again about a plan that was becoming clearer by the second—a plan that could deliver them from Joshua's evil.

"I've got something to say," he exclaimed after the small talk surrounding Kathy's news had waned. "Like I said before, it's pretty farfetched. It's like something out of an H. G. Wells story, but I think I can do it. If it works, we won't have to worry about Joshua anymore . . . it might even save my dad."

He saw Kathy's eyes tear, and then he quickly added, "It's maybe not really possible. If a whole lot of strange things hadn't happened, I'd say it was definitely impossible. But, well, here's what I'd like to try."

They listened. At any other moment in their lives, they would have laughed at his idea and called it ridiculous. Time travel. It was, indeed, the stuff of science fiction and not the real world.

Yet, Blackwinter Inn resided on the borderland between dimensions.

"I'll take myself back there if I can . . . to the death of Joshua. Remember, he told me it was the spring that gave him his powers, his immortality . . . so what I'm thinking is I'll wait till those men bury him and then I'll dig him up and move his body away from the spring . . . so he'll stay dead . . . and everything that's happened . . . it'll be like nothing horrible ever happened."

They wanted to believe him. They tried. And for several minutes they talked—all but Larry, who remained silent.

"When will you go?" asked Maria.

"I'd better do it right away," said Kevin.

He glanced at Kathy and she touched his hand softly.

"Bring him back. Please. If you find him, bring your dad back to me. To us."

He felt weak all over, and yet more determined than ever to attempt the crazy, unbelievable plan.

For Maria and her father.

For Kathy.

And, perhaps most of all, for his dad and the coming child.

"I'm going to turn off the flashlight for a while—save the battery. If the creatures don't come back soon, then

323

I'll head for the cellar."

"Let me go with you," said Maria.

"No. You should be here. Your dad and Kathy need you."

He clicked off the flashlight; the room blackened into almost palpable darkness.

He thought he heard Larry groan.

Poor damn guy.

In the darkness, Kevin conjured up pleasant images of his three companions: Larry, laughing, talking, can of beer in hand; Kathy, soft, pretty, yet an inner fabric as tough as steel; Maria, becoming a woman—he thought of her in her gymnastics outfit tiptoeing atop a balance beam.

Minutes slid by, mostly in silence.

Kevin reasoned that his plan could work; though not all of his reluctance had dissolved.

They're counting on me.

Maria and Larry.

Kathy and the child inside her.

Dad.

"I wonder where the cat went."

It was Maria's comment, an innocent one, and magically, it changed the tenor of Kevin's concerns.

"Geez, I hope it got away," he said.

"I should have carried it up with us," Maria murmured.

"Cats can take care of themselves," said Kevin. "It's down there, hiding somewhere."

"Sorta like us," whispered Maria.

There was a note of sadness in her voice; Kevin groped for her hand, wanting to squeeze it, a gesture of reassurance. But at that instant, they heard a thump.

"Listen!" Kathy exclaimed.

A second thump. And a third.

The creatures.

They were at the door of the first landing.

Then a noise like that of marbles rolling across a hardwood floor.

"Kevin, they're on the roof," said Maria.

God, no.

Stay calm, Kevin told himself.

He would have to be ready to exercise his will again. That realization sent a chill jagging up his spine.

Before he could switch on the flashlight, he heard them at the windows, tapping like raindrops; then a more intense clatter. Kathy and Maria scrambled into the center of the room.

The flashlight beam captured the first wave of the creatures; they amassed on the window ledges, clawing, clambering over one another until they virtually covered the glass.

Again, the light excited them, sending them into a frenzy of clicking.

Kevin swung the beam around, catching the figure of Larry as he sat staring at the massing of the creatures. The man's expression was that of an insect placidly feeding upon a leaf.

Kevin shuddered and reflexively pressed his thumb on the off switch.

Darkness seemed to quiet the creatures somewhat.

Hands trembling, Kevin set the flashlight down and it rolled to one side.

"I'm going below," he exclaimed.

Maria followed him through the opening.

"Can they break the glass?" she asked.

"I don't know. Hope to God they can't."

He positioned himself over the door leading from the lower landing to the third floor of the inn. The clatter of the creatures had lapsed into a less terrifying degree of sound—something like the drone of crickets or other night insects.

"I can't hear them below us," said Maria.

"Me either. I think it might be a good time for me to go to the cellar."

"What if they hear you? We have to do something to distract them first."

Maria was right, he reasoned.

"Kevin!"

Kathy's voice, balanced on a rim of fear, pressed down upon them from the upper landing.

"Kevin, come up here quickly. Hurry."

He and Maria negotiated the steps as rapidly as the darkness would allow. Kathy met them at the opening.

"He's been at the glass . . . talking to them. He has the flashlight. I think he's going to break the glass."

A blinding fear held Kevin in its grip.

"Daddy!" Maria exclaimed.

Kevin instinctively clutched at her.

"No, stay away from him."

Here was the scene: Across the room, Larry had switched on the flashlight and had positioned himself close to the glass where he was muttering at the creatures and teasing them by clicking the light on and off.

Good God, Kevin thought. *What's he trying to do?*

"Daddy?" Maria whispered.

She and Kevin began moving very cautiously toward him.

When the beam was on, they could see the creatures flood against the glass . . . they could see the glass appear to sag inward.

"God, they're gonna break it," Kevin hissed through clenched teeth.

And everywhere Larry put a hand and arm upon the glass, the creatures would swarm, forming there an outline of his appendage.

It was a breathless scene of horror.

Then Larry saw them approaching. He raised the

326

flashlight threateningly.

"Keep away from me," he said.

Kevin managed to free his tongue.

"If you excite the creatures, they're gonna break the glass. Don't get them all upset. Please, please don't."

"Break the glass?" the man echoed.

He half turned. The beam captured the wild, disoriented look in his eyes.

And then he did something which lifted the terror of the moment to a new level: He took the head of the flashlight and tapped it against the glass—two or three times—hard taps.

"God, stop it!" Kevin cried.

"Daddy, please!"

"Break the glass and let them in?"

Kevin silently calculated whether he could rush the man and wrest the light from him—or would it possibly trigger Larry to smash the glass?

The man laughed softly. A small boy's giggle.

He continued to tap at the glass, each tap echoing the sound of a near break.

"Oh, please, do something," said Kathy.

Suddenly Maria pulled away from Kevin's hold.

"Daddy? Daddy, listen to me."

She stood within a few feet of him.

Momentarily he ceased tapping.

"Would you like them to come in?" he murmured. "They want to come in. I hear the voices in my head. They're asking me. Begging me."

"Daddy, it's Maria. Your daughter, Maria. Please look at me."

Confused, the man held the flashlight with both hands. The hands trembled.

"They're begging me," he whispered.

"This is Maria, Daddy. Please hand me the flashlight."

327

The display of courage on Maria's part created a warmth in Kevin's chest.

Beyond the glass, the creatures softened their clatter.

"Daddy?"

Maria slowly extended her hand.

For what seemed an eternity to Kevin, Larry stared at that hand before speaking.

"Maria, is it you?"

"Yes, Daddy. Hand me the flashlight. Please."

"Here, Maria. Here it is. Help me out, couldja?"

It was an excruciating span of seconds which passed as the man finally handed over the flashlight to Maria.

Kevin felt all the air being punched out of his lungs as he watched father and daughter embrace.

How close had they come to having the creatures pour into the room?

The thought caused Kevin's stomach to roil.

There was a stunned silence as Maria continued to hold her father, much as a mother would comfort a son.

"I know how to draw the creatures away," said Kathy. "Draw them away so you can make it to the cellar."

She stepped forward and took the flashlight from Maria.

Kevin followed her to the panel of glass which looked out upon the roofline.

Pooling the light at her feet, Kathy explained what she had in mind.

"The creatures will go wherever the beam is directed. If I stand here and aim it at the end of the roofline, then I think they'll be drawn to that spot — like moths. And you can get away to the cellar and try your plan."

Kevin hesitated. He was doubtful, but he didn't have a better idea.

"OK. I'll go to the landing below us and watch what they do."

He glanced from Kathy to Maria and her father, realizing that he might never see them again.

"If this works, you'll know," he said. "Take care of yourselves."

Kathy forced a weary smile.

"We will."

He slipped through the opening, climbing down into the darkness of the lower landing.

No turning back. Got to try this.

He wished he had said something to Maria. Something more personal.

Don't think about it.

Some of the creatures filled the blackness beyond the windows, but when Kathy directed the beam out onto the roofline, they stirred.

Come on, damn you. Go to the light.

The beam slanted down from above, spearing through the fog and the chill night air. The clicking and clawing sounds increased, and then, gradually, the creatures began to gravitate toward the oval of light.

God, it's working.

His nerves were hot needles.

He heard someone coming down the steps from the upper landing.

"Maria?"

"Be careful, Kevin. I just wanted to tell you to be careful."

It occurred to him that she had been so strong in the face of horror. Some tears, but they had been expected, normal tears of grief. She had lost her sister, her mother . . . and perhaps her father.

"Thanks," he said. "You be careful, too."

He wanted to say more; feelings warred within him. And though Kathy had bandaged the cuts made by the creatures, he felt the sting of those wounds and the dull ache of exhaustion.

"You'll find him. I know you will," said Maria. "Your dad, I mean. Somehow your plan will work."

Shadows covered most of her face.

She sounded older. More mature.

"I'm probably wrong," he said. "If you think about it . . . going back in time. It's impossible. Maybe I dreamed up what happened earlier. Maybe I'll get down to the cellar and see that I was wrong."

"No. Because it's our best chance."

Confidence was couched in each of her words.

"Listen," he said. "You watch out for Kathy and your dad, OK?"

"I will."

Kevin turned his attention to the beam of light beyond the window. The creatures were not gathering at the end of the roofline as rapidly as before. Some, in fact, were spinning off to one side or the other as if confused; some were wandering back toward the tower.

And Kevin thought he noticed something else.

"Does it seem to you like the flashlight's gettin' dimmer?"

"Yeah, a little, I guess," said Maria. "But it's working, isn't it? It has to work."

Kevin sighed.

"As soon as more of them pull away from the windows, I'll go."

"I wish I could help," Maria whispered.

"You can. You are. Help the adults."

Perhaps it was the tension of the moment, perhaps it was the way in which he had said the word 'adults,' but whatever it was, both of them chuckled.

"I feel like we're the adults now," she said.

"Me, too."

And that stone cold realization ended the mirth.

"Daddy . . . he needs lots of help," said Maria, absently, changing the subject as if her mind were some insect which couldn't remain long on any resting place.

"We gotta keep up hope, Maria. When daylight comes, we'll get free of here."

"Daddy's all I'm gonna have."

"Don't start cryin'."

"I won't."

Kevin went to one of the windows; of course, Maria had every right to cry. He simply wished she wouldn't. Not then. Not at what seemed to him to be such a crucial moment, one requiring as much concentration and good judgment as possible.

A few of the creatures stirred, lifting their claws, inviting him to open the window and join them. He shuddered at the thought of being out there with them.

"Kevin, the light!"

The anxiety in Maria's voice jolted him.

Then he, too, saw what had provoked her exclamation: Kathy's flashlight was growing dimmer by the second.

"Damn," he whispered.

What now?

God, what can we do?

"Get ready to go, Kevin."

He looked toward his companion, searching for the outline of her face in the shadows.

"What?"

"Open the door and start down. I can draw them off."

"How?"

"Never mind. Just do it. We're running out of time, Kevin. We have to do something. Trust me. I can do this. I want to do this."

There was so much authority in her words, such a convincing tone to them, that Kevin hesitated only briefly, and then he cautiously pulled open the small door.

331

"Tell me what you're going to do, Maria."

"No. I can't," she replied. "Go on."

She was right about one thing, he admitted—there was little time. Who could anticipate what Joshua might do next? Something worse than the spider creatures perhaps.

"Be careful. OK?" he said to her as he began to squeeze through the opening and to touch the rungs of the steps.

Maria moved away from the opening.

Kevin could hear the clicking of the creatures.

And then he heard something almost beyond his comprehension: a window sliding open, followed by the sound of that same window shutting resolutely.

For a second or more he felt paralyzed.

Kathy's scream freed his legs to move.

"Maria!" he shouted.

He scrambled back onto the landing.

The scene reeled forward, devoid suddenly of sound, devoid of dimension except for the single image of the girl balancing herself as she made her way along the roofline just as he had seen her one day at gymnastics practice.

She was drawing the spider creatures.

Mercifully, the flashlight blinked off before Kevin could witness their attack. Above him, Kathy was screaming and crying. He never heard Maria make a sound.

Run, an inner voice demanded.

The cellar.

Now.

He turned. He clambered down to the third floor and continued as fast as the darkness permitted.

And he forced himself not to think.

About Maria.

About anything except getting to the cellar and executing his plan.

One word. Only one word clawed at his throat, wanting desperately to be given voice:

Dad! Dad! Dad!

Chapter XX

1

The cellar ticked with a ghostly silence.

A light in the stairwell faintly showered down upon Kevin as he sat on the steps to catch his breath and control his emotions.

He wanted to race back to Maria. But his heart-sickening realization was that it would be too late. She had sacrificed herself so that the rest of them could survive. Her action had stunned him.

Now I have to go through with the plan.

For her. For Maria.

And what about Kathy and Larry? he wondered. Would they make it?

Dad. Dad, help me.

He looked around.

This was no time for hesitation, for thinking rather than doing.

Time to concentrate and gear up to go for it.

He moved down into the center of the cellar.

For Maria, he reminded himself.

He closed his eyes.

And because he was concentrating on stopping time and floating free of reality, he did not hear the distant clatter, did not hear the frenzied skittering, and did not see the first wave of the spider creatures as it spilled into the stairwell.

It broke upon him like a sudden burst of rifle fire.

God, what is it?

He was immediately, preternaturally alert. And afraid.

The creatures threaded their way around him, weaving a circle he could not escape. Their clamor was so deafening, he fell to his knees and clasped his hands over his ears.

He cried out in pain.

He feared his eardrums would burst.

The circle tightened. He could feel the creatures, sense their nearness.

Concentrate.

He fought to control his will, to direct it toward the creatures and fend them off, but they had surprised him, throwing him out of balance.

I can't do it.

An awareness of his impending doom came upon him as a clear and distinct image: a heavy, black ball sinking inexorably in crystal blue water, down, down, down.

But then, by degrees, he intuited a change, a relenting of the pandemonium. He took his hands away from his ears. He opened his eyes. The circle of creatures ran upon itself at a point beyond him. It converged, and from that convergence another form arose, solid and dark.

"My friend, we meet again."

The figure of Joshua stood within ten feet of Kevin. There were no signs of the creatures.

The boy's ears continued to ring from the horrible din.

"Did I frighten you?" Joshua prodded.

Kevin, weakened, detested the sight of the demonic young man.

335

"You can't stop me," he murmured, though there was little strength or command in his voice.

"I know your plan," said Joshua. "Quite ingenious. Unfortunately, it cannot succeed."

"It will," said Kevin.

"Truly I admire your effort," Joshua continued. "And the action of the girl, Maria . . . she was brave. Foolish, too."

"I'm going back," said Kevin, as much to himself as to his nemesis. "To lay you to rest forever and erase all the horror."

"Yes, of course. Your father is waiting for you."

"Don't try to stand in my way," Kevin warned.

"But why should I? This will be a perfect revenge for me. I wouldn't think of stopping you."

Momentarily, Joshua's words puzzled the boy.

Is this some kind of trick? he asked himself.

Concentrate.

He redoubled his effort to stop time, float free, journey back in time. In the quiet space of his own concentration, he struggled for a minute or more.

It wasn't working.

God, I've lost my power.

For several more minutes, he tried. Doubts flamed within him. And all the while, Joshua looked on.

Dad. Dad, help me.

Kevin thought of Maria, too, and the others. But nothing happened.

He had failed.

He lowered his head.

Suddenly he felt the touch of a hand upon his shoulder.

"My friend," said Joshua.

Kevin glanced up, but he did not see the complete figure of Joshua, only a single eye, large and liquid.

He concentrated upon that eye and time slowed.

336

He reached out of himself. He rode a spiral of darkness.

He let go of the moment.

Far off he could hear the angry voices of men.

Torches glowed eerily.

Several men were carrying a body to the rear of the cellar. He stole closer to watch as they worked deliberately with pick and shovel to dig a shallow grave in the soft stone where the spring purled like a whisper.

They laid the body there and covered it and walked away as if they had completed a just and righteous act. Kevin felt the pangs of an inner conflict: The person of Joshua might have been innocent before his death—his murder. The men had accused him of bearing the touch of the Red Death. But was he evil?

Kevin stared at the finger-width of the spring inching its way toward the grave, reclaiming the area disturbed by the digging. And he knew he had to act, despite his confusion; he also knew he would need help.

He surveyed the cellar. Apparently all the men had left as had the servants and kitchen help. The man who had risen to defend Joshua remained unconscious, slumped against a wall.

Above him, Kevin could hear music, the lilt of a waltz, a glorious sound which the ballroom could not contain. He could imagine gaily costumed gentlemen and ladies gliding about the floor.

"A whole different century," he whispered to himself. *I'm not hallucinating. This is real.*

Then, over near one of the wine racks, he saw movement. Cautiously he walked in that direction, wishing the torchlight were brighter.

Closer.

"Who's there?" he stammered.

Shifting of feet upon the stone.

A man emerged.

"Kevin?"

"Dad!"

The boy rushed to his father, but the man, disoriented, deeply confused, appeared not to believe his senses.

"What is going on here? This is the cellar at Blackwinter, isn't it? Who were those men? And the boy. They murdered a boy. I saw them. I've been hiding."

As best he could, Kevin tried to explain how Joshua had used his powers, how some kind of time warp had been created.

"They buried Joshua and we have to dig him up and move the body."

But his father, slowly suspending his disbelief, did not understand.

"The spring," said Kevin. "It gave him his powers . . . made him evil . . . made him so he couldn't die. He wants Blackwinter, and that's why the Davenports and Sophie and Mrs. Bozic . . . and probably Maria . . ."

God, he doesn't know.

"What's happened?" his father demanded. "What about Kathy?"

Kevin agonized that there was so little time; they should be moving Joshua's body, and yet the tragic events had to be recounted.

In the shadows created by the torchlight, Kevin reconstructed the night of horror.

He concluded by saying, "Kathy and Larry are in the tower . . . I don't know about Maria."

"God help us, it can't be true," his father muttered. "These things can't happen. They can't be. My friends."

He took Kevin by the shoulders and shook him angrily as if the action might somehow cause the boy to recant the macabre narrative. And then, seeing the truth in his son's eyes, he pressed him into an embrace.

Kevin held onto Kathy's secret.

338

I'll tell him. I'll find the right time and tell him. Not now.

"Dad, this is our only chance . . . to destroy Joshua's evil and change what's happened."

He could feel the tremendous doubt his father harbored.

"Trust me. Please, Dad, trust me."

The man nodded weakly.

The old antagonism, the former rift between them was dissolving. Once again they were becoming father and son.

"We don't have much time," said Kevin.

He led his father to Joshua's shallow grave.

"We have to move him before the spring water starts changing him."

Pick and shovel in hand, they began to work, digging eagerly.

Kevin felt a rush of energy: *We're doing it — we're doing it!*

When they had uncovered the body, his father paused to catch his breath.

"Where can we take it? Where can we rebury the body?"

"I know a place," said Kevin. "The flower garden out beyond the kitchen."

"But how do we get the body out of the cellar? We can't go up through the house."

"There's an opening to the outside. It has an iron grate across it — in the wall past the wine racks. We can lift the body out through there."

"OK, let's do it," said his father. "You get a hold of his feet and I'll take his head and shoulders."

And then Kevin leaned down closer to Joshua's body, positioning himself to lift.

"Son . . . my God . . . look . . . look at his face."

Kevin glanced at where his father had gestured.

The grotesque mask of the Red death lay upon Joshua's features.

Father and son stood as if paralyzed by the sight. And Kevin heard his father whisper,

"I can't touch him . . . my God . . . I can't do it."

2

"But we have to," said Kevin, though even as he spoke he felt something weakening his volition. It was as if the diseased body of Joshua were sending out invisible lines of power, making it difficult for anyone to dislodge the corpse.

Kevin's father stepped back. He wiped at his mouth as if he were becoming physically ill.

"I'm sorry . . . this is just too . . ."

He looked at his son, a curious defeat in his eyes.

"No, Dad. We have to."

But Kevin could sense that a transformation was already under way—the spring water weaving its dark magic upon Joshua.

"Help me," Kevin pleaded.

He leaned over and grasped Joshua's boots.

"Dad!"

"No . . . I'm sorry."

The man was shaking his head slowly, decidedly.

A foul odor of disease—the lingering stench of the Red Death—filtered around them like smoke.

"Dad, we're so close. We've gone too far to stop now. Everything depends—"

"I can't do it!" his father shouted, and then he turned and began to scramble away from the corpse, stumbling, falling hard onto his knees.

Joshua's won.

The words blazed through Kevin's thoughts like fireworks at night.

The plan didn't work.

He ran to his father and hunkered down beside him. There seemed nothing to say; the man was trembling, his eyes dilated and shimmering in the amber spray of the torchlight.

Kevin thought of Maria. Her apparent sacrifice was made in vain. The boy wanted to cry. All their chances to escape the horrors of Blackwinter Inn had come down to this: defeat in the presence of forces perhaps no one could truly understand.

Yet, the irony. Kevin could feel that he and his father had been drawn as close as ever before. That new bond, however, lacked something.

"I'm sorry, son. I am. Believe me, I'm sorry. I want to do what has to be done . . . for Kathy and . . ."

Kevin didn't hear the remainder of his father's words. His heart was drumming so loudly, blood rushing into his ears so rapidly that he felt as if he were beside the ocean as a huge wave gathered fury to pound against the shore.

He grabbed his father's wrist.

God, I know what will help him.

The answer had been there waiting for the boy to realize it, an answer housed in a single word. A name.

Kathy.

Good feelings streamed through him; he had to calm himself before he could speak coherently.

"Dad . . . Dad, there's something I haven't told you."

The man slowly lifted his eyes; he seemed confused by Kevin's animated tone.

"Dad, it's about Kathy."

"Kathy?" the name was whispered.

"She told us . . . she told us she's gonna have a baby."

His father mumbled something.

Kevin clutched his dad's shoulder and leaned to within a few inches of his face.

"Did you hear me, Dad? Kathy's gonna have a baby."

The metamorphosis unfolded at an excruciatingly slow pace—Kevin had to repeat himself, had to fill in the narrative blanks, and had to reassure his father that he spoke the truth.

Eventually his father smiled.

And then tears came to his eyes. A mushrooming of emotion.

A nervous laughter. An exclamation of surprise and joy and, perhaps, hope.

He hugged his son.

"Come on," said Kevin, riding upon his father's happiness. "We have some work to do."

This time there was no hesitation.

Joshua's embryonic powers had no effect upon them.

They worked quickly, casting their magnified shadows upon the wall. They found the opening leading out of the cellar and pried loose the iron grate.

3

First light.

It stole upon them like a memory.

And for Kevin it was the memory of the birthday willow.

Pick and shovel tore into the flower-garden plot. They dug eagerly, with a sense of purpose—a mission. The ground was hard, but it yielded to their effort.

They did not feel the chill in the air.

And when they had completed a hole four feet deep or so, they rested, leaning upon their tools, watching the pinking of dawn.

"Do you remember the willow, Dad?"

"Willow?"

"The birthday willow — for Mom."

His father thought a moment. Then a smile creased his lips.

"Yes, I do. Is there some connection here?"

"No . . . except, we did it together."

"Will you ever forgive me for leaving your mother and marrying Kathy?"

Kevin looked away, his gaze touching the corpse of Joshua.

"Part of me won't," he admitted.

"I understand that. But it was something that couldn't be helped. And Kathy has changed my life . . . more so now than ever."

"I like her. She's not Mom. I mean, I can't love her the same. Not the same way."

"You and me . . . we going to be better friends? I was wrong, Kevin. You were aware of so much more than the rest of us — about Blackwinter and Joshua. If we had listened to you . . ."

"Let's finish it."

His father clasped him warmly upon the shoulder. Then they lowered the body of Joshua into the grave and mounded dirt over it as if they were burying the source of all the world's evil.

They cheered each other. Smiled. Laughed. Felt good. Very good.

We've won. We've beaten Joshua.

Or was it that they had beaten Blackwinter Inn?

Morning light drove away more shadows.

"Back inside," Kevin exclaimed, gesturing for his father to follow.

It was a dizzying moment — the expectation of triumph.

They clambered through the opening, reentering the cellar.

"Hold onto my hand, Dad."

Concentrate.

Stop time.

Float free.

Hand in hand, they stood in the center of the cellar. Joshua's body rested in peace. Past horrors could be erased.

Concentrate.

They lifted free of themselves — father and son — in a spiral of time, spinning, swirling, leaving behind a century in which the Blackwinter Inn gloried despite its hidden darkness.

Everything was going according to plan until suddenly Kevin heard his father say, "I have to let go."

Panic flamed instantly in the boy's mind.

"Dad, no!"

But he could feel the man's grip loosening.

"Go on without me. I'll try to make it alone."

With those words Alan lost contact. Kevin momentarily grasped a ghostly hand. Then nothing.

He snapped back into his body.

And jolted awake.

"Dad?"

The boy dropped to his knees.

He was alone in the cellar.

"Dad?"

Tears came even as Kevin tried to reason through what had occurred. Perhaps, he considered, it had been a trade off: To eliminate Joshua's evil, a price had to be paid. It wasn't fair, he told himself — hadn't they already paid enough?

"Dad, you can make it," he whispered.

But the cellar responded only with silence.

Then he thought of the others.

He ran to the stairs. Had the rest of the plan worked? Would he find all of them still alive? The

Davenports? Gina and Sophie Bozic? Maria?

Heart in his throat, he ran.

On the first floor, he received his answer.

The bodies of Sophie and her mother remained where the Red Death had claimed them. Stunned, Kevin sat for a time on the stone ledge by the fireplace; only ashes survived the previous night's fire.

Eventually he remembered Kathy and Larry and Maria.

He made his way up the stairs, expecting the worst.

It seemed that the very silence of the old inn crouched in hiding as he climbed higher and higher, that it watched him with predatory intent.

When he pressed his shoulders through the opening into the lower landing of the tower he called out.

"Maria? Kathy?"

The names spun out into the dusty shadows and hung in the air by single threads of hope. The roofline, bathed in an intense sunlight, gave no appearance of anyone or anything having been there. No spider creatures. No courageous girl.

By the slant of the sun, it was approaching noon.

Maria, God, the plan didn't work.

He wondered where her body was. But he forced himself not to think about it.

"Kathy?"

Cautiously he pushed his way into the upper landing and saw immediately that it was empty.

God, no one got saved.

Crushed by the reality of it all, he hesitated there in the opening, not even certain he possessed the energy to go farther.

Until he heard something.

The deep bellow of some kind of horn.

It was coming from out on the lake.

Revitalized, Kevin scrambled free of the opening and

found himself astonished by the sight which greeted him: It was a beautiful November day; high, bright sun, and sparkling lake. And there, riding atop the surface of the lake, a magnificent boat—the Catlin County paddle wheeler.

And more.

A rescue boat rowing back toward the gaily bedecked vessel.

In it were Kathy and Larry.

Oh, God . . . they did make it! They did!

A small voice within him, of course, told him to race down the stairs and call for his own rescue. But a cold moment later his gaze drifted to the upper deck of the paddle wheeler where, against the railing, a familiar-looking young man leaned.

"No, it can't be. Can't be him," he whispered to himself. "We buried him. Dad and I."

He had to find out. Had to be certain.

The joy of seeing Kathy and Larry being rescued dissipated some as he bounded down the stairs at breakneck speed. Then out through the kitchen to the flower-garden area.

The mound of earth showed signs of being freshly dug.

Kevin smiled. He clenched his fist in triumph and whooped.

The stranger at the railing of the boat was not Joshua.

The paddle wheeler steamed onward, diminishing in size as it stayed on course for Jackson Lake. And, again, the boy was gladdened by the thought of Kathy and Larry being carried to safety.

If only Dad . . .

He knelt beside Joshua's grave. All that had happened. The horror. The mystery. And the prospect of picking up the pieces, creating new bonds—it would be the most difficult time of his life.

How would any of this be explained to the authorities?

He brushed the question aside.

Considered another: Would he always feel as tremendously lonely as he did at that moment?

He lost himself in reflection.

The cat's meowing brought him out of it.

"Nat King Cole? Hey, look at you. You made it through the night."

"So did I."

Surprised by the voice, Kevin spun around.

He couldn't believe his eyes.

Chapter XXI

1

Together, scouting along the shore, they found Flo-Jo's fishing boat, derelict and, thankfully, empty. They used tree limbs to help them pole out, away from the island.

"Didn't you believe me? I told you I'd try to make it alone. It just took your ole dad a little longer, that's all."

Kevin had to keep clearing his throat and fighting off a strange sensation that, if he looked away from his father for more than an instant, the man would disappear.

"I never quit hoping," said the boy.

Nat King Cole snuggled close to him.

Alan Holmes stopped poling once or twice to glance over his shoulder at Blackwinter Inn.

"Dad . . . we won't ever go back there, will we?"

"No, son."

Kevin told himself he wouldn't look, that he should keep his eyes upon the opposite shore — on the future, as it were. They would help Larry Bozic find himself. And, most of all, they would have Kathy and the promise of a new family. A starting over.

348

But it was impossible not to look just once.

At first he saw the magnificent old inn perched proudly atop the pine-clad island, a striking edifice waiting to be ushered into the twentieth century. Yet, there he also saw darkness, a vision of a hideous mask; a demon's eye, large and liquid, gleaming through the shadows of time.

TERROR LIVES!

THE SHADOW MAN (1946, $3.95)
by Stephen Gresham

The Shadow Man could hide anywhere — under the bed, in the closet, behind the mirror . . . even in the sophisticated circuitry of little Joey's computer. And the Shadow Man could make Joey do things that no little boy should ever do!

SIGHT UNSEEN (2038, $3.95)
by Andrew Neiderman

David was always right. Always. But now that he was growing up, his gift was turning into a power. The power to know things — terrible things — that he didn't want to know. Like who would live . . . and who would die!

MIDNIGHT BOY (2065, $3.95)
by Stephen Gresham

Something horrible is stalking the town's children. For one of its most trusted citizens possesses the twisted need and cunning of a psychopathic killer. Now Town Creek's only hope lies in the horrific, blood-soaked visions of the MIDNIGHT BOY!

TEACHER'S PET (1927, $3.95)
by Andrew Neiderman

All the children loved their teacher Mr. Lucy. It was astonishing to see how they all seemed to begin to resemble Mr. Lucy. And act like Mr. Lucy. And kill like Mr. Lucy!

DEW CLAWS (1808, $3.50)
by Stephen Gresham

Jonathan's terrifying memories of watching his three brothers and their uncle sucked into the fetid mud at Night Horse Swamp were just beginning to fade. But the dank odor of decay all around him reminded Jonathan that the nightmare wasn't over yet. The horror had taken everything Jonathan loved. And now it had come back for him!

Available wherever paperbacks are sold, or order direct from the Publisher. Send cover price plus 50¢ per copy for mailing and handling to Zebra Books, Dept. 2704, 475 Park Avenue South, New York, N.Y. 10016. Residents of New York, New Jersey and Pennsylvania must include sales tax. DO NOT SEND CASH.

ZEBRA'S GOT THE FINEST
IN BONE-CHILLING TERROR!

NIGHT WHISPER (2092, $3.95)
by Patricia Wallace
Twenty-six years have passed since Paige Brown lost her parents in the bizarre Tranquility Murders. Now Paige is back in her home town. And the bloody nightmare is far from over . . . it has only just begun!

TOY CEMETERY (2228, $3.95)
by William W. Johnstone
A young man inherits a magnificent collection of dolls. But an ancient, unspeakable evil lurks behind the vacant eyes and painted-on smiles of his deadly toys!

GUARDIAN ANGELS (2278, $3.95)
by Joseph Citro
The blood-soaked walls of the old Whitcombe house have been painted over, the broken-down doors repaired, and a new family has moved in. But fifteen-year-old Will Crockett knows something is wrong — something so evil only a kid's imagination could conceive of its horror!

SMOKE (2255, $3.95)
by Ruby Jean Jensen
Little Ellen was sure it was Alladdin's lamp she had found at the local garage sale. And no power on Earth could stop the terror unleashed when she rubbed the magic lamp to make the genie appear!

WATER BABY (2188, $3.95)
by Patricia Wallace
Her strangeness after her sister's drowning made Kelly the victim of her schoolmates' cruelty. But then all the gruesome, water-related "accidents" began. It seemed someone was looking after Kelly — all too well!